Praise for the novels of Rosalind Noonan

TAKE ANOTHER LOOK

"Noonan grips readers in this suspenseful novel . . . worth picking up." —*RT Book Reviews*

ALL SHE EVER WANTED

"Noonan has a knack for page-turners and doesn't disappoint . . . a readable tale." —*Publishers Weekly*

THE DAUGHTER SHE USED TO BE

"An engrossing family saga and a suspenseful legal thriller. Noonan covers a lot of narrative ground, with a large cast of characters whose situations involve morally complex issues, as well as knotty family dynamics. This novel would fuel some great book-club discussions." —*Shelf Awareness*

IN A HEARTBEAT

"Complex, intriguing characters and an intensely emotional plot make *In a Heartbeat* compelling." —*RT Book Reviews*

ONE SEPTEMBER MORNING

"Written with great insight into military families and the constant struggle between supporting the troops but not the war, Noonan delivers a fast-paced, character-driven tale with a touch of mystery." —*Publishers Weekly*

"Reminiscent of Jodi Picoult's kind of tale . . . it's a keeper!" —Lisa Jackson, *New York Times*–bestselling author

Please turn the page for more praise for Rosalind Noonan!

ONE SEPTEMBER MORNING

"Noonan creates a unique thriller that is anti–Iraq War and pro-soldier, a novel that focuses on the toll war takes on returning soldiers and civilians whose loved ones won't be coming home." —*Booklist*

"Gripping and emotional, the story could not be more timely." —*RT Book Club*

"Carefully plotted, well-paced, and taut, this novel builds to a stunning conclusion." —*The Romance Readers Connection*

"This is an intense and emotional story that readers are sure to enjoy. Grab a hankie; you will need one for *One September Morning*." —*Romance Reviews Today*

DOMESTIC
SECRETS

Books by Rosalind Noonan

ONE SEPTEMBER MORNING

IN A HEARTBEAT

THE DAUGHTER SHE USED TO BE

ALL SHE EVER WANTED

AND THEN SHE WAS GONE

TAKE ANOTHER LOOK

DOMESTIC SECRETS

Published by Kensington Publishing Corporation

DOMESTIC SECRETS

ROSALIND NOONAN

KENSINGTON BOOKS
www.kensingtonbooks.com

KENSINGTON BOOKS are published by

Kensington Publishing Corp.
119 West 40th Street
New York, NY 10018

All Kensington titles, imprints, and distributed lines are available at special quantity discounts for bulk purchases for sales promotion, premiums, fund-raising, educational, or institutional use.

Special book excerpts or customized printings can also be created to fit specific needs. For details, write or phone the office of the Kensington Special Sales Manager: Kensington Publishing Corp., 119 West 40th Street, New York, NY 10018. Attn. Special Sales Department. Phone: 1-800-221-2647.

Kensington and the K logo Reg. U.S. Pat. & TM Off.

eISBN-13: 978-1-61773-328-4
eISBN-10: 61773-328-8
First Kensington Electronic Edition: March 2016

ISBN-13: 978-1-61773-327-7
ISBN-10: 1-61773-327-X
First Kensington Trade Paperback Printing: March 2016

10 9 8 7 6 5 4 3 2 1

Printed in the United States of America

*In memory of Ruby,
who brought us joy
and unconditional love
and kept our secrets*

O, that this too, too sullied flesh would melt
Thaw, and resolve itself into a dew!

—William Shakespeare, *Hamlet,* act 1, scene ii

PART 1

Chapter 1

Early May

The salon was hopping with all the music and conversation and laughter typical of a Saturday afternoon when his text came. The ambient noise was so loud that Rachel Whalen would have missed the message if she hadn't seen the screen of her cell light up on the counter as she swept up her station.

Maternal pride and fear swelled inside her when she saw that it was from Kyle James. Her oldest son, a junior in the home stretch of spring term at Green State, had been playing a friendly game of touch football with some friends when he'd hit his head and gotten his third concussion in eight months. The coach had immediately responded with concerns about his ability to play football next year. His role as the team quarterback was in jeopardy.

Rachel's pulse pinged a little faster as she opened the text. KJ had called back the coach that morning to clarify things.

Not kicking me off yet, but I think they want me to resign. I'm totally screwed. Meeting with them tomorrow. What do I do?

Her heart sank. She hadn't expected this—at least, not so soon—and she didn't have time to watch her empire crumble now. She texted back: **At work. Let's talk later.** Although it hurt to blow him off, she couldn't spare the time to talk with him now, without keeping customers waiting. Even when they did talk, there was nothing she could do to help him besides listen, and Rachel hated conceding to the unfixable. She was the fixer, dammit. But there was no easy solution to the situation, and the consequences on both sides were significant. Poor KJ. The sin of failure settled heavily on her shoulders. A mother was supposed to take care of her kids.

As she cleaned up her station, Rachel checked herself in the mirror—the beauty of working in a hair salon. She was having a good hair day, her dark-chocolate hair falling in fat curls at the bottom while the side bangs flipped back from her brown eyes. That new product covered those stray grays well. She smiled, glad that her dimples still appeared after forty-three years. "Mom's happy dots," the boys used to call them.

Her customer came out of the changing room to say good-bye, dragging Rachel back to reality.

"It's going to take a while to get used to it so short, but I love it." Mae Yang swept a hand over the back of her neck, then wrapped on a checkered scarf. "I feel a few tons lighter."

"It suits you." Rachel wiggled her fingers in a casual wave. "And I'm putting the Memorial Day Concert on my calendar. That's so exciting. You must be busting your buttons."

"Yeah." Calm as ever, Mae paused to check her hair in a mirror and outline one of the triangular sideburns with a fingertip. The subtle smile told Rachel that she was pleased. They had taken off a good six inches, "lightening the load," as Mae called it. Rachel had touched up the flaming crimson and combed Mae's red hair into a dense, wild stack atop her head. The new hairstyle seemed to represent Mae's new incarnation as a survivor, an artist, and a free woman.

Mae had looked quite different a year ago when she had appeared at the salon door, frightened as a trapped mouse. Her long, thick hair had been greasy on top, snarled and matted around her neck. Even Rachel had been at a loss for where to begin with it, but she had kept mum, sensing the young woman's pent-up anxiety.

"Just take a load off, and tell me what style you're thinking of," Rachel had said gently.

Instead, Mae had told her a tale of domestic abuse, the psychological kind. While Rachel worked conditioner into knots and detangled from the bottom up, the girl talked of a boyfriend who refused to marry her but refused to let her go. There were mornings in which Mae could no longer drag herself out of bed and into work, and nights of waiting up for him and then cowering when he finally came home in a drunken rage. With tears streaming down her face, she had admitted that she would leave except that she still loved him. She was sure that he loved her back. It was the booze that kept him from showing it.

"But you need to love yourself first," Rachel had said softly, seeing her own past in this broken young woman.

"God first, yourself second," Hilda had added from the next station. "But this man, he does not deserve your love. And he's not allowed to threaten you this way. . . . This is no good."

That day, Rachel had extracted a simple promise from Mae; the girl vowed not to let her hygiene deteriorate again. It had been a small start, but as Hilda said, "You do what you can." Mae had kept her part of the bargain, returning every two months for a haircut and a check-in. Within four months she had gotten out of the abusive relationship and moved in with some girlfriends. After that, she had enrolled in evening classes, formed a band with some friends, and earned a promotion at work. At this point, all of the stylists had some knowledge of her past, and they joined in to celebrate her progress.

Rachel kept quiet for a moment, savoring the ladies' love for Mae.

"Wait," Sondra said, lifting her gaze from her scissors. "You're playing here on the square for Memorial Day?"

Mae nodded, her fiery-red hair bobbing as she shared the details of her band's upcoming gigs at farmers' markets and charity events. Most of the women in the shop were watching now, interested, promising to attend.

"Well, now you've got the right hairstyle to be a performer," Hilda said. "Very dramatic."

Mae tilted her head to one side, peering shyly from behind a lock of hair. "Thanks."

"Good luck to you, young lady," called one elderly customer, Trish Dwyer's mother, Hazel, and the group joined in a chorus of cheerful good-byes as Mae headed out.

"Rihanna's got nothing on her!" someone commented. "She's adorable."

"Right? She's got a great energy," Rachel said. "I can't wait to see her perform." It was moments like these that kept Rachel Whalen in the game at the hair salon she owned in the Portland suburb of Timbergrove. Rachel recognized the fact that women came to her because she was equal parts truth-teller and ass-kicker, and she knew they came to the salon because it was one place in town where they could get what they needed. Love and advice, therapy and transformation, all for the price of a haircut. This was how they rolled.

Her bit of euphoria was cut short when she checked the appointment book and saw that Tootsie Dover, grand dame of Timbergrove, was up next. The older woman with a penchant for plastic surgery and wine was one of the few customers who enjoyed reminding Rachel that she worked in a service profession. After an hour or two with Tootsie, Rachel felt like one of the scullery maids in *Downton Abbey*.

As usual, Tootsie was late. Rachel looked up from the appointment book, hoping to steal a minute to catch up with KJ, as Tootsie slinked in, jaw clenched and shoulders back in that imperious stance. All that was missing was her royal scepter.

"Hey, there. How's it going?" Rachel flashed her usual smile, extending a casual greeting as she came around the reception desk and pointed Tootsie toward her station.

"I'm so busy I hardly have time to breathe," Tootsie muttered, her puffy lips barely moving. A few years back she had gotten some sort of implants that made her lips bulbous and swollen. For months Rachel had thought of a bad bee sting reaction whenever she'd looked at Tootsie. "I'm trying to plan a European vacation and it's so hard to get what you want these days."

"I can imagine." Rachel did not have that problem. The last vacation she had taken was with her boys at the coast, and even there they had stayed in a friend's cottage. "Can I get you something to drink? Coffee or tea? Wine or soda?"

As usual, Tootsie wanted wine. While Tootsie switched her blouse for a gown, Rachel poured a hefty goblet of white wine. Tootsie took the glass without acknowledgment. *You're welcome.* Since when did money become an excuse for lacking manners?

With a small flourish, Rachel wrapped the cape around Tootsie. As she moved she caught a glimmer of silver in the part of her own dark hair. Damn. Time to freshen up her own roots. Usually Ariel helped her out with that, but her friend had been busy lately, coaching kids for the spring show.

"I'm looking for a little wow factor." Tootsie tipped up her well-sculpted nose and swirled her glass of white wine as Rachel pumped the chair higher. "Can we go blonder this time?"

Any blonder and your head is going to glow in the dark, Rachel thought, though she bit the words back. Some women wanted to hear the truth, but Tootsie Dover was not one of them. And if Rachel Whalen had learned anything in twenty years of styling hair, it was to give the customer what she wanted.

"We can put more umber into the golden highlights," Rachel suggested. "That will give it more contrast, more shine."

"I want that instant bling thing. That sparkle and pop, you know? I want people to notice when I walk into a room."

You mean, when you stumble in, Rachel thought, pretending to ponder a strand of the woman's hair. It was the consultation, the moment when Rachel listened, then proposed a fabulous transformation of her client's hair and, hence, life. Not everyone went for the dramatic consult. Some wanted just a trim, a color touch-up, a little chitchat, and a couple of laughs. But Tootsie always demanded the deluxe package: flattery, asskissing, and a magical transformation.

"I have some product with gold sparkles in it."

The plump lips curled into a beak that reminded Rachel of Donald Duck's. "I want that. Pour it on."

"And we can finish with a Brazilian blowout."

One of Tootsie's painted brows arched as she sipped the wine. "Mmm. What the hell is that?"

"A deep conditioning treatment we use after the color. It adds a layer of protective protein that gives your hair a smooth, healthy sheen. Lasts for weeks, and it'll bring out that golden-honey glow in your hair."

"Yes, yes. Do that, too."

"Perfect." Ka-ching, ka-ching. Rachel tabulated the rising profit on Tootsie's hair treatment as she started to mix the product in plastic containers. Right now Rachel really needed the money. She was a single parent operating her own business, and every month she seemed to come up short. With Jared heading off to college in September, she spent many late nights staring at the computer screen showing her online bank accounts and wondering how she was going to sew together the budget holes. And that was before she'd learned KJ's scholarship was in jeopardy. On the other hand, Tootsie Dover, heir to the Dover Pumpworks fortune, had money to burn. All was fair in love and commerce.

As Rachel applied color to layers of hair separated by waxed papers, Tootsie nattered on about her latest renovation, her newest car, her royal treatment at the country club, her wunderkind Cooper.

"He's made his final choice," Tootsie said. "Winchester College, down in California. Maybe you've heard of it?"

"I know it well. That's a great school." Rachel brushed the pale muck of dye into the roots of Tootsie's hair as she pictured the college with its low-slung adobe buildings, mosaic-tiled artwork, swimming pools, and lawns bordered by tall palm trees. It had been the first choice of her younger son, Jared, who had been accepted, but not offered a scholarship.

"Did you hear that Cooper's been given a football scholarship? A full ride," Tootsie tossed in, toasting Rachel with the wineglass.

"Fabulous," Rachel gushed, though inside she was seething. That scholarship was wasted on a wealthy family like the

Dovers, who had the money to send their son to Stanford and build him his own dormitory, too. But Rachel had kept her mouth shut. Maybe she'd sounded just as greedy when KJ has gotten his football scholarship to Green State two years ago. Had she actually bragged about it back then?

Well . . . maybe.

"Of course, I told him he doesn't have to play football, but he just loves it."

So does KJ.

"And I must admit, it's nice having a celebrity in the family. Have you been at the high school games when they chant Cooper's name?"

"I have." Back in October, Rachel and Ariel had attended the homecoming game. In a town the size of Timbergrove, a Friday night football game was quite the social event, with tailgate parties, marching bands, cheerleaders, and helicopters hovering overhead for TV coverage. Although it had been a fun, cheap night out, Rachel could not say she enjoyed hearing the crowd chant the name of their current quarterback. It had reminded her too much of her own son's ride to glory two years earlier, when the roar of fans had rumbled through the bleachers.

"KJ!" Clap, clap. "KJ!" Clap, clap. "KJ!"

At first KJ had asked people to stop chanting his name, explaining that he was no hero, that the entire team deserved a rally cry. But no one listened or cared. The chant was intoxicating and contagious.

"KJ!" Clap, clap. "KJ!"

For a seventeen-year-old kid who had grown up playing tackle football since he was five, the cheering fans were part of the thrill of football. KJ had admitted that, even as he'd tried to stay modest and focused, keeping his head in the game. "Football is my life," he'd told her, and Rachel had been so pleased and proud that her son had found a good, solid foundation in his life.

A foundation on the verge of crumbling.

Snapping herself back to the conversation, Rachel was relieved to find that the topic had changed to prom.

"Cooper is going with his girlfriend, and I've got to tell you, it's not cheap. I was going to book the limo, but then Cooper told me they needed a party bus. An entire bus? Can you imagine? Cost me a damned fortune, but I don't care." Tootsie was nearly growling now, her voice low as a sleepy tiger's.

"Usually the guys chip in for that," Rachel said. "I bet you'll get reimbursed for most of it."

"I don't care. I don't need the money. Not as long as my boy's happy, and he's happy as a pig in shit these days. Absolute shit."

Rachel was aware that her client was beginning to sour, typical of the degeneration during Tootsie's visits. She shot a look over to the next station, where Hilda was blowing out a young, pink-faced woman in the chair. A new mom who had left the baby with her mother to get a haircut, Irene had her eyes closed in meditation, and the noise of the dryer probably drowned out Tootsie's nastiness.

"Cooper's got a girlfriend." Tootsie let out a dry cackle. "A regular screw, is what my husband calls it."

"Come on, Toots. That's no way to talk about a seventeen-year-old girl." *Especially a girl who's like a daughter to me.*

"He's joking. I think you know the girl. Remy . . . something or other. Indian girl."

"Native American," Rachel corrected, despising Tootsie for the not-so-subtle put-down. "Remy is a doll. But then, her mom is my best friend in the world, so I'm a little prejudiced."

"Well, she'd better be worth it, because I'm sinking a boatload of money into her. We're taking her on our family vacation this summer. Five weeks in Europe. England, France, Spain, and Italy. And some of those small countries that no one knows the names of."

"Sounds like a dream vacation," Rachel said. The chance for Remy to see Europe was the only bright light in Tootsie's brag. Rachel had known Remy and her sister, Cassie, since the girls were preschoolers. Many a summer day Ariel's girls had splashed around in the kiddie pool with Rachel's boys, and throughout the years there had been countless camping trips and sledding and hikes and picnics that drew their two families together. Rachel had always hoped that one of Ariel's girls would end up with either KJ or Jared, but you couldn't make that sort of thing happen.

"I've never been to Europe," Rachel said. "What's your favorite spot there? Like, if you could only go to one place."

"I don't know. A bunch of tourist traps, if you ask me. It was Cooper's pick, and it's his graduation trip. But first we have to get through graduation and prom." Tootsie finished her goblet of wine, leaving her lips moist and drooping open. "Who's your boy taking to prom? You have a senior, right?"

Rachel nodded, taken aback by Tootsie's sudden interest. In all the years that she had cut Tootsie's hair, she'd rarely fielded a personal question from the maven of mean. "Jared." Honestly, how could Tootsie not know his name? He was in Gleetime with Cooper. "I'm not sure he's going to prom."

"No girlfriend?"

"I'm just not sure he's interested in all the hoopla of prom."

"That's right, he's in theater. *That* type."

"He's in theater, but he likes girls." Rachel had blurted it out before she could stop herself, but she was not going to let the likes of Tootsie Dover start rumors about her son.

Tootsie covered her wet lips as she snorted, a lame attempt at a laugh. "Now don't go getting all defensive, Mom. I just know that theater crowd answers to a different drummer. Bohemian types."

"Right," Rachel said flatly, glad that she was finished applying the color. She couldn't stomach much more of Tootsie Dover. "You're good for now. Let's give the color twenty or thirty minutes to set."

"And I'll take another glass of wine while I'm waiting."

"Okay." Rachel took the goblet into the kitchen and poured another glass of wine cut with water.

"Oh, my God, are you watering that down?" Tiffani rolled her eyes. "That's hysterical."

Rachel didn't find it funny at all. "It's called limiting your liability. This client has a history of DUI." She couldn't bear to think that she might be contributing to Tootsie's intoxication, especially since the woman would slither out of here and slide behind the wheel of the big-ass SUV that had replaced the Mercedes she had totaled a few years ago when she'd slammed into a parked car. Fortunately, no one had been injured in the crash.

"Yeah, well, she needs to own up, be responsible for herself," Tiffani said, running the zipper on her black leather vest up and down. At twenty-four, Tiffani Delgado was the youngest stylist, and she still held tight to that know-it-all smugness of youth.

"In a perfect world, she would," Rachel agreed.

"You know . . ." Tiffani hoisted herself onto the counter, the butt of her jeans inches from a platter of cookies ready to go out front. "We should stop serving the wine and get a latte machine. That would get more young people in here. It's only the old ladies who drink that cheap wine."

"Maybe next year. Unless you want to buy the machine, and operate it. For now, if people want fancy coffees, they can go to the café two doors down. Now take those cookies out to the waiting area, please. Thank you."

Striding from the kitchen with the goblet held high as a gauntlet, Rachel contemplated telling Tootsie about Jared's new girlfriend. How she would love to rub that hot news in, grind her heel over it.

But it was too early, premature news. Rachel didn't even know who the girl was, only that she existed. And they were involved. Sexually involved. The disappearing condoms and his dirty laundry didn't lie. Granted, it had been a sporadic thing over the past few months, but whatever the circumstances, Rachel was thrilled.

Rachel handed over the wine along with three recent *People* magazines, then turned away and chuckled to herself as she took her pots of dye to the sink for rinsing. Some mothers of teens would have been horrified to learn that their kid was having sex. She sort of got that. But since it was such a natural, healthy part of life, she was glad to know her seventeen-year-old son had finally jumped that hurdle. She knew that Jared had longed for a girlfriend since junior high, when he had confided in his cocky older brother for advice. That hadn't gone so well. One afternoon Rachel had overheard KJ laughing at his brother for using Oreo cookies as an entrée to conversation. "Really?" KJ had scoffed. "You couldn't think of anything better than sharing your cookies?"

Sweet, kind Jared. He wasn't confident and popular like his brother, and he was not a star athlete. After a few frightening bullying incidents during junior varsity football he had dropped out of sports and fallen into a geeky group of male friends who spent weekends doing online gaming and probably smoking weed. That part she couldn't be sure of, as the get-togethers rarely happened at their tiny house. But Jared kept his grades up and sparkled onstage, so Rachel never found any reason to complain.

He was still as uncommunicative as ever—typical teenage boy—but his confidence had risen and just the other day she'd caught him smiling for no reason. Whoever she was, that girl had put her son in a perennial good mood. Oh, he had a girlfriend, all right, and Rachel was tickled pink.

Jared had even started talking about going to college in nearby Portland next year, wanting to be close to home. Rachel didn't want to pressure him to do that, but secretly she was jumping for joy at the prospect of having one of her boys nearby for the occasional lunch or dinner. And he could come home to do laundry. It would help her stave off the empty nest for a while.

She cleaned up the sink, then went to the desk to spell their receptionist, Kit, who wanted to run out for a slice.

While she was going through her appointment book, three girls, all bright eyes and long hair, came into the shop and made their way to the desk.

"We need appointments for prom," said the tallest, a brunette. "The last week in May?"

"Timbergrove?" When the girls nodded, Rachel leafed through the book and added, "My son is a senior there. Jared Whalen?"

"Oh. Jared's my friend," said the medium-sized girl. She had cinnamon-colored hair that fell in curls around her face, and green eyes that reminded Rachel of a summer lake.

Could she be the one? Jared's secret girlfriend?

"He draws me pictures in AP Stats."

Rachel smiled, careful not to overplay her enthusiasm. Her sons had taught her that teens did not go for the zip-a-dee-doo-dah parents. "I don't know how you kids survive those math classes." She scheduled appointments for the three girls, making a note of the cinnamon girl's name, Aubrey Sweeney.

Probably not Jared's girl, she thought as the teens left the shop. Really, what were the chances of that? Still, she thanked God for Jared's mystery girl.

She was left wondering if Jared was planning to go to prom with his new girlfriend. He had never attended a school dance; he didn't know all the steps and rituals. What would they need to plan in advance? Transportation. Well, if they were sharing a limo, arrangements would have to be made, as limo services booked up months before prom. On the other hand, Jared could drive his own rust bucket, or else borrow Rachel's car.

Of course, Rachel could trim his hair, but he would need to rent a tux. And flowers. No problem. Rachel had a client who worked at the florist on Maple Street. Wendy would cut her a deal.

Maybe she was getting ahead of herself, but she would need to press Jared for an answer, since he was turning eighteen the day before prom. If he wasn't going to the dance, he definitely deserved a bit of private celebration.

The image of her son's smiling face lifted Rachel's mood as she answered the phone and booked a few appointments for the other gals. Prom or no prom, this girl made Jared happy. And with time, KJ would find his moral center again, life beyond football. Everything was going to be just fine.

Chapter 2

Just across the square, in the small bridal shop called Stardust Dreams, nineteen-year-old Cassie Alexander sat on the large, puffy, white leather bench shaped like a flat mushroom, waiting for her sister to try on gowns. Although prom was more than a month away, the search for dresses was on.

"Can I get you something?" asked the clerk, a brutally thin woman with big square teeth that reminded Cassie of a documentary she had seen on herbivores. "Some water or tea?"

"No, thanks." Cassie knew she didn't deserve a drink when they wouldn't be buying any of these pricey dresses. And she could feel the clerk's disapproval, which was typical. Women in their forties who worked in shops usually expected only one thing of young shoppers in their teens and early twenties: shoplifting. Of course, Cassie would never, ever, and she wouldn't allow Remy to go there, either. But the whole dynamic made shopping really suck. Looking down, she picked at the peeling cuticle on her thumb and willed the woman to go away.

It didn't work, because the woman walked past her and tapped gently on the louvered dressing room door. "How's it going in there? Can I give you a hand with something?"

Like what? Tuck in bra straps or labels? Cassie squinted up at the woman. What moron couldn't dress herself?

"I'm fine," Remy answered.

"My name is Shanna if you need me."

Cassie felt her level of annoyance ease as Shanna whisked herself out of the dressing room to the front of the store. "Let's get out of here," Cassie told her sister. "You know these dresses are too expensive, and that Shanna sucks the air out of the room."

"She's just doing her job." The door popped open and Remy lifted a hand, draping herself in the stall doorway. "This is the perfect dress." The dress was a striation of color, moving from emerald to a vivid moss green; it complimented Remy's golden-brown skin and dark hair. Remy did a runway turn to show the back of the dress, then faced the mirrored wall and took a selfie. "I'm feelin' this one, Cass."

"It's nice," Cassie conceded, moving into Remy's mirror shot to check the price. "Three seventy-five." She dropped the tag as if it burned her hand. "Not gonna happen."

Remy didn't seem to hear. She moved away, twirling, so that the hem of the gown billowed open like an upside-down tulip. A rare green tulip. "But I love this one." Her voice was soft and joyous, so in the moment.

Cassie could think of a million responses: *You can't love an inanimate object. You'll only be wearing it a few hours. It'll be ruined once you start dancing and break into a sweat. And most of all, it's too expensive.* Most girls had their moms in the dressing room to tell them these things, but Ariel Alexander had given up the reins of the family long ago, sometime between closing herself into her bedroom to grieve over her husband and scrambling to step up her business as a voice teacher so that she could earn enough to buy groceries for the family.

"It's really beautiful," Cassie admitted, "but you can find something as nice for a third of the price." It was a little annoying that Remy kicked ass in every dress she tried. Remy had inherited Mom's petite but ripe body and exotic Native American beauty. Her silken black hair looked fabulous with every dress in the shop.

Cassie, on the other hand, had been cursed with their father's gene pool, something Russian or Yugoslavian; Mom wasn't sure about it. Cassie knew she would probably never see her dad again, and she really didn't care, except that she wished he had given her more than broad shoulders and a horsey body and curly hair that looked ridiculous on her huge head. *Thanks for the gift of ugly, Dad.* Paul Alexander had left for Alaska to work on the pipeline when Cassie was five, and apart from two late Christmas cards, Cassie had never heard from him again.

Her memories of those times were a little spotty, though she could still picture herself tending to her sister, holding Remy's hand to keep her from straying in the mall, comforting her in the car when Mom was inside a store. Always the big sister, Cassie had known that she needed to take care of Remy because little Rem was a baby and Mom was . . . distracted. A few years later, Ariel married Oliver Ward, a local firefighter, and Cassie quickly learned what it was like to have a father. Ariel got pregnant, and the family grew with Trevor and Maisy. Oliver had been totally in love with Mom, and he'd brought their family some security. He didn't mind "holding down the fort" while Mom went to LA for walk-on roles and auditions. He seemed to get a charge out of seeing her on TV. Those were good times; sometimes Cassie kicked herself for not appreciating what she had back then. Oliver had freed Cassie of the burden of worry and let her have a childhood. Unfortunately, that had ended when Oliver died four years ago.

"Can we go now?" Cassie asked, trying to keep the annoyance out of her voice. She wanted to help her sister find a dress—she'd gotten up early and driven home from college just for that purpose—but they were kidding themselves to think they would find anything here. "I know a nice thrift shop on Hawthorne," she said, trying to make the prospect sound irresistible.

"Just let me finish trying on what I have here," Remy said. Although Remy sounded reasonable, Cassie knew it was just a stall tactic. Like maybe, if Cassie stared at that gorgeous green dress long enough, she might cave.

Nope.

"So what is Cooper wearing?" Cassie asked. "The classic black tux?"

"I don't know." Remy's voice was slightly muffled by the door. "And I don't care."

"Wow. That's a little cold. You two have a fight?"

"Not really." The door popped open and she emerged in an indigo dress with crystals sewn into the sheer bodice. Another heavenly dress, though it had a tuft of fabric that draped in the back like a tail. "I love the front." Remy held up her cell phone and smiled for a photo. The varied shades of blue bleeding from indigo to turquoise hinted of distant, exotic seas. "But what's that weird thing in the back?"

"Is it a train?" Cassie tried to unravel the fabric and realized that it was just part of the skirt that had torn away. "It's damaged," she said. "I hope they don't think you did this."

"Calm down. It's probably something that can be fixed." Remy smoothed the ridge of the fabric along the waistline, holding it into place. "If this part weren't ripped, I would love it."

Cassie loved the price. "Seventy-five dollars, as is. So I guess they know the dress is damaged."

"But I bet I can fix it. Mom can help me. She has that experience sewing costumes." Remy twirled in the sparkly dress, her face bright with enthusiasm.

"So let's get it."

"I've just got two more to try," Remy said, shutting herself into the dressing room.

With a groan, Cassie collapsed back onto the giant white dumpling. "So what's the deal with Cooper, anyway? Did he do something to annoy you?"

"It's just that . . . I don't know. I don't think it's working out for us. We probably won't end up going to prom together."

"What?" Cassie sat up straighter. "Why not?"

"Because I'm going to break up with him. Soon."

"You are kidding me."

"I wish. Don't say anything."

"Obviously," Cassie agreed, thinking that Cooper shouldn't

be the last to know. "But wait. If you're not going to prom with Cooper, why are we shopping for a dress?"

"Because it's my senior prom." Remy's voice was pinched with annoyance. "I'm not going to miss that."

"But we don't have that kind of money." This opened a whole new can of worms. Cassie began to calculate costs in her head. "You'll have to pay for the prom ticket and dinner and flowers. And you need to pitch in for a limo. Oh my God, Remy. We can't afford that."

"I will figure it out."

"I don't see why you have to go if you're not his date."

"You make it sound like I don't exist without Cooper. The same controlling shit he's trying to sell me." The door opened and Remy stood there, suddenly dressed in her own jeans and T-shirt.

Cassie sagged against the cushion. "Please, allow me a moment to recover from the crushed dream of my sister being swept away by this gorgeous, incredibly rich guy."

Remy put her hands on her hips, standing her ground. "Looks aren't everything."

"I know that, Boo. Want to tell me what happened?"

"Not really. It's just . . . I'm going to break up with him, okay? I'll tell Cooper soon. And knowing him, rich, generous guy that he is, he'll probably give me my ticket."

"Don't count on it. He'll need it for some other hottie who wants to jump into your shoes. Guys like Cooper do not stay home from prom and cry on Mommy's shoulder."

"Whatever." Remy held out her hand, axing the topic. "Cooper can take care of himself, and so can I. I'm jumping into a limo with some of my girls. Maddie says I don't have to pay. And I'll order soup at dinner and make a corsage from the garden. I've got it all figured out. Okay? So don't you worry about me, Mama Bear."

Cassie let out her breath in a deep sigh. "You know I will." It had been a long time since Remy had called her Mama Bear, and something about it tugged at Cassie's sense of responsibility for her sister. She hated the fact that Remy would now be cut off from all the extra goodies she'd been privy to as Cooper's girlfriend. But at the same time, she didn't want her sister begging charity from the rich kid. It was getting harder and harder to take care of little Rem.

Remy sank onto the settee beside her and leaned in, giving her a hefty nudge. "So . . . ? Are we getting the blue dress? I can fix it. You know I can."

Leave it to Remy to bring it back to the all-important dress. "Is that the one you want, Boo?"

"Hell, yeah."

It was the right price, and perfect for Remy. "Then let's do it."

It was impressive the way that Remy dealt with Shanna. Cassie hung back as Remy praised the dress, then lamented over the damage, her small fingers smoothing over the edge as they discussed ways to repair it. She pretended to be undecided about the purchase, which prompted Shanna to knock another twenty bucks off the price. Sweet!

As Cassie swiped her credit card and Shanna wrapped the delicate garment in tangerine-colored tissue paper, Cassie felt herself warming up to the salesclerk, who seemed to have a rapport with Remy. The screen on the credit card keypad flashed: *PURCHASE DENIED,* and Cassie figured the store was having trouble with its scanner. Shanna told her to swipe the card again, but the same message came up.

"What does that mean?" Remy asked.

Shanna shrugged. "Either the account is maxed out or closed. Do you have another card?"

Cassie tried to tamp down the creeping feeling of dread as she exchanged a wary look with her sister. Had Mom overspent the card again? Cassie had a very specific monthly budget on the card, and she was still two hundred short of reaching it.

"Can you hold the dress for a day or two?" Remy asked. "I'll come back for it."

"I'm afraid not. We don't hold clearance items. Once you leave the store, it will go back on the sales rack. No discount."

"Okay, then." Cassie turned away from the counter as mortification flared, warming her cheeks. She hated it when Mom put her in positions like this. "Maybe we should keep looking. There's still a month till prom."

"No." Remy grabbed her arm. "Cass, no. We won't find anything this good."

Shanna put the wrapped gown behind the counter. "Let me know when you figure it out," she said, heading toward the door to greet a new customer.

"I am so embarrassed," Cassie muttered when the clerk was out of range. "Why does Mom do this to me? She knows the spending limits. She's the one who does the budget."

"We have to get this dress!" Remy kept a firm grip on Cassie's arm. "We're buying it. Today. How much cash do you have on you?"

"Not much." Cassie knew she had a twenty that was meant for groceries. Of course, with her stockpile of nonperishables, she wouldn't starve, and she had a small paycheck waiting for her at the café, where she had cut her hours back until after finals. Resigning herself to a steady diet of lentil soup and mac and cheese for the next few weeks, she opened her wallet and forked over the cash. Remy had sixteen, which left them around twenty bucks short.

"Okay, one of us needs to run home and get the money from Mom, while the other waits here and watches the dress."

"And I get to be the runner, right?" Cassie winced as she glanced out the shop window over the town square, picturing herself jogging in her flip-flops through packs of shoppers, dog walkers, elderly couples, women with strollers. She was not a runner, even in sneakers. She'd been stupid not to take the car this morning, but it had been a beautiful day to walk, and she'd figured it was wise to save the gas. "I'll walk home, and bring the car back. And I hope Mom has cash in the house." Their mother was giving voice lessons in the studio this morning, and no doubt she'd be annoyed at being interrupted.

"Okay, but hurry," Remy was saying as Cassie gazed across the square at the large church with a white clapboard façade and a spire. Next to the church was a smaller building with the same white clapboard and roof pitch. Years before the little building had been part of the church, but a few years ago Rachel had turned it into a hair salon.

"Holy Snips." Cassie lifted her hand toward the window. "Rachel will throw in for us. I'm sure she won't mind, and she always works Saturdays. I'll run over and talk to her."

"Oh my God, yes!" Remy's amber eyes were full of light. "Great idea! And tell her thank you for me."

"Be right back." Cassie ducked out of the shop, relieved to avoid a confrontation with Mom for now. These days, everything Ariel did seemed to piss her off. Leaving her sister to watch the dress, Cassie hurried down the street, moving as fast as her flip-flops would allow.

Less than a mile away in the space designated as her studio, Ariel Alexander was about to wrap up Kristina Lee's voice lesson. Kristina stood erect, her dark hair swept back in a twist so taut that you'd think it would hold her mouth open. She was a super-achieving senior in Gleetime Company, the high school performing group that had become Ariel's bread and butter in the past few years. All the students in the song-and-dance company came to her for vocal coaching because the music teacher "strongly recommended"—meaning, required—that all his performers take private voice lessons, and Ariel was the only vocal coach this side of Portland. God bless Craig Schulteis. The Gleetime kids paid Ariel's mortgage and grocery bills, leaving any money she earned from TV or film gigs to go for incidentals. And there were a lot of incidentals when you were a single parent of four kids.

"Don't move your chin," Ariel instructed, then watched as Kristina sang: "La-ga, la-ga, la-ga, la-ga, la."

"Nice. I know it sounds silly, but it's just an exercise to relax the larynx. That creates more space in the back of your throat for beautiful sound."

Kristina nodded brusquely and then continued the exercise with fierce concentration. The girl definitely got an A plus for effort. Kristina Lee was one of the most erudite and determined students Ariel worked with. Precise and disciplined, yes, but talented? Not so much. Granted, her voice had improved in the past few years. Technically, she was hitting her notes with a full, clear tone. But the girl lacked artistry and emotion. Her best performance was like *Madame Butterfly* played on Muzak.

"That's good," Ariel said, ending the exercise. "Great, actually. Your tone has really improved. So let's spend the rest of our time working on your solo audition for the Spring Showcase. Did you pick a song from the list I gave you?"

Kristina frowned, shaking her head. "I'm not so sure about a solo."

"Really? Your mom seems to think it's important." Nan Lee was the classic tiger mom, hovering, coaching, prepared to pounce on her daughter for any missed opportunity. For Kristina's mother, getting a solo in the spring performance was all about winning. "Did you talk to her about it?"

The student averted her eyes and flushed with embarrassment. "Not really. But I don't like being onstage alone, and there are so many kids who are better singers. They should do the duets and solos."

"Mmm." Ariel agreed with that, but she knew Kristina's mom would blow a gasket if she heard her daughter talking that way. Ariel walked a fine line, trying to please the parents who paid her and the students who sang in Gleetime to fulfill their parents' expectations.

"Well, how about we work on one of the solos?" Ariel suggested. "If you have something prepared, you can audition and know that you tried."

"And what if I'm not so good?" There was fear in Kristina's lovely dark eyes.

"Well, then, you get to sing in the group numbers, which is exactly what you want, right?" Ariel got up from the piano and slid an arm around the girl's shoulder. "You know, kiddo, everyone has their gifts. You can do equations and lab experiments that would melt my brain."

The girl gave a little snort of appreciation.

"Some kids excel at sports. You've got filmmakers and artists, and soon computer geeks will be ruling the world. I think we all have to play to our strengths. You know where you rock. So if I were you, I'd just do the solo audition to keep your mom off your back."

Kristina grinned, covering her mouth with one hand. "I can't believe you would say that."

"Yeah, well, don't repeat it." The last thing Ariel needed was an ass-kicking from a tiger mom. She leafed through her collection of sheet music until she found the one she wanted and handed it over. "So let's try something you can embrace. Pour your heart into it." Ariel went back to the piano keyboard as the girl scanned the music. "It's a song from *Wicked*." She played a few chords and sang, "It's time to try defying gravity. . . ."

"You chose a science lyric for me," Kristina said, then joined in on the next line.

So she had learned the lyrics. Damn, but this girl was scary good. Ariel imagined Kristina's future in a molecular lab, concocting a cure for cancer or a way to get to Mars and back in three days. One of those *Star Trek* beam-me-up thingies.

They went over the song twice, once for mechanics and the second time for flow. "Don't worry about the technical elements this time. Just let it go. You're pouring jars of paint over a giant canvas. Swirling stars in a pot. Dancing in the daisies."

Again Kristina pressed a hand over her lips to hold back giggles, but she began to relax a bit, diving into the song. It was better. Still pedantic and measured, but a bit of energy was beginning to come through. When she finished, her face was bright and animated, like a child who'd gotten her first peek of the night sky.

As she rose and smoothed down her pleated gray skirt, Ariel felt good about the lesson. If nothing else, it had been therapeutic for the kid.

"That song is going to come together quickly," Ariel said as she ushered the girl toward the mudroom, where students entered and exited. The entrance off the driveway was a good way to keep the business separate from family and home.

"What's my homework?" Kristina asked as she handed Ariel a few crisp twenties. "Some breathing exercises?"

"Nope. You've mastered the technical aspects. Instead, I want you to find a comfortable spot in your room, sit in front of a candle, and meditate on how wonderful it would feel to defy gravity."

Kristina squinted at her. "Really?"

"I kid you not. You need to own the emotions in that song." Ariel pushed open the door to find Kristina's mother waiting in her car by the curb. "There's your mom, right on time."

"See you Wednesday," Kristina said.

Grateful for a break between sessions, Ariel let the door close behind her and went back to the studio, where she made herself a cup of mint tea from the water cooler. Alone, she let out a melodic cry of frustration. She hated these Saturday sessions! Yes, they paid the bills, but in all her studies and the personal discipline of her craft, all the auditions and long gigs and waiting around on TV sets, she had never once seen herself reduced to the mediocre, routine life of a suburban tutor.

She tossed the tea bag into the trash, wishing she could toss away her ingratitude and discontent. Ennui sucked. It was part of the reason for her mistakes with men. Too many of them. Now that she had kids, she had learned to be discreet, at least most of the time. The public incident with Stosh last week, well, that had been simply a bad ending to a mutual trade. Commerce. She had provided him with great sex and arm candy, and he had given her access to the life she loved in Southern California: TV gigs and small film roles, parties and red carpet award nights.

Although she had vowed not to see him again, Ariel was already aching for the life she missed. She sipped at her tea, telling herself to cool it. Take a breath. Have an attitude of gratitude.

With the cup lifted to her lips, she caught a glimpse of herself in the gilt-framed mirror that she used to help students isolate and control the parts of the throat.

She lowered the cup, stabbed by the sight of the dejected

woman in the mirror. Sad, sallow eyes like dull beads in a sagging face. How did her eyes get so bloodshot? She needed to run upstairs for her Visine. And her face was flat and washed-out. The damned Oregon weather. She should have spent more time on her makeup this morning. Some bronzing and concealer, more color on her lips. She used her free hand to lift her ruddy hair near the part, trying to crimp some body into it. What happened to those great copper highlights that Rachel had woven in for her?

With a last sip of tea, she was about to dash upstairs to paint on a face when the click of the opening door came from the mudroom.

Who the hell was that? Her next student wasn't due for a good thirty minutes. Or had she screwed up her scheduling? She opened the studio door and peeked in.

He was sitting on the bench of the mudroom, as if waiting for his own appointment.

Wariness tugged at her, a mixture of alarm and acute interest. "I told you not to come," she said, turning away from him. Her clogs clicked on the wooden floor of the studio as danger and desire cut through her. She pressed her hands around the hot paper cup, willing herself to remember what was real and what was an illusion. The heat was real; desire was a jokester. Sexual cravings bobbed and weaved, tricking a person into dangerous, dark places. She knew that. She had to remember that.

He followed her into the studio as she knew he would. Quickly, she processed that all the children were out of the house; no one was around to hear. But also no one was around to come to her rescue if he refused to listen. Did he know that?

"You can't be here. Did anyone see you come in?" she asked, staring out the window, not trusting herself to face him, because when she looked into his eyes, she always caved.

"I can't stop thinking about you," he said. "And I think you feel the same way." Suddenly, he was behind her, pressing against her, drawing her to his hard warmth. "You want me, don't you? Say it."

"This is wrong," she said, even as she molded her bottom to him. Even through the thick fabric of her skirt she could feel the rigid swell of him. She gasped when he yanked her skirt up in the back and thrust against her.

"Tell me you want me. Tell me."

She was about to step away when his hands swept over her hips, capturing her, claiming her. Her hunger was expressed in a small sigh that escaped her throat before she could check the reaction. How could she? She knew how to channel emotion, pouring it into a song or a scene. But how did a person mask a physical need, ignoring hunger and thirst and desire?

"I do want you," she groaned. "Why do you do this to me?" When his hands skimmed down over her thighs and then up along the thin material of her tights to her center, she was lost to sensation. Once the teeth burst the skin of a succulent cherry, there was no tearing it from the lips.

Her knees sagging, she lowered the shade. "Just one more time. A farewell fuck."

He groaned, his lips pulsing into her neck. "I love it when you talk dirty."

Her conscience hounded her, a barking dog. This was so wrong. She had been right to end it. She knew that.

But no one was home; the teens were out shopping and the kids were visiting their grandfather for the weekend. No one would ever know if, just one more time, they took each other. One more hot, passionate ride.

Chapter 3

When Cassie had burst into Holy Snips looking for Rachel, she had stopped in her tracks at the sight of Tootsie Dover in Rachel's chair. There was no mistaking her pink, puffy eyes and wrinkled face under the layers of white papers and dye resembling vanilla pudding. Fortunately, Mrs. Dover had her nose in a magazine, giving Cassie a chance to turn away unnoticed. The last thing Cassie needed was to go broadcasting the need for money under the nose of Cooper's mother. That would be so wrong.

"Hey, honey!" Rachel had called from the reception desk. "What's up?"

Cassie had asked to talk, in private, and Rachel had ushered her into the salon's small kitchen.

"Take a load off. I've got a few minutes before I have to get back to Tootsie. Want something to drink?"

"No, thanks. Actually, I came to ask you a favor." Cassie leaned against the kitchen counter and explained that Remy was in the bridal shop across the way, held hostage with her beloved prom dress.

"Sure. I can spot you twenty." Rachel reached into the pocket of her apron. "Take forty, just in case. Geez, I haven't set foot in Stardust since KJ had prom. Do you know if they still do tux rentals?"

"I think so," Cassie said, pocketing the cash. "This is so great. Thanks. Mom will pay you back."

Rachel waved her off. "No problem. I'm glad Remy found a dress. And I'm glad to see you. I need the scoop." She kicked the door closed behind her and cocked her head so that her long chestnut hair fell over one shoulder. Rachel wasn't model-chic like Cassie's mom, who had acted in a few TV shows and modeled in her younger days. But Cassie always found reassurance in Rachel's ordinary features: thin lips, wide nose, and warm brown eyes. There was a softness about her that was very huggable. And then there was that attitude, her quick jokes, her giddy smile, her need to please. Rachel was genuine, never acting or posing as a mother, which Ariel sometimes did in public. KJ and Jared didn't know how good they had it.

"I just wanted to check in, see how you think the fam is doing after that fiasco with Stosh last weekend."

"That mess." Cassie pressed a palm to her forehead and groaned. It was the real reason Cassie had come home this weekend; she had been concerned about picking up the pieces. "I'm fine, but Trev and Maisy are still a little rattled. I'm so glad I missed that ordeal."

"You and me both," Rachel agreed. "More the merrier is definitely not true at a domestic dispute."

A *domestic dispute* . . . that was what Mom had called it when she'd dropped that bomb over the phone last Sunday while Cassie had been trying to finish a paper in the university library. Apparently, the cops had been called to the house Saturday night when Mom and her boyfriend, Stosh, had gotten in a fight. So embarrassing. Stosh—actually Nick Anastasio—was Mom's latest boyfriend, a Hollywood producer who'd been making big promises of revitalizing Mom's television career. Years ago, before Cassie had been born, Ariel had been the star of *Wicked Voice,* in which she played a witch who used her voice to charm people into doing what she wanted. It was a pretty lame show, though Cassie and her sibs sometimes enjoyed watching episodes in syndication, grinning as a younger

version of their mother sang her boss out of a grumpy funk or
calmed two football rivals into forgetting a grudge.

The kids never dreamed that anyone would want to see
more of *Wicked Voice,* especially not with a singing witch pushing forty. But Stosh had a way of working himself into a
dreamy frenzy when he talked about pitching a remake of the
witch series. Cassie never quite believed a grown man could
have that much enthusiasm for a TV show like *Wicked Voice.*
More likely, Stosh had pretended interest to hook up with
Ariel. Cassie didn't like to think about that stuff, but in the
years since Oliver had died, Cassie had become aware of her
mother's power over men. She had seen more than a few men
stumble in the presence of Ariel's sexual charms. So gross.
Even though the master bedroom was off in its own wing
above the studio, it was no secret what Mom and Stosh were
up to.

Being away at school most of the time, Cassie wouldn't
have cared if it weren't for the younger kids. Trevor was eleven
and Maisy was only eight, and they needed a mother who wasn't
so distracted all the time. Besides, it could be really damaging to
have strange men coming and going at home. Cassie knew that;
she had studied child development in a psych course.

Rachel's voice pulled Cassie back to the present. "Oh, honey,
you don't look so good." There was an awkward moment until
Rachel slipped an arm over Cassie's shoulders and gave a gentle
squeeze. "You look like you have the weight of the world on
your shoulders."

"I was just thinking that Mom has never really gotten over
Oliver," Cassie said softly. "I guess none of us have." Oliver
Ward had been Trevor and Maisy's real father, but he'd treated
all the kids like his own. When he died four years ago, Ariel
fell to pieces. Cassie had held things together for the family,
stamping down her own grief over the loss of the only father in
her life. But now and then, the pain slipped out. She would
hear his laugh in the halls at school, smell his aftershave in the
checkout lines at the store. She'd shiver a little when someone

said, "No worries," his favorite expression. Every time she came home from school, she expected to hear his low, rumbly voice greet her.

"Oliver was a stand-up guy." Rachel patted her shoulder. "Every man your mother has dated since is just a shadow of Oliver Ward. But then those are big shoes to fill."

Cassie leaned in to hug the older woman, soaked up comfort, then stepped back with a sigh. "Stosh would have never lasted," she said. "I'm glad he's gone, but I wish the end wasn't so ugly. I can't believe the police came to the house."

"The cops always respond in cases of domestic violence. I understand Stosh and your mom were throwing things. The candlesticks were flying."

"I know, I heard, that's what Remy said. It sounded awful."

Rachel's brown eyes grew wide with concern. "I'm just glad that the cops came before anyone was hurt."

Cassie nodded, not wanting to contradict Rachel to point out that the kids had been hurt. Trevor's eyes had been shiny with gathering tears when he told Cassie about the incident, and Maisy, obviously scared, kept asking about Stosh. Questions like, "Are you sure he's not coming back?" and "Why was he so mad?" Ariel didn't answer her questions; she just told her to calm down and everything would be fine.

Bullshit, Cassie thought. She hated it when Mom treated them like idiots.

"Have you talked to Mom about him?" Cassie asked.

"We had a heart-to-heart Saturday night, after everyone piled into my place and the kids went to sleep. Your mom was sure it was over."

"I think he's gone for good," Cassie said. "When I got home Thursday, while Mom was giving a lesson, I sneaked into her room and the master bathroom. No sign of his stuff anymore, and I looked through all the drawers. I think she really did kick him out this time."

"I sure hope so." Rachel adjusted the loop of the apron around her neck. "I used to like Stosh, but he and your mom are a toxic combination."

"Yeah." Cassie had a feeling that everyone her mom dated from here on was going to be a problem for the kids. "I know you have to get back," she said as Rachel opened the kitchen door. "Thanks for the loan."

"Anytime." Rachel paused in the doorway. "When are you heading back to school?"

"Tomorrow." Right now Cassie's separate life at school was her escape from the highs and lows of life with Ariel Alexander, the freakin' singing witch. "How's KJ liking Green State?"

"He likes it just fine. I can't believe Remy and Jared are heading off in the fall."

They talked about college choices for a minute, and then Cassie made her exit. "Tell the guys I said hi," she said, heading out.

Cassie pushed out through the door and escaped the buzz of hairdryers and conversation. Outside she broke into a jog as childhood memories of KJ and Jared floated through her head. Those boys had tortured Remy and her with water guns, lizards, and skateboard challenges, but they were all grown up now. The guys were like brothers, Rachel like a second mother.

Well, with a mother like Ariel, Cassie and her sibs could use a second mother.

Back inside the bridal shop, she found Remy sitting with an elderly Asian woman who gingerly fingered the torn fabric of the dress.

"I got the money," Cassie said, pleased with herself.

"And Mrs. Seng says the repair won't cost much."

"For you, five dollars," said the elderly woman. "It's a slow time for me."

And no doubt Remy was getting the Miss Congeniality discount.

"Plus she's going to take it in at the waist."

"Just a little bit," the seamstress said. "Such a pretty dress for a pretty girl."

"You are so sweet," Remy told the older woman. "Thank you so much."

As Mrs. Seng took Remy's measurements, Cassie paid for

the dress, giving simple yes and no answers when Shanna tried to make small talk. Cassie wasn't falling for that fake friendship crap. With Rachel's loan, Cassie was able to pocket fifteen bucks after she paid Mrs. Seng the five dollars. She smiled at the thought of the groceries she could buy: eggs and cheese and fresh fruit. Things were taking a turn for the better.

"Yup, that's one of my adopted daughters," Rachel joked when someone asked about the dark-haired girl who had dropped in.

"That's so nice." Hilda stood in the next station, blowing out Becca Handwerger's copper bob. "You have an extended family."

"Yup. Three daughters and another son, too." Rachel smiled as she cut layers into the back of Tootsie's hair. If she could draw Tootsie into the group conversation, maybe she wouldn't find the woman so irritating.

"And her sister is dating my Cooper," Tootsie said. "She's coming to Europe with us this summer."

Rachel refrained from telling Tootsie that they'd already had this conversation.

"Europe?" Hilda perked up. "I grew up in Austria. Are you going there?"

"Well, let me see. I have the itinerary here."

As Tootsie searched her cell phone for the information, Rachel focused on the haircut and the conversation around her. One customer confided in her stylist, Sondra, that she recently had ended a bad relationship, while another talked about her sister needing a hysterectomy. People did that all the time: spilling their guts in the salon about awesome recipes and breast cancer, bad husbands and the kinky sex that someone else was having, evil teachers and online scams. If she ever had the money to go to grad school, Rachel figured she'd be a perfect candidate for a degree in psychology. Hell, she'd had years of experience as a counselor.

It was amazing how a woman would share her secrets when you had her hair in your hands.

Of course, not every bit of information shared by the gals in the shop was suitable for public consumption. Rachel had a mind for remembering women's personal stories, but she wasn't one to spread gossip. Hell, most women put their own shit out there on Facebook or Twitter or whatever, which was fine, but Rachel didn't want to be the one broadcasting personal bits.

And then there were the secrets she shared with Ariel, another category altogether. "Lock that up tight and throw away the key," she used to tell her friend. Over the years they had taken turns leaning on each other, helping each other through the gnarly spots.

Last Saturday night, it had been Rachel's turn to help. She flashed back to the late-night call from Remy, the feeling of panic as she'd hurried over to the Alexander house at three in the morning, nightgown ruffling under her jacket. The cops insisted that Ariel and Stosh be separated, but Stosh was drunk and standing his ground.

"So Ariel will go to my house," Rachel had told the cop, a good-looking one someone had called Boss. His wife must have been pissed about him working a Saturday night. Rachel had gathered her friend's brood like a mother duck, hustling Ariel, Remy, Maisy, and Trevor into her car, driving them the few blocks to her house.

At the time, it would have been selfish to admit it, considering the circumstances, but Rachel had enjoyed having Ariel's crew under her roof. Remy and Maisy had shared the double bed in KJ's old room, Trev had unrolled a sleeping bag on Jared's floor, and Ariel had shared Rachel's big king-sized bed. Their two families fit together so well.

"I am so sorry." Ariel's voice had been a low drawl. "Way to ruin your Saturday night."

"Are you kidding me? This house hasn't seen this much action on a Saturday night since KJ threw himself a graduation party."

"I remember that," Ariel said. "It was a whopper. Another time when the cops were called."

"Nothing like flashing lights and sirens to get the blood

going," Rachel said as she punched a pillow and propped it behind her back. "Talk about an adrenaline rush."

"Too much drama." Ariel stared off as if trying to make out a distant sign. "It's time to let him go. It's over."

"Are you sure?" Rachel asked, testing her friend's resolve. It wasn't the first time Ariel claimed to be done with Stosh.

"I am so done with him. Do you know what he wanted me to do?" Ariel told of the witch costume Stosh had brought this weekend, hoping that Ariel would reprise her role as the singing witch and give him a private performance.

Rachel wiggled against her pillow, not wanting to hear the rest of this. "And did you?"

"Hell no. That was twenty years ago and I'm done with that shit. And when I told him that, he kept needling me and . . ."

Rachel found her mind wandering back to the scenario of her friend dressed in a witch's costume. Had Stosh wanted her to perform the song as a striptease? Or was Rachel reading into it? Sometimes, hearing about Ariel's escapades, Rachel felt like a dried-up old prune. In the two years since she'd lost Jackson, she had been completely focused on her shop and her sons; there hadn't been time to think about dating, much less the desire. And even if she were looking, it would be hard to find a man to follow Jackson Simmons. A former marine, he'd been a good provider, a good man who'd died far too young. Cirrhosis. Yes, he'd always hit the beer hard, but he was never a nasty drunk. Never mean, the way Stosh was with Ariel, but then Rachel had gotten a full serving of cruelty.

"Alcohol turns men into crazy bastards," Rachel said. "I should have learned that back in the day with Gage." Rachel had seen the withering effects of alcohol on her first husband, Gage Whalen, who had gone from being a teen heartthrob to a menacing, bloodshot, philandering fool in a matter of years. For a while she had tried to ignore his late nights at the bar and make their marriage work for the sake of the boys. Then, one night when he brought home a tart from the local saloon and she confronted him, he slapped her so hard that all fear flew out of her. One swing of his arm and she saw the only path: If she wanted to survive and save her kids, she had to cut him loose. That was when she knew it was over. The next morning she loaded his clothes into his sexy little Mazda and sent him packing, warning him to stay away from her and the boys. To her surprise, Gage disappeared, cutting the kids off without a birthday card or a penny of child support. Last she heard, he had headed down to Arizona to get in on the building boom down there.

The memory still swelled her throat; sometimes the past was a bitter pill to swallow. "The beer destroyed Gage," she told Ariel. "And though Jackson was never that nasty, it was alcohol that killed him, too. I wish they would make it illegal."

"I don't," Ariel said sternly, "and it killed my daddy, too. But I like to enjoy a glass of wine now and again, and so do you. And Stosh isn't really an alcoholic. He's got control issues."

"Right." Rachel lifted her head from the pillow and nailed her friend with an uncompromising look. "Stosh loses control when he drinks. Same thing, honey."

"I'm too tired to argue with you." Ariel stretched out on the bed, her complexion smooth as a whipped latte, her hair falling back in curly tendrils, despite the ordeal she had been through that night. "All I can say is that it's over with Stosh. Really. I swear."

"Good." Rachel had closed her eyes, vowing to remind Ariel of her resolution. Stosh was a lightweight in Hollywood and in life. A producer on a crappy little show, the man had been clueless when it came to Ariel's kids. Callous toward Trevor and downright cruel to eight-year-old Maisy, who didn't have a bad bone in her little body. The man was an ogre.

Rachel had been glad to come to Ariel's rescue last Saturday, especially if it helped Ariel slam the door on Stosh. The next morning, Rachel had been up at six to make pancakes, bacon, and eggs—a labor of love for her full house. How she adored feeding the little ones. She could sit at the table and chat with them for hours. Ariel and Jared had rolled their eyes at Rachel's doting, but the situation had been a novelty, and it had driven home the point that she would be an empty nester soon. After twentysome years of parenting, the prospect of having an empty house rattled through her with equal parts excitement and trepidation.

Tootsie's Brazilian blowout took additional time, and suddenly Rachel found herself running late. No breaks for her this afternoon, but then that was a typical Saturday at the salon. She thanked God for Tootsie's skimpy ten percent tip—better than five, which she had once tried—and directed the woman over to Allegra's station for a mani-pedi, breathing a sigh of relief to have Tootsie's negative karma a few yards away.

With one customer after another, Rachel couldn't allow herself to think too much about the problem with KJ. Sure, she found herself calculating numbers while the blow dryer ran: If she cashed in Jackson's IRAs, and subtracted the taxes, what would that leave her? It might work, but money wasn't the only problem here; KJ was being pushed to give up his passion, and that was a dilemma that no amount of money could fix for her son.

After a quick trim for a teenage girl, she touched up the color for a fiftyish woman who thought she was channeling seventies Cher. One of these days, Rachel would convince Madeleine to ease up on the jet-black color and give up the waist-length hair.

She was just cleaning up after Madeleine when Jared opened the door, a patient smile on his face as the other stylists cooed over him. Rachel couldn't help the flash of motherly pride that filled her.

"You got so tall!" Sondra said. "I barely recognized you."

Hilda reached up for a hug, and Shanna offered him some cookies from the tray. The backpack slung over one shoulder reminded Rachel that he was here to do a short sales pitch for her customers. Jared had begun selling Flashco knives last year, with a modicum of success. The freelance job was perfect because it forced him to step out of his shell and he could squeeze it in around his AP classes, Gleetime rehearsals, performances, and competitions. And Jared, old soul that he was, clicked with older adults, unlike KJ, who was respectful but horrified at the prospect of spending time with "old people."

"You can't be here for a haircut. Your mama keeps you well clipped, I see." Hilda reached up to run her hand over Jared's hair, the stubbles on the sides where it had been buzzed. These days he wore it trim on the sides and thicker on top, a look that emphasized his wide brown eyes and bold dark brows, which Rachel longed to shape a bit.

Jared blushed, smiling down on Hilda. "No haircut. I actually came to do a demonstration for anyone interested."

"What are you demonstrating?" Hilda asked, clapping his shoulder.

"Flashco knives." Jared lowered his backpack to the floor, unzipped it. "I brought along a kitchen set and some Flashco scissors."

"Ah, yes. This we must see."

God bless you, Hilda, Rachel thought, grateful that she didn't have to be the one coaxing her son's sales pitch. Rachel cleared a space on the rolling cart for Jared to set up, and he opened his vinyl knife roll, gaging his audience with questions about who liked to cook and who had trouble chopping vegetables with the dull knives in the house. "And one more question," he said, with a well-timed pause. "Who likes to save money?"

That hooked them. Even the women on the fringes of the group looked over.

"Well, who doesn't?" Tootsie called over from the pedicure chair.

Spying her next client, Rachel cut over to the reception desk and greeted Brianna Crafton, another Gleetime mom, who said she didn't mind the demonstration going on.

"It's great to see the kids all grown up," Brianna said as they stepped over to the sinks. "Jared's really come into his own. Sometimes we need to send the older ones off to school to give the younger sibs a chance to shine."

"Ain't that the truth." In a mist of strawberry-scented shampoo, Rachel listened in as Jared had Lexi Collins cut an apple with the mini-chef.

"It's effortless!" Lexi raved as Jared handed out apple slices.

Off in the corner, Rachel noticed Tiff and her client hanging back, shooting critical glances at the group. That Tiff was such a buzz kill. You would think that, as the youngest stylist, Tiffani Delgado would be a bit more open-minded. Instead, she put a negative glaze on everything. The girl had even had the nerve to advise Rachel to get rid of the "Holy Snips" name and theme, saying that religion was just not in anymore and nobody liked cutesy themes. Cutesy. Oh, that girl tested Rachel's patience.

By the time Rachel led Brianna back to her station, Jared was talking about the ease of cutting a chicken with the help of Flashco scissors.

"With these shears, separating a chicken into parts is quick work, which means savings for you, since we know it's cheaper to buy a whole chicken than parts."

"Let me see those." Tootsie gestured him closer, her mouth a downward slash of skepticism. "They don't look very sharp."

"That's the beauty of it. You can run your finger over the serrated blade without cutting, but when put to the test, these scissors get the job done."

The women nodded politely, except for Tootsie, who scowled. "You look dubious, Mrs. Dover," he said. "Here. Let me show you. Mom, do you have a penny?" Rachel provided a shiny penny from her apron pocket and, with a flourish, Jared cut through the coin as if it were made of clay.

Hilda gasped with delight and a few women applauded.

"Wow, thanks," Jared said with a mild smile. "But it wasn't me; it's the scissors."

Even Tootsie softened in her sardonic way. "You are one s-s-smooth salesman," she said in a loose voice that was a little too loud. And was that drool on her lips? Rachel looked away in dismay.

Jared must have known that she was tipsy—he'd seen enough of that with Jackson—but he didn't seem bothered by Tootsie's altered state.

"So, ladies, I have just one question for you." Calm but attentive, Jared held them in the palm of his hand as his gaze swept the room. "How many knives would you like to order today?"

In the end, half of the clients bought single knives or scissors, and Sondra ordered a small set of steak knives as a house-warming gift for her daughter.

For a few minutes Tootsie fingered all the knives, admiring her new manicure as she tried out the faux-ivory handles. She told Jared that one of these days she was going to replace her old stuff, and she really liked the feel of these knives.

Apparently, today was not that day; the drunken maven bought nothing. After Tootsie left, Rachel ran into Sondra in the kitchen. Sondra Stegman was a chameleon of hairstyles. Today her shoulder-length hair was jet-black with a bluish sheen, styled in an A-line bob.

"That Tootsie sure is a cheap one," Sondra murmured under her breath as she piled her dirty Tupperware containers into a bag. She was on one of those macrobiotic diets that Rachel didn't understand. "I think the last time I saw her open her wallet, moths flew out."

Rachel laughed. "Jared knows that he's not to put on the pressure. I don't want the ladies to feel obligated in any way."

"I know, but still." Sondra tossed an empty water bottle into the recycling bin. "If I was loaded, I'd buy one of every-thing. Charity begins at home."

"You bought a whole set. That was so nice of you."

"Sammy will think it's a real score, and I'm sick of trying to cut vegetables with a table knife whenever I visit her."

"Well . . . you know I appreciate it."

"My pleasure." Sondra beamed, her green eyes sparkling with compassion.

Rachel melted a little inside, and for the zillionth time she considered what an enigma this woman was; she ran hot and cold, friendly and distant, up and down. Rachel had learned to simply steer clear of her on the bad days.

Jared hung out, chatting with the ladies as customers said good-bye and stylists began to clean up their stations. When he offered to help Rachel close up the shop, she accepted with a little pang of regret that he didn't have plans on a Saturday night. When was he going to go on record with this mystery girl? She bit her question back and started sweeping up her station. That was the drawback of having a son who was an old soul; the weekend-party racket held no appeal for him.

After the last stylist left, she latched the door, leaving the keys hanging in the lock. "So how did sales go?"

"I did okay today." Jared shrugged with the low-key coolness typical of tall teen boys. "Thanks for setting me up with your clients, Mom."

"It's fine, as long as you don't put the squeeze on."

"Mom? Like I would ever do that?"

"I know, honey." She pointed to the stained glass window. "Use the special glass cleaner on that. It's in the kitchen, under the sink."

Although every stylist was responsible for cleaning her station and a crew came in and did a thorough scrubbing each Monday night, Rachel couldn't abide the cobwebs and dust that migrated into the common spaces during the week. She ran the duster along the shiny wooden pews in the waiting area, then ran the electric broom over the floor. When she turned off the vacuum, she heard him humming as he wiped the stained glass.

"What's that song?"

"It's one of the group numbers for Gleetime. Called 'Seasons of Love.' It's got great harmonies."

"I think I know it. Are you doing it for the Spring Showcase?"

"Yeah. And the state competition." He swiped the rag over the windowsill, then paused. "About that. There's sort of good news, bad news."

Rachel braced herself. "Oh, God."

"The good news is that this guy from Winchester College, he's going to be at the state competition."

"This guy?"

"From admissions. A recruiter."

She wrapped the cord on the electric broom and looked up. "Wait. Really? How did you find out?"

Another subtle shrug. "He e-mailed me."

"You personally? Honey, that's great! It means he's looking at you for their performance group. Which translates to scholarship money."

"Yeah, well, that's the bad news. He's not going to be able to find me at state since I didn't make it to the finals for the solo competition, and I don't have a partner for a duet. I mean, I'll be in with the company, but you know how that is. One head in the crowd."

"Oh no! That can't happen. Did you tell Mr. Schulteis a recruiter is coming? I'm sure he'll let you solo."

"Mom, that's not going to happen. Every single kid in Gleetime auditioned for a solo, and cuts were made, fair and square. Schulteis can't rig the competition just so that I can be seen."

"I can't believe this." She tucked the electric broom into the closet and closed the door with a petulant thunk. "Winchester is your first choice. It's a dream school." She had never seen Jared so happy as when he'd been walking on that campus, past sparkling fountains, green lawns, and low-slung buildings with colorful mosaic tiles, sandstone arches and arcades, and roofs of red-clay tiles. It had killed her that she could not afford to send him there. But with a scholarship . . .

"We've got to get you a duet," she said. "Schulteis is still auditioning for duets, right?"

"Mom, I don't have a partner. None of my friends are in Gleetime. It's not going to happen." He folded the rag, grabbed the can of spray cleaner, and headed into the kitchen to stash it away.

"We can get you a partner," she called after him. "What about Remy? I bet she'll do it in a heartbeat."

"Just give it a rest, okay?"

"You're giving up on your dream too easily."

"I'm just being realistic." He emerged from the kitchen and

joined her at the door. "We talked about this. I don't need to go to a private college, and we can't afford it. I'll be fine at a state school. I might even stay here and go to Portland."

"Stop, stop, stop! Don't even say that."

"It's a good school."

"And live in your mother's back pocket?" She opened the door, and waited for him to step out. "I know you don't want that."

"I could get a place with some friends."

"And always feel like you missed out on going away to college? That's no good, honey. You need to do a duet at state." Rachel stepped through the door behind him, reaching back to turn off all the lights but one, a spotlight shining on the stained glass in the window.

"Mom . . . don't make this a problem."

"When you see a problem, I see an opportunity to grow."

Jared rolled his eyes and turned toward the parking lot. "Wow, Mom. Hallmark called. They need you to write some inspirational cards."

"They'll just have to wait." Rachel smiled as she locked the door and jangled the keys in one palm. "Right now I'm devoting my life to raising my sons and beautifying the world, one head at a time."

"See you at home," he said, heading toward his ancient car, a distressed Volvo in a sad shade of rust.

Rachel paused at the door of her car, watching her son amble toward his car with the lanky swagger of a kid struggling to catch up with the large man-body that contained him. God, she loved that kid. "I love you to the moon and back," they used to say to each other at night when she tucked him into bed. Back in the sweet kiddy days. She loved KJ, too, though admittedly in a different way. Jared was the dear teddy bear that required only occasional attention, while his older brother had a kinetic, popping personality that demanded engagement and sacrifice.

Of the two of them, Kyle James was more like Gage in the raw physicality of his presence. God help him. But KJ had substance under that sex appeal, and both boys had good souls. It was Jackson's intervention eleven years ago that had turned their family around. A former marine, Jackson had taught the boys respect and discipline. Oh, they'd complained that he was harsh, but who else was going to teach them about courage and integrity? And football, too. When they'd lost Jackson two years ago, both boys had mourned him as if he'd been their real father.

As she drove home, she speed-dialed Ariel, eager to get her best friend cued in on the new goal for Jared at the state competition. Jared could protest all he wanted, but Rachel would not give up. Nope. Easing down the street past a dense green laurel hedge that gave way to a lawn bordered by bright peonies, she thought of Jared's dream of Winchester College and KJ's concerns about getting pushed off the team. Somehow, some way, she was going to pull things together for her boys.

Chapter 4

Tuning out the television and the kids sprawled on the sofa behind her, Ariel crossed her pajama-clad legs and let them hang in the air over the side of the comfy leather chair. Her feet, couched in white, fluffy socks, hung limp like lamb ears. Lonely lambs. Sunday mornings used to be the best, staying in bed late, snuggling up to Stosh, talking quietly and giggling and trying some new hot lotions and silly sex games. There was a certain athleticism to having sex with Stosh that put the "sun" in Sundays.

She sighed. Sunday mornings were dull without him.

Not that it wasn't charming to have her little lovies around, watching old Harry Potter movies on TV or working on school projects at the kitchen table. Maisy was a cuddle monster and Trevor was a good buddy, observant and inquisitive, always relaying advice from magazines and Googling the ingredients of snack crackers to make sure the family wasn't ingesting harmful chemicals. Remy was creative and patient but rarely around these days, drawn away by activities and friend commitments. And smart, stubborn Cassie had played the role of housemother until she left for college nearly two years ago. Kids made good company, but they could also be a pain in the ass. An expensive pain.

Adjusting the romance novel in her lap, Ariel scanned a few lines, trying to move past the slower parts. Sometimes the snappy dialogue amused her, but the love scenes, those were the parts that really snagged her interest. Romance writers understood how sex felt for a woman—not the physical wham-bam that men were mired in—but the rich springtime of emotion, with all its spice and color and sensation and splendor.

Damn but she missed having Stosh here. She turned the page and scanned on and turned another page, searching for the vicarious thrill of someone else's lovemaking.

"I miss soccer already," Trevor said wistfully from behind her. He came over to the arm of the chair and positioned himself between her calves, grabbing hold of her socks to maneuver her feet as if they were gearshifts. "I wish I had a game today."

"You can play a game with your friends." She clamped her calves around him, giving him a little jostle.

He grinned. "I know, but I want a real game."

"You're done for the season, buddy." As evidenced by last night's team spaghetti banquet that had stretched on and on until, in a haze of red wine, Ariel had steered Trevor out the door. She was glad to be done with the same old faces that fringed the soccer field, mediocre people making stupid conversation. Most annoying was Nan Lee, Kristina's mother, who also had a son on Trevor's team. That Alex Lee, what a superstar! If you believed Nan, you'd think that Alex played the field singlehandedly.

Fortunately, Ariel was close enough to walk home with Trevor, but she would have to go back and pick up the car this morning. "That was the best banquet ever," Trevor had told her. He'd loved the mundane spaghetti, the presentation of trophies and homemade awards and the endless rounds of billiards and foosball. Ariel wished that she could relate to the parents half as well as Trevor bonded with the other kids.

"I was just getting good and they ended the season." Trevor pushed away from her legs and plodded toward the kitchen. "What am I going to do today, Mom? A kid my age needs exercise and I wanna play soccer."

"So play, honey." Her phone began to buzz from the side

table. "Get some of your friends together at the field." It was time for Trev to take the initiative. She glanced at her phone and felt a tug of longing and regret.

It was him.

Trying to keep her voice even and calm, she answered. "I told you it was over."

"You said a lot of things you didn't mean."

"Don't flatter yourself. I meant every word I said." Though, honestly, she didn't remember everything from that night. Too much wine, too little sleep.

"Then let's talk about it," he said, his voice low. "In bed. I'll come over."

"Nope." She couldn't have him here anymore. "Where are you? Are you still in Oregon?"

"I'm in Glendale, but I can catch the noon flight."

"Don't even think about it," she said in a singsong voice.

"Come on, baby. Don't you miss our Sunday sex?"

His voice cracked her cold resolve. Stosh may not have been the best-looking man she'd ever dated, but the man had a voice like warm, drizzled honey. A voice that could make her so hungry. Starving. "Maybe," she said, thinking she could creep up to her bedroom, take the rest of the call up there. No way was she bringing him back into the house, but what was the harm in a little phone session? "Give me a minute." Her body sang with adrenaline as she swung her legs down and rose from the chair. "I need to slip into something nice and flim—"

Her oldest daughter, Cassie, stood in the archway leading toward the stairs. She wore an oversized Oregon State T-shirt and those godawful baggy sweatpants that made her butt look too large for her square body. Hands on her hips, her dark hair wild and tousled from sleep, she was a formidable barrier. "Who are you talking to?" she demanded.

"No one," Ariel said, feeling guilty and defensive as she brushed past Cassie.

"Is it him?" Cassie called after her.

Ariel ducked into the downstairs restroom, locked the door,

and leaned against it. "I'll have to call you back," she said, though she knew she wouldn't. The heat of the tease had chilled; the moment was lost.

"Aw, come on, babe. Don't leave me hanging here."

Out in the hallway, Cassie's voice boomed. "You're talking to Stosh, aren't you? Mom! You promised."

"I gotta go," Ariel said, recognizing that this had always been the real source of the conflict between Stosh and her. Ariel was always being pulled between her hot, single Hollywood producer and her four kids, and for now, the kids needed her more. At least, for the next few years. Stosh was protesting, but she ended the call, put her phone on the edge of the sink, and splashed cold water onto her flushed face to cool the remaining embers of lust.

There. Patting her face dry with the fluffy white towel, she peered into the mirror and tried a slight smile. There it was; her glow was back again. A sort of bronze sheen of her skin that contrasted so beautifully with the white of her teeth and eyes, and complimented her auburn eyes and hair. No Visine needed today. She had her mojo back.

She flung open the bathroom door and came face-to-face with a very scary, angry young woman. "That was him, wasn't it?"

"Since when do you monitor my phone calls?" Ariel kept her voice low, knowing there was power in restraint. "I'm the adult here, and when two people end a relationship, there tend to be loose ends that need to be sorted out." *But you wouldn't know that, since you're still an uptight virgin,* she thought, though she kept the barb to herself. Cassie's bitchy armor kept men and some women at bay, but Ariel knew it was all about insecurity. One of these days, Cassie would relax enough to be in a relationship. Until then, the world would have to put up with her castigating comments.

"You promised, Mom, and I'm holding you to it. The police were here because of him. You guys had to leave the house." Cassie's face was a pale portrait of propriety as she pointed toward the kids in the family room. "You can't put them through that again."

"It's not going to happen again. Don't you worry." Ariel patted Cassie's shoulder and stepped around her to get back to her novel. "I've got it under control."

"Oh, yeah? Like the credit card we were supposed to use for Remy's prom gown?"

"What are you talking about?" Ariel asked as she found her empty purple mug and brought it to the coffeemaker.

"The credit card was declined at the dress shop."

"It shouldn't be. I paid that bill." Ariel poured half a cup and palmed her mug, soaking up warmth as she tried to recollect what last month's bill had looked like. "I think I paid it. Wait . . . I know I did." She put down the mug, yanked out a drawer, and fished through a heap of bills, coupons, and junk mail.

Cassie drew closer, took one look in the drawer, and let out a huff of disgust. "Are you kidding me? That's your billing system, a mound of crap in the kitchen drawer? You have got to start getting organized and show some responsibility. You're the mother of four; why don't you start acting like that for a change?"

Little Miss Cassie Know-it-all was beginning to piss Ariel off. Ariel found the Visa bill tucked under a recipe for shrimp stir-fry. "Here it is." She slid it out and pushed the drawer shut with her hip. Even without reading glasses she could make out her note at the top. "Two hundred dollars, paid." She waved it at Cassie. "See? I didn't screw up. Their computers must have blipped out."

Still skeptical, Cassie took the bill and stared at it as she sipped coffee.

See? Ariel wanted to say. *Your mother is not a total idiot.* Fortunately, her attention was diverted by a knock on the family room's sliding glass door, where Rachel stood, holding up a paper sack and pointing to the Bagel Dell logo.

"Rachel's here." Trevor was already at the door, tugging the slider to the side. "Are those for us?" he asked.

"Yup. I hit the bagel shop after Mass. Plus I got three kinds of cream cheese and fruit salad." Rachel was already beginning to unload the two bags on the table that separated the kitchen from the family room, but then she didn't need an invitation to come in. Rachel was like family; no, better than family. She was family without the dysfunctional hang-ups.

"Bagels! Yay!" Maisy popped up and went over to hug Rachel. "Thank you very much," she said, resting her head against Rachel's chest.

"You are very welcome." Rachel beamed a winning smile, looking cute, despite her getup, which was dowdy enough to compete with Cassie's: zebra-striped leggings, a tent of a T-shirt, and a quilted green vest. Half elf, half wild animal. Obviously, she'd been out running and hadn't taken the time to change clothes. Well, thank God her hair looked fabulous. The gold highlights gave her brown hair a subtle sparkle and her side bangs feathered back to her ponytail in a flattering angle. At least Rach hadn't turned into a total suburban ruin.

Ariel brought over some forks, knives, plates, and bowls, as everyone came to the table to grab for food. Dishing chunks of melon, pineapple, and orange into a bowl, Ariel figured she'd start with the fruit and maybe take half a bagel. Once the thirties hit, no one could afford to load on the carbs, and she liked to save her guilty pleasures for martinis and wine.

"I'm not using the whipped cream cheese," Trevor said as he slathered butter onto his bagel. "I like butter, and I can use the extra fat since I still have some growing to do and I'll probably play soccer later."

"Good for you." Rachel tore a piece from her bagel. "Personally, I'm trying to stop growing."

"Good morning." Bright as a sunflower, Remy came through the arch. Looking adorable in a white Coachella T tied off at the waist over a pair of blue denim jeans, she came to the table and leaned down to place a kiss on Rachel's cheek. "Hi, Aunt Rachel. How's it going?"

"All good. Sit. Eat." She pulled out the chair beside her. "Oh, and I want to see that kickin' prom dress."

"It's so gorgeous." Remy scrolled through her phone as she sat down. "Thanks for loaning us the money."

"What?" Ariel stabbed at a cube of pineapple. "You hit Rachel up for money?"

"Just forty bucks."

"The dress was discounted," Remy explained. "I knew someone else would snatch it up if I didn't." She tipped her phone toward Rachel. "What do you think?"

Rachel swooned, squeezing Remy's arm. "Just heavenly. You will be the belle of the ball."

Ariel leaned toward the cell phone. Seeing the way the vibrant blue of the dress lit up Remy's skin tone, Ariel had to agree. In the first photo, two of the crystals on the dress had caught the light, winking with a gleam almost as bright as Remy's smile. "You look beautiful, my darling," Ariel said, passing it down the table to Maisy.

"Aw. So pretty." Maisy cooed as if she were reassuring a kitten.

"Oh my God! I know why they denied the card," Cassie piped in, snatching up the bill. "It's over the limit. That's got to be it. See?" She held the bill toward Ariel, tapping it with one jagged fingernail. "See? You paid the minimum, two hundred dollars, and you were less than a hundred dollars away from the limit."

"Really?" Ariel took the bill from Cassie, but the print blurred, and she wasn't going to fetch her reading glasses. She folded the bill and tucked it under her bowl. "Can we talk about this later?"

"Can you keep the payments up-to-date so that we don't get humiliated by salesclerks?" Cassie's dark eyes pinned Ariel, stern as a warden.

Remnants of fruit juice suddenly went sour in Ariel's mouth as she held back the urge to blast her oldest daughter from here to Timbuktu. She didn't like to let loose on her kids. Temper tantrums sucked up so much energy. But Cassie, with her condescending attitude and accusatory statements, pushed all the wrong buttons. Maybe it was the fact that Cassie had her father's square nose and wild hair, always a reminder of the man who had squeezed Ariel dry of money and passion, then abandoned her with two kids and a mountain of bills. Ariel would never forgive that bastard. Never.

"At least you got the dress." Rachel's calm voice smoothed over the edges of the confrontation. "Why don't you model it for us, Remy?"

"It's still at the shop being altered," Remy explained. "But I'm sure you'll see it."

"And you got it from Stardust Dreams." Having lost her appetite, Ariel took her bowl to the counter. "I'm glad you bought local. It's got to be hard for a shop like that to make it."

"Absolutely," Rachel said, turning the conversation to the two Timbergrove stores that had gone out of business last year.

Times were tough all around, Ariel thought, thrusting the folded bill onto the kitchen counter, the twelve-thousand-dollar debt burning a hole in her conscience. Crap. Somehow her expenses had crept up and toppled over the limit, and she no longer had Stosh to bail her out. While he'd been spending weekends here, he had thrown her two grand a month toward expenses. Two thousand awesome dollars. Stosh had that kind of money to throw around. Now it was hard to make ends meet without that stipend.

When Cassie brought her plate to the sink, Ariel reached for a clean mug, busying herself with pouring another cup to avoid her bitchy daughter. But when she replaced the coffeepot and turned away, Cassie had cornered her once again.

"So what's the plan for paying that off, Mom?" Cassie's voice was lower now, almost sympathetic. "I know most of the tutoring money goes toward the mortgage."

Raking a hand through her hair, Ariel lifted her head to face Cassie. "I've got an audition coming up this month," she lied. "A couple of commercials would take care of that bill."

"*If* you get cast," said Cassie, nineteen-year-old stick-in-the-mud. "There's no guarantee."

"Thanks for peeing on my parade." Ariel palmed the mug, trying to absorb some warmth. "When did you get so negative?"

"I'm just realistic." Cassie took the milk carton from the refrigerator, gave it a shake, and frowned. "Who put this back empty?"

"I didn't do it," Trevor insisted, giving himself up.

With a grunt, Cassie crushed the carton. When she went to pitch it into the recycle bin under the sink, she missed and gave a petulant groan. "Nothing works around here."

"Yah think? So count yourself lucky that you don't have to live here anymore." Ariel picked up the milk container and stuffed it into the trash. Cassie didn't appreciate what she had going for her. She'd be getting a college degree and a chance to make a steady income for herself.

"You could probably get a real job if you tried," Cassie said as she dug the instant creamer out of the cabinet beside the stove. "It's not like you haven't had the chance. You should have taken that teaching job in West Green when you had the offer."

That was the least of Ariel's regrets.

"You could get a job like that."

"I make more tutoring the Gleetime kids." Ariel took the creamer from her, and shook some of the white powder into her mug. "And I'm not the schoolmarm type."

"I get it. Because you're forever young, right? Forty is the new thirty?"

That cut a bit too close. "You're just full of piss and vinegar today, aren't you?" The girl was on fire, all right. "And by the way, I'm only thirty-eight. Not quite forty yet."

Cassie held her hands up in a stopping motion. "I'm just being honest. Come on, Mom. You know it's time to grow up and take care of this family. It's a miracle that something horrible hasn't happened to us while you were out doing your thing, acting and dressing like you're twenty instead of forty." Cassie stirred her coffee slowly. Calculating. "Oh, sorry. I meant thirty-eight. Like that makes a difference."

Ariel sucked air in through her clenched teeth, staring at her oldest girl. Staring and seething. The high-and-mighty brat thought she knew everything, which made her all the more infuriating.

"Yeah, you're right. Thirty-eight, forty-eight . . . what's the difference? After thirty you're just staring down the barrel of a gun at wrinkles and a box of Depends."

Cassie flinched, ever so slightly. "I didn't say that."

"In so many words, you did. And as long as we're handing out advice, I've got a bit for you. Take the stick out of your ass and open your eyes to all the things I do to make everyone happy around here.

"If you think you can do a better job raising these kids and keeping a roof over their head, then go right ahead. Be my guest."

"Whoa." Cassie's brown eyes grew round, all wide-eyed innocence. "I didn't say that. I mean . . . you're twisting my words."

"You got attitude, girl. That's not a bad thing. But right now, you're turning on the wrong person."

"You're the one who didn't pay the bill!"

"Oh, are we back to that again?"

Letting out a huff of air, Cassie looked away. "I've got to finish my laundry and get on the road. And homework, too. I'm meeting some people on campus for a project."

"Yeah. Don't let me keep you from that."

Cassie stomped up the stairs, taking a bundle of tension with her. Damn, but that girl was a ball of twisted accusations and guilt.

Taking a sip of lukewarm coffee, Ariel lingered in the kitchen and ticked through all the ways Cassie did not understand her. Yes, she still wanted to look good. Just because she had a few kids and forty was coming at her like a freight train did not mean she had to let it all go. All the modeling, acting and voice lessons, the years of paying her dues on television sets and in cheesy theater productions had to have some payback. Not to mention the workouts and diets, expensive cosmetics and deprivation. She still had a tight butt, killer abs, and a perky rack.

Not bad for thirty-eight. And she would never leave the house in sweatpants or zebra leggings. That was who she was. And she was not going to let her snotty daughter shame her into being some granola-eating Madonna.

She looked back at the bill, felt a sting of adrenaline at the hefty $12,000 figure, one of the few things she could read without her glasses.

It was not supposed to turn out this way. She'd had it all: a family, a home, work she loved, and a man who loved and cared for her. He protected her. He put this roof over her head. Her darlin' Oliver. She missed him every day.

At least Ariel had restrained herself from blasting Cassie. Remy and Maisy hated confrontation. Those girls were gentle souls. Trevor didn't mind it so much; he had that boy's understanding of holding your ground and wrestling horns to protect your territory. The male-aggression component.

A glance at the clock told her it was coming up on eleven and she was still lounging in her silk pajamas. She darted upstairs, slipped on some jeans, a tight black T, and a thin black cardigan with white polka dots. Quickly, she applied the basics of her makeup until her skin, eyes, and lips shone with a healthy glow. That was better. Just because she lived in the suburbs didn't mean she had to look that way.

Back downstairs at the table, Rachel had kept the conversation going with the story of a woman who always got her hair cut with her Chihuahua sitting in her lap. "She's a nice lady, but that dog sure likes to talk. One day he yapped through the entire haircut."

"Can I bring my turtle in next time I get a haircut?" Trevor asked.

"Uh, no thanks. Reptiles aren't my thing."

Maisy's dark eyes opened wide. "Can I bring my pet rhinoceros?"

"Of courseros," Rachel answered without missing a beat.

There was a flash of light from the other side of the table, where Remy was photographing herself with her cell phone.

She was holding a flat bagel up to her face, peering through the large hole.

"Gimme that! I want to do it," Trevor said.

Remy handed him the bagel and scrolled over her phone. "I'm calling this one, 'Bagel Monocle.' "

"How about 'I spy with my little eye'?" Maisy suggested.

"I'm calling mine, 'The bagel sees all,' " Trevor said.

"And I need one with Aunt Rachel." Remy leaned close to Rachel and snapped a photo, which she would post with a nice caption thanking Rachel for bringing breakfast. That was Remy, documenting her life on social media.

"So, I've got good news and bad news," Rachel said.

"Bad news first. Let's get the worst over with." Ariel tore off a small piece of a salt bagel as her friend told her that KJ's scholarship and place on the football team were in jeopardy.

"That's awful," Remy said. "Poor KJ."

"But he's such a good player," Trevor pointed out. "He's the best quarterback Timbergrove ever had."

"I know, Trev, but he's had a lot of concussions, and now he can't even practice for a while, until he gets better."

"That is a bum deal," Ariel protested. "So they're kicking him off?"

"Hard to say." Rachel shrugged. "I'm heading out to Bend this afternoon to talk and figure things out. He's pretty broken-up about it."

Ariel put on a pouty face as she rubbed her friend's shoulder. "I feel his pain. You're a good mother to drive down there just to talk."

Rachel sighed. "What else can I do?"

"I'm sure it'll work out. Mark my words. Come this fall, we'll be in the stadium at Green State, watching him play."

"I sure hope so."

"So what's the good news?" Remy asked.

Rachel cocked her head to one side, her smile returning. "Jared is being courted by a recruiter from Winchester. The man is coming to the Glee State Finals, and it's Jared's chance to shine. But he doesn't have a solo. Do you think he'll qualify for a duet in the competition?"

"I'd say he has an excellent chance if he can get a partner," Ariel said. "That's the crux of the matter." Jared was still so painfully shy about reaching out to people. Ariel had thought he might grow out of that, but the kid was still an introvert.

"I know, I know," Rachel agreed. "It's a problem for him, without any of his friends in the class. And believe me, I think he told me about the recruiter in a moment of weakness, because my son tells me nothing. Did he mention it to you during his last voice lesson?" she asked Ariel.

"Not a word," Ariel said. "He hasn't brought in new material to rehearse for quite a while. But . . . wow! This is a great opportunity. He'll kick himself if he lets this go by."

"I know. That's why I'm wondering if you might work on a number with him." Rachel turned pleading eyes on Remy. "I know you've got your scholarship to Southern Oregon all sewn up. But you guys have worked together before, and there wouldn't be any weirdness for Jared. God knows, you're like brother and sister."

Remy's brows rose as she considered the prospect. "That'd be fun. Except I've got my solo, and Siri and I are rehearsing 'Kids' for the duet audition."

"That's a pretty full load," Rachel admitted. "I don't mean to put pressure on you."

"But this is really important for Jared, and Remy is a quick study." Ariel sprang up from the table and pointed toward the door with a flourish. "Everybody in the studio. We need a major brainstorming session."

"Can I come in my pajamas?" Maisy asked as she popped up from the table.

"Sure. There won't be any clients coming in today." Ariel had trained her kids to stay out of the studio unless invited, and if they came in because of an emergency, they needed to be presentable. It was important to her to maintain professionalism in her home studio.

"Off the bat, I'm thinking of some super-romantic duets."

Ariel set out a stack of sheet music for duets and sat at the piano while the others gathered around. The day was overcast but the studio lighting hit the cut-crystal vase on the piano, forming squares of light along with translucent prism shades of red, blue, and purple.

Ariel played a few chords and then began singing the show tune "If I Loved You" from *Carousel*.

Rachel pressed a hand to her chest and joined in, singing fervently of a love that defied words and description.

When Ariel noticed Trevor rolling his eyes, she stopped singing but continued playing. "What's wrong?"

"It's an old fart song," he said flatly.

Laughing, Ariel hit a sharp chord as Rachel gave a dramatic gasp, saying, "My heart, be still. You dare to defile Rodgers and Hammerstein?"

Ariel pulled out another piece. "If that's too heavy, how about this?" She launched into "People Will Say We're in Love." Rachel sang along, but as soon as they sang the title line, the kids objected.

"No way! No way!" Maisy waved her arms. "It's too corny."

"I love that song!" Rachel exclaimed.

"But Jared and I don't have the chemistry to sing a sappy love song to each other." Remy twisted her long hair back into a bun, then let it drop on her shoulders. "How about something comedic?"

Ariel pulled out the music from *The King and I*. "How about this?" she asked, breaking into "Shall We Dance?"

Rachel knew all of the words, and she took Remy and Maisy by the hands and whirled them around in a dance. Soon Trevor was moving in rhythm, an odd mixture of break dancing and calisthenics. At the end of the song Rachel and the kids collapsed on the yellow velvet couch in a cloud of laughter, while Ariel hummed and searched her sheet music for other possibilities.

"You know lots of songs, Aunt Rachel," Maisy said.

"It's true," Remy said, adjusting her hair against the yellow sofa to take a photo. Selfies were such a big part of her life, that girl. She was a natural-born publicist. "Are you a big Broadway musical fan?"

"Sure. Back when I was in high school, I was in the Glee Club. But I guess I learned a lot of music when I went to work in New York City after I graduated college. I worked in some small theaters as a hair stylist."

"That sounds so glamorous," Remy said.

"Not really." Rachel wrinkled her nose, explaining that most of the actors wore wigs. "I spent hours and hours working on mannequin heads that never talked back."

Ariel revived them with "Singin' in the Rain," and Trevor brought an umbrella out from the mudroom to open and close beside Ariel at the piano. At the end of the song, when Remy took the umbrella and performed a little dance with it, Ariel could see that her daughter was getting into it. This was the perfect song for them. If Remy was willing, Ariel would devote herself to making this musical number sparkle.

Everyone was feeling bubbly and giddy and loose when Cassie appeared at the studio door. Weighed down by her duffel bag and backpack and a dour expression, she explained that there was too much noise to study here.

"So I'm going back now."

The kids went over to give her hugs, but Ariel remained in place, pretending to be engrossed in her search for sheet music. She knew she would get over it, but at the moment she wasn't feeling particularly affectionate toward Cassie, and she sensed that her eldest daughter felt the same way.

"Drive safe," Ariel said. *And don't let the door hit you on the way out,* she thought as Cassie plodded through the mudroom like a peasant climbing the Matterhorn. Such a martyr.

Inspired by Cassie's dark exit, she started playing "Don't Rain on My Parade." When Remy and Rachel linked arms and attacked the lyrics, Ariel was glad all that batshit-crazy family conflict dissolved away in the music.

Chapter 5

The old Ford whined as Cassie kept it pointed south on I-5, heading back to school. She pressed the gas pedal and the car made a weird scrambling noise. Nothing new; the engine had been doing that a lot lately. She had meant to tell Mom, but once the credit fiasco happened she'd realized the timing was all wrong.

"All right, then," she said, easing off the gas, coaxing the car into a slower cruising speed. "If you need to be babied, we'll take it easy. Just keep yourself together." She needed Old Red to last for two or three more years, until she was done with school and making a salary.

A solid salary, unlike her mother's dribs and drabs of income. She rubbed her index finger over the cuticle of one thumb, worrying over the sour end to the weekend at home, which had revealed Mom's monster debt.

Cassie was in the nursing program at Oregon State, and so far she was doing pretty well with her classes, though she was just finishing up her sophomore year. She had wanted to be a doctor, but there was no money for med school, and she knew that a nursing license with a BS guaranteed her a job pretty much anywhere she wanted to live. On her application she had written a pandering essay about her need to help people, but Cassie's main motivation was money. She needed a big enough salary to gain independence and control her own life away from Ariel.

As she drove, she could hear Oliver over her shoulder, telling her that she would be just fine. "You can do anything you put your mind to," he used to tell her. "When you get going on something, you're unstoppable." Just like a real father, he had recognized her best qualities and encouraged her to utilize her gifts. Oliver had been a good stepfather, kind and steady, just what she'd needed. What everyone had needed.

When he'd died of cancer four years ago, everyone in the family had been heartbroken. The kids had turned to their mother for comfort, but Ariel had retreated into a fragile shell, distant and unresponsive. Just fifteen, Cassie had tamped down her own wobbly emotions and stepped up to take care of everyone else. She had been forced to take over the family duties, getting the little ones to school and day care, helping Remy and Trevor with their homework, cooking and cleaning, even figuring out how to pay bills while Mom wallowed in grief.

At times, like this weekend, Cassie still resented her mother for dumping everything on her during that difficult period. But mostly, Cassie had gotten over it by giving up on her mother. If you had no expectations, you could never be disappointed, right? Well, she still needed some financial help from Ariel, but she was working to break free. And when Cassie left for college, she'd tried to move past her annoyance with Mom and build her own life at Oregon State. At last she had friends of her own and a life that was miles away from the Venus flytrap of Mom and the sibs in Timbergrove.

She pulled into the driveway of the Chick Shack, the little house she shared with five other girls, and cut the engine. The car sputtered and bucked, as if chastising her for pushing it too far. Not good. She tried to start it again, but the engine just coughed and wheezed, refusing to turn over. Crap.

"Fine. Take a rest," she told the car.

At least Old Red had gotten her home, and now that she was back on campus she wouldn't need it for a while. She lugged her stuff inside, liking the sound of the dubstep music coming from the little kitchen at the center of the one-story house. Amelie stood at the stove, swaying to the music as she added salt to a pot of water.

"Hey, how's it—" Cassie scowled at the mess of pots, pans, and dishes rising like a tower from a pool of brown water in the sink. "What the hell?"

"I know. Maya did it to us again. She made a big breakfast." Amelie extracted a wooden spoon from the jar of utensils and rapped it against her hand. Tall, trim, and athletic, with a short crop of sandy blond hair, Amelie was a Danish student who had come to Oregon to study agriculture. Her straightforward, cool demeanor made her an awesome housemate, though her visa required her to return to Denmark at the end of the semester.

"Maya said she would come back and clean up after her run," Amelie reported, "but she's been gone for hours."

"Really?"

Amelie tore open a box of macaroni. "I think she ran right over to Jessie's house." Maya's boyfriend, Jessie, lived a few blocks away, and the girl seemed to have trouble breathing when he wasn't around.

"Probably. And she figures we'll clean up after her, the way we always do."

"I had to wash out this pot to make my meal," Amelie said. "Do you want some pastas?"

"No thanks. I just ate." Cassie pulled a paper sack of bagels out of her bag, marked her name on it with a Sharpie, and then stored it in the refrigerator for later that week. Her limited budget had taught her how to stretch and utilize leftovers.

After dumping her stuff in the room she shared with Olivia, her friend from Timbergrove who spent Sunday afternoons at the library, Cassie returned to the kitchen, tossed off her jacket, and approached the sink.

"You can't do it for Maya," Amelie said, stirring her pasta. "She gets away with killing." Amelie's English was fairly well polished, but sometimes she got mixed up on idioms.

"The expression is 'gets away with murder.' " Cassie winced as she plunged one hand into the cool, murky water. "I'm just going to clear the quagmire."

She unplugged the sink, removed the two greasy pans, and stacked the dirty dishes on the side as the sink cleared. She waited for Amelie to drain her pasta, then scrubbed the sink with cleanser and set the dishes back in hot, soapy water. She left the two pans to soak on the side.

"That's the best I can do. I've got to get some schoolwork done." She had an anatomy quiz to study for, and a meeting for a group project in sociology.

"I will do the dishes so the sink can be clear," Amelie said. "But this is the last time."

"That'd be great. I wish we could get rid of piggy Maya, but we need her share of the rent."

"And piggy Maya needs a place to live," Amelie said as she took a bite of pasta over a fashion magazine stretched out on the kitchen table.

"True dat." There was no such thing as a perfect housemate, and overall Cassie knew they had a good group of girls. Olivia was caring and fiercely loyal. Keisha, an education major from Coos Bay, was a party girl, always fun to be around. By contrast, Ellie Wong was serious and low-key, so distant that Cassie sometimes wondered what went on behind those big black glasses. But just when she began to think the girl had detached from her housemates, Ellie would make them all dinner or suggest a movie night.

As Cassie unpacked her clean clothes, she quizzed herself from a diagram of the human skeleton on her laptop. Two hundred and six bones in the human body, and she had to memorize every single one. "Tibia, fibula, patella," she recited as she hung her hoodies on a hook in the closet. "Metatarsal. And then the lateral, intermediate, and medial cuneiform."

Her cell phone pinged with text messages. She stashed her clean socks in the top drawer and grabbed the phone. Hadley, the other girl in the soc group, was begging for them to carry her weight.

Just put my name on the project this time and I swear I'll do the whole thing next time.

Nice offer, but this was the last project of the semester. A second group text from Andrew, the painfully quiet guy on the project, told Hadley not to worry, she was covered.

Really? That was nice of him. Was he going to cover for her, too?

The next text was a private message from Andrew. Did Cassie still want to meet at the library?

Well, she didn't want to, but they had to get this thing done. **Meet you there in 20 minutes.**

At the last minute she'd been afraid she wouldn't recognize him, as he wasn't the kind of guy to make a strong impression. Thin, freckled, and geeky had stuck in her mind, but today as she had spotted him in the sea of studying students in the main gallery, the angles of his face had seemed sort of regal and, well, even chiseled. The blue plaid flannel brought out the periwinkle of his eyes and gave him a rugged outdoor look. And now that she was sitting beside him, she noticed a sweet fragrance that made her want to draw closer. Either he was wearing kick-ass cologne or else he had found the yummiest-smelling fabric softener in existence.

"I was a little surprised that you let Hadley off the hook so easily," Cassie said as she placed her laptop on the table. "I mean, she totally blew us off."

"She said it was an emergency." He stopped writing and tapped his pen on the notebook. "Here's the thing. For what-ever reason, she was bagging out. I figured that the choices were to A) let her off the hook; B) make a big deal about it and try to shame her into helping; and C) tell her she was out of the group and probably getting a zero. B requires too much en-ergy and C is heartless. So A was really the only choice."

"I guess you're right," Cassie admitted, flipping her long hair out of the collar of her jacket. Although she wouldn't have minded making Hadley squirm a little before letting her go. "But it's more work for us, and I wish I had a brilliant idea for this, but I've got an anatomy quiz tomorrow."

"Breitman?" he asked, and she nodded. "You'll do fine. It's straight memorization. She doesn't pull any tricks."

"Good to know."

"And I've got a few ideas I've been tossing around. I was thinking about the culture of San Francisco's Chinatown, which is still a center for Chinese immigration."

She thought about it as she noticed the handful of books on the table about Chinatowns and Chinese immigration that he'd already scanned and bookmarked. "That would work well," she said, picking up one of the books.

As they began to outline their approach, she had to make an effort to keep her eyes on the screen of her computer so that she wouldn't stare at Andrew. She had always found him a bit socially awkward and silent as a stone, but today, with just the two of them, he talked easily, showing her the research he'd found on Chinatown. She liked the way he'd prepared. The books were marked with sticky notes and he'd written out a sheet of notes outlining the research.

"This is great," she admitted. It was the first time someone else in a group had done all the work for her. Well, most of it. "You must have put some time into this, culling research. I feel kind of bad. Do you want me to do the PowerPoint presentation?" she offered.

"You don't have to. I'm fine with doing it together."

"Okay." More than okay, she thought as she set up the PowerPoint on her laptop. This was fun. Something about Andrew made her bubble up inside. He was so smart, and not embarrassed about it. That was a weird turn-on.

Her fingers clicked away on her laptop as he talked about the mythical tale of chop suey, the bubonic plague epidemic denied by Governor Gage, and the fire that destroyed much of San Francisco. Andrew had managed to zero in on the details that were pertinent to their project.

Periodically, she paused to show him a PowerPoint page and discuss design or decide on a photo. She liked the way he leaned forward, alert but serious as he studied the text. The screen illuminated his face, highlighting his amazing lashes, his freckles, his thoughtful eyes.

Not as geeky as she'd thought. He was an engineering major. Wow. She couldn't even imagine the kind of mind-boggling classes he was ticking through. And he was taller than she was, by a few inches. Nice.

As they polished up the presentation, they began to laugh over some of the photos that came up in the search. They talked about San Francisco, which she'd visited once on a field trip. Andrew had been there a few times to visit his aunt and uncle. When the conversation turned to world travel, she learned that his father was an air force officer, whose assignments had taken the family to England, Japan, and Germany.

"What's it like to live in so many foreign countries?" she asked, feeling a bit starstruck.

"Not as exotic as you might think."

"Well, I'm envious."

"And I envy you growing up in suburbia, able to have lasting relationships and stay in the same school."

She closed her laptop. "Not as great as you think. My high school rewarded mediocrity."

"The American way. We'll have to compare stories sometime," he said as they packed up their stuff.

When Andrew offered to walk her home in the dark, she hoped that she was not mistaking a common courtesy for interest. They talked all the way to the Chick Shack, and when she invited him in for coffee, he accepted.

She felt a mixture of pride and awkwardness as she led him into the house. This was a first for her, bringing a guy into the house. She introduced him to Amelie and Keisha, who were watching some reality show on television in the living room.

"You want to hang here?" Keisha, who had been reclining, bundled her blanket onto her lap and swung her feet down to the floor. "We'll make room."

"We're just going to have some coffee," Cassie explained, leading Andrew into the kitchen. She kind of wanted Olivia to come out of the bedroom to meet Andrew, but otherwise she hoped the other girls would leave them alone for now. It was hard to get something going on with housemates flitting in and out.

"So." Cassie lifted the lid on the coffeemaker. "We've got a machine here. And K-Cups. Regular and hazelnut." The girls had to put money in the blue jelly jar for coffee: 80 cents for each K-Cup. Cassie would pitch in after Andrew left. "What would you like?"

"Actually, just water." He lowered his backpack and sat down in one of the kitchen chairs. "I'm not really a coffee drinker."

Her eyebrows rose as she shot him a curious look.

"To be honest, I just wanted to hang with you a little longer," he said, studying her face for a reaction.

"Oh. That's cool." A warm feeling radiated from her heart to the extremities of her body. He liked her. And she had a crazy desire to wrap herself around him and never let go. But for now, they both had to play it down, play it cool.

She was leaning toward the sink, filling a glass with water, when her stomach growled. Dinnertime.

"I'm kind of hungry." She placed the glass on the table in front of him. It was touching, the way he worried his fingers over a button on his flannel shirt. He was nervous.

Well, she was, too, but in a good way. "You up for some cracked-egg ramen?" she offered.

He nodded. "That sounds great."

Cassie turned away to hide her pleased smile as she rummaged in the cupboard for a pot. This was going to be good.

Chapter 6

Rachel knew that she was like a bulldog with a chew toy when a problem was tossed her way. She would grind and maul and gnaw with single-minded focus until she saw the satisfaction of a solution. Sometimes that made her a bit overbearing. But when it came to parenting, she thought it helped her stay focused on showing her kids how to deal with obstacles.

As she drove east toward Bend and Green State, she tried to weigh the various possibilities for KJ's future minus the thick glaze of emotion that distorted things for him right now. She had gone over finances and figured out that, if her oldest son lost his scholarship, there was a way to patch together student loans and savings to cover the next two years. Yes, it was more debt than she wanted to take on, but she believed college was vital to a young man's future. She had made it through Oregon State back in the day when things weren't so expensive, and she was grateful for the experience.

Sunday afternoon traffic was light as she drove along the ridge road that offered the cool shade of mountains on the left with occasional glimpses of Detroit Lake through the tall fir trees on the right. From up here the water was blue, sparkling, and inviting. Tapping on the steering wheel in time to the music, she thought of other possibilities for KJ. He could do a gap year in Washington, D.C. As a political science major, a year as an aide in the Capitol would be great on his résumé. Or maybe they would redshirt KJ, give him a year off from football—time to heal. KJ had plenty of options.

But the young man she found pacing the kitchen of his apartment was not going to see new possibilities. KJ was in crisis.

"I can't believe this is happening to me," he muttered. Barefoot and wearing athletic shorts and a stained T-shirt, he was on a rant. His dark hair was disheveled and oily, his skin blotchy and red. A new growth of dark hair curled on his chin, the beginnings of a soul patch if he trimmed it. What really smote her sense of hope was the stillness in his eyes. Hollow and tired, his eyes had lost their light. He hardly resembled the handsome, clean-cut quarterback that had led his high school team to a state championship. "Everything I've worked for—everything—is turning to shit. My life is over."

"Aw, honey . . ." Rachel reached up to press a hand against his cheek, then hugged him. "Looks like you're not up for going out to dinner."

"What do you expect?" He pulled away from her. "I can't eat or sleep. So, no, sorry if I don't feel like going out."

"No problem. I'll order us some sandwiches from Jimmy Johns." Long ago she had learned that food and sleep took the edge off every crisis. Even when Jackson was dying, in those last days when he'd been confined to a bed in their living room, he had awakened with renewed spirit after dozing off. Yup. What KJ needed was less drama, more sleep and nourishment.

"First, how are you feeling? How's that head?"

"The headache's still there, but the ringing in my ears has stopped. And I didn't throw up this time." He rubbed his hand over one bristly side of his short dark hair. "The doctor told me to rest until Tuesday. I can't believe I got a concussion in a pickup game. I must have a thin skull, like a useless eggshell."

"It's kept your noggin together for more than two decades." She slipped off her jacket and propped herself on a kitchen stool, noticing no sign of the roommate around. "Where's Bowler?"

"He went to a movie with his girlfriend."

That was good. No one to interrupt. "So tell me about the meeting," she said. "What's the takeaway?"

Never one to condense, KJ went through a play-by-play description of how the coaches expressed their appreciation for his team loyalty and leadership, and then went on to cut his heart out. They wanted KJ to get checked out by a neurologist, a Dr. Ginsberg.

"That's a great idea," Rachel interrupted. "Maybe this doctor can be more definitive than the last neurologist you saw."

"Or maybe they want to use whatever she says to write me off," he said, explaining that the coaches were planning to recruit a freshman quarterback for next week. "They're already trying to replace me."

"That's not true. They're just trying to cover all possibilities. They need to give the team some depth—an alternate, in case you can't play." Rachel, with her glass-half-full attitude, understood what the coaches were trying to do.

"But you weren't there, Mom," he snapped. "They told me there were no guarantees."

"There never are. They could redshirt you or drop you completely. But the coaching staff doesn't have a crystal ball. They don't know what's going to happen in the fall, any more than we do."

He hung his head and sighed. "This is so unfair."

"It is what it is. You need to let it go for a while. Things are still fuzzy for you. Right now you need to take it easy and stop thinking about football."

"I can't. It's my future. It's everything to me."

"I know that, and your obsession with football is another concern. But let's dial it back for a second and order some food. Hunger adds stress to the situation." She opened the app on her phone and looked up at him. "What sounds good? Roast beef, turkey? Or do you want the Gargantuan?"

They decided on two turkey sandwiches, and she placed the order. She coaxed him into the living room in an attempt to get him to relax and stop pacing. "And how about a cup of tea?

That always settles my nerves." When he started to get up she waved him down. "Let me wait on you. I can only stay for a few hours, so you might as well take advantage of it." As she heated up a mug of water in the microwave, she asked about his girlfriend, a sophomore journalism major, whom he'd met when she had interviewed him for the school newspaper.

"Lindsay is a disappointment, just like everything else," he said. "She's been around, but she's no help at all." He complained that she didn't understand what he was going through.

"Cut the girl some slack. She's not your therapist or your mother."

"I think she should be here for me."

"You said she's been around, and that says a lot. You're not a very fun person right now. Look, it's fine with me if you want to cut Lindsay loose, but don't blame her for your unhappiness."

He was sitting back on the couch, staring off with a sour expression when she handed him the tea sweetened with sugar.

"You're welcome, Cookie Monster," she said, referring to one of his favorite characters from childhood.

"Yeah, thanks. I appreciate what you're doing, Mom. I just know everything's a lot worse than you think it is."

"You've always had a flair for the dramatic, and you've got a concussion. Confusion is one of the symptoms. And speaking of cookies . . ." She turned toward her tote bag, where she had stashed a tin of cookies. "I made these last night. Oatmeal chocolate chip. I figured you could use some cheering up."

"Mom." He lowered his voice as his head lolled back against the sofa. "I'm too old for this. There are some problems that cookies can't fix."

"Shut up and drink your tea. Not to burst your bubble, but we are not talking about curing cancer or ending a war here. I take your problems quite seriously, but I also know that some things in life work themselves out." She went back into the kitchen and returned with her mug of steeping tea. "So. Now it's time to recuperate. And when you're feeling better, you'll work to change the things you can, and you'll have to let go of the things beyond your control."

KJ took a sip of tea and lowered the mug. "So you're saying I'm an asshole."

"No, honey." She took a cookie for herself. "Right now you're acting like one, but I'm confident that you'll get over it."

It was dangerous to let him into her house. Ariel knew that. But with Cassie gone back to school and the younger kids up in their rooms, Ariel knew no one would be the wiser. Her kids had been taught to leave Mom alone when she was in her studio, and with the door locked, there would be no accidents.

She was free to take him, explore the hard lines and planes of his body, and share the ripe, soft curves that defined her. She needed this. In a suburb of sameness and routine, a family community where everyone was so focused on the kids, the students, the damned SAT scores, and the car wash for the soccer team, Ariel needed an outlet... her own secret pleasure. And damn those PTA warriors if they couldn't accept that a hot middle-aged woman still enjoyed sex.

"Tell me you want me." His voice was an enticing whisper that demanded she stay close. "Tell me how much you missed me... how much you missed this."

She told him with her lips, her hot mouth, her hands, and finally, that primal connection that filled the empty places inside her with satisfaction.

He was one of the few men who liked to cuddle afterward, and that was fine by Ariel. Most of the others dozed off or found some excuse to head off. But he liked to stay, holding her close in his strong arms, flesh on flesh. The feel of his chest rising and falling settled her in a surprising way, and she had to admit that she liked being held. There was a reassuring message in his embrace that said:

I've got you. I can take care of you. I'll hold you together.

Their entangled bodies sank into the lemon velvet sofa, and she closed her eyes and imagined them drifting together through space.

"I want to stay with you," he said. "Wake up beside you. I want to hold you through the night."

Much as she would like to be held, Ariel knew she couldn't take him up to her bed. "I can't let my kids see you. There'd be hell to pay."

"Your kids love me."

"It's not going to happen."

He didn't understand about the kids. He never had. Guys never did. It pissed her off, the whole gender thing. Women were born with the ability to give birth and after that they got stuck with all the nurturing assignments that followed. Men were born with the need to mark their territory and move on to the next conquest. No nurturing there. Except for Oliver. He had cared about her girls, loved them like his own daughters. He had been one of a kind.

"And anyway, you have to go." She rolled back, hating the cold air that rushed between them, the separation that signaled a return to the mundane routine of life. He had stuff to take care of, and so did she. Society had built in complex ways to keep people apart, snuffing the flame out of sexual creatures like her. She got up from the couch and reached down for her jeans.

He looked at the time on his cell phone, then sat up abruptly. "Yeah, I'd better get going." His hand cupped one cheek of her backside before she could slide her jeans up. "But I don't want to."

She glanced back at him, at his thick erection, and that male body, all muscle and bone and raw sexuality. Desire licked through her as she thought of giving it another go. It'd be sweet, but stupid.

"You'd better get out of here," she said. Damn, but she hated being the voice of reason.

Chapter 7

Where the hell was Ariel? The meeting was about to start. Rachel took inventory of the moms and one dad assembling in the green room for the Gleetime parents' meeting. Plenty of strident conversation, perfume clouds, and stylish glasses with black, blue, or bright red frames. But no Ariel.

She probably forgot, and now it was too late for Rachel to back out of the room and make a beeline over to her friend's house. Rachel wanted to kick herself for not shooting her friend a reminder or swinging by to pick her up. Last time they had talked about this meeting, Ariel had joked about coming down with a cold or a hangnail or bubonic plague; showed you how much Ariel hated these community things. Rachel could think of plenty of things she would rather do on a Tuesday night, and after a day on her feet, she needed to get horizontal. She pulled a chair out from one of the round tables and took a load off.

Without Ariel by her side, Rachel felt out of sorts among the soccer moms and parents, many of whom acknowledged Rachel as their stylist but had never bonded with her outside the hair salon.

Some of them Rachel had known since her kids were in grade school. Women like tiger mom Nan Lee and perennial volunteer Margaret King, who was a self-righteous know-it-all, had pushed Rachel and Ariel to form a bond to survive.

"Are we going to start?" Margaret held up her cell phone like a beacon, showing the time displayed on the screen. "It's five after seven. Let's go. Where's Craig?"

"He'll be right back," said Nora Delfatti. With a squat face and body, Nora was solid and level—probably the most solid, centered woman in the bunch. Cutting Nora's hair was always a calming experience. If it weren't for Nora's job writing university grants, which consumed much of her time, Rachel felt sure they would have been better friends. "He went to the office to get some flyers."

"He should have done that before," Estee said. "I don't have all day." Standing like a statue in the corner of the room, gaunt and darkly glamorous Estee Sherer was majestic, cold, and unapproachable, much like the Sherers' lakefront palace, which very few of the high schoolers had ever been allowed to enter. When Sage Sherer had made it into Gleetime, the other moms had assumed that Estee would offer up one of the cavernous rooms as rehearsal space. Estee had quickly put the kibosh on that. "I don't like kids," she had told Rachel without an ounce of shame. "Why would I invite a bunch of loud teenagers into my home?"

"Ladies, I say if he isn't back in five we all go for margueritas at Wimplebees," said Dawn Opaka, a big-talking mom who always had a million ideas but never actually did anything. That elicited a big round of giggles from the other do-nothing moms huddled with Dawn, who proudly flipped her spun-gold hair out of her eyes. Considering the amount of product it took to maintain that golden sheen of Dawn's hair, the woman should have purchased stock in the company.

Rachel didn't really know the other women in Dawn's group, mostly because one of them was friends with a stylist at a salon in Portland, and the three of them made the trek into town for what they considered to be more cosmopolitan haircuts. She did avert her eyes from Patti Cronin, the mother of Matty, who used to tease Jared back in junior high, always threatening to beat him up and calling him "homo boy." Rachel had handled that little turd and his sidekick, Tai Belnavis, through the principal. Another woman was the mother of Armand Ahari, a brilliant kid who was bound for Cornell; the other had a son named Riley who was a talented drummer.

"In another ten minutes, they'll be doing the late happy hour at Stanford's!" Dawn announced, garnering a hoot of laughter from her friends.

To hide her lack of amusement Rachel turned away from them and locked eyes with the one man in the room. Anthony Lopez gave a polite smile, but he did not budge from his spot in the shadows at the edge of the room where he leaned against a wall, arms crossed. The only man in the group, Anthony was a carpenter who had taken on the design and construction of most of the sets since his son Rick had been cast in a play last year.

Rachel was headed over to thank Anthony for all his hard work on the sets for the Christmas show when the theater director, Craig Schulteis, flew into the room.

"Is this our group? Nice turnout!" Craig Schulteis had the flashing blue eyes of a Hollywood star, embedded in the face of "Mr. Normal," as Ariel called him. Of medium height and stature, with a bland face and shoulders that seemed a bit wide for his frame, Craig was saved from mediocrity by his enthusiasm and his amazing eyes.

As one of the few passably attractive single men in Timbergrove, Craig seemed to bring out the flirt in the high school moms. Admittedly, Rachel had fallen under his spell a time or two with simple fantasies. She could see herself pressed up against him, melting in the light of those blue eyes and taking comfort from that strong wall of a chest. Yes, she could. Other times, she wondered if the whole flirt campaign was just an act. Maybe he had no interest in well-preserved and -oiled suburban moms.

"Thanks for coming out, everyone. I've got flyers with all the pertinent information for our Spring Showcase, which is right around the corner." As he spoke, Craig passed the stack of flyers to Nora Delfatti. "So we'll need someone in charge of publicity, costumes, makeup, and hair. Anthony, I'm trusting that you'll manage our set construction, as usual. I promise you, we will keep it simple," he said, clasping his hands in prayer position as he faced Lopez.

Anthony nodded. "Will do."

"This year I'm going to have the students manage the house and take care of ticket sales. Some of our tech students built a Web site for purchasing tickets, and we'll have students man the box office. What am I forgetting? Anything?"

"I'm sure there's more, but we'll figure it out as we go along," Dawn said with a flirty little smile. Was her skin actually shimmering? Yup. The woman was wearing one of those glitter sheens, here at a parents' meeting.

"Of course. What would I do without you, Dawn?" Craig opened his arms in a gracious gesture of thanks. Or was there more to it? Definitely a vibe between Dawn and Craig.

Nora Delfatti raised two fingers. "Since I already placed some ads in the *Timbergrove Times,* I'll handle publicity."

"It's all yours," Craig said.

"I'll do hair," Rachel volunteered, knowing that no one else would want it.

Dawn circled one red-lacquered finger, as if lassoing her posse. "We'll all do makeup."

That would mean plenty of lined crimson lips and glittering faces. Rachel sank her teeth into her lower lip. If Ariel were here, she would have jumped on makeup and gotten the job done correctly.

Other moms signed up, and Craig made a list of each group on his phone. Nan Lee and Liz Luchter signed up for costumes, though there would not be much work to do there. The Gleetime kids received matching costumes in the fall—formal attire for the boys and sparkling, full-skirted dresses for the girls—and the same costumes had to last until the end of the school year. The kids would need wardrobe for the duets and sketches, but often the students used their own clothes.

"I'll help you with the costumes," offered Angela Harrell, a stoic-faced woman with hair in a long braid down the back of her neck. Rachel felt sure that, if she ever unraveled that hair, moths would fly out. The Harrells were strict Christians whose objection to evolution warranted them pulling their daughter Mary out of some history classes and prohibiting her from taking Anthropology. And yet, Angela didn't seem disturbed by her daughter's penchant for low-cut sweaters and costumes that resembled hookers' attire. Rachel didn't get the woman, so she just smiled and tried to keep her distance.

As details were ironed out, Rachel stood by quietly speculating about Craig. Was he gay? Secretly dating? Divorced and bitter? Maybe a serial dater. Nothing wrong with that. Rachel, who had no sex life, liked to imagine that someday a responsible older gentleman with charisma would find her. But since she did not do the bar scene and she was not going to hook up with a psycho through that online dating garbage, her new lover would have to be someone like Craig who was already a part of her life.

When the meeting ended, Rachel went up to the table to take an extra flyer for Ariel. To her surprise, Craig excused himself from the supermoms and stepped in to intercept her. "Rachel . . ." His eyes were blue as a summer sky. "You've been hiding something from me."

Her throat was suddenly dry as she faced him, not a clue as to what he was talking about. Unless, of course, he was privy to her fantasies. "Have I?"

"Just that dynamite 'Singin' in the Rain' number your son is putting together with Remy Alexander. Or hasn't he mentioned it?"

There had been one rehearsal at Ariel's studio. "How did you know about it? Auditions aren't till next week, right?"

"I saw them working out some choreography in the school studio at lunchtime, and they did a short run-through for me." He held up one hand to shield his words from the others. "Don't quote me, but they're a shoo-in for state. In fact, I'm thinking of incorporating the number in the Spring Showcase if they have it ready in time."

"Craig . . ." She felt a surge of gratitude at his support. Did he know about the recruiter coming to state? "That would be wonderful."

He nodded, shifting his eyes over to the ladies, then lowering his voice. "I think so. Might be just the boost our showcase needs."

Rachel knew that was code for, "The showcase is drowning in a sea of lackluster talent!" Jared had mentioned that Sage Sherer was doing an operatic song that made his balls ache— his exact words—and Blake Luchter was doing a country solo, despite the fact that he had trouble staying on key. That was high school politics: To the big donors go the spoils.

"I don't know how you do it," she told Craig, nodding toward the gaggle of ladies.

"Oh. Well. I love my job." He flicked at his cheek, a nervous habit. "Just not every aspect of it."

"I bet. Someday, we'll have to get together and swap stories." There. She'd given him the perfect entrée. He could suggest a cup of coffee or a glass of wine.

"You bet." He winked at her—not a sexy gesture; more of a grandpa wink.

What did that mean? "So what do you—"

"Excuse me." He was already looking over her shoulder. "I've got a fire to put out." He stepped toward the costume ladies, waving one hand. "Did I hear someone mention budget? Because we don't have one. We're using costumes and props from our inventory."

She headed to the door, wondering if that was just bad timing or a way for him to avoid her overture. Dang it. If only Ariel were here to put her two cents in.

Three blocks from home, Rachel turned off her usual route and headed toward Ariel's house. She was dying to get her friend's input on the Craig situation, and she needed to drop off the flyer.

The house seemed dark as she pulled her Subaru up to the curb and cut the engine. The second-story windows were dark, the younger kids probably in bed. After all, it was almost ten. From here she couldn't see Remy's back bedroom or the master, though there seemed to be some muted light coming from the studio. She texted Ariel, saying that she was here, just came from the Spring Showcase meeting, didn't want to bug her, but would leave the flyer in the mudroom.

Come get me if you're up for a chat.

She held on to the phone for a minute or so as she watched the house, expecting a light to go on in the studio, or maybe even the mudroom door to fly open to reveal Ariel in her silk pajamas, waving her inside. Both Ariel and Rachel were night owls compared to most of their neighbors, who rose before sunrise and hit the local coffee shops or jogging paths. Bored, Rachel opened the console and gathered the old gum and lozenge wrappers into a ball, which she shoved into her travel cup. She liked to keep her car tidy; even though the vehicle was six years old, sometimes it still had that new car smell.

The seconds ticked away in her ears, the silence in the car overwhelming. No use waiting. Ariel was probably in the shower or working on a song, which she did from time to time. She'd never had much luck selling one of her creations, but you never know. Best to drop the flyer and go.

The mudroom door was open, as always, and recorded music pulsed through the adjoining wall and door. The narrow room with a long bench and cubbies served as a place for Ariel's students to wait while Ariel was finishing a lesson in the studio. Rachel put the flyer on the cubby counter by the door, holding it in place with the deep-mauve-and-blue plate Remy had made in ceramics class. She was halfway back to the door when the throbbing bass of the music caught her attention. That was no show tune. Sort of a sexy Meghan Trainor. Maybe Rihanna? Pausing to listen for a moment, Rachel heard the deep rumble of a man's chuckle.

"Oh. My. God," she whispered, pressing a hand to her mouth. "Stosh." What the hell was he doing back in town, back in Ariel's house?

Still as a stone, she listened intently. She could hear their voices, but they were muffled by the wall and the music, keeping her from making out anything beyond the tone, which was decidedly smooth and low.

At least they weren't fighting.

She edged closer to the door and waited. Now the playful noises were giving way to moans and . . . spanking?

Not a beating, but the torturous, rapturous, rhythmic sounds of two bodies engaged in an active sexual romp.

Rachel felt stung, curious, and intrigued, all at the same time. A voyeuristic part of her wanted to stay and listen; this was the closest she had gotten to any sign of passion since her husband had taken ill.

But the moral part of her wanted to barge in and demand that Stosh leave her friend alone. How dare he come back here? She should march in there and drive him out the door, straight out of town.

But she couldn't do that. It was not her call, even if the man was a worthless abuser. Rachel loved her friend dearly, but all the good intentions in the world could not protect Ariel from her own decisions, her own desires.

Damn it.

Maybe just a little scare? Rachel considered stomping around the mudroom in the hopes that the lovers would hear her and have the mood ruined. Coitus interruptus. But really? It was none of her beeswax. Feeling a mixture of guilt and alarm, she fled the mudroom.

As she drove home, she wondered how Ariel pulled that off, entertaining a man while her kids were asleep. Remy had to be up and about still. Didn't Ariel worry about her kids barging in or overhearing? Apparently not. It reminded Rachel that, next fall, she would be an empty nester with two sons away at school. She could entertain her imaginary gentleman friend all night long, swinging from the chandelier and making love on the rug in front of the fire.

Too bad he was just imaginary.

* * *

The next morning Rachel pushed herself out the door into the misty rain to get her run in. In Oregon, if you waited until the rain stopped to go running, you would never get outside. The last few months had been so consistently wet that Rachel had taken to putting her running shoes on the heat vent. She knew it wasn't good for them, but stiff shoes were preferable to wet ones.

With a baseball cap and her hood staving off the drizzle, she jogged her loop along the trails that cut through the park with the totem sculpture and around by Briar's farm. Rachel hated exercise, but she did it for the relief of being done with it. One of these days she was going to get an exercise bike and take a load off her feet, but right now, with two in college next fall, a big purchase like that was out of the question.

She was warmed up now, enjoying the sensation of flying as she passed through the park on the return trip. The trail spilled out of the park and past the elementary school. She leaped over a puddle and forged ahead, happy to be in the home-stretch and loving her neighborhood. Where else could she feel safe running alone amid trees and grass and art in the park? Fat baskets of flowers hung from the lamppost on each corner, and she drank in the bright shades of poppy and lemon yellow, royal purple, and lipstick pink. Rain or shine, life was good in the town of Timbergrove.

A line of cars eased into the school parking lot: moms and some dads dropping their kids off for school. It seemed like yesterday that Rachel had been waiting in that line with both boys in the car, and then, two years later, just Jared, her scraggly little guy who'd caused her so much worry. Ironically, these days it was the older kid who'd been keeping her up nights with his fatalistic comments about life while Jared seemed to be moving toward his dreams. You never knew how things would turn out.

She spotted Ariel's BMW pulling up to the elementary school for the drop-off. Grinning, she called out a greeting to Kath Monahan, who worked the crosswalk with her flag and orange vest. She cut into the school driveway, jogged up to the over-hang, and ran in place, mugging for Ariel and the kids as the beamer approached.

"Aunt Rachel, what are you doing here?" Trevor asked as he popped out at the curb.

"Just happened to be in the neighborhood," she answered, patting his shoulder.

"I knew that was you!" Maisy said, reaching out to hug her. Rachel felt a gush of joy at the contact. Oh, she wished she'd had just one girl.

Quickly, she sent the kids on their way and jumped into the vacated passenger seat.

"Hey, honey!" Ariel's dark eyes were bright, her smile re-flecting her vibrant good mood. "Wanna go for coffee?"

"Absolutely. My first appointment isn't until eleven and we need to catch up." Wednesday was Rachel's late day at work, so she usually started around noon and went through till nine p.m. or as late as her clients needed her.

"I saw the flyer," Ariel said as she swung out of the school parking lot. "I meant to drop you a text. I had a phone confer-ence with a producer."

"Really?" Rachel worked the zipper of her hoodie up and down. "Well, you didn't miss much at the meeting. Except I wasn't sure if you wanted to sign up for hair with me or join the Walking Dead Moms on the makeup crew."

"Like that's a choice. I'm with you, girlfriend. But I'll bring my makeup box, just in case." During lean times in Holly-wood, Ariel had worked as a makeup artist, as well as a sales-clerk at a pricey department store. One of those gals who pulled you aside for a quick makeover to hawk their products, and you bought their whole line because you thought you might turn out looking half as gorgeous as the salesperson. Rachel suspected Ariel had done well with that.

"Well, that's good." Rachel let the Craftsman homes and trees blur beyond the window as she decided to go for it. "'Cuz I'd hate to let a little angry sex come between us."

"What the hell are you talking about?"

"You. Doing the nasty with Stosh when I dropped the flyer off last night."

"What?" Ariel's head snapped around, her features strained for a moment before softening into a grin. "Oh. That."

"Yup. You were pretty far into it when I stopped by. And honestly? I was worried all night. You know Stosh is bad news for you."

"Yes, he is," Ariel agreed.

"And you know I don't approve. I won't lie about that, but please, don't let him come between us. No man is worth that."

"Right again. But you don't need to worry, Rach. It's not Stosh."

"What? It's not?" It was Rachel's turn to be taken by surprise. It did not occur to her that Ariel could have hooked up with someone else so quickly. "Well, aren't you a fast worker. I am relieved and amazed. Who the hell was it?"

"Someone I've known for a while." Ariel kept her eyes on the road, the mauve lacquer of her nails reflecting light as she smoothly turned the wheel of the BMW. "But it's a relatively new thing."

"Who?" Rachel could barely contain her curiosity. "Tell me. I need details. You know I haven't had sex since the mullet was in. Help a friend out here."

"Stop putting yourself down, and give me a little space."

"Seriously? You're not going to tell me?"

Ariel shook her head. "He doesn't want to go public yet, and I'm good with that. I'm not sure he's going to be around too long. Maybe it won't last."

"I'm not asking you to marry him, I just want to know who he is." Rachel turned in her seat, totally focused on her friend's response. "Okay, you don't have to tell me, but when I say a name you can shake it off."

"Nope."

"Is it Dave Tang?" Dave was their insurance agent, single and attractive, but socially awkward. Lived with his mom and worked out of a little shed in the backyard.

"I am not going to play this game," Ariel said.

"You didn't even blink. It's not Dave," Rachel said, study-ing Ariel's face. "Let's see, what other single men do we have in town? Come out, come out, wherever you are. Craig Schul-teis? No, never mind, can't be him. He was at the meeting. How about the pharmacist. That guy is loaded. What's his name? Sam something."

"Sam Hornbecker, and it's not him."

Rachel squinted at her friend. "It's got to be someone with money. Is it that estate lawyer, Ron Bolen? No, no, it couldn't be. That man is so old that his dingle berries must be dried peas."

That made Ariel laugh. "You know, older can be quite sea-soned and aged, like a fine wine."

"Or a stinky cheese," Rachel responded. Although she made light of Ariel's affair, she was a tiny bit jealous. Here she was holding on to daydreams about Craig Schulteis, a sexually neb-ulous drama teacher, while Ariel was having hot sex, acting out her fantasies with a mystery man. And all this had hap-pened barely a week after dismissing her Hollywood producer boyfriend. Rachel had to know who this guy was.

"Is it someone from out of town?" Rachel asked.

"My lips are sealed." Ariel pinched her fingers together and made a gesture of zipping closed her lips.

"If you're not going to tell me who, at least tell me how," Rachel said. "I could sure use a few pointers on how to get from first base to home plate."

"You're fine, honey. You know how to talk to men. You make everyone feel comfortable and so good about themselves."

"So what is it about me that sends men running in the other direction?"

"It's not you, it's . . . men. They're so confused about what they want. Sometimes you just have to take them by the hand and tell them."

"Tell them what? What do they want?"

"Besides sex? Not much."

"I was afraid of that. That ship has sailed for me. I'll never have your luck attracting men."

"I'm not sure *luck* is the right word." Ariel frowned. "Men want me. They want to possess me and have their way with me. I don't know what it is, but I'm telling you, it's a gift and a curse, too."

"Mmm." Rachel slipped off her seat belt as they arrived at the coffee shop on Main Street. "A terrible curse." She struck a haughty pose. "Don't hate me because I'm beautiful. I'll take some of that."

"You *are* beautiful," Ariel said, though it seemed a bit forced and pat.

"But not voluptuous." Stepping up to the coffee shop window, Rachel caught a glimpse of their reflections. Ariel was a trim line of curves, her jeans hugging the swell of her hips, her suede-collared hunting jacket cinched in at the waist, her black T cut just low enough to reveal a hint of bountiful cleavage.

Next to Ariel, Rachel was hardly the picture of femininity. She was all thighs in her running tights, her jacket straining over her wide hips. A big lump of spandex. She tugged her zipper up and shoved her hands into the pockets of her jacket. To everything there was a season. And apparently, she was way beyond the season of feminine wiles.

Chapter 8

"Let's take it from the top, one more time," Ariel said, leaving the sheet music for "Singin' in the Rain" open to the last page, as she now knew the song by heart. She should, after a solid week of daily rehearsals. Despite Rachel's concern that Jared would be annoyed at being pushed to partner with Remy, he had been pleased by the whole setup. Which did not surprise Ariel at all. These kids had known each other since diaper days, and they could find a groove together when they both put their egos aside.

"Wait. Hold on. Let me get this closed," Remy said as she fumbled with the red umbrella.

"Let me. And you get a sip of tea," Jared said, taking the umbrella and nodding toward the table by the sofa. "You need to keep that throat lubricated."

"I know," Remy said, scooting over to grab her tea dosed with honey and lemon to soothe her throat. "I can't fall apart now." She had a handful of numbers to perform in for the showcase and state finals, not to mention her other classes. It was a lot of pressure for a young person, but Ariel had confidence in her daughter.

"No one will be falling apart," Ariel said firmly. "Keep breathing with your diaphragm; no more of that head voice. It's too nasal anyway."

"Right. Got it." Remy put the cup down and scurried over to take her place beside Jared. "Okay. Hit it, Mom."

Ariel launched into the song's intro, tapping the piano keys as she watched Jared start the number. He danced past a frozen Remy, bringing her to life to join in. They used the closed umbrellas as canes, moving in unison. Some of the jaunty dance steps were inspired by the movie; others were innovated by the kids. They traded off verses and shared the chorus, building to the finish, in which they popped open the umbrellas, and then tossed them aside to dance in the rain.

The burst of energy and delight between them was awesome. Fantastic! So dynamic that Ariel longed to push away from the piano and dance along with them. She missed being in the limelight, on stage or on camera. Suburban life was good for her family but toxic for her creative soul.

"Just singin'!" Jared sang in a jazzy echo to Remy's melody. The kid was holding his own, really shining next to Remy, and that was the greatest surprise here. The chipmunk of a boy who had been bullied off and on since junior high now exuded charm and talent. Despite his odd walking gait he was literally dancing circles around Remy, moving with a spring in his step.

"Very nice," Ariel announced when the song ended.

"I think we nailed it, J-dawg." Remy snapped selfies with Jared as Ariel rose from the piano and mulled over the best way to refine their routine. She leaned in to smell the sweet scent of her coral roses in the crystal vase. The blooms would only last another day or two, but these cup-shaped blossoms were among her favorites. The crystal vase was always filled with flowers; it was one of the few accents in the studio. Sometimes when she was struggling through a tedious lesson she needed to focus on the flowers to remember that beauty and art still existed in the world.

"So whaddaya think, Mom?" Remy asked, sneaking a photo of Ariel leaning into the flowers.

"You guys have come a long way in a week. Really. The number has great energy, and the choreography is totes adorbs."

"Yay!" A smile lit Remy's face as she did a little happy dance.

"But . . ." Jared held up one finger. "There's always a but, right, Ariel?" He pushed the hair back from his dark eyes, challenging her. "A few more changes?"

"Umm-hmm. In the biz, we call them notes. You guys are ninety-five percent there. I'm here to help you with the last five percent."

"Fair enough." Jared put his hands on his hips. "Let 'er rip."

Ariel gave them a few notes on timing and pitch. Jared was rushing the intro, Remy was belting too much, and they needed to modulate their volume. "Don't belt until the finale."

Jared cast a disapproving look at Remy. "I told you we were singing too loud."

"So we'll scale it back. Calm down."

"You're the one who's got all the answers."

"I know you are, but what am I?" Remy taunted him.

"Cut it out, you two." Ariel pressed the butt of one hand to her forehead. "Stop acting like real siblings. You were getting along so well."

"She's got a stubborn streak," Jared said.

"And you're not the boss of me," Remy replied, then took a deep sip of tea to seal the conversation.

"Figure it out, brats." Ariel walked away, rolling her eyes. These two really did belong together.

As the kids dropped their beef and swung back into their dance routine, Ariel went to the water dispenser and opened a tea bag. As the orange pekoe steeped, she went to the window and gazed at the green leaves of the laurel, glimmering with rain. They had endured a cold, rainy May, with hardly a whiff of summer in the air. Could she take another year of this rain? Wishing herself out of this place, she cupped her hands around the mug and stared out at the dripping buds on the trees.

She had come to Oregon for her girls, knowing that their lives would be too difficult and expensive in Southern California. How many years ago was it that she landed here and met Rachel and her boys? It would be fifteen years this summer.

She flashed back to their first meeting at the swim park, two young moms trying to coax their kids into the water. Ariel had moved here after she'd dumped Paul Alexander, her tattooed road worker who'd given her a place to sleep when she first arrived in Hollywood. How she'd loved his gruff, hard demeanor; inside he'd had a good heart. When they had first met, Ariel possessed the skills to melt the mean off Paul, but as her attention was drawn away by the sitcom role and their babies, the hearty handyman had lost his luster. Paul wasn't a bad person, but he'd had no patience for babies and he was the kind of guy who felt threatened by his woman's success. Although he'd given up drinking for her, his addictive personality had not changed. When Ariel caught him using the money she'd set aside for the nanny on meth, she gave him the boot. Her own zero tolerance policy. Damn him.

When she kicked him out, he said he was going up to Alaska. She tossed him a wool cap from the closet and wished him good luck. After that he'd sent a few messages, which she'd passed on to the girls with a little sugarcoating, but she had never seen him again, and she wasn't sorry about that. She wasn't going to play a part in an addiction melodrama.

Ariel had suffered through enough of that shit with her father. Yas had been a smooth talker with big dreams and an endless appetite for alcohol. As a kid she had loved his stories. She had loved him, a lot more than she cared for her mother, who was coldhearted and unhappy, her lips always pinched tight, as if she had just swallowed vinegar. That sour heart had seized a few years back. Ariel had gotten word from an aunt in Oklahoma, but she hadn't cared to attend the funeral. She had missed her father's funeral, too, but with him she had stayed long enough to say her good-byes.

The last time she saw her dad, she was only a teenager and he was so reduced and shriveled that she could hold him in her arms like a pet. Once a strong, solid Navajo man, he had been reduced to skin and bones . . . and then dust. Yas Dehiya was his name. Their surname, Dehiya, was Navajo for "one who went upward," but, unless you counted that ecclesiastical rise to heaven, that had not been true of her dad. He never went far from the bottle.

When she left home, Ariel vowed that she would manifest the family name through her success. Onward and upward. The day after she graduated from high school she got on a bus headed west. It took her three days of riding buses with armrests tacky from dirty hands and upholstery smelling of human soil. But she made it to Hollywood and scrambled to make "friends" and get auditions. Producers, nearly all of them male, were attracted to her exotic dark looks, and she was happy to be arm candy in exchange for a few parts. Her experience with her father had taught her how to work people to give her what she wanted. She bartered with sex, but she never gave away her soul. Sex was a game, an animal instinct that was miles apart from the delicate web of true love.

Success had happened fast for her. A series of solid roles had helped her land a show of her own, a singing witch, a role that optimized her vocal talents and sexuality. Not even twenty, and she'd been a star. Ariel had embraced the process of starring in a sitcom. She had loved the weekly routine that began with a table reading and wound up with a high-energy show performed in front of an enthusiastic audience. The cast of *Wicked Voice* had become her family for those fabulous years, during which she'd gotten pregnant with both her girls. They had shot around her belly both times, and Ariel had barely had to work to get her body back after childbirth. She'd maintained her iconic role as America's sexy singing witch . . . until reality programming slammed into their time slot and killed the show.

By necessity, she had brought her girls to the Northwest for a brief hiatus . . . which had lasted fifteen years. Some of those years had been good ones, especially after Oliver came along and pulled Ariel and the girls into a sweet little family. Dear Oliver. She still couldn't allow herself to think of him without getting weepy.

Turning away from the window of the studio, she sipped her tea and observed Remy and Jared working on some dance steps. Once upon a time, Ariel and Rachel had hoped that one set of their kids might get together. "Wouldn't that be the bomb?" Rachel used to say. "Then we could be in-laws together." With two sets of kids the same age, they thought it might happen. But then KJ, Rachel's oldest, had hooked up with a girl in junior high, and Cassie was cold and leery of men. With Ariel's luck, that girl would join some sort of severe religious order. And now Remy and Jared looked cute together, but Remy had a boyfriend and, with his newfound confidence, Jared was going to be breaking hearts soon.

"You guys are looking great," Ariel told them, "but I need to get ready for my next tutoring session. Let's pick a time for tomorrow." She went over to the table by her window and checked her appointment book for Friday. "Ooh. Tomorrow is a little tight."

Gripping Ariel's arm, Remy leaned in for a look. "Wow, Mom. Your schedule is jam-packed."

"That's typical before the spring show," Ariel admitted.

"But you've got Graham Oyama every day! That's a little extreme when he's already perfect." Remy cocked her head, her dark curls tumbling to one side. "Perfect at singing. Perfect at baseball, academics, and debate."

"He'll probably end up being President," Jared agreed, though the comment was laced with criticism, as if that would be the worst occupation in the world.

"Let's retract the claws." Ariel reserved comment on gorgeous Graham and scheduled them in for later in the evening and closed her book.

Jared grabbed his backpack and headed out, but Remy remained hunched over the piano keyboard, playing "Heart and Soul" while Ariel threw open a window and pulled out a quick mop. She had noticed a few dust particles flying in the light as the kids danced, and the only thing she hated more than cleaning was living in dust.

Remy stopped playing long enough to snap a photo of herself at the piano, then continued. "Mom, can I ask you a question?" Remy said, staring off into the distance like a philosopher. "Did you ever break up with someone and you regretted it afterward?"

Grabbing a clump of dirt under the piano with the Swiffer, Ariel considered the question. *Certainly not your father,* she thought, though it would be cruel to share that with Remy.

"I did break it off with a guy once, when I lived in California. And afterward I worried that I'd let a really good one get away." Back in the Hollywood days when a convertible, a house in the hills, and a studio job made a man a catch. "So I went back to him and told him I was wrong."

"Really? What happened?"

Ariel laughed. "We got back together. But then I dumped him again two months later. The guy had a lot of perks, but he was too full of himself." It amused Ariel to think back on that story. "What was that guy's name? Ray? Or maybe Gray."

Remy played a sharp chord. "I may have made a mistake breaking up with Cooper."

"What? You broke up with Cooper? When?" It was the first Ariel had heard of this, and her initial reaction was to tell her daughter to get that guy back. Cooper's family was loaded, and although money did not buy happiness, it could pay for a lot of nice things, including financial security. And that trip to Europe this summer.

"I told him this week, and he's not taking it well."

"And you're thinking of getting back together?" Ariel leaned the sweeper against the wall.

"Sort of. I didn't mean to hurt him; that makes me feel awful. And I miss being Cooper's girlfriend. It's like a titled position, like prom queen or something."

Remy turned worried eyes to Ariel, then hunched over the keys again. "Which is all so stupid, because one of the things that annoyed me when we were together was the way he acted like he owned me. Like I was arm candy. And now, I miss that."

"It's nice to belong," Ariel agreed, trying to stay unbiased though she couldn't deny feeling a pinch of regret. Ariel had been able to relax, knowing her daughter was with Cooper.

"Breaking up isn't always a clear-cut thing. Sometimes you know he's bad for you, but still, you miss him."

"I don't miss Cooper," Remy said quickly. "He's not a bad guy, but he's not for me. No chemistry. Or maybe I expect too much."

Ariel slid onto the bench beside her daughter and slung an arm over her shoulders. "Welcome to the big-girl world. When it comes to relationships, there are a lot of gray areas." Ariel wanted to encourage Remy to stick with Cooper for a while. Through prom and graduation . . . and that trip to Europe. Not to pimp her daughter out, but that guy had some nice benefits. "Do you think you'll stay with Coop for a bit?"

"I can't be his girlfriend." Remy was sure of this. "It would be like tricking him, when I know our relationship won't last."

Somehow, my daughter has her own strong sense of morality. Ariel knew it did not come from her.

When Remy shifted, Ariel had to turn away to hide her disappointment. Her eyes went to the yellow sofa, where she had ridden him relentlessly last night. Entangled in a relationship that was wrong, a relationship that wouldn't last, Ariel knew what she should do about it. But she wasn't ready to take the moral high ground like her daughter. At least not today. Not tonight.

"Checking the clock?" Remy asked. "I'm sorry to lay this on you. Here, do you want me to help you finish cleaning up?"

"Sure. Grab the duster and hit the piano."

They made quick work of finishing off the studio.

"I'm proud of you, Remy." Ariel coiled up the cord on the small vacuum and wheeled it into the closet as her daughter carried over the caddy of cleaning supplies. "You're a good person."

"Not really. A person doesn't deserve credit for doing the right thing." Remy stashed the bucket in the closet. "It's what we do."

Ariel patted her shoulder. "It's what you do."

They hugged, and then Ariel held Remy close for a mother-daughter-moment selfie.

"The post-cleaning selfie," Ariel teased. "And by the way, Cooper will be here for his lesson in an hour. In case you want to avoid him."

"Totes." Remy raked her hair back as she headed toward the door connecting to the family room. "Last time I saw him, he was really mad. I hope he's not mean to you."

"He wouldn't dare."

Watching her daughter go, Ariel was a little bit in awe of Remy's composure and maturity. "Don't know where she got that," Ariel muttered under her breath as the door opened out in the mudroom, and Rosie Delfatti appeared in the doorway.

Next.

When Cooper Dover plodded his sad ass in for his lesson later that afternoon, he was definitely out of sorts. His blond hair was dark, still wet from his shower, and instead of his usual sporty attire he wore an old gray T-shirt that drooped on one side and baggy cargo shorts. Not a great look for him, though Cooper was handsome enough to pull off distressed clothes, but the pout of romantic distress made him resemble a big baby.

Ariel ignored his sullen mood and pushed on with the lesson. Damn it, she wasn't Dr. Phil or Dear Sugar. And right now, she didn't want to be the mother of the girl who'd just broken up with him. She was his vocal coach, end of story.

"The song is deceptive," Ariel told him, motioning Cooper closer to the piano so that he could look at the sheet music.

One corner of his mouth curled in a surly frown as he came around the piano.

"The melody is simple, yes, but the lyric of the song provides the rhythm of the piece. Use your hands to tap out the lyrics."

His jaw set firmly, he began to knock on the piano as she spoke the words: "You gotta have heart, all you really need is heart. . . ."

Suddenly, he stepped back from the piano and waved his arms. "Stop. Just cut it, all right? We both know the song will work itself out. That's not what matters here. I'm here because of Remy. You need to talk to her."

She folded her arms across her chest. "About what?"

"About me . . . and her. About us getting back together. She made a mistake, breaking up with me." He stubbed a thumb at his chest. "I'm the best thing that ever happened to her."

His arrogance knew no bounds. "Apparently she doesn't agree. And that's her choice."

He cocked his head to one side, that ragtag look that probably turned girls' knees to jelly. "Talk to her. Do me a solid. She'll listen to you."

"Remy makes her own decisions. I don't interfere in my kids' lives; you know that."

He held up a finger like a TV preacher. "But you could."

"Remy is her own person, and the truth is, if she were my puppet, you wouldn't be interested in her." She turned her gaze to the sheet music and stretched her hands. "Can we get back to the lesson?"

"Screw the lesson." He turned away, shoved his hands into the pockets of his shorts, and strode toward the door.

Was he leaving? She'd never had anyone walk out on a lesson before. She would have counseled a discouraged student, but in this case Cooper wanted something she could not give.

Maybe it was best for him to go. Ariel picked up the sheet music, pretending to leaf through it as he flung open the door to the mudroom, then paused.

"Just saying," he said, "she's better than you."

At first she didn't know what he meant, but then it came into sharper focus. Their sexual adventure had happened right here in the studio. This damned studio. It had become her prison in more ways than one.

"I'm glad," she said coldly. "A mother wants that for her daughter."

"I wonder what would happen if I shared our secret." He came back into the room, walking thoughtfully toward the piano. "You know, I was under eighteen." He cupped his hands over the fly of his shorts. "Maybe I was taken advantage of," he said in a whiney voice. He reached toward the flowers on the piano, touching a rosebud. "I was a young bud, not ready to open."

"Oh, cry me a river." She got up from the piano bench and went to the water dispenser, trying to fake indifference.

"You know, I could make a lot of trouble for you. But I've kept my mouth shut. And I'll continue to keep our secret, if you patch things up with Remy."

"That's not going to happen." When she turned toward him, he was right on her, intimidating her. But she spoke in a firm, calm tone. "Right now you are going to go home and take a cold shower. And next year at college you will meet a beautiful young girl and you'll forget all about having your heart broken in high school. You'll get married, have babies, and use your daddy's money to buy a McMansion."

He snickered. "And you're going to land in jail."

"No, Cooper. If you so much as sweat one drop of what happened, I will cry rape so loud that your ears will be bleeding. A big brute of a guy overcoming little old me. You can forget that football career. You'll be living in the shadow of your criminal behavior. Bye, bye, football hero. That gorgeous girl won't go near you, much less marry you. You'll be the scourge of campus. You wouldn't want that, would you?"

"You're a piece of work." His nostrils flared, but he was in check now. He was a skilled-enough player to know when to retreat. "Tell Remy I asked about her," he said in a bitter tone before storming out.

She watched him go. It was only after she heard the outer door slam that she allowed herself to breathe again.

Chapter 9

Kaboom! Cassie felt like the roof had blown off her life to reveal a sky full of fireworks. She finally did it—she had sex!—a few times now, and after that awkward and painful first time, she has come to see what all the hype was about. Kapow!

It really helped that Andrew was so sweet and thoughtful. When they were making love he spoke to her softly, telling her what felt good and praising her skin, her breasts, her body. His words washed away any self-consciousness, allowing her the freedom to enjoy the sensations, embrace the journey.

But now it was Friday morning and she was in Andrew's bed and he'd woken up with an unbelievable boner and there were no condoms left. Oh no.

He was cupping one of her breasts and rocking his pelvis against her, sending a ribbon of desire curling through her. But she couldn't. She wouldn't. She couldn't risk it.

A whimper escaped her throat as she scooted back from him. "I can't." She sat up and scrambled back on the bed, bumping into the wall with a thump that set her bare breasts jiggling. "I can't do this. Can't take the chance." She could not ruin her life with a baby now. No, no. She was not going to follow her mother down that path.

"It's okay." Andrew rolled away from her and pulled the

quilt up to his waist. "I just . . . I wake up this way. It'll go away."

"Okay." She gave up her stance against the wall and sidled close to him once again. "I want to, but, like I said, I'm not using the pill, and I can't risk getting pregnant." Feeling more relaxed now, she snuggled against his back and slid a hand around his chest, which had enticing indentations of muscle that she had not expected. Andrew was one of those guys who seemed thin and bony in clothes, but with everything stripped away you could see the definition of his muscles. "Sorry."

"It's okay. I'll get more condoms."

She let her arm slid down over his tight abs.

But she landed on . . . it. So hard and high.

He groaned.

"Sorry." When she started to pull away he covered her hand with his and held it there.

"Maybe we can try something different?" he whispered. He guided her palm over him, up and down. Slowly. Then picking up the pace.

Oh. Okay. She could do that. Attentive and on alert, she was a student of the process, a woman in training. She could learn this. She had an excellent teacher.

The week before finals was not the best time to hook up with someone. Sex was a huge distraction when you could have it just about any time, all the time. Besides, when Cassie wasn't with Andrew she found herself obsessed with thoughts of him and of her new self and of the potential of the two of them together. Cassie had two papers to write and a mountain of material to review for next week, but that was nothing compared to Andrew's workload. An engineering major, he had a few classes that she didn't even fathom, one involving algorithms, and one called Quantitative Physiology. He called it Quan Phys. So cute. As in, "I've got a Quan Phys study group this afternoon. Want to come to the library with me?" he'd asked her over lunch. Grilled cheese and tomato soup, which he had made for her since they were at his house.

"Sure," she told him. She had a poetry analysis essay to write, and it was easier to work in the library. When they arrived at Valley Library, she was headed toward the cubicle when he grabbed her hand, linking his fingers through hers.

"Come on upstairs with me. You should meet my brainiac friends."

She had called him a brainiac as a joke, and it had stuck. Now she felt oddly touched that he wanted her to meet the smart kids after just a week or so of them being together. He liked her, and he sort of wanted to show her off. No one had ever wanted to show her off before. That was kind of cool.

All three of the guys shook her hand, which was not something kids in the U did. Darren shook her hand and then returned to searching for something on his iPad. Seth, the bearded one from Spokane, Washington, seemed painfully shy, while Shiv, a slight young man from India with jet-black hair and gorgeous mocha skin, was very personable. When he found out that she was a nursing major, he teased her. "That is a far more noble profession than anything we might engage in. Andrew, you have a good girl here."

"I know," Andrew said, his pale blue eyes holding her gaze in such an intimate way, even here, in front of his friends.

She chatted with Shiv a little longer, then bowed out of the small conference room to whittle away on her essay. As she worked she texted with Remy, eager to talk with her. At this point, all of Cassie's roommates knew about Andrew, and Remy knew they were dating, but Cassie hadn't shared many details. Now, with concerns over birth control for the very first time, Cassie needed to talk to her younger sister. Knowing that all her roommates had lost their virginity in high school, Cassie didn't want to bring up the topic of sex with them. It was too embarrassing to be the only novice in the group.

When Remy texted her that she was free to talk, Cassie packed up her things and ducked outside to the gray drizzle. Tiny droplets hummed through the air, and the grassy lawn was soaked. But the moisture was a refreshing reminder of spring—of new things. Cassie lingered under the library's over-hang as she called Remy's number.

"Hey, wassup?" Remy sounded cheerful as ever.

"Actually, a lot of things. Remember I told you about that guy, Andrew? Well, things have moved fast." Details spilled forth as she brought her sister up to speed on her relationship with Andrew. Remy wanted to know which actor he most re-sembled—Michael Cera, but more distinguished—and what his sign was—Sagittarius.

"That's a good match. A Sagittarius man needs a strong woman, and that's you, Cassie. Leo and Sag go well together."

"Nice." Cassie didn't really follow astrology, but she was happy to have the stars on her side.

"When are you going to send me a picture of you two to-gether?" Remy nudged her.

"I will. It's all pretty new right now. And that's not the only thing that's new." Cassie explained that they had been having sex. "We've been using condoms, but you know that's not a hundred percent effective. And I can't get pregnant. What should I do?"

"Go to the school clinic, or else get a referral for a free clinic. They'll give you BC pills."

"How much will that cost?"

"It should be free. I've never paid for them. And you're over eighteen, so you won't need consent. You're in a college town; it'll be super easy."

Of course it would. Cassie wondered if they'd still be open now, Friday afternoon. She would call the school clinic for in-formation as soon as she got off the phone with Remy.

"Thanks. How's your day going?"

"Kind of sucky. Cooper is being a shit."

"Aaah! I can't believe he's being so mean to you. What did he do now?"

"He poured a bottle of cologne inside my locker. Bad co-logne. Now all my books reek."

"What an ass. I guess his true colors are shining through."

"He was always so nice to me. I know he has a good heart, and he's just hurt."

"Don't defend him, Remy. He's acting like a ten-year-old."

"I know, and it makes him impossible to reason with. But I'm going to talk to him. I'm not going to let him scare me, and I'm not going to be the victim here. We don't have to be friends; I just want a truce between us."

Cassie frowned at the thought of that big brute pushing her little sister around; Remy had always been way too nice for her own good. "A truce is fine, as long as you stand your ground with him. Don't let him push you around just because he's a big bully, twice your size," Cassie warned.

Remy let out a laugh. "Spoken as a big sister. Don't worry about me. I know how to handle Coop, and I don't even want to waste time talking about him anymore. You go do your birth control shopping. I've got to get over to the bridal shop to pick up my prom dress. The alterations are done."

"Nice. Are you looking for another prom date?"

"Nope. Not feelin' it. I'm going with some girlfriends. Keepin' it in the posse."

Cassie smiled as they said good-bye. That was Remy, always landing on her feet, like an agile cat. Taking her sister's advice, she hung up and dialed the number of the school clinic. The sooner the better.

Chapter 10

Rachel slogged along the path Friday evening, grimacing with each damp squish of her running shoes. Her mood was darkened by the pointed edges of recent conversations that haunted her. Her sons and their problems. In the dusk, gray clouds parted to reveal the moon surrounded by translucent rings. Her mother used to say that a ringed moon was a sign of bad weather and trouble.

Right now Rachel had plenty of both.

Although she was able to put her personal worries on a back burner when she was at the salon, turmoil over her sons' issues ruled her personal life. That was nothing new, but recently she'd begun to wonder if she was part of the problem. Rachel had always been involved in their lives, not really a helicopter parent, but a disciplinarian and a cheerleader. A pusher. She had always acted in their best interests, but maybe it was a mistake to have her hands all over their lives. KJ was twenty and Jared would be eighteen soon. Had she carved them into mama's boys? Was it time to back away? Or maybe just begin to extract herself. Good Lord, she couldn't walk away from KJ when his health was at risk.

"There's a concern about brain-stem injury," the neurologist Dr. Susan Ginsberg, had told Rachel over the phone earlier that afternoon. The doctor had explained that KJ had given consent for her to talk with Rachel. "And that might be the best thing he ever did, Mrs. Whalen, because he seems to be in denial about the consequences of continuing to play football. KJ's chances of brain damage are worse than he realizes. And once the brain is damaged, we don't have the means of fixing it."

Stammering a response, Rachel had encouraged the doctor to go on, and the woman had compared the brain to a head of cauliflower. When the top of the cauliflower was hit, the stem softened and weakened a bit more. Repeated blows to the top of the cauliflower damaged the stem. With enough damage, the stem would no longer function.

Rachel's heart had been racing like a nervous rabbit by the time the doctor had finished her description. For the first time, she had realized that her son's health truly was at stake here. Gummed up with concern, she had dialed up KJ to tell him about Dr. Ginsberg's warning.

"Yeah, I met with her. She and one of the coaches double-teamed me," he'd complained, as if it were a bad thing. "They went on and on about the possibility of brain damage from re-peated concussions. They really tried to sell me on quitting football. And I told them that I don't care about the risk; I'll never give up football. Never."

"Oh, it's worth winding up brain-dead?" she had blasted him.

"Mom . . . I may never get another head injury again."

"You don't know that, and I am not willing to see you re-duced to being a vegetable just so you can play a stupid game for a few more years. I am not going to be around to feed you pudding while you breathe through a tube!" That was Rachel, always overboard, hammering away at her point.

In truth, she knew she would stand by her boys through thick or thin, but that was no excuse for KJ to make a stupid decision because of his ego.

"Mom! You told me to keep my options open. You drove out here Sunday night and told me to wait on it."

"That was before I learned about the smashed head of cauli-flower."

"What the hell? You're not making any sense."

"I just spent thirty minutes on the phone with a neurologist who was kind enough to reach out to me because she's concerned about your health. A lot of people are putting themselves out there to save your quality of life, KJ. Don't you think it's time to take the advice you've been blessed with and minimize the damage? Dr. Ginsberg says the hazards of playing football outweigh the benefits of playing for another year or so. It's time to give it up."

It was not the pep talk KJ had wanted to hear. He'd hung up on her, and she had let it go for today. Well, she wasn't calling him back, but unfortunately, she was unable to let go of the stress and fierce worries.

With a rush of breath through her teeth, she sprinted for a few yards. Slacking off, she realized that the source of her worries had shifted to Kyle James from Jared, who had spent years navigating an entirely different set of issues. The quiet son had attracted more than his share of harassment. In junior high a handful of kids had interpreted Jared's naïve shyness to be effeminate, starting a groundswell of rumors that he was gay. Jared had been stung to be branded for being himself, and she has swiftly stomped out the bullies' fire with the help of the vice principal.

Then, in high school, a new brand of bully had emerged on the football team. That year there had been a shortage of players, so the freshman team had been merged in with junior varsity players. The combination put innocents like Jared in the sights of a handful of conniving sophomores and juniors who were jealous of KJ's success and quick to recognize Jared's weakness.

Looking back, Rachel could see that Jared did not belong in sports. His lack of athleticism made him destined to fail. But between Jackson's passion and KJ's talent, they had become a football family, and there was no easy way out for Jared. A second-string player, a bench warmer, Jared quickly became the victim of choice for the pack of hungry boys. They homed in on his weakness and made him the butt of locker room jokes. On the field, the players banded against Jared. Whenever Jared got a chance to run the ball, his teammates were suspiciously detained elsewhere, unable to block for him.

In the first two weeks of the season, a handful of hazing incidents masked as practical jokes went unnoticed by the coaches and parents. After that the attackers narrowed their focus and accelerated the frequency and intensity of their assault. In a short amount of time, all strikes were aimed at Jared.

Of course, Jared tried to fend them off with insults, good humor, nonchalance. He went to the school counselor for help, but the administrator misconstrued his request and referred a therapist. Isolated from his friends and menaced daily, Jared began to shut down in September. He stopped speaking during dinner, stopped seeing friends on the weekends. In October, when the church choir director called to see if there was a conflict that was keeping him from attending practice, he had no answer.

"It's a phase," Jackson said when Rachel pointed out that Jared was sleeping more, staying in his room, maintaining an emotional distance. "This is what boys do when they're separating from their parents."

He made it sound like a good thing, but Rachel could feel the darkness swirling around her son, tugging him away from her.

In the twisted jumble of barbed incidents that eventually came to light, Rachel believed the worst was the time the players held Jared facedown in the men's room toilet, threatening to drown him. Sometimes she awoke early in the morning and imagined Jared choking and gasping for air. What would it be like to hold your breath while thrashing helplessly in captivity? Guilt forced her to relive her son's fear and revulsion in that critical moment when his head was plunged into the toilet water.

How she longed to strangle those monsters. . . .

Rachel hated labels like the word *bully,* but Jared's experiences had opened her eyes to the pack mentality in American schools. Like a group of wild wolves, bullies marauded through the halls and classrooms, sniffing out fear and pinning down the weakest prey. A nerd here, a loner there. Bullies forced kids with learning disabilities to pretend they didn't care about the answer, even as they swept individuals hungry for identity into their ranks. At Timbergrove High, bullies ruled the popular groups and clubs, and the alternative groups like the ceramics club and the debating team were branded as "freaks, nerds, and losers." Rachel had no reason to believe it was any different outside their suburban haven of hanging flower baskets and old-fashioned lampposts. Fresh and pristine and photogenic, her beloved town put a happy face on turmoil.

She dug in and stepped up the pace as the path went uphill, ignoring the water sluicing down the pavement. Lights on the ridge ahead marked a string of mansions, glimmering like a jewel necklace in the night. Dutton Hill, often called Diamond Hill. Craftsman homes with hand-carved cedar, contemporary castles with walls of granite and glass, chalet-style villas with cheerful window boxes. From the outside looking in, those houses seemed perfect. No one knew the secrets lingering behind a home's threshold, the fear creeping beneath the bed, the discontent that hung in the air, the shame splattered on the walls.

And the sorrow. Sorrow that slashed a boy's innocence and left him wanting to end his life, an early exit, a way to squeeze the pain off until it withered to a slow, wheezing whistle. Suicide. Her son had thought of killing himself.

"Death by suffocation is on the rise among teens trying to commit suicide," the doctor had told her. "Usually in combination with an overdose of prescription drugs."

There had been no sign of drug use, but she had seen the bulge of plastic bags in Jared's desk drawer. White garbage bags along with that clear plastic sheeting cleaners used to cover clothes. She had thought the odd collection involved a school project or a recycling drive. She reasoned that it was a boyish hobby that didn't matter, something like the giant foil ball Jared had assembled in sixth grade.

Until the day she found the suicide note on his computer.

To whoever reads this, I'm sorry. I didn't want to gross any-one out, but I had to do it. There's too much pain to make it worth staying.

"Too much pain!" she had ranted to Jared's pediatrician, Jeff Palmer. "He's only a freshman in high school and already he doesn't think life is worth living."

She had sobbed in Dr. Palmer's office as the older man had calmed her, promising to talk to her son, suggesting a trusted counselor, and gently pondering the delicate balance between guiding a child and letting him falter in his flight from the nest. "You know, the human species is the only one that doesn't know when to kick its offspring out of the nest."

Despite Dr. Palmer's advice and Rachel's pleas, there would be no counseling. Jared flatly refused help from strangers, and he would not discuss his thoughts of suicide with Rachel. But Jared did confide in his older brother. Although the boys had never been particularly close, Jared felt safe explaining some things to KJ. Which forced Rachel to pump her oldest son for information on Jared's state of mind.

"Is he doing better?" Rachel had asked KJ one cool December night when he was home for the break. They stood in the yard, taking in a sunset that painted the sky in phosphorescent pink and orange. Jackson was inside on the couch, fighting to maintain a façade of good health, and Jared was doing home-work at the computer nook in the kitchen. "Does he still talk to you about it?"

KJ shushed her, nodding toward the house. They had been keeping the details of the crisis from Jackson. The tough-guy mentality that Rachel had once found so appealing had hard-ened into a brittle shell around Jackson, stripping him of com-passion and tolerance as his disease worsened. After he had told Jared to "stand tall and stand your ground" in response to the very first hints of hazing, the entire family had kept Jackson out of the loop.

"He doesn't talk about it much," KJ murmured in a low voice. "But yeah, I think the crisis stage is over."

"Thank God. I keep praying that it's over." Rachel had been stopping by at the church on her way to work in the morning, putting quarters into the box, lighting a candle, and praying for her youngest son. "I mean, if this is the worst thing that ever happens to Jared, then he'll have a really good life, right?"

"Weird, Mom, but I guess that's true."

"I don't understand any of this," she admitted. "I don't even get how it's possible to suffocate yourself. How does that work?"

KJ folded his arms, looking away. "Well, did you see the rubber bands in the drawer, too?"

Rachel shook her head. "With the plastic?"

"Somewhere in his desk," KJ muttered. "You put all that plastic over your head and tie off each layer with a rubber band."

"Oh my God." Rachel had clutched KJ's arm.

He nodded. "But you need to drug yourself first so you fall asleep instead of fighting it. Apparently, the natural instinct is to take another breath."

Rachel hugged herself as she stared at the colorful sky, fighting the impulse to run inside and wrap her arms around her youngest son. "How could he want to do that to himself?"

KJ had shrugged. "I don't think it's something he wants. It's like he's been driven to it."

"By those kids at school." Rachel's heart thudded in her chest. "I should have known. I wish he had turned those meatheads in." Although Rachel insisted that the school needed to know about violence on school grounds, Jared had refused to name names and get involved in their investigation. Tim Hoddevick, the school counselor, had been receptive, but without Jared's cooperation, his hands were tied.

Which infuriated Rachel. Everyone knew the ringleader and his henchmen.

"Damn it, I'll run them down with my car and sue their goddamned parents blind for what they've done to him."

"Mom." KJ winced, gesturing for her to lower her voice.

"Don't. It's over, okay? The football season is over, and Jared will probably never play again. Jackson is going to freak out about that, but he'll have to deal with it."

"I'll smooth it all over when the time comes," Rachel said, realizing that it was getting easy to keep things from Jackson, who had withdrawn into a fog of pain and medication. "The important thing is that Jared is okay."

"He's moved on. The plastic is gone from his desk, right?"

It was. She had checked that day. And ever since that scare, she had made a daily ritual of slipping into Jared's room when he wasn't there, sliding the drawer open to find a tumble of papers and books and phone chargers and earbuds.

Every day, every drawer, like a mantra to ward off death.

Those had been dark days, with Jackson sick and out of sorts, missing a lot of work, hiding his cirrhosis diagnosis so that he could eventually drink himself to death. Rachel shuddered at the memory of that dismal, isolating time. Ariel had been by her side for much of it, but Jared had sworn the family to secrecy over his issues. Not even Ariel knew the depth of her problems with Jared.

Thank the Lord, love and perseverance had brought her youngest boy back to the land of the living. Now he had his first girlfriend—a good thing—but he was sneaking around with her, and denying it—a very annoying behavior. Fed up with the lies, Rachel had approached Jared last week with an invitation to legitimize his relationship.

"It's okay to have a girlfriend," she had told him when they'd crossed paths at home at lunchtime. She had been polishing off a container of Greek yogurt, a quick break before returning to the shop, when he had come in the side door with a giddy smile. That head-over-heels contentment. She figured it was as good a time as any to bring up the girlfriend topic. "It's okay to have sex if it's in a committed relationship," she had said, looking down at her yogurt to avoid his awkward frown. "We've talked about this . . . the precautions and the need to respect a girl's wishes."

"I'm not having sex."

"Jared, don't."

"I'm not doing anything, Mom."

"Don't lie to me. I know what's going on. A mother knows. Why can't you let me in?"

At first he'd seemed hurt. Then his expression had hardened to disdain, his dark eyes glimmering.

"Because it's my life, not yours. Back off!" He had wheeled around and bounded up the stairs, slamming the door behind him.

Well played, Rachel! She could write the manual on how to alienate your high school senior in one quick conversation.

Shoving the spoon into her mouth, she had stared up at the ceiling as his music came on. Strains of "Black Hole Sun" added to her gloomy mood. She probably had the only son at Timbergrove High School who listened to Soundgarden, Pink Floyd, and Jethro Tull. Jared always complained that he had been born a few decades too late.

Hoping to escape the domestic drama, Rachel had returned to the shop and walked right into a ridiculous ripple with Tiffani, one of the younger stylists. While Rachel had been out of the salon, Tiff had been telling some of the customers about her plans to open a salon of her own just across Timbergrove's main square.

Not one to beat around the bush, Rachel confronted Tiff, whose hair was currently spiked on top and shaved on the sides, with a tail of feathers dangling from one ear. "Are you serious about opening another salon on the square?"

Tiffani had rolled her eyes awkwardly. "Wow. Word sure travels fast when you have a good idea."

"Really? *Really?*" Rachel had looked the young woman squarely in the eyes; she wasn't afraid to get right up in her grill. "And what might be the purpose of that?"

"I think this town needs something shiny and new, and I'm just the person to do it," Tiffani had said with relish. "Actually, I'm pretty shiny and new myself," she had added with a giggle.

"At least shiny." Rachel would give the girl that. "You got the capital to put up for that kind of venture?"

"What, a few months' rent and a couple of mirrors?" Tiffani's neck had turned a rosy pink; she was blushing under her spiderweb tattoo. She knew she was out of her league. "I could figure it out," she muttered. "Get some friends to throw in."

"Sure thing. We'll talk again when you've got investors."

Rachel had moved away from Tiff's station, using restraint not to stomp across the salon.

A few months' rent and a couple of mirrors. If only it were that simple. Timbergrove wouldn't allow Tiffani to open up a shop until her wiring and plumbing was up to code, not to mention the amenities like sinks and adjustable chairs and proper lighting. Little Miss Tiff, who didn't have a pot to piss in, didn't have a clue what it would take to open a new salon.

Ungrateful little thing. Tiff seemed to have forgotten that Rachel let her use a chair for three months, rent free, when the girl had come to her down-and-out, just out of cosmetology school. It killed Rachel to think that, after all that, Tiff would stab her in the back and become her competition. Well, no, that would never happen. The cocky, well-inked upstart was going to fall flat on her face.

That possibility also irked Rachel. Some people just refused to be saved by good advice.

And all the running in the world was not going to get these boulders off her shoulders. KJ, Jared, and Tiff. "Why are you guys busting my chops?" she ground out, realizing that she'd been clenching her jaw. Too much tension.

Darkness was closing in as Rachel jogged past the famously tall ponderosa pine marked with a plaque. Had she started her run too late? Too bad Ariel hadn't been able to come along. Her friend always had a story or two to distract Rachel from her own crap. But Ariel was overloaded with Gleetime kids this weekend. Everyone was cramming in extra practice sessions for the Spring Showcase and the state competition.

She was thinking that it would have been wise to have Ariel along for safety's sake, too. What were those noises behind her? The scrape of footsteps? She darted a look over her shoulder, but no one was there.

It reminded her of an unsolved attack two years ago when a masked man with a knife came out of the woods, grabbed a female jogger, and cut her face. Didn't kill the poor girl, fortunately. The police never did catch the guy, but that was on the other side of town. Not that the attacker couldn't travel a few miles.

She braced herself as the trail turned into a wooded area, cool shadows on shadows. Damn, but the brush was invasive. Dense laurels twisted this way and that in a thick wall of green that effectively hid the path from the road. Anything could happen here and no one would be the wiser. She sprinted past the lower brush, panting until she reached the tall trees once again. At last the trail emerged from the woods to run alongside the country road. At least, on this part of the path, people from the road could see her if some pervert came along. Then again, it didn't instill a lot of confidence to be striding alongside the road in this fuzzy light. One texting driver could send her flying like a bowling pin.

"Never again." Rachel chastised herself for starting her run too late. Friday was supposed to be her easy day at the shop. Her day to set aside some "me" time for exercise and pampering. Apparently, the cosmos wasn't in the mood to pamper her today.

A car slowed on the road, trailing along behind her. A chill came over her as she shot a glance over but couldn't make out the driver. She half expected the occupants to call out and ask directions, but the car simply lingered, its motor humming.

Oh, Lordy. Should she turn around and launch herself back into the woods? At least that would get her away from the road. She picked up the pace to a run, but the car accelerated easily, staying on her heels.

"Get the hell away from me," she muttered. She heard the low whir of the passenger window rolling down, and her perverse mind imagined a rifle pointing out the window, the shooter raising the weapon until she was smack in the middle of his sights.

A moving target.

Chapter 11

"**R**achel? Is that you?"

Fear spiraled into surprise as Rachel slowed her pace and turned toward the vehicle.

There was no rifle. The console light inside the black unmarked car revealed a uniformed officer leaning over the passenger seat, squinting toward her. "Little late to be out on your own, isn't it?"

Rachel stopped running and gaped at the sheriff, Mike McCabe. "Mike, you just about gave me a heart attack!" she said, clasping her chest as the car stopped on the shoulder.

"That would defeat the whole purpose of running, wouldn't it?"

"I guess it would." Rachel couldn't help but smile as a mixture of relief and amusement slowed her racing pulse. "I wasn't planning to be out after dark, but time got away from me."

"I know how that goes." He pushed open the passenger side door and waved her toward the car. "Come on, now. I'll give you a lift."

"Well, that sort of defeats the purpose of a workout, too." She shoved her fists into the pockets of her thin running jacket as she sauntered closer. "But since it's getting dark, okay." She slid into the passenger seat, feeling a mixture of intimidation and excitement to be sitting in a patrol car with lights, gadgets, a squawking radio, and a fat computer with a bright monitor. "I live on Woodburn, not far from Pine Elementary."

The space in the seat was tight; the computer on the center console jutted out, taking up much of the knee room. But she was grateful for the warmth of the vehicle, and a little nervous to be so up close and personal with the town sheriff. The last time she'd spoken with him at length had been a few years ago, when she had been called to pick KJ up from a senior class party where alcohol had been present. At the time, she had thought it was kind of him not to hit the kids with charges or fines, which he could have done. McCabe had said he didn't want to put a hurting on them. "They're good kids," he'd said.

Recalling his kindness, Rachel settled into the warm car and exchanged witty jabs with Mike, who had been quickly transformed from a stalker into a Good Samaritan.

"I was surprised to see you out alone in the dark," Mike said as he pulled onto the road. "That path is pretty isolated in spots. I wouldn't trust it at night."

"I won't be doing that again," she assured him. "I just got a late start, and time got away from me."

"That makes me feel better. We live in a relatively safe community, but a woman alone is bait for some nefarious types."

So he remembered that she was unattached; that was flattering. She got a chance to check him out as he kept his eyes on the road. Despite a large head of wildish brown hair, he was a handsome devil with a strong jaw and stark blue eyes. As they talked she let her eyes wander to his hands on the steering wheel, noticing that he was not wearing a wedding ring. Hmm. She knew he was married. Maybe he was one of those men who didn't wear jewelry. Most women kept that wedding ring on.

She asked him about recent incidents on the path, and he said none had been reported. No random assaults in Timbergrove since that case with the masked man, who was still at large. They discussed local crime, and he expressed surprise that Rachel was aware of most of the town's burglaries, thefts, and acts of vandalism.

She prided herself on staying aware. "Between the gossip at the salon and the crime blotter in the *Times,* I keep my finger on the pulse."

Mike sang the praises of Timbergrove. He was grateful to be policing in a town where the chief hazards were ice on the roads and teen parties that got out of control.

"You're preaching to the choir," she said. "I love this town. I've lived in a few different places, east and west, and nothing can beat the quality of life here. The schools. The downtown area with a stunning backdrop of Mount Hood behind it. The flowers and trees. The way the sun sets over the crest of the hills."

"You get it," he agreed.

"I do. I'm glad my kids got to grow up here." He asked about her kids and she told him one was in college and her youngest was finishing his senior year. She told him about the Gleetime Spring Showcase—a must-see! He told her about plans for a summer concert in the town square. It was hard to imagine that July, post-graduation, would really come around. So much would be changing for her after the summer.

As the intimidation of the cop car wore off, Rachel fell into an easy patter with the sheriff. There was something open and All-American about his broad shoulders, low-key demeanor, and wide, easy grin. The conversation was so relaxed she found a graceful segue to the topic of his wedding ring. "Are you not allowed to wear it on patrol?"

"I'm not married anymore—divorced three years ago."

"I'm sorry to hear that," she said, pausing before adding, "I guess."

Her timing was perfect. He turned his head aside and chuckled. "No need to be sorry about that. Believe me, it was a good thing; sometimes people are better off apart."

"Well..." She smiled. "That explains your haircut." No woman would let her husband neglect his hair like that. "Stop by Holy Snips sometime and I'll clean you up back there. Your hair is hitting your collar."

"Is it? Time to go to Larry's. You know Larry, the barber over in West Green? That's where I go." He rubbed his chin, a spark of mirth in his blue eyes. "That's where manly men go for a haircut."

"Apparently, not often enough." She directed him to her house up ahead, and he laughed softly as he pulled up to her driveway.

"You got me. Maybe I will stop by your place sometime. Maybe I can get you out of the shop for a cup of coffee."

"Maybe." She slid out of the dark car, her heart trilling in joy. She'd just made a date for the first time in years.

Ariel moaned as their entangled bodies dropped onto the quilt that had been spread on the studio floor. Saturated with pleasure, she rested in the thrum of deep satisfaction.

As he gently stroked her hair away from her face—he always did that in the afterglow—she soaked up the excitement and fear of possessing him, of treading into forbidden territory.

Sometimes it seemed ridiculous that her involvement with a younger man had the potential to bring her entire world tumbling down. Really. She could see the leagues of disapproving women, the Timbergrove moms, pointing her out on the sidelines of soccer games, whispering over the potatoes in the produce aisle at Safeway, smirking as they lined up behind her at the ATM.

Oh, she's the one.

Sex with a younger man. In fact, more than one.

She was their tutor. Apparently, she gave them more than voice lessons.

In the so-called age of tolerance, her sexual appetite should not be such a big deal. The new political correctness dictated that it was fine to be gay and lesbian, black, Hispanic, and mixed race. Every individual was supposed to celebrate his or her identity; fly the banner high! One Oregon high school had just built a special restroom for transgender students. Everyone claimed to be "free to be you and me." But when it came down to it, any deviation from the "norm" could be toxic. Sometimes she felt like packing up and hightailing it out of this town, but then she reminded herself that she would encounter the same disapproval wherever she went. Besides, there were the kids, Trevor and Maisy, and she knew that the teachers and parents of Timbergrove gave them the stability that their mother couldn't offer. Since Oliver's death, it had taken most of her energy to keep herself functioning. She had little left over for nurturing the fledglings.

But this, these sessions of stolen pleasure, were utterly invigorating. Who knew?

Five minutes of stretching and relaxing, like cats in the sun, and he was ready to go again. Ariel liked that about him, the fact that he could get hard just looking at her. She wanted to believe that it was her luscious breasts and soft curves that stoked his fires, but she knew that his age figured into it.

"You young guys, you get hard when the friggin' wind blows," she said, looking down at him.

"Doesn't seem to be a problem for you." He leaned down and covered her nipple with his lips, evoking a tug of desire deep in her groin. How quickly he had learned how to melt her resolve.

He was right. She was always up for a second helping. "It's all good now," she said on a sigh. "But someday, when you're older, all this is going to go away. Hard to believe, I know, but the wood just wilts."

"Yeah? That's gotta suck."

"Sucks for you," she teased.

"But you won't care." He propped himself on one elbow, latching his gaze on to her eyes with that weird X-ray vision of his. "You'll stay with me, no matter what."

"Nope." She didn't want him mistaking sex for a relationship. "You'll be on your own, bud."

"You're kidding." He rolled on top of her, and she relished the feel of skin on skin, as well as the curves of his shoulder muscles as he held a plank position over her, his strong arms flexed. "You'll never leave me. We belong together."

She was about to deny that—reality check, kid!—but he was already working her, nuzzling her, finding his way in. Conversation was lost in the art of the moment, the swing and sway and rocking of their search for pleasure and release.

Later, she would wonder if she was giving him the wrong idea about their future together. They had no future as a couple.

Later, she would fantasize about a true relationship with him, a sweet romance that would breathe new life into her deflating hopes.

Later.

Chapter 12

"**O**ur last dress rehearsal. *Ever*," Ariel said when Rachel picked her up to drive to the high school Sunday evening. She let out a wistful sigh as she buckled her seat belt. "I can hardly believe it."

"It's hitting me harder than I expected," Rachel admitted as she pulled away from the curb. She was feeling the shift more acutely than Ariel, but then she was a few years older, and Ariel still would have two younger ones in the house after graduation. "You may have another few rounds of this if Trevor and Maisy decide to try out for Gleetime."

Ariel pressed her palms to her face as she sank down in the seat. "Don't remind me. Little Miss Maisy is already showing a theatrical bent. The other night as she went up the stairs to bed she sang 'So Long, Farewell' from *The Sound of Music*. That kid kills me."

The Gleetime kids were in high spirits when Rachel and Ariel arrived in the green room. Most kids were already in costume for the opening number, Simon & Garfunkel's "59th Street Bridge Song," better known as "Feelin' Groovy." The bright colors and wild designs of the "hippie" costumes seemed to vibrate with energy. Some kids gathered for group selfies, while others stretched and danced to the music.

"We got a sixties explosion going on here," Ariel commented, placing her makeup box on the long counter in front of the lighted mirrors.

A few of the moms had already hung sheets to screen off two changing areas in opposite ends of the green room, where they assisted with quick changes. Traci Harper was the enforcer, batting boys away from the girls' section. As if these boys weren't getting near-naked views of these girls with the pre-summer attire the kids trotted around in this time of year. Nora was stitching something by hand, while Nan Lee pinned up the hem of a formal gown.

Dawn Opaka and her posse sat at a round table, sipping iced latte drinks and poking at boxes of donut holes that they had pretended to bring in for the students. "Anything consumed while in the line of duty does not count for calories!" Dawn insisted, prompting laughter from the moms at the table who had parked their asses as if they were waiting for a show to begin.

Whatever. Rachel would be happy to be free of that crew after Jared graduated. She turned away and dug into her bag of hair supplies, determined not to let the sluggards get to her. This was going to be a fun show, made even better by working backstage with her best friend.

Someone was playing sixties music on portable speakers, tunes like "For What It's Worth" and "Fortunate Son," and Ariel had jumped into the fray of dancing kids to demonstrate classic moves like the Twist and the Mashed Potato. Malika was whooping it up with Riley, and Tia was jitterbugging with Sophia. Jared was in that group, laughing with his dance partner, Allison Samwick, as they tried to do the Monkey. Dressed in faded jeans and a multicolored mod shirt, Jared seemed to fit right in with the other students.

Such a huge improvement from a few years ago, when he had been targeted, bullied, and isolated. Jared, the shy nerd, who would never match up to his older brother. She still felt bad about her lack of involvement in those early days when

she had thought the bully phase would pass without her intervention. By the time it blossomed into an excruciating situation for Jared, Rachel's mind had been elsewhere, wrapped up
in Jackson's diagnosis, his treatment. His illness had knocked
her off her feet, sent her tumbling in the surf. Even now, years
later, she sometimes felt the sands shifting beneath her feet
when she tried to move ahead.

Rachel turned away quickly, not wanting to be caught staring by her son, who was less than thrilled with her involvement here. "You don't embarrass me," he had told her a few
weeks ago, "but I need my own space."

Already committed to helping out with Gleetime, she had
promised to keep her distance. She didn't want to do anything
to disrupt the good mojo that had begun to swirl around Jared
recently. Finally, in the last few months of high school, kids
began to value academic achievement and talent. The kids
who had once dominated because they were captain of a team
or because Daddy owned a house with lakefront property now
took a backseat to students being courted by prestigious col-
leges because of their accomplishments and skills. The kids
who had once mocked Jared relentlessly for yodeling in a song
from *The Sound of Music* now whooped it up when he belted a
lyric to "Fortunate Son."

Rachel allowed herself a quick, proud glance at the young
man who had come so far; these days Jared seemed happy
with his life. Granted, Rachel still checked that drawer in his
desk, her eyes on alert for any sign of plastic bags or rubber
bands or drugs. But these days she checked more out of habit
than fear. Somehow the act of checking seemed to ward off the
irrevocable choice of death. Somehow, her vigilance seemed to
guarantee that the laughter and joy of that young man dancing
with his friends would go on. Doug Harper backed toward
Jared, doing "the Bump," and the two guys cracked up.

Smiling, Rachel got to work helping some of the girls with
their beaded headbands. The whole scene brought back a fond
memory of working on a revival of *Hair* during her crazy years

in New York City. Those had been good times, free times. Well, it had been a blast in the first few months, before the financial reality of city living had hit her. The last month there, she had probably gone through cases of beans and ramen noodles. The allure of New York City had worn thin when she'd returned home for Christmas to find her high school boyfriend, Gage Whalen, looking better than ever. His uncle had gotten him a job in construction, framing houses, and the hard labor had pumped up his muscles and filled his wallet with cash. Good Lord, they'd both been kids then, just a few years older than Kyle James was now, but Rachel had thought she'd had it all together. Rachel had fallen hard, choosing the security of his strong arms and the thrilling sex in his silver RX-7. So much sex and beer; she should have realized it was a toxic combination.

"Are you really Jared's mom?" A tiny wisp of a girl with white-blond curls brought Rachel out of her reverie. A new face.

"Indeed. I'm here to do hair, but you look like you've already got it going on."

The girl raked back her bouncy curls with a smile. "Thanks. I just love Jared in the rain song. I think it's the best song in the show."

"Thanks. Did you mention that to him?"

The girl looked away. "He doesn't really know me. I'm just a junior."

"I'm sure he knows who you are." Rachel talked a while with the petite girl, Miranda, who obviously had a crush on Jared. Although Rachel knew he had a girlfriend, her heart swelled at the realization that Jared's cachet was on the rise.

Bell-bottoms in plum and lime green and passion pink were the pants of choice, broken up by some worn jeans. There were large, clunky, peace symbol medallions and fringed vests over peasant blouses. A few of the girls wore mod-print dresses with white go-go boots that seemed to be absolutely authentic.

"I just can't get over your costumes," Rachel told Remy as

she parted the girl's thick dark hair down the middle and began to tie off pigtails. She noticed a shiny gold-leaf tattoo that formed a band around Remy's arm. "Is this new?"

"It's temporary. It'll be gone before the show," Remy said. "But I thought it was very Cleopatra."

"Let's try these pigtails with your flower-power headband. I'm really impressed with the costumes. Did Mrs. Luchter put all this together?" Even with a talented seamstress like Shelly Zinnert you couldn't come up with all this.

"Shelly sewed the dresses and bell-bottoms. But Mrs. L gave us money to go shopping in thrift stores. Rosie totally organized everyone to do a sweep of second-hand shops around Portland. She researched the hippie era. You can find a lot of photos on Google. Rosie called around and found out where to get the boots and stuff."

"Mrs. Whalen, have you ever heard of Goldie Hawn?" Tia Harper interrupted, brushing her blond bangs back and making googly eyes in the mirror. "My mother says I look like Goldie Hawn."

"From *Laugh-In*." Rachel grinned. "Yes, I see the resemblance, especially when you're looking so groovy."

"I don't even know who that is," Tia said, flustered.

"It's a compliment. She's Kate Hudson's mother." Rachel used some mousse to tamp down the flyaway hairs around Remy's face. "Finito."

"Thanks." Remy popped out of the chair with a smile that faded when she looked over Rachel's shoulder.

Rachel was pretty sure she knew what that was about. Glancing behind her, she spotted Cooper Dover with a dour expression. You'd think the boy had just eaten dog doo. Rachel and Ariel had talked about that boy and the difficult breakup. Some kids handled breakups worse than others. Ignoring him, Rachel leaned close to Remy, as if sharing a secret. Well, it was, in a way. She didn't want Jared overhearing.

"Honey, I can't thank you enough for working with Jared on the duet. Mr. Schulteis thinks it's fantastic, and I'm so excited about the prospects at state. You're a lifesaver."

That spark of enthusiasm returned to Remy's eyes. "It's been fun. Jared has changed a lot."

"You think so?" Rachel looked down, trying not to show her delight that Remy had noticed. "The mom is always the last to know."

"He's confident now. He seems to know what he wants. Do you think he'll get that scholarship?"

"You never know. But if he does, he has you to thank."

"Nah. He's his own person. I'm just a partner."

"Well, I'm very grateful. It's got to be hard to do all these extra things when your scholarship to SOU is all wrapped up." Remy was shrugging when the air in the room seemed to change as Estee Sherer blew in the door.

"Okay, boys and girls, attention please!" Estee was toting two large paper shopping bags, which she put on the table smack in front of Dawn. "Here are the flowers for the opening number. Everyone needs to wear one if you want to maximize the blacklight effect." Estee looked down at Dawn. "You. You can hand them out." With that, she left the room.

Dawn's face scrunched up in disdain as kids surged forward, each vying for a paper flower.

"Wonders never cease," Ariel muttered in Rachel's ear. "Estee finally stepped up and did something. And Dawn's about to get her donuts squashed."

Rachel laughed aloud, biting back a comment as kids began streaming back to the mirrors, trying to figure out a way to get the flowers to stay put in their hair. Nora Delfatti, always prepared, produced a box of safety pins so that some of the kids could pin a flower to their costumes.

Meanwhile Dawn was making a scene, objecting when her daughter Sunshine complained about the positioning of the flower in her hair. "They say girls are easy, but this one is never happy. I'd take a houseful of boys any day," Dawn said as she dropped back into her chair, leaving her daughter standing there on the verge of tears. Rachel gestured for Sunshine to come over, and she helped the girl solve the problem, rubbing the center of her back to soothe her. She would definitely not miss having to deal with the Dawn Patrol.

As the stage manager, Sophia Nyro, called the kids out to the stage to begin the run-through, Ariel and Rachel began taking photos with their cell phones, trying to document as much as they could for continuity and future promos.

"You guys sure look groovy to me," Ariel commented as she hustled kids out to the stage, reminding them to tuck their cell phones into a cubby.

"But what if someone takes it?" one girl asked. "My parents will kill me if I lose my phone again."

"Don't worry," Patti Cronin intervened. "We're going to be sitting right here. We'll keep watch."

"See that? The Dawn Patrol has finally found a mission," Ariel said under her breath as she patted the girl on the shoulder and shooed her out the door.

Rachel bit back a laugh. "What's the second number? Have you seen a set list?"

"I don't know and I don't care. Come on." Ariel took her by the hand and pulled her out the door. "We are gonna get us some front-row seats."

They moved past the craziness of kids taking their positons on the stage and escaped out the side stage door and into the dusk of the auditorium. Craig sat alone, sixth row, center, with three students hunching in seats in the row behind him—his assistant directors. None of them looked too happy.

"Hey, there, Craig." Ariel cocked her head to one side, cordial and warm. "How's it going?"

"Not quite on track yet. We've got to finalize lighting and blocking and choreography, and we haven't even run the opening number. I'm getting ready to tear my hair out here."

"You always manage to pull it together, Craig." Ariel didn't let his tension ruffle her. "The kids were taking their places when we snuck out here. I think they're ready to go."

"They'd better be." Craig turned around and barked to a student, a lanky kid with freckles and a black T-shirt with a

Jimi Hendrix graphic. "Milo, would you please see what's holding things up?"

Milo was jogging down the aisle when the curtain began to open and the music track started to play. Rachel and Ariel slid into seats in the second row to watch.

As the sweet Simon & Garfunkel song washed through the auditorium, Rachel held her breath until she spotted Jared. There he was, stage right, twirling his dance partner Allison Samwick. It was a bad habit Rachel had had since Jared got into the song-and-dance troupe; she couldn't enjoy a company number until she had picked out her son in the pack. But then, she'd always kept a close eye on KJ while watching a football game. Somehow, keeping watch over her boys, she fooled herself into believing she could keep them safe through sheer will.

"Very cute," Rachel whispered to her friend.

Ariel's gaze searched the stage. "Who?"

Rachel nudged Ariel's arm. "I meant the song."

"Right." Ariel nodded. "It's a fun number, though the choreography is a little mucky."

Rachel hadn't noticed. Her eyes found Jared once again. He was holding Allison's hands, swaying from side to side as they stared into each other's eyes. All the couples onstage were doing the same step, but there was such tenderness between Jared and Allison—a certain chemistry. Allison's blond curls bounced as she moved, and the girl's smile could light up a room.

Could she be the one? Allison seemed like a nice girl, and Rachel had seen her name on the list of honor roll students published in the *Timbergrove Times*. Jared could do worse for a first girlfriend. Where was she going to college? Would Jared get pissed off if she approached Allison? He might. He'd made it clear that he didn't want his mother encroaching on his relationships. Damn. She wanted the pleasure of being Jared's cool mom. She had learned from KJ that there was no stopping teens from experimentation with sex and alcohol. She would let Jared and Allison hang out in his room with the door closed, and she would discreetly place herself in the living room with the TV volume up. Jared didn't understand that she could make his life so much more pleasant if he just trusted her.

Rachel was still lolling in the possibilities when the song ended and the students gathered on the stage apron for notes from their director.

Craig praised the energy, the costumes, and hair. "But, people, there's a hole in the choreography. In the bridge, you look like you're doing some sort of monster stomp." He talked with the student choreographer, a beanpole of a girl with freckles, who showed a few alternative steps.

"Nope. Nope. No." Craig shook his head, frowning. "We need something more lilting and dramatic. It's a quiet little song, and you run the risk of putting us to sleep with the choreography."

"How about a little more contact?" Ariel was on her feet, moving toward the stairs at the edge of the stage. "I think a little could go a long way here."

Rachel waited for Craig to object. After all, Ariel was their vocal coach, not a choreographer.

But Craig was nodding, grateful, as if Ariel had lifted a weight from his shoulders.

Ariel moved through the kids staggered onstage like trees in a forest until she spotted what she wanted. "Graham. Come be my partner," she said, motioning to Graham Oyama, the class heartthrob. Tall and solid, Graham had dark, exotic looks from his father's side and mad skills as a fielder that had earned him a full-ride scholarship to Tulane University.

"Let's pick it up from the second verse," Ariel called, as the students formed a semi-circle around Graham and her, ready to watch and learn. Ariel leaned forward to whisper in Graham's ear, no doubt giving him instructions, though it looked a hell of a lot like she was flirting. Ariel's shoulders were back in perfect posture, and those silicone boobies were perfect perky peaches.

Shifting in her chair, Rachel sucked in her abs, hating the seven pounds she'd put on in the past few years. Well, seven to ten, a belt on her belly. It was time to start cutting out the dark chocolate, stop telling herself it was good for her because it was loaded with antioxidants.

Uneasiness rippled up Rachel's skin as she saw Graham's arm slide over Ariel's shoulders with ease. What a smoothie that boy was. The big, flashy grin on his face transmitted his enjoyment as he pulled her to him, grinding pelvis to pelvis in a bit of dirty dancing.

The kids found this all to be hysterically funny, but Rachel thought it inappropriate. Yes, it was just a dance, but Ariel was not a dance coach, and as a voice teacher to young people, she needed to conduct herself with professionalism. Rachel had warned her friend about this. In this day and age, sexy did not translate well in the public school curriculum. Ariel needed to be above it all, detached . . . chaste.

Well, *chaste* was a stretch for Ariel. But she could maintain her aura of sexuality without looking like she was mating with a teenage boy onstage. Although she kept her face frozen in a stoic expression, Rachel could feel the heat flaring in her cheeks. God, this was embarrassing.

And the hoots from the kids, the big grin on Graham's face, the way Graham's hands commanded Ariel's hands, thighs, and hips, grinding together in their most intimate places . . . it was as if he owned her body. As if he'd ridden that highway before.

No! Rachel covered her mouth with one hand as her jaw clenched. It couldn't be. Ariel would never date a student. These days Ariel's livelihood relied on students, and to cross that line and breach the trust of the community would spell disaster.

That conversation about Ariel's hot new squeeze came back to her. Was that why Ariel refused to mention him by name? Please God, let her be wrong.

Ariel didn't know what she'd done to be chosen for the rarified position at the director's right hand. Well, of course, Craig knew that she had worked in Hollywood and starred in her own show for a while, and yes, she was the vocal coach for these kids. But normally he didn't play favorites, and Ariel wasn't sure she wanted the honor of sitting out the rest of the rehearsal in the dark auditorium. She'd been having a blast backstage, playing with makeup and hair. It had brought her back to the old days on set, with that giddy excitement and nervous tension. Except tonight, she didn't have to suffer the anxiety, because she wasn't going onstage. And it had been a long time since she and Rachel had rolled up their sleeves and laughed together. Damn, the woman was a fun sidekick. Maybe she could finagle a way to get Rach out here, make it more of a directing committee so that Craig wouldn't get any ideas.

However, Craig was the man who buttered her bread. It was his referrals and his insistence that the Gleetime kids take voice lessons that brought Ariel most of her steady income. And as for the choreography that these kids had dreamed up— many of the moves stolen from the school dance team, which took the football field at halftime—Ariel had more than a few suggestions for dance steps that went beyond shakes and wiggles. So if Craig wanted her riding shotgun to help critique and boost the kids' confidence, all she could say was giddy-up.

Chapter 13

Rachel returned to the green room with a twinge of regret. Having lost Ariel to Craig, Rachel worried that she would be shorthanded in the green room. The last thing she wanted was to be forced to ask one of the Dawn Patrol for help. God forbid. If worse came to worst, she knew she could rely on Nora, if she could track her down. Last she'd heard, Nora was supervising the frazzled lighting crew, a group of newbies who didn't yet know their way around spotlights and gels.

The second number in the show, now being rehearsed, was an a cappella version of "Blackbird" performed in choir robes. No hair styling necessary, minus removal of headbands.

A quick triage revealed Rosie Delfatti, who needed a fancy up-do with braids and twists to play Frau Blücher in a number from *Young Frankenstein*. "But I can wait," Rosie said, nodding toward a cluster of boys. "These guys go before me."

The handful of boys dressed in flowered board shorts and coconut bras for "Kokomo" needed help getting their wigs on. One of the wigs was impossibly small for the good-sized student who wanted to wear it. Isaiah Denton, a hefty tackle on the football team, was trying to pull a small platinum wig over his large head.

"Never gonna happen," Rachel said. "Here. Try one of these."

He shook his head. "I want the blond for shock effect." The pale golden strands of fake hair were a sharp contrast to his dark mocha skin.

"But it's too small. You need a large, even an extra-large."

"Who knew wigs came in sizes?" Isaiah flung the blond wig onto the vanity and chose one in the auburn red. "Dover! Why'd you buy me a small wig?"

"Just put one on and stop complaining," Cooper said, wincing as he batted the flyaway hair of his dark wig away from his face.

"I don't complain." Isaiah picked up the auburn-red wig and frowned down at it. "I just wanted a blond wig. Is that too much to ask for? I don't think so."

"This is freakin' annoying." Cooper tore off the wig, flung it to the floor, and stormed off.

"What got his shorts in a bunch?" Rachel muttered.

"He's a moody bastard," Isaiah said.

He sure is, Rachel thought as she helped Isaiah with the red-haired wig. If Cooper's petulance was any indication, this was about more than wigs. "There you go."

Isaiah grinned into the mirror. "I'm a red-haired Oprah."

Rachel laughed. "Oprah would die for your muscle tone, honey." For a big guy, he was light on his feet and often stole the show.

He adjusted his coconut-shell bra, flexed his biceps in the mirror, and grinned. "Yeah. I'm killing it."

"Save the charisma for onstage." Rachel sent him off with a pat on the back and turned to the cluster of girls who were waiting for some minor adjustments: frizz control, ponytails, and primping.

"Rosie first, and then I'll get to you girls," she said, directing Rosie into the hot seat and rolling her shoulders back to relax for a moment as she assessed. "You know, I have a hairpiece that might be helpful." Digging in her bag, she found a sandy-brown hair extension that was a fairly close match to the girl's hair color. "We'll braid this and use it as a crown. The rest, we'll just pin up. How about that, Frau Blücher?"

"Perfect." Rosie reached for the hairpiece. "I'll braid it while you do the rest."

"Deal." As Rachel dug out hairpins and began combing Rosie's hair, the other girls seated at the lit vanity were talking among themselves, lamenting a rift in the company. It reminded her of the way kids talked in the backseat of the car, honest and unfiltered, completely forgetting that a parent was listening from the front seat. Ever the invisible therapist/hair stylist, she kept her mouth shut and soaked it all in.

Rachel's heart faltered when she heard that little Remy was at the center of the conflict. The girls were upset that Cooper was feuding with Remy, who didn't seem to be fighting back at all. Angry and hurt over their breakup, Cooper had enlisted a bunch of his friends to tune Remy out, refusing to include her or speak to her.

"I'm afraid something bad is going to happen when they're dancing together in the show," Kristina said. "I wish they weren't dance partners."

"But they became partners because they were going out," Sage Sherer argued. "It's partly her fault."

"You can't blame Remy," Rosie added, flashing a warning look at the other girls. "She's free to break up with him. He's the one being a turd. Like she's really going to get back with him just so he stops torturing her."

Some of the girls agreed that Cooper was rotten; others felt sorry for him.

"Can't you see he's in pain?" Tory Gifford squeaked. "He's dying of a broken heart."

Some of the other girls swooned over that romantic notion, but Rosie wasn't buying it. "He'll survive. He's just a big baby."

"But Remy chose the worst time to break up with him," Tory added. "Right before prom? That's just cold."

Rosie glared at Tory. "It's her right to make her own relationship choices, whenever and wherever. Wow. You act like he's got some rights over Remy, which he doesn't."

"Just saying, I feel sorry for him," Tory said.

"I do, too," another girl agreed.

"Well, I don't," Rosie said firmly.

Thank God for Rosie's stubbornness. Although Rachel kept her mouth shut, annoyance simmered inside her as the girls expressed their varied opinions on how to deal with their boyfriends and dancing partners and bullies. How she would love to take Cooper by the strap of his coconut bra and give him a good scolding. To target Remy, sweet, kind Remy, the girl who released spiders to the yard! That boy needed a reality check. A good kick in the nuts.

Too bad it wasn't Rachel's place to reel him in. He wasn't her son, and he wasn't acting out in front of her. But she was going to make sure Ariel knew about this hot mess.

Some thirty minutes later, one of the kids on the production team delivered a message to Rachel. "Mr. Schulteis wants to talk to you out in the auditorium," the young man said.

"Thanks. Milo, right?" Rachel remembered him from out in the auditorium.

"Yes, ma'am."

"Oh, you can call me Rachel," she said, chatting him up as they headed out of the green room. She found out that he was a sophomore, interested in theater, but not so much acting.

"That's fine. There are plenty of jobs behind the scenes in theater. I worked for a few years, doing hair in off-Broadway productions in New York."

"Really?" He brightened. "Did you meet any famous people?"

Her mind raced as she grappled for the memory of a celebrity that Milo would have heard of. Wow, did that make her old? "Have you ever heard of Robert Downey, Jr.?"

"You met him?"

"Yup. He's a great guy." Okay, she hadn't actually met him, but she'd caught glimpses of him eating a salad in a restaurant on Sixth Avenue. And from every interview she'd seen, she was convinced that he was a great guy.

"Cool," he said as they entered the dark auditorium, where Sage Sherer stood alone on stage in a formal gown, carving out a song from *Les Misérables*. She wasn't off-key, but the unpleasant nasal quality of her voice reminded Rachel of a woman trapped in a diving bell. It had taken Sage four years of lessons and donations from her parents to make it to a faltering solo. Rachel wondered if the girl realized that the only reason she was onstage now was because of her parents' financial clout.

Milo scooted into the row with the other students, while Ariel perked up and motioned for Rachel to sit beside her. Craig watched the performance with a bland look. He didn't seem to notice Rachel sliding into the row.

"Hey, there," Rachel whispered, sinking into the upholstered seat. "How's it going out here?"

"All good. Craig and I just wanted to make sure you got a piece of the pie," Ariel said, tipping her chin toward the floor.

There was no pie, just a bottle of red wine that Ariel and Craig were drinking from travel mugs.

"Oh." Rachel felt trapped as Ariel bent down to fill a third cup for her. She didn't want to be a party pooper, but there would be kids who needed help backstage. Four girls doing an a cappella rendition of "Mr. Sandman" dressed in footie pajamas would need their hair tied up in pigtails, and she could only imagine the styling work needed for the Part One finale, "Walking on Sunshine."

An impassive Craig watched with a glazed look in his eyes.

"I really need to get back," she whispered.

"Relax," Ariel said, handing her a cup as the song ended. Without missing a beat Ariel joined in with Craig to give Sage notes about breathing from the diaphragm and keeping the energy light.

Rachel took a sip of wine, which seemed to sit on her tongue, bitter and dark. Although it felt good to take a load off her feet, she felt useless sitting here, and it seemed kind of crappy to be sneaking wine in front of the kids after all these years of trying to enforce the rules on booze and drugs.

As Sage departed and the stagehands reset microphones and props, Ariel added more wine to Craig's cup. "The only way to survive a number like that is through the filter of wine," she joked.

"But you gotta admit, she has improved. Leaps and bounds from last year," Rachel pointed out.

"True," Craig agreed. "Nice job," he said, toasting Ariel.

It seemed like such a pompous attitude, Rachel thought, shifting in her seat. What had she ever seen in Craig? She looked over Ariel's clipboard, checking the upcoming songs and plotting her escape. "Singin' in the Rain" was next, with Remy and Jared. That was worth staying for. After that, she would bow out.

The music came up and Jared appeared in the spotlight, whistling as he swaggered across the stage. Rachel was glad that he wouldn't see her in the darkened auditorium; he hated when she was the übermom, cheering him on.

He played it low-key in the beginning, slow and calm and smooth as silk. Special effects lighting shimmered over him, simulating rain glimmering down from above. The confidence in his manner, the glee in his voice, the spring in his step— Jared seemed to own the stage with a presence Rachel had never before witnessed. He danced past a shop window where Remy stood as a mannequin, and when he paused and reached out to her, she came alive and joined in the song.

Watching them sing and dance in unison, Rachel could not recognize the sensitive boy and the babbling young girl they used to be. They moved onstage as a joyous couple, celebrating love and life. Mixing in a few tap steps, they jazzed it up a bit as the routine rose to a finale then tapered off. Jared danced Remy back to the shop window, kissed her hand, and bowed to her as he turned away with a regretful smile and strolled off in time to the music.

Tears clouded Rachel's eyesight as the number ended, but

she quickly swiped them away, pretending to look down at her phone as Craig and Ariel delivered comments to Remy and Jared. Rachel could not process their words. The song was still swirling in her head, and her heart was swollen with love for those two kids. So much love for the boy who was finally coming into his own and the girl who was helping him get there.

To the moon and back.

Chapter 14

By the time the penultimate number—"Heart" from *Damn Yankees*—was wrapping up, Ariel was checking her cell phone and hoping to be out of the school by ten. The show was in decent shape, but it was nothing more than a showcase of hopeful kids. Save a few performances in church choir, most of these students would never sing in public again. The evening had filled her with a stale feeling of ennui.

Then it happened. The two girls onstage, Remy and Rosie, leaped up into the arms of their dance partners. Graham caught Rosie, but Remy landed on the stage with a sickening thud.

Ariel bolted up in her seat, wanting to rush onto the stage and tend to her daughter, who seemed to be resting there. Had she lost consciousness?

But the performance continued, the kids singing, "All you really need it heart!" Even Cooper swayed in time with the other singers dressed as baseball players while Remy lay crumpled at his feet.

Seconds later she pulled herself into a ball and rose to her feet. She seemed okay as she stepped into place and resumed singing. A little rattled, maybe, poor thing.

As Ariel's fears eased, her full-blown wrath turned to Cooper Dover. That vindictive bastard. Give him a few years and he would be beating women behind closed doors.

Ariel became aware of Craig bristling beside her, a scorching frown on his face. "He just bought himself a ticket out of the show," he muttered as the kids powered through the end of the song.

"Maybe he missed the cue," Ariel murmured in Cooper's defense. She knew it wasn't true, but dropping Cooper from the show at this point would spell disaster.

When the song ended, Craig got up from his seat. "I've got Cooper. You'll check on Remy?"

She nodded and moved to the edge of the stage as Craig unleased a curse. "What the hell happened up there? Cooper?"

Remy stared down at the floor as Cooper mumbled some excuse. "Let's step outside," Craig ordered the young man. "Now."

Relieved to see Craig take action, Ariel hurried onto the stage and reached toward her daughter. Remy collapsed in her arms for a moment, like a small bird that lands briefly then flies away.

"Are you okay, honey?" Ariel asked, rubbing the thin crease between Remy's shoulder blades.

"I'm fine. It was no big deal."

"But it is a big deal. Come here." There would be no privacy backstage, so she whisked her daughter off to a dark, quiet corner of the auditorium, promising Remy that Cooper would pay for his actions. "This is not okay at all. We both know why Cooper is acting like a little shit, and I'm not going to let him hurt you. You can't let him hurt you."

"I told you, I'm okay. I don't think he meant it."

Of course he had; she hoped her daughter recognized that much. "Well, it's not going to happen again. Craig is going to want you to switch partners, that is, if he even lets Cooper stay in the show."

"Because I fell onstage?" Remy tilted her head to one side, the dark waves of her pigtails bobbing. "That's an overreaction, don't you think?"

"That was no fall. He didn't catch you. Didn't even try."

"Separating us will screw up all the choreography, for everyone. We have to be dance partners," Remy insisted. "Mom, don't let Mr. Schulteis split us up."

"This is out of my hands. And Cooper needs to learn that there are consequences for his actions."

"But those consequences are going to hurt me and the other Gleetime kids a lot if Mr. Schulteis makes major changes now." Remy's hands were clasped together in a gesture of prayer. "Please, Mom. I can deal with this. Let me talk to him. Trust me."

Ariel stared at her daughter, wondering how such a civil, calm creature could have come from her family's gene pool. "Oh, honey, you are not the one I don't trust."

Whether it was exhaustion or anxiety over Remy's tumble onstage, the high spirits that had infused most of the rehearsal dissipated. The closing number, "Walking on Sunshine," was anything but sunny and bright. Craig told the kids that the finale required some fixes, which they would focus on the following morning in class.

"Let's get the hell out of here," he said under his breath. "We can talk at my place."

They did need to talk, and Ariel felt no need to go home. Remy would ride with her friends. Trevor was old enough to be in charge, and those two younger ones had been putting themselves to bed for a while.

On the way out, Rachel called after her. "Am I giving you a ride home?" Rachel asked, jogging to catch up with Ariel and Craig at the door. Apparently Rachel had been playing with the stage makeup as two bright triangles of pink glimmered from her cheekbones.

"I'm heading out with Craig to discuss the show." Ariel knew she should have texted her friend an excuse, but it had slipped her mind. "We'll connect tomorrow."

"Oh. Okay." The timbre of Rachel's voice changed, as if she were swallowing a hot potato. "It's just that we have to talk. Didn't you see my text messages?"

"I did." Ariel had seen the oblique "Call me when you can" messages, and, frankly, she had found them annoying. She figured it was Rachel's way of trying to tug her away from Craig.

Rach was a great friend, but she was quick to reel Ariel in when anyone else threatened to get between them. "But we've got to figure this situation out tonight."

Rachel grabbed her by the wrist. "You're talking about what Cooper did to Remy? That's exactly what I meant. I heard some things backstage."

Craig cleared his voice, brisk and a bit mean. "Are we ready?" he asked Ariel.

"We'll talk tomorrow, first thing," Ariel promised her friend.

"Okay. Um, I guess I'll bring home your makeup kit."

"Please. Thanks, Rach." Ariel forced a quick smile for her friend before turning away in relief. Sometimes it was best to duck away from Rachel's dogged determination to fix things in her own way. Good intentions did not always amount to a positive outcome.

At least Craig held a position of power in this situation. They spent the car ride discussing whether to split up Remy and Cooper as dance partners. That damned ex-boyfriend was a domestic felon in the making, and Ariel wasn't sure what to do about him.

Craig shared her apprehension. "I don't know what to do with this conundrum," he said as he shifted gears in his Mazda coupe. "The school has a zero tolerance policy for bullying. Zero. Some might say that requires me to suspend Cooper from Gleetime Company."

"Which would mean the collapse of half the numbers in the showcase," Ariel pointed out. "It's a hot mess, all right."

"You said Remy was okay, but what was her reaction?" he asked.

"She thinks it can be patched over. Remy wants a chance to talk with Cooper and smooth things out."

"It's not her fault," Craig said, flicking at his cheek three times, as if shooing off a cobweb.

"Of course it's not, but she suggested that it might have been an accident." Remy had said nothing of the sort, but Ariel knew that Craig needed to cover his ass here. He couldn't overlook a blatant act of bullying. "Maybe Cooper lost his grip," Ariel suggested. "We don't know for sure. He did express remorse, didn't he?"

"When he realized he was in big trouble. But he played dumb. Didn't know how it happened. Said he's under too much pressure. Exams and grades. No date for prom. The usual complaints."

"No date? Oh, please! Cooper could have any girl he wants."

"Except the one he wants," Craig said pointedly.

Ariel sighed. "I don't feel sorry for him. Not a lick. But I do think that it would be an overreaction to dump him from Gleetime. And as far as changing partners, I don't know."

"It would throw off a lot of the dance numbers, and we have no time to make the adjustment. We are four days away from opening night."

"I wouldn't mess with the dance partners. For now, let's give Remy a chance to talk some sense into the big nutball."

By the time they arrived at his place, Craig had decided to give the situation twenty-four hours before taking action. That would give Remy the time she needed, and Ariel was confident that her daughter would strike some sort of peace accord with Cooper. No one could resist an appeal from Remy.

Ariel tried to keep the tone light and friendly as she followed Craig into his apartment, a downstairs unit in a four-story cluster of apartments set in the hills overlooking Portland. When Craig had invited her here, she had suspected he had an ulterior motive. She figured that Craig, like most single men in this town, wanted to have sex with her, and she had been mentally preparing ways to wriggle out of it. Despite her mottled moral scruples, she tried to be monogamous; in the past, trying to juggle relationships with two people at one time had landed her in a pickle. She tried to be a one-man woman. And although her current relationship was fleeting, that didn't give her justification to be a slut.

But as they'd entered his living room of square, modern sectional furniture, she realized that there would be no brushoffs. There were no lingering looks, no loaded touches as he handed her a wineglass. Craig chose the chair opposite the sofa and launched into the topic of his career, pointing out his college background, his experience in local theater, and his grave sacrifice to earn a wage as a teacher when his dream was to be onstage himself.

"Right now, I'm feeling kind of stifled," he said, putting his wineglass down on the glass coffee table. "I feel like it's time for a change. The things I love the most are getting short shrift these days." He was on his feet, moving toward the fireplace. As she watched he took a framed collage from the wall. "Here, let me show you what I've been up to in the past few years."

Ariel accepted the framed collection of photos, programs, and news clippings. "Here's me in *The Man Who Came to Dinner*. Sheridan Whiteside."

"You played that old coot Sheridan?" Ariel squinted at the photos. "How did you pull that off? You're way too young."

"Acting, my dear. A little spirit gum, a good beard, a few penciled-in wrinkles." Craig beamed with pride as he leaned in and studied the collage. "And this was at Portland Center Stage, a fabulous play by a local author. That one was called *Vitriol and Violets*. About the Algonquin Round Table, in New York. I played a number of characters, including the irrepressible Harpo Marx."

"That must have been a blast," Ariel said, infusing her voice with optimism she did not feel. *Acting, my dear Mr. Schulteis.*

"It was fun, but it's not a hobby," Craig said. "I'm a serious actor."

"Of course you are." She put her wineglass down, calculating her timing. Another ten minutes of listening to his career goals and then she could leave. It was a relief: envisioning her exit.

"Lately, I've been feeling that it's time for a change. Maybe a move to New York or LA. Do you ever get that restless feeling?"

She grinned. "Every day. Every hour. It's hard to get show business out of your system."

"But you could get back into it if you want. You must have stayed in touch with agents and casting people. And everyone knows who you are."

"I don't know about that," she said modestly. "Some of your students have never seen my show."

"But that's the beauty of television. They can see reruns. DVDs. I'm sure the kids know that you used to be a star."

The positive energy fizzled with his use of the past tense. Well, it was true. She'd been a celebrity once. Now she was a domestic goddess.

How had she slipped down so far?

"So . . ." He plopped down in the chair. "Not to get really personal, but do you still have an agent?" He brushed at his cheek with two fingers, bringing to mind a fly with flickering legs. "Or maybe you know someone who's taking on new clients. I'm thinking of spending the summer in Hollywood, going on some auditions. It's time, and that might be just the boost my acting career needs."

Acting career? A handful of roles in community theater did not amount to a career. But she couldn't tell Craig how bad his chances were.

"I know a couple of talent agents," she said, lowering her voice as if preparing to reveal the secrets of the universe. "But you know they have different specialties. First, you need to decide what's right for you. Are you going for a film role? Or do you see yourself in commercials or TV? You know, they are three very distinct worlds."

"I'm very versatile. I could do all three."

"But you need to start with one, Craig. Focus your talents. Get a foot in the door, and then you can branch out."

"Start with one." He was nodding vigorously. "See that? I would never have thought of that. Good idea. Perfect." He leaned toward the coffee table and poured more wine into her glass. "You are going to be invaluable to me."

Ariel held back a sigh as she realized this would be her payment for all those voice lesson referrals. Quid pro quo.

* * *

An hour later Ariel stumbled out of a cab and staggered up the dark driveway. There were two arcane messages from Cassie, the second one asking where the hell she was. Ariel turned the mike on and dictated a text message to Cassie. "I'm home. Good night." The heels of her boots sank into the soft soil as she made her way to the mudroom door. She liked to use the side entrance at night so that she wouldn't disturb the kids, whose bedrooms were on the opposite end of the house. She wasn't so much tipsy as weary, so tired of having her time wasted with other people's problems.

There'd been the issue with Remy and Cooper, and then she'd endured two hours of Craig droning on about his limping acting career, and then she'd had to perk up and play the life coach, steering him toward commercial work. He had pushed until she'd sacrificed the name and number of a talent agent in her phone directory—Glinna Jenneli. Not that she'd ever really liked the woman—a cold, blond ice princess who may have already aged out of the business—but every contact was like a gold coin in your pocket. You never knew when an agent or producer would come in handy.

She pushed her way into the mudroom and paused. Although the outer door was never locked, a sliver of alarm prodded her when she noticed that the door to the studio was cracked open. Light streamed out, casting sinister shadows over the dark foyer, making coats on the hooks resemble thugs waiting to spring into attack mode.

What the hell? Who had left this door open? Her kids knew better than to play in the studio, and they always went in through the back door. She reached up and fumbled on the shelf in the corner, her fingers creeping along for the spare key. Nothing there. Someone in the know had taken the key.

Crap. Was Cooper in there, trying to make up with Remy?

Nothing to be alarmed about; bad things didn't happen in Timbergrove, Oregon. Most people didn't even bother to lock their doors, but Ariel did it out of habit, having lived in places where a locked door was the only thing separating you from the mean streets.

As she pushed her way into the studio, alarm skittered up her spine. Her red roses had been ripped apart, the petals scattered on the wood floor amid naked stems and shriveling green leaves. Glass crunched underfoot as she approached the carnage around the piano. Her crystal vase, a gift from Stosh, had been smashed. Although the piano was wet it seemed undamaged but for the shards of glass that sparkled like scattered diamonds on the baby grand's black surface.

"Oh, God." It wasn't the fact of the broken vase but the signs of fury that frightened her.

Fear sent her bounding up the stairs, first to Maisy's little closet of a room, then to Trevor's bedroom with its slanting ceiling. She found the little kids sleeping peacefully in their rooms, the steady sound of their breathing a salve to her panic. When she cracked Remy's door, she could just make out the lump in the bed of her daughter and . . . someone else. A guy. Remy was snuggled up to a guy.

Ariel closed the door, a little miffed. So Cooper was back? That had happened fast.

But he must have come back with a vengeance. Perhaps Remy had brought him into the studio to keep from disturbing the kids. It made sense that they wouldn't have heard anything, as their rooms were on the other side of the house, and years ago Ariel had done some sound-proofing on the studio so she could noodle around on the piano at night.

As she headed back down the stairs the scenario played out in her head. Cooper had shredded the flowers, probably likening it to the shredding of their love. And he'd smashed the vase for what—sheer petty anger? Or dramatic effect?

Either way, the boy was a self-absorbed brat.

Her heartbeat began to slow to a normal pace with the rhythm of sweeping. As the big chunks of crystal landed in the trash can with a thud, Ariel thought of the new vase she would be getting from the Dovers. Waterford crystal. Or Baccarat. Or maybe both. It was the least they could do to make up for their delinquent son's tantrum.

Ariel lost her footing as she tried to reach under the piano. Well, that was good enough for now. She would do a more thorough job in the morning. Better yet, she would get Remy on the task. With a sigh, she stashed the broom and trash in the closet, locked the door, and slipped off her boots to avoid tracking broken glass upstairs.

Up in her bedroom, she moved in the dim light from the bedside table, tugging off her shirt and stepping out of her skirt. She splashed water onto her face, brushed her teeth, and buried her face in a plush white towel for a moment of meditation. Shutting off the bathroom light, she stripped off her bra and panties, leaving them where they fell onto the carpet. She was turning down the comforter when the groan of the closet door came from behind her. Suddenly, she was grabbed from behind, a silver blade flashing before her eyes. The air rushed from her lungs in a spastic gasp as his arms clamped around her and the knife moved to her throat.

"Tell me why I shouldn't kill you now."

Chapter 15

The three-word text from Remy had made Cassie's heart sink: **Stosh is back.**

It all started two hours ago when Cassie was sitting in the kitchen, trying to block out the noise from the thrumming music in Keisha and Maya's room so that she could squeeze in some study time before Andrew came over, when she got the first text. The news brought the cheese raviolis she'd had for dinner right up to the top of her stomach. Acid churned there, threatening to rise up her esophagus.

At a time like this Cassie felt guilty about being away at college, unable to help Remy and Trevor and Maisy. Yeah, it was a relief to be outside the scope of Mom's craziness, but she'd had to leave prisoners behind: her siblings.

Her immediate reaction had been to jump in the car and speed north on the Interstate until she got home. Someone had to protect the kids, and if Mom was going to be part of the problem, that left only Cassie to enforce some sort of solution. But it was late, after ten, and if she made the ninety-minute drive now, she would never get back to campus for her morning classes.

The words of Cassie's psych textbook blurred as she texted a response to Remy.

Cassie: **Wtf! Are they fighting again?**
Remy: **Stosh got violent.**

Cassie: **Call the police! Is he there? Is everyone okay?**

Remy: **We're okay. Stosh came in while Mom was gone and smashed her vase. Left this mess.**

The photo from Remy showed a puddle of glass over the top of the baby grand. A second photo showed a mess of rose petals and leaves on the floor. Yeah, he'd trashed Mom's flowers, all right. Jerk.

Cassie texted: **Is Mom freaking out?**

Remy: **She's not here. She's meeting with Mr. Schulteis.**

"At this time of night?" Cassie said aloud. "I know what's on *their* agenda."

"Are you okay?" Keisha asked as she swung open the fridge. "You're looking a little freaked out."

"Trouble at home." Cassie scraped her long, thick hair into a ponytail, then let it fall on her back. "My mom's evil boyfriend is back."

"Aw. Is he a bad dude?"

"They were really bad together."

"Yeah." Keisha twisted open a bottle of kombucha and took a sip. "That sucks. I feel bad for you." She gave a little pouty face, her lower lip protruding.

Cassie shrugged it off. She talked with her roommates, but she never let on to the depth of her emotions or fears. Nobody really got it. "I need to call my sister."

"I hope everything's okay," Keisha called over her shoulder as she went back to her room.

Remy didn't answer her phone, but texted that she would call back in a bit. Great. Nothing like being stalled when you're in an agony of worry.

It was at least fifteen minutes until Remy called back.

"What's going on?" Cassie asked. "Are you okay? Are Trevor and Maisy home?"

"I'm fine. We're fine. I don't think they know anything happened."

"Why couldn't you take my call?"

"I had to take a shower. I'd just gotten home from rehearsal when I texted you."

"What did Stosh say to you? Was he really creepy?"

"I didn't see him. I just found his little gift to Mom when I came in."

"That's so awful." Cassie felt bad for her sister; sweet Remy, who wouldn't hurt a fly. "You must have been so scared. I know I was. I was about to jump in the car and head up there."

"I'm glad you didn't. There's really nothing anyone can do tonight."

"There would be if Mom was around. It's her job to protect you guys. You should text her to come home. Aren't you scared that he's going to come back?"

"I was a little creeped out, so I called a friend. He's going to stay with me, and I know Stosh won't give him any trouble."

"That's good." Cassie couldn't resist asking, "Who is it?"

"He's here now, so I'm going to go," Remy said evasively. "But don't worry, Mama Bear."

Cassie had come to dislike that nickname, but tonight it endeared Remy to her.

"I just wanted you to know what was up," Remy continued, "but we're okay here. I'll talk to Mom about it tomorrow. Maybe you can call her, too. Your word has more sway with her."

"Of course I'll talk to her, but lately everything I do seems to piss her off."

"She's mad at the world right now."

"She needs to grow up." Cassie didn't check the venom in her voice. She'd had it with her mother.

"I gotta go," Remy said. The girl who was obsessed with selfies thought it was rude to ignore a friend to be on the phone. "I'll call you tomorrow."

"Okay." As Cassie ended the call, worry gave way to annoyance and relief. Now that the crisis was averted, she felt tears welling in her eyes. She couldn't stop thinking of Maisy and Trevor asleep in their beds while Stosh, all red in the face and bulging eyes, was downstairs smashing things up. Slouching over the table, she rested her head on her arms as a small whimper slipped out.

"Hey, there." Andrew's voice, tentative and low, came from behind her. "Olivia let me in. I guess you didn't hear the bell."

"Sorry." She lifted her head and swiped at her eyes. "I'm so stressed."

"The psych exam? I can help you with that."

"No. Problems at home."

"Oh. I can't help you with that." He took a seat beside her and leaned close. "What's going on?"

"I got a scary text from my sister," she began, then spilled the whole story, filling him in on the problems between Stosh and Ariel, as well as her mother's tendency toward "hands-off" parenting.

"Wow, you've really been through hell night," he said, running his thumb over a groove in the kitchen table. He told her that he wasn't surprised to hear that she was the responsible one in the family, though it was hard to imagine having a parent who didn't enforce discipline. "I would have loved that freedom in high school."

"No, you wouldn't. There's no safety net with my mom, no one to catch you when you fall."

"Yeah, but at the other end of the spectrum are the parents who act like jailers. I'm not saying my parents were that bad, but I was always sneaking around, trying to duck my mother's radar. She runs the house like a training camp. Both of my parents were in the navy. I don't think they'll ever get that lifestyle out of their system."

"There's nothing wrong with a little discipline," Cassie said.

"Yeah. I guess we want what we didn't have." He reached over and squeezed her knee, and the gesture made her realize how far they had come. They had become comfortable with each other's company and familiar with each other's body. "You're so grounded. Hard to believe you were raised in the wilds."

She snickered. "It wasn't always so crazy. When my step-father was alive, he kept things on an even keel. Oliver was a rock. He was always there for us, always in a good mood. He worked out of an office at home, and each afternoon he'd pick up Remy and me from school, and then take a break to have a snack with us. He made dinner almost every night, and we'd eat together. We were a family."

"How long has he been gone?"

She shrugged, trying to keep it casual despite the tight knot growing in her throat. "Four years." And she missed him. She missed the family they used to have. It wasn't something she had ever talked about with friends or family. But Andrew was different. He cared. He wanted to listen. And she trusted him. For the first time in her life, Cassie trusted someone enough to really open up. She knew that the truth sometimes drove people away, but so far Andrew didn't seem daunted by her admissions of her weird family life.

"My stepfather was a great parent," she said. "It's my mom who lacks emotional stability." With that, she began the story of Ariel Alexander, opening the Pandora's box of family secrets. With any luck, none of the escaped demons would bite her in the ass.

"Don't hurt me. Don't hurt me, please!" Ariel gasped as the intruder ensnared her in his arms, pulling her back against him. Her body went stiff as the cold blade of his knife pushed into the flesh of her neck. Her pulse pounded, hammering in her ears, and her mind buzzed with the shrill whirr of adrenaline. She braced for the brutal slice of the sharp edge, but there was only pressure. That meant he was pressing the blunt side to her skin; maybe he didn't mean to kill her. Or maybe he just wanted to scare the hell out of her first.

"Please, let me go." She could feel his erection pressing into her bare bottom. "I'll . . . I'll do anything to . . ."

"You already did, you whore." That voice, that low growl. It was someone she knew.

The realization allowed her to draw a breath of relief. She could reason with someone she knew. One of his hands moved across her belly and hooked over her hip bone in a hold that was possessive. Familiar. The detail shook loose some of the scales of fear, allowing the truth to surface.

"It's you," she hissed, reaching up for the hand that held the knife. "You bastard." Careful to avoid the blade, she clamped her fist over his and pushed, moving the knife away from her. "Oh, my God, look at that blade! You could have sliced me from here to heaven. Are you crazy?"

"I'm pissed. If you didn't guess that already."

"Give me that knife!" Ariel nearly spat the words out as fury sputtered forth. How dare he? She squeezed his hand until he released, letting the blade drop to the thick pile carpet with barely a sound. "I can't believe you pulled a knife on me. I can't believe it!" She picked up the knife and marched to the window. "What the hell were you thinking?"

"That you're fucking around behind my back, you bitch."

"What?" She tugged the window open and flung the knife out to the backyard. "And don't think I won't throw you out, too. Pulling a knife on me! What kind of person are you?" She wheeled around and shoved him in the chest. "What are you, a tough guy? Think you're going to abuse me? Slice me up? Or just manipulate me." She pushed at his chest again, and though his face remained stoic, he stepped back. He was wearing jeans—only jeans—and the sight of his bare chest, the feel of muscular ridges beneath baby-smooth skin, was definitely getting to her.

"I saw you go off with him. You left with Mr. Schulteis."

"To discuss the damn show."

"You went to his house, didn't you? Did you fuck him, too?"

The jealous tension in his face, the clench of his jaw, the strain in his body—all combined together to arouse her. Granted, the knife scenario was way over the top, but adrenaline still thrummed in her veins, amplifying the anger and desire. This time, instead of shoving him, she grabbed him by the waistband of his jeans and pulled him closer.

"What if I did?" she murmured, unclasping the rivet and freeing his erection. "What if I did fuck him?"

"I'll kill him." Fury had dilated his pupils, making the circles so wide and dark you could get lost in them.

Oh, he talked a big game, she thought as she dipped into his pants and stroked him over his boxers. "I think you're all talk." Though his talk was eliciting a warmth that throbbed through the core of her body.

He reciprocated, sliding his fingers over the slick folds between her legs. That light buzz of contact made her knees go weak.

"Did he do this to you?" he asked as his fingers teased her, stoking the flames.

"I saved myself for you," she murmured, leaning into him. "Nothing happened with him. I told you, I'm a monogamous creature: One man at a time."

"Yeah, well, you'd better stay that way. Loyal to me."

"You're so possessive," she teased. "But you need to get that temper in check. I can't believe you broke my vase. You idiot. That was a gift from a good friend of mine."

"How good?" He sank his teeth into the side of her neck, working the sensitive tendons, melting her tension to wanton longing. "Who gave it to you? I want to find him and kick his ass."

"You're just full of piss and vinegar tonight." She pushed him onto the mattress, climbing on top.

As she ran her mouth down his chest, sucking the salt from his skin, she wondered how she was going to give him up. Oh, the end was coming, dark clouds gathering with impending thunder and pounding rain.

It was inevitable, but not imminent. For now, she would mount him and screw him like a tigress. Tomorrow be damned. Tonight, she would close her eyes and enjoy the ride.

Chapter 16

The dream kept tugging Rachel back to the roiling, dark waters of the lake. Panic trilled in her chest as she kneeled on the dock at the swim park, reaching into the water, grabbing at the small bodies that kept surfacing. Whenever she had a chance, she would pluck a child from the water, grabbing a pickled hand or a stretched-out T-shirt or the waistband of a pair of pants.

Where were they all coming from, these drowning children? They kept emerging from the inky blue depths, bloated and immobile, and yet when she pulled them onto the deck they sprang to life and walked away as if she'd merely helped them down from a ladder at the playground. She was grateful that they were surviving, but when would this end? When would the churning waters stop coughing up the bodies of Timbergrove's children?

Again she reached down toward the silvery sheen of a white belly and found a little girl's arm. She recognized the gold band of the temporary tattoo on her arm. "Oh my God, it's Remy!" she shouted to Ariel, who knelt beside her, rescuing children with methodical precision.

"No, it's not." Cool as a cucumber, Ariel seized the girl's arm, popped her out of the water, and plunked her little body onto the dock, landing her like a fish. The girl's long curls, barely wet, swept aside to reveal Maisy.

"Told you," Ariel said with a scowl, then leaned back over the side of the dock.

"Maisy, honey, are you okay?" Rachel's hand shook as she reached to the limp girl.

Maisy's head swiveled toward her like a doll's, her eyes falling open to reveal a flat, icy stare. "I'm fine." Her body bucked once, and then she bounced up onto her feet. Her skin was pink and healthy now, her clothes dry. Without another word she ran off the dock, disappearing behind a shrub in the park.

Rachel wanted to follow to check on the girl, but she couldn't turn away from the lake, where the black waters were even now spitting up another young body. . . .

She awoke moaning, trying to say no but unable to form any words as the vise around her chest seemed to crush all breath and circulation from her body.

Only a dream, of course, but a brutally dismal one.

Rolling onto her side, Rachel checked the clock on the nightstand and groaned. Four twenty-two. Way too early to get out of bed, but too scary to return to that morbid dream world.

She flipped her pillow and tried to burrow into the cool, pristine surface. Tried to wipe her mind clean of the dream and the rotten incident that had inspired it. That crappy rehearsal. Her backstage job had been under control, most of the kids ready for the finale, when Rachel had slipped out to the wings to watch the second-to-last sketch, "Heart." She'd seen it all:

Cooper's callous expression, a flicker of evil shadowing his handsome face as he'd stood back and let Remy drop to the stage. She'd caught the look of shock on Remy's face and the horrible sound of her bones banging against the wood.

And she couldn't get it out of her head, as evidenced by that awful dream. Rachel was concerned about Remy and a little pissed with lackadaisical Ariel, who'd breezed off for a hookup with Craig instead of doing the right thing.

Rachel threw back the covers and sat up with a scowl. "You sound so judgmental." She wasn't that way. Blame it on sleep deprivation, not firing on all pistons. It would be wise to go back to sleep, but she couldn't risk falling back into that dark lake dream.

She grabbed her phone from the nightstand and checked the string of texts to see if Ariel had answered her.

Rachel: **I'd love to smack Cooper Dumbass back to last Tuesday. What's Craig doing about it?**

Ariel: **Keeping cool. Don't want to make things worse.**

Rachel: **This is not going away. Kids say he's plotting against her.**

Ariel: **I got this. Don't worry, Mother Hubbard.**

Rachel: **You know me. Talk soon. Coffee in the AM?**

No answer. Well, sure. Only a crazy person would send a text at four in the morning. Only a crazy person was up at this time of night.

With a sigh of resignation she grabbed her robe from the hook and scrambled into socks to keep her feet warm on the cold kitchen floor. What had happened to her? She usually slept like a rock. It felt a little creepy, switching off lights to fend off the night. The overhead kitchen lights were stark white, so she switched them off and measured coffee and water in the dim glow of the bulb over the stove. A few minutes later the coffeemaker was steaming away.

She scrolled through the television guide—another waste-land at this time of night—and settled on a mundane but reas-suring rerun of a family sitcom. Trying to be quiet on the stairs, she went back up to grab the novel she'd been reading. Half-way down the hall, she paused as she noticed the dim bar of light under Jared's door. Was he up, or had he fallen asleep with the light on?

"Jared?" Her voice was soft as she gave two gentle knocks and turned the knob. The lamp on his desk illuminated his stack of schoolbooks, an empty plate and glass, his laptop and neatly made bed.

What the hell?

Moving into the room, she sensed from the eerie stillness that he had not spent the night here. Still . . . she had to check.

She slid open the desk drawer, the one he'd used to store his stash of plastic bags and rubber bands. Now it contained two old binders and a Nerf football. Relief sighed from her lips.

She went to the bedroom window and looked down at the street. His old ruddy Volvo was nowhere in sight. He had never come home last night.

She tugged her cellphone from the pocket of her robe. His last message had been about going for pizza with some of the Gleetime kids. Okay. Deep breath. No one had called, so he was probably fine. Maybe staying the night with a friend?

Actually, Jared wasn't super friendly with any of the Gleetime kids. She didn't even know who in the group she would call to ask about Jared.

But his star was rising, and kids were beginning to see the kind, loyal person he had become. She had seen him goofing around with some kids at rehearsal. Malika Little and Doug Harper and Riley What's-his-name. And Allison Samwick.

Was Jared spending the night with his dance partner? The girlfriend, no doubt.

He is seventeen, she reminded herself. By the time she'd been that age she'd already done some things in a guy's car that would curl a mother's toes.

Retreating downstairs, she poured a cup of coffee and paced. The kids in the TV sitcom resembled chipmunks, spry and cute, so unlike real kids who thwarted your plans and insisted on tearing their own jagged path. This was so unlike Jared. There'd been plenty of times when Rachel had to track down KJ, but Jared had always reported in and rarely stayed out with friends.

Should she call the police? She could try Mike. No, no, no. She didn't want to get her son in trouble with the law if there were some shenanigans going on. Best to stay put. Jared had school this morning, and she doubted that he would miss that.

Ten minutes later, she was dressed in yoga pants and a hoodie and filling a thermal flask with coffee. Too restless to hang around, she was going to head over to Allison's house to look for Jared's car. Not to confront anyone or raise a fuss. Right now she just wanted to know that he had made a safe landing somewhere.

When she didn't find Jared's car near Allison's house, she looked up Doug Harper in the school directory and headed over to Jasmine Lane, a street that ran along the town's small lake. Parking was limited on the narrow road, but the houses set down on the lakeside were sumptuous and airy. The Harpers' home presented a Northwest cedar front, but Rachel could see that the side and back were dotted with yawning windows that would provide great water views. Timbergrove was such a beautiful place to live. Someday her sons would thank her for bringing them to this suburban paradise.

With no sign of Jared's car she drove around town, checking the park, the school parking lot, the twenty-four-hour diner. As the sky softened into a pewter mist, she pulled up and parked on Ariel's block, planning to wake her friend as soon as it reached the decent hour of six a.m. to check on Remy and share her worries about Jared. She and Ariel had a deal that they could wake each other any time, but this hardly constituted an emergency.

Her Hydro Flask was drained of coffee and she longed for more. She opened the screen on her phone and checked the weather app, which said sunrise was due any minute. On this breezy, gray day, the sun would have trouble breaking through.

Just then there was a flurry of motion in front of Ariel's house. Or was it just the shadow of a flickering tree?

Squinting, she made out the figure of a person, a young man, striding away from the Alexander house. He tucked in his shirt-tail as he came up the driveway, moving with a distinctive clipped gait.

Rachel's jaw dropped. Jared. She'd found him.

Once he hit the street, he broke into a jog and climbed into a car parked up ahead.

The dark Volvo pulled away, its taillights glowing red in the dissipating gray mist.

So he'd been there overnight, and Ariel hadn't told Rachel? Because . . . because Ariel didn't know.

Holy cow! That was it. Jared was seeing Remy. Remy was the secret girlfriend.

It made sense for them to keep it secret, because God only knew what Cooper Dover would do once he found out. The big bully. Already he was torturing Remy just for breaking up with him.

With that problem solved, Rachel headed home. She would check in with Ariel later. Better yet, she could ask Jared about Remy.

Jared and Remy. The idea of those kids together made her heart just about burst with joy. But as she pulled into the driveway, she saw a new hurdle ahead. How would she confront Jared without shutting him down? He'd been emphatic about maintaining his privacy with Remy. And now . . . now he was going to think that she'd been spying on him.

She clambered through the cold mist, grateful for the warm kitchen and the smell of coffee. The sound of water running upstairs told her Jared was showering. She rinsed her thermos and poured a fresh cup. Once he came downstairs, he wouldn't have a lot of time to spare before he headed off to school. She had to hit him up today. Let him think what he wanted; she was not going to tiptoe around and play games now that she knew the truth.

She sat in front of the cheerful buzz of a morning show, waiting to confront him.

"Hey, Mom." He came down the stairs at 7:05, his usual morning schedule, and put his backpack on the counter.

"Good morning." She rose from the sofa. "We need to talk."

"Really?" He frowned, moving around her to get to the fridge. "I've got to get to school."

"Just for a minute." She put her empty mug on the counter, struggling to find a way to connect with him. "Look, I know you're going to think I was spying on you, but I wasn't. Bottom line, I was sitting in my car this morning, just beyond Ariel's driveway, when you came out of her house."

His spine went stiff. "You were?"

"Yup. So now I know. I know about your girlfriend."

"What the hell? Mom!" His cheeks burned red as he slammed the refrigerator shut and stomped away.

"Just calm down. You're the one who stayed out all night. I went looking for you when I saw that you hadn't come home. I was worried, honey."

"I'm almost eighteen, Mom. Almost a legal adult. I can handle myself."

"I know, and I trust you. But I worry."

Avoiding eye contact, he opened the pantry door and grabbed a package of peanut butter crackers. "You need to get over that."

"Anyway, I didn't expect to find you at the Alexander house, but I'm glad I did. Thrilled. It's wonderful that you and Remy have found each other. Remy needs support. Especially now. Honey, I'm so glad that you've been there for her."

He let out a breath, shifting to lean against the counter. At last, his gaze flickered over toward her, allowing a moment of connection. In his eyes she saw so much: fear and grace and determination. It was a quick glimpse of the man he was becoming. "Okay. Okay so . . . now you know." His mood shifted, more relaxed now as he slipped the crackers into a pocket of his backpack. Maybe he, too, was relieved to have the truth out.

"Now I know." She turned away to hide her gloating smile. She couldn't help it. The thought of him dating Remy brought her delight. "Want a piece of toast?"

"I don't have time."

"Right. I don't want to make you late, but I just wanted to put it out there. You know I don't like secrets."

"Yeah." His face was composed now; the storm had blown over. "About that. Could you not broadcast it to the world?"

She snickered. "You mean the gals at the shop?"

"I mean everyone. Not even Ariel. Keep it to yourself until I say so. If word gets out, it'll ruin everything."

That seemed a bit dire, but teens had a penchant for hyperbole. "I won't tell anyone," Rachel promised. "Scout's honor."

"Don't forget. You're always forgetting stuff," he said, a little too tersely, before heading out the door.

"Yeah," she said to the closed door. "And thanks, Mom, for being so understanding." She put her mug in the sink, feeling a little lighter despite Jared's dour mood.

Or maybe it was lack of sleep and a surge of caffeine. Planning for the day, she hoped to squeeze in coffee with Ariel and maybe even a cup with Mike McCabe. Suddenly the prospect of empty-nesting didn't seem quite so lonely.

Chapter 17

That morning Ariel awoke to a spate of concerned texts. Rachel was ultra-concerned over Remy, and Cassie had sent a few pompous gems like: **Your family needs you home NOW** and **For once I wish you would think of others when you make your bad choices.**

Ariel agreed to go for coffee with Rachel after drop-off. Then she texted **WTF?** in response to Cassie's barbs. What had inspired Cassie to rise up onto her soapbox, and so early in the morning? Ariel's head throbbed from lack of caffeine and too much wine and too little sleep. She yawned, losing track of how many scoops of coffee she'd measured, and threw in two more. When given the choice, sex always won over sleep. And her boy toy had ducked out a few hours ago, giving her time for one REM cycle. She would survive.

She filled the coffeemaker, cursing as she sloshed water onto the counter. She needed one of those new coffeemakers. A quick injection of caffeine.

As the coffee was brewing she went upstairs to wake the little ones.

Maisy opened her eyes, smiling through her tousled downy hair. "I love the morning in my cushy bed," she said sweetly.

"Me, too," Ariel agreed. If only she could have stayed there.

Twenty minutes later, Ariel was leaning against the kitchen counter, nursing her headache with coffee and aspirin, when

Remy came down the stairs. Ariel lifted her gaze from the guest host on the *Today* show, a vibrant, sexy young actress whose winning personality was pissing her off. She scrutinized her daughter, realizing they hadn't really been alone since the incident with Cooper.

"How're you feeling this morning? Any bruises or bumps from last night?"

Remy shook her head as she filled her Hydro Flask with cold water and shoved it into the side pocket of her backpack. "All good, and I straightened things out with Cooper."

"That's what I thought." Cradling her mug for warmth, Ariel recalled that lump of man she'd spied in Remy's bed last night. "So you two are back together again?"

"What?" Remy scraped her hair back from her shoulder and hitched up her backpack. "No."

"Then, who..." Ariel wanted to ask, but that would violate the unspoken deal. She didn't keep score on her girls, and in turn, they didn't pass judgment on her relationships. The deal had worked well with Remy, not so much with Cassie, who was a walking cop, judge, and jury.

Ariel took a different tack. "I thought I saw Cooper here last night."

"That was just a friend."

A friend? Ariel massaged the tender spot beside her right eye. *Throw me a bone. A tiny hint.* Maybe Cooper had been the boy in her bed, and Remy just wasn't ready to admit they were a couple again.

"He came over to keep me company because I was freaked out about the smashed vase." Remy glanced cautiously toward the studio. "That scared me, Mom. I didn't see him do it, but I know it was him."

Ariel tightened her grip on the mug as the bottom dropped out beneath her feet. "You do?" How could Remy know? Ariel had covered her tracks; she'd insisted on caution with him.

"Just connect the dots. He knows where we keep the key, he loves drama, and he gave you that vase, right? Stosh was always vindictive."

"Stosh? Oh, honey, no. I'm done with him."

"Are you sure?" Remy cocked her head. "It seems like the sort of thing he would do."

"No, no, it wasn't him. He's past tense." Ariel pressed a hand to her right temple as she squinted through the ache between her eyes. It was hard to track this morning. "It was an accident. It happened earlier in the day during a voice lesson. One of my students knocked it over."

"And you just left it like that?"

"I didn't have time to clean it up. I had to get to rehearsal." Ariel took a sip of coffee, but already it was tepid and kind of muddy. "So what's the deal with prom now? Are you going with this new guy, or is it back to Cooper?"

"I'm still going with my girls, Sophia and Siri. It's more fun to go in a group, anyway."

Also more expensive, Ariel thought, though she kept that jibe to herself. Still, the old days were better, when guys paid for girls and played the role of protector. Things made more sense back then. Prom had become a moneymaking machine with expensive invites, flowers, gowns and tuxes, limousines and buses with stripper poles. Thinking fondly of her senior prom, in which she'd worn a corsage made from flowers in her boyfriend's garden, Ariel felt a shiver of nostalgia. Crap. She was getting old.

Trevor came bounding down the stairs. He propped some sort of Lego invention up on the kitchen table, explaining that it was his geography project.

"The three-dimensional city map," Remy said. "I remember doing that." They talked about it while Trevor poured himself a bowl of cereal and Maisy handed Ariel an apple to slice for her.

"When are you going to learn to do this yourself?" Ariel asked her youngest.

"I'm afraid of cutting myself," Maisy responded, shifting from foot to foot in a little dance. "I don't like pain."

"It's not that hard. Here. I'll do half, and you can do the rest. Just move the knife away from you." Ariel was tossing slices into a plastic bowl when her cell phone began to jingle. She wiped her hands on a towel and snatched up the phone.

"Cassie, what's up?" she answered. Might as well get this over with.

"I've only got a few minutes before my exam. It's finals week, but I've been worried sick. Remy told me that Stosh is back."

"She did?" Ariel turned to nod at Remy, who was ruffling Trevor's hair on her way out the door. "Well, he's not. Look, one of my students broke the vase in the studio by accident."

"Really." Cassie did not sound convinced. "How did that happen?"

"It's a long story, but everything's fine. Remy saw the mess and jumped to conclusions. I don't know why she would call you. It's not like you can do anything about it."

"She was scared."

"You know, if I got scared every time I found a mess in this house, I'd be a walking heart attack."

"Wow. Thanks for understanding."

"Cassie girl, you need to learn how to discern the difference between legitimate fear and teen drama." Ariel was getting a little sick of Cassie blowing things out of proportion, especially when it came to criticizing Ariel's parenting skills.

"Oh come on, Mom! Remy was freaked out last night and you were nowhere to be found."

"I was working on the show. Volunteer work. And you know what? I don't need to answer to you, missy."

"Mom. Mom. Mom," Trevor called. He stood at the door, his arms wrapped around the colorful Lego sculpture. "Come on. I need extra time to drop this off in Mr. Goebel's class."

"I gotta take the kids to school," Ariel told Cassie, glad for the excuse.

"Can't they take the bus?" That was Cassie, always second-guessing her.

"Trevor is carrying in a project. It's very delicate." Besides, Ariel was planning to meet Rachel along her jogging route to the coffee shop, but Cassie didn't need to know that. "Call me later if you need me."

She knew Cassie wouldn't call, and that was fine with her. Nobody liked a critic.

That large dose of early-morning caffeine was kicking Rachel's run up a few notches. She was on her second lap past the elementary school when Ariel's BMW slowed at the curb.

"Hey, girl!" Ariel called through the open window. "Climb aboard! I'm going your way."

Rachel slid into the seat and closed the door.

Ariel punched the gas pedal in that annoying manner of a reckless driver. "Did I see you sprinting past the field there?"

"Yeah, girl." Rachel was actually sorry to end the run. The skies were clear and the sun had already warded off the morning chill. It was going to be a green grass, fresh air day, and Rachel would have to spend most of it inside at the salon. "I was really kicking it this morning."

"Looks like it." Ariel fished in the console, coming up with a pair of sunglasses. Despite her chipper tone, Ariel was a little off her game. Her frosted-rose lipstick made her skin seem yellow, and her eyes were bloodshot.

"You look a little tired," Rachel said. "Did Craig keep you up late?" Last night Rachel had been a little annoyed that Ariel had made Craig a conquest after Rachel had mentioned a casual interest in him. Not that it mattered now. She'd already gotten over it. Way over it.

"Craig kept me up, all right, but no fun was had. Apparently, my gaydar has been malfunctioning. Craig wants a career in show business. Other than that, he's not interested in anything you or I can give him."

"I suspected as much. Whenever Craig's around, there's a certain awkwardness in the air. I thought it was me, being so rusty with dating and all. I'm glad he's gay." Rachel folded her arms, feeling vindicated. "Wow. If you couldn't turn him, the guy must be devout."

"I'm flattered, but honestly, I wasn't that interested. Craig is a little too by-the-book for me." Ariel pressed a finger to one temple as she slowed to turn into the parking lot. "My head is pounding."

"You need some aspirin."

"More aspirin. More caffeine." Ariel sighed. "It was a wasted night, and now I'm ruined for the day. I'm going to need a nap."

"If it's any consolation, I didn't sleep, either," Rachel said reassuringly. "I was so worried about Remy." Not so much anymore. With Jared by her side, Remy no longer seemed so vulnerable and alone. "How's she doing?"

"She's fine. You know Remy; she bounces back quickly. She's already on to another guy."

The image of her son leaving the Alexander house brought Rachel a flicker of pride as she followed her friend into the coffee shop. She was bursting to celebrate the news, but she sensed that Ariel wasn't in on it yet, and Rachel would not break a promise to her son. "Do you know who he is?"

"Nope. And I don't probe about those things. I give my kids privacy, and in turn I expect them to respect mine."

Rachel stepped up to the counter to order a decaf cap, glad for the conversation stopper. Ariel's claims of privacy didn't jibe with the way Rachel saw motherhood. That sort of removal had never worked for her with her boys. She was their mother first, their friend second. But who was she to judge? If the proof was in the results, then Ariel was doing a great job.

As they moved to the next counter to pick up their drinks, Ariel shoved her sunglasses up on her head, pulled out her phone, and scowled. "Freakin' Cassie. She just can't leave well enough alone."

"What's that about?"

"She texts me all the time, criticizing the way I handle the kids. I'll be glad when she has a bunch of her own kids to freak out over. That'll teach her that there's no mothering manual." They settled at a small marble table, where Ariel rambled on, complaining about her oldest.

As Rachel pretended to listen, she imagined Ariel as a girl herself, a toddler left abandoned in a playpen. It had been three or four days until someone had come for the little girl, who'd needed two days' treatment for dehydration in a hospital. Although Ariel had no memory of the event, she had always told the story in a cavalier manner, pegging herself as a survivor.

But you don't understand the joys of being a mother, Rachel thought as she sipped her hot drink. *Your parents robbed you of that.*

A few years ago when Ariel's mother had passed away, it was no surprise that she didn't return to Oklahoma for the funeral. Ariel downplayed it all, saying that she'd raised herself, but there was no denying the effects of neglect. Parents mattered.

"Cassie must be getting ready for finals soon," Rachel said when Ariel's rant wound down. "I know KJ is almost done. Is she coming home for the summer?"

"I sure hope not." The sour tone was not very flattering. She popped two aspirins and washed them down with her latte.

"KJ's doing summer school. And I'm starting to think about empty nesting." She met Ariel's gaze, hesitant. "I texted Mike McCabe this morning." Oh, God, she'd said it! An odd warmth suffused her cheeks. "That sounds so junior high."

Ariel grinned. "Rachel and the sheriff, sitting in a tree, k-i-s-s-i-n-g..."

"Thanks for that. It makes an awkward admission mortifying. And we're just meeting for coffee."

"I've had coffee dates that ended up in the horizontal tango. Just be prepared. Shave and wax and all. And how's your lingerie collection?"

"Chez Target's finest cotton briefs."

Ariel's head lolled back. "Hopeless. I'm taking you shopping. Thongs and slinky camisoles are your friend. The tease is everything."

"I'm planning to get to know him first." Just the thought of getting naked with a man made her palms sweat. "You know I like to take it slow."

"You moved at a pretty good pace when you met Jackson."

"That was different." It seemed like ancient history, though it was only twelve years ago. "The first day he pulled up on his motorcycle to read our meter, I knew it was right."

"What a great line." Ariel arched one brow. *"Sweetheart, I've come to read your meter."*

Rachel waved her off, but conceded with a smile. Those had been the glory days: falling in love, watching him engage her sons with kindness and patience. After that first meeting Jackson began to stop by the house while on his route. He showed KJ how to hold a football, he moved a fallen tree from the driveway, and he helped Rachel climb in through a window when she locked herself out. Back then, all the women in the neighborhood had looked longingly after Jackson Simmons as he pulled away on his bike, and Rachel had counted her blessings at the attraction that was so natural between them.

Around the same time, Ariel had met Oliver while filming a commercial in LA. That had sweetened the experience. They had shared their lives as single moms, their dating secrets, and then their new marriages.

"Remember how we used to joke about having a double wedding?" Ariel toasted with her paper cup. "That would have been a fiasco."

"Those were good times." Rachel smiled, recalling the surge of love she had felt when she'd met Jackson, a man who'd been able to straighten out the things in her life that had been going sideways. Her kids, her finances, her home. Even her disposition. She'd been such a man-hater after the boys' father had left her for another woman.

"We used to have a lot of fun together. Playing hooky together, driving out to the coast, or sitting around watching soap operas. Too bad that ship sailed." Ariel's voice held an edge of criticism. "What happened to us?"

"We got older," Rachel said, "and we lost our husbands."

"Yeah, but that doesn't mean we can't still have fun." Ariel's stern gaze lit on Rachel, chastising.

Tension crackled in the air between them; a good time to take a sip of cappuccino and hope that Ariel would calm down. No such luck.

"You're not going to answer me?" Ariel asked.

Rachel lowered her drink. "What was the question? Can we still have fun? Sure. We do. But every day can't be a holiday."

"That's a cop-out."

"We both have jobs, thank God. So we've become respectable members of society. As boring as that may seem, it's a good thing."

"I'm not so sure about that." Ariel's anger was palpable. "Responsibility is so boring. Every day I wake up to a day that's the same as yesterday, stuck in the box of the calendar day. Same appointments, stuck in the studio. I might as well be in prison."

"Is it that bad? Oh, honey, I didn't know—"

"Stop. I don't want your pity or your judgment. Don't you see? I hate domestic bliss, but you like it. You're doing your thing. You go to the shop and play judge, jury, and therapist to half the women in Timbergrove."

"I don't judge my customers." Rachel smiled to slough off the sting of the accusation, which held a grain of truth.

"That's all okay. You found your niche. But I'm . . ." Ariel's train of thought seemed to melt away as she pressed her fingertips to her temples. "I'm so tired of this suburban crap. Just so tired."

Rachel was nodding sympathetically, though she was annoyed by the way Ariel had slipped into self-indulgence and, in the process, identified Rachel as part of the suburban army. But this was no time to defend herself, with Ariel falling apart. Sometimes you just had to cut your losses.

"Let's get you home," Rachel said. "And I'm afraid I've got to get to work." She'd been up since four and there was no time to nap. But was she complaining?

Ariel didn't realize how good she had it.

Chapter 18

By Thursday night, the tides had shifted for Ariel. Last night's premiere of the Spring Showcase had bowled the audience over, and by Thursday noon the entire run of five performances had been sold out. Just like that, they had a smash hit on their hands, with "crisp, bright vocal performances worthy of a Broadway stage," wrote the *Oregonian*. The review was nice, but the most powerful tool of suburbia was word of mouth, and the grapevine was abuzz with praise. Craig attributed the success to a "talented group of students," but Ariel knew the truth. This show was all her. Working with these kids for months, some of them for years, she had drawn out their talents and polished them to a brilliant luster.

Bravo, Ariel.

The success reminded her that she still had it, even if her talents were currently cloaked in suburban ennui. And the actual performances filled her with the rush of adrenaline she had been missing in the past few years, reminding her that it was high time to rattle her agent's cage and book a flight to Los Angeles for some auditions. This singing witch had a bit more magic up her sleeve. She could do commercial gigs to start. Then, if a show came along, she would hire a nanny for Trevor and Maisy, and commute home on the weekends. Hell, her kids were so independent, they'd barely miss her.

For now, there was joy in flitting about backstage, checking the acoustics from the back of the auditorium, encouraging her students, and soaking up the praise of parents, who had lined up in the lobby to share hugs and thanks after last night's performance.

"Blake loves the country song you recommended," Liz Luchter had raved. "What a great pick for him."

"Isn't it fabulous?" Ariel had agreed. She'd had to find a song that Blake could talk his way through, but since his parents had bankrolled their son's lessons for the past three years, it had been worth the effort.

"That number with the four girls in their jammies is a hoot," Deanne Little had said. "Malika's got everyone in the house singing about the Sandman."

"Our Kristina never sounded so good," Rich Lee had told her. "You're a miracle worker."

True dat, Ariel had thought, responding only with a gracious smile as she recalled the grueling hours of squeezing water from a stone.

Tonight everyone was in high spirits. With opening night jitters behind them, the kids seemed to be enjoying themselves, in the groove. Everywhere Ariel turned, students still asked for advice and pointers, wanting that last-minute boost before going onstage. The audience lapped up every performance, applauding wildly over the a cappella performance of "Blackbird," roaring in laughter over the boys' coconut-bra choir of "Kokomo."

Ariel moved past a group of stagehands to the wings to get a bead on Sage Sherer in the spotlight at center stage. This gem of an audience even seemed to buy into Sage's performance of "On My Own." Sage usually managed to make the lovely song pedantic, but tonight she had tapped into a vein of emotion that even struck a chord in Ariel. The song of a woman pining for her man reminded Ariel of Oliver, who had taken her to see *Les Mis* in Los Angeles.

Suddenly, Ariel was bumped from behind and would have fallen forward if hands had not snaked around to catch her, landing squarely on her breasts.

"What the hell?" She tried to wriggle loose, turning her head to see Graham Oyama.

His square teeth gleamed. "Don't worry, Ariel. I got you." So damned confident and strong. Every female swooned when he came near, but he wanted her. That fired her up in the best ways.

"Apparently so." She placed her hands over his, pausing a moment to savor the warmth of him, the fullness of her breasts against his palms. Arousal radiated from his fingertips straight to her core, tempting her to go for it here and now. The chances of getting caught were fairly high, but the risk factor heightened the excitement.

"Come on, now." His breath was warm against her ear. "You know you want it."

She did. But she could see the stage from here, and countless people could probably see them from the lighting booth, the catwalks, the wings.

"Not here. Not now." She moved his hands down to her waist, hating the fact that she had to be the responsible one here. "How many times have I told you? We can't do this anymore."

"Nobody can see."

"Just the stagehands."

"They don't care."

"You naughty boy. All it takes is one person seeing us together to set tongues wagging." She stepped away from him, her voice low and sultry. This was killing her. "Now stay away."

"Killjoy." The hunger in his dark eyes was hard to resist.

"You need to learn to keep your hands to yourself in public." Ariel had to scrape together all her resolve to fix him with a stern look. "Go get ready for the group number. It's coming up. Get the hell out of here. And if you're lucky, I'll see you later."

She pretended to ignore the tantalizing hand that trailed down her back and cupped her butt as he pulled away. He always did like to have last licks. With a deep breath, Ariel straightened her black dress, making sure her bra straps weren't showing. Onstage, Sage finished with a crescendo, just as Ariel had taught her. Nicely done. She clapped, checking around her. The stagehands wheeling out a tall table and bar stools for the next number were preoccupied for now.

Just as Ariel turned away, she caught the gaze of someone in the wings across the stage. A woman. Had she been watching? In the flurry of movement onstage, the contact was broken. Well. Ariel would need to come up with an explanation, just in case.

In the large dressing room backstage, Rachel was still humming "Singin' in the Rain" as she did a few last-minute comb-outs for the Part One finale. Although she remained backstage to help out the kids through most of the show, each night she had stolen into the wings to watch Jared and Remy perform their musical duet, and the joy that bubbled up inside her at the sight of those two always left her feeling a little lighter on her tired feet. The recruiter for Winchester College was going to be bowled over when they did that number at the state competition.

"You're done." Rachel was sending one out of her chair and ushering the waiting girl in when Angela Harrell strode in from the stage area, twitching mad.

"It's not right. I'm telling Craig. Or no, not him. I'm going to the top. The principal," Angela told Nora Delfatti, who motioned Angela toward the girls' dressing area, just a few feet beyond the lighted vanity mirrors. "Is Dr. Balducci here tonight? She needs to know about this."

"Are you sure of what you saw?" Nora lifted the white privacy sheet and waited for Angela to step through. "I know you don't want to start a rumor that might get people in trouble."

Pretending to focus on combing out Sunshine's hair, Rachel listened intently to the two women who had disappeared behind the sheet. Apparently, they thought that since they were out of sight, they were out of earshot.

"I saw Dr. B last night," Nora said in a level voice. She was maintaining calm, Rachel could tell. "Not sure if she's here tonight."

"Well, there must be a way to reach her." Angela's tone grated on Rachel's nerves. "An emergency number."

"But is this really an emergency?" Nora asked.

"She's their voice coach. She's spending time alone with all those innocent boys."

Ariel. They were talking about Ariel.

"We've entrusted our sons and daughters to her care," Angela went on, "and she's abusing them."

"We don't know that."

"There's definitely something going on between her and Graham. Have you seen the way he touches her? Right in front of God and everyone."

So other people had noticed Graham's familiarity with Ariel. It could be a huge problem for Ariel. Huge. Angela Harrell was not one to back down. She had nearly knocked the anthropology curriculum out of the high school based on her family's religious beliefs that dinosaurs had never roamed the earth because they were not mentioned in the Bible.

"I did notice that he was kind of hands-on, but maybe that's his style."

"It's inappropriate. Immoral. Illegal."

"Even if something was going on between them, they're not breaking the law. Graham is eighteen."

"Well, there ought to be a law. It's appalling, even the way those boys look at her. The other day I heard Blake Luchter make a comment that scalded my ears. It's creating a very unhealthy environment for our kids."

There was a grain of truth in the complaint. Much as Rachel hated to side with Angela Harrell, she couldn't deny the discomfiture that made her look away when Ariel mixed with the male students. It wasn't just the way that Ariel jumped into their groups like a hot girl at a fraternity party. The ease with which they touched her suggested a visceral familiarity with her body. That was Ariel's gift and curse, as she always said;

when you had a body that rang of sexuality, men thought the bell was tolling for them.

As Rachel tied Sunshine's hair into low pigtails, she stole a glance around the room to see who else might be listening. Except for essential helpers, parents were out in the audience. The girls at the vanity were having their own discussion about false eyelashes, and the bulk of the students waiting for the Part One finale were outside sitting at tables in the adjoining cafeteria, which was the only way to contain the noise of the kids' chatter. No one else seemed to be listening.

At least, containment was still possible.

But with Angela now going on a tirade about other boys Ariel might have "touched," Rachel wasn't sure if she should make a move. Knowing that she was best friends with Ariel, Angela was likely to amplify her protest if Rachel intervened.

"I would start by talking to Craig about it," Nora advised.

"At least. If I had a son, I wouldn't leave him alone with her. I shudder to think of what's going on behind closed doors." From Angela's dramatic pitch, Rachel suspected she was deriving some perverse pleasure from this. She heard it all the time from clients who told stories of someone else's "outrageous" scandal that got their own juices flowing.

"There's got to be another teacher in this town who can give voice lessons," Angela went on. "Maybe someone in West Green or Mirror Lake."

"I doubt there's anyone as experienced as Ariel." Nora's tone was calm, just the right amount of indifference to diffuse the situation. Or so Rachel hoped.

As soon as she finished with Sunshine's hair she swept up her cell from the counter and shot off a text to Ariel: **Angela Harrell talking trash about you and Gleetime boys. Wants to go to the principal.**

For now, it was all she could do. Hoping that Ariel would come swinging through the door to nip this thing in the bud, she put her phone down and helped Armand Ahari adjust his hippie headband.

*   *   *

It was amazing how quickly Ariel defused the situation. When she came backstage during the intermission, with Craig at her side, they tracked Angela Harrell like a gossip-seeking missile and escorted her out, down the hall toward the band and choir rooms.

That night, Rachel got a text from Ariel saying that they'd corrected the situation. It wasn't until Friday morning, while shopping at the mall with Ariel, that Rachel got the full story. Craig had taken charge of the situation, sitting down in his office off the choir room with Ariel and Angela and cutting to the heart of the matter.

"Angela the angel said she saw Graham touching me inappropriately, which was true." Ariel recalled the incident proudly, glad to have squashed Angela's bit of drama. "I told them that naughty boy grabbed me backstage and I got him in line, which Angela didn't really buy at first. Craig promised to have a talk with Graham about boundaries, and I gave her the speech about how I keep an open-door studio. Like anything could happen in there with the big window facing out on the street. I told her there's often a student waiting in the mudroom. My kids are home, and parents are welcome to sit in on their kids' lessons. That shut her down."

"Good for you," Rachel said as she reluctantly followed her friend into a lingerie store. She knew what was coming, and she dreaded it.

"Thanks for the heads-up, my friend. You saved my skin." Ariel slung an arm around Rachel for a quick hug, then reached into a display of silky triangles. "Look at these V-strings, on sale, two for ten. I'd grab six of them if I were you."

Trying not to be a curmudgeon, Rachel picked one up by the pink elastic band. "But they don't cover anything."

"Well, you wear clothes over them, honey. I would stay away from the lace, though. That can be itchy. You need to be comfortable."

As if having a string between your buttocks was going to be comfortable. Rachel picked out four V-strings, avoiding the cheetah prints but allowing stripes. She had to be prepared for the prospect of being seen in her underwear for the first time in years. Her current stock of polyester or cotton briefs was starting to fail, with gummy threads bunching on the sides. Not that she would abandon her steady-eddies. But from now on she would have to wear fancy underwear for those "maybe" occasions.

"Do you like the bikinis, or do you want some thongs, too?" Ariel asked from the next multilevel display of satin patches and strings.

"I'm good here." Rachel's feet seemed to be glued in place by the underwear bin as Ariel zigzagged through the tables, pinching the lace trim on bras, testing the smoothness of a camisole, and holding items up for size. "So you never finished your story about Angela," Rachel said. "What was the up-shot?"

"Nothing. Craig will talk to Graham, and Angela gets to eat her words."

"But she wasn't making things up," Rachel said, trying to tread delicately. "And I understand her concern. Someone who didn't know you well might think you're a little too physical with the guys."

Ariel held a tiny silk dress up to her chin. "People can think anything they want. I can't stop them."

"But you do have a reputation to protect," Rachel pointed out. "Maybe you want to put on a more conservative appearance. Cover the cleavage. Throw on a blazer."

"Like a pantsuit?" Ariel puckered as if she'd just bit into a lemon.

"Maybe at school events. It wouldn't be so bad."

"Sorry, dear Prudence, but I'm not hiding this light under a bushel. Do I criticize you for wearing sweats and mom jeans?"

That stung. Rachel didn't expect that kind of criticism from her friend.

"Just a thought," Rachel said, hoping that Ariel would pay some attention to her warning. "Angela is not someone you want as an enemy."

"I am not dressing for Angela Harrell," Ariel said. "And

you, my friend, are not allowed to buy that cotton nightshirt. When the hell would you wear that?"

"To bed."

"No, no, no." Ariel turned to a rack of clothes and removed a little purple-and-blue camisole. "You want something like this. Babydolls, with matching undies. Look at those cutouts!"

"It's beautiful, but I would never be able to sleep with those spaghetti straps."

Sighing, Ariel shook her head. "Who's sleeping? This is all about the tease. He'll love peeling it off you."

"Oh, please. I am so not ready to be peeled."

"Like a banana." Ariel handed her the babydoll pajamas and pointed her to the fitting room. "Trust me, this is gonna be great."

As Rachel turned away from the mirror of the dressing room and stripped down, she wondered if Ariel had any idea how cutting her remarks could be at times. Sometimes Ariel was all about herself. Suddenly, she was glad she hadn't broken her promise to Jared and spilled the beans about Remy and him. Ariel would find out later, when the kids wanted her to know. For now, Rachel would treasure the secret.

Chapter 19

The end is always bittersweet.

Ariel felt a mixture of exhilaration and melancholy as she held court in the theater lobby during intermission, smiling as two of the moms thanked her emphatically for her craft and dedication. The floor-to-ceiling windows of the lobby's outer wall provided a reflective surface for Ariel to turn and catch her own reflection from time to time. She saw herself radiating power and light throughout the crowded lobby, with the glimmering smile and sparkling smooth skin of a starlet on a red carpet at a Hollywood film premiere. Tonight, she was sizzling hot.

This was their last show, a Sunday matinee, and Ariel was soaking up one of the last interludes of praise from the Gleetime parents. Some of the parents appreciated the genuine progress their kids had made, while others simply enjoyed the glad-handing, being part of the inner circle of the Gleetime troupe. Patti Cronin thanked her for drawing out Matthew's talents, and Elizabeth Gifford revealed that Tory had talked endlessly about Gleetime. And of course, there were those dads (and one mom) who enjoyed talking to Ariel's cleavage. No offense taken. She was glad the girls still got their share of attention.

She was going to miss this—the attention, the adult conversation, the adulation. After the show closed this afternoon there would be a company party tonight, and then there would be a bit of a break until fall, when she would be back to the grindstone leading vocal exercises for the next round of Gleetime performers.

This summer, she was going to get herself back to Los Angeles for auditions. It was time to do something for herself for a change.

Traci Harper was just discussing the merits of her son's summer job at Giant Burger when someone grabbed at Ariel's arm.

"There you are!" The trollish voice growled as something sharp clenched over Ariel's biceps.

Ariel swung around and came within inches of the staunch mask of Tootsie Dover's face, puffy and immobilized from inebriation. A heavy whiff of alcohol enveloped Tootsie, and she dug her lacquered nails into the flesh of Ariel's skin.

"Easy, Toots," Ariel said, wrenching her arm free. The motion sent the older woman teetering back, wobbling on her high heels. She smacked a hand against the windows and braced herself there, a tipsy bacchanalian goddess.

Traci and Patti had the good grace to excuse themselves and disappear, leaving Ariel to face Tootsie on her own.

"Jesus, Tootsie. I think you broke the skin."

"I wasn't going to let you slip away this time. You've been avoiding me."

"Not quite. I've been so busy with the show, I haven't had a moment to myself."

Tootsie tried to straighten her spine, but her head wobbled on her neck. "Your daughter should be ashamed of herself, the way she's treating my son."

"Last time I checked, a girl had the right to break up with her boyfriend. Remy tried to let him down easy. It's not her fault if Cooper is taking it badly."

"Her timing shh . . . shtinks. You know we booked the trip to Europe. Three weeks, seven countries. I can't believe she would be so irresponsible." Her head lolled against her shoulder until she jerked herself upright. "What am I supposed to do with her ticket now? It's too late to get a refund."

That old news? Ariel wanted to tell Tootsie to stick that ticket up her surgically enhanced ass. It hurt Ariel to think that her daughter might be missing out on the chance of a lifetime—a grand tour of Europe—but Remy had made her choice, and Ariel supported her daughter's decision. "I'd say you have two choices. You can give Remy the ticket to use on her own sometime." Ariel knew Tootsie would never go for that. "Or you can have the ticket reassigned to Cooper's next girlfriend."

One of Tootsie's well-painted eyebrows lifted at the prospect. Perhaps she hadn't considered that her son might find a replacement girl.

"Or is Cooper having trouble finding another girlfriend?"

Tootsie swayed forward, catching herself against one of the windows. "Of course not."

"Then your problem is solved."

"My problem is solved," Tootsie mimicked with false cheerfulness. "My son just needs to find a new fuck-buddy."

Ariel steeled herself to keep from pouncing. "Now, now. Let's keep it clean, Toots. This is a family event."

"Oh, right." To her credit, Tootsie cast a doleful look to the side, though the momentum sent her swaying again.

"Look, I've got to get backstage," Ariel lied.

"Bye, then. Tell your daughter not to cry herself to sleep on prom night. I heard that she hasn't been able to find another date."

It felt too lame to admit that Remy was going with friends. "She has her choice of dates. It's so hard to decide which guy to choose."

"That's not what I heard," Tootsie said in a singsong voice. "Poor little Remy. No one will go near her now. Damaged goods."

Ariel felt annoyance buzzing in her head. "What the hell?"

"You know I'm kidding." Tootsie's fat lips parted into a

toothy, wicked grin. Despite her inebriated state, she could see that she'd gotten to Ariel, and oh how she savored it.

That bitch.

"So this is where you work your magic during the show?" Mike surveyed the vanity counter with the lit mirrors. "Nice. But I noticed you were standing in the back of the auditorium for Jared's duet. The rain song?"

"God help me, I love that number. They do such a good job, don't they?"

"Fantastic. Everyone sitting near me was tapping their toes in time to the music. They had the audience in the palm of their hands."

Rachel lined up her hairbrushes as she basked in Mike's praise. "It's a great show this year," she said, trying to be magnanimous in case the other kids hanging out in the green room were listening. "These kids have done an awesome job."

Mike nodded, catching the attention of a few students. "Hey, guys. I liked that Beach Boys number. That was some getup."

"Yeah," Isaiah said. "I think we turned some heads."

"You definitely got some laughs. You know, Cooper and Isaiah, I've seen you play football, but I didn't know you could do this kind of stuff, too."

"We're like renaissance dudes," Isaiah said.

A few girls joined them, and Mike mentioned something about the "Mr. Sandman" song. The kids seemed to enjoy talking with him, and Mike knew most of them by name. Rachel was impressed by his easy rapport.

As the kids began to gather toward the end of intermission, Mike leaned close to Rachel. "I guess I'd better get back to my seat, but I was hoping to see Jared back here. Where is he?"

"As far away from me as he can be," she said with a small laugh. "He sort of just tolerates my involvement here."

"Sounds typical." Mike surveyed the room. "And what about your friend Ariel? I haven't seen her around."

"I really want you two to meet, but she's all over the place right now, putting out fires and calming nerves."

"I'll catch her some other time." Mike kept his voice low, discreet. She liked that. "See you after the show?"

"Meet you outside." She had already made plans to skip the cast party and go for an early dinner with Mike. It was time to let Jared have his space while she did her own thing. She had already indulged herself in fantasies of Mike McCabe giving advice to Jared and KJ over the next few years. Finally, she had found a warm, engaging male role model for her sons to look up to. A good, kind man. Granted, she hadn't known him long, but when things were right, you just knew.

Mike leaned closer and winked, just for her. The gesture was both old-fashioned and endearing. Watching him go, Rachel straightened her black blouse over her new candy-cane-striped bra, a purchase Ariel had insisted on. Rachel had to admit, she looked damned sexy in it. She hoped to give Mike a chance to agree.

Ariel descended the staircase leading down to the music rooms, her spiky heels echoing in the empty steel-and-concrete tomb. She paused on the landing, hating this glum prison of a school.

Gritting her teeth, she continued down, letting her footsteps hammer out her fury. To hell with it; no one else was down here.

She should have lashed out at Tootsie while she had the chance; now, the haggard lush had disappeared back into the dark auditorium, leaving Ariel smarting over the comments about Remy. It was one thing to take it on the chin yourself, quite another to endure nasty comments about one of your kids.

And Tootsie was way off the mark. Remy was adorable. She had inherited Ariel's style and grace, and she was a much kinder person. Everyone liked Remy. She was far from a dateless reject. Couldn't find a date! Well, she would show Tootsie Dover, and anyone else who took nasty shots at Remy.

Where the hell was he? She needed him. Now. This anger had left Ariel on edge, roiling with a passion that had to bubble over before it would subside.

It was dangerous. Risky and foolish. But weren't the best moments in life amplified by bursts of adrenaline?

She had told him to meet her right after the Part Two opening. Once he finished the group number, there were five songs in a row that he did not appear in. He would not be missed upstairs. And this entire section of offices and rehearsal rooms was quiet as a morgue. She had realized that earlier in the week when Craig had asked her to come down to his office to work out the kink with Angela Harrell. With two walls built into the hill, this wing had been chosen to house the choir and band rooms because noise was so well absorbed underground.

Perfect.

"What do you want, woman?" he asked, cocking his head to one side with a surly look in his eyes.

So he wanted to play? Sure. He didn't realize that she always got what she wanted. She always won.

"I think you know." She reached for his hand, pulled it to her chest, and then tucked it into the bodice of her dress, sliding his palm over her breast.

He smiled as he cupped her, teased her. "I don't have a lot of time," he said.

"I know some shortcuts." She led him into the band room and closed the door behind them, sliding a desk over to prop against the door.

"Turn the lights off," she ordered. There was enough ambient light filtering through the slender window of the door, and it would be more exciting to take him under the cover of darkness.

She gave him some teeth when they kissed, and he answered with a thrust of his hips against her pelvis. A surge of want tugged at her when she felt him come alive for her, hard as a rock. She was already wet for him, stoked up from urgency and danger. It was a brazen violation, taking him in a classroom at the school. So bad. Adrenaline fired in her veins as she hitched up her dress and mounted him.

Scandalous.

Furious.

Frenzied.

She would show them.

Fuck them all.

Chapter 20

Monday afternoon, Cassie sat at the kitchen table scraping the last of her mac and cheese from a bowl as she checked in with Remy on things at home. "I'm sorry I missed the Spring Showcase," she said, trying to sound sincere. Her finals had ended Friday so she actually could have made it home, but with Mom putting her fingerprints all over that production, Cassie really wasn't that interested. "But...you know how crazed I've been with finals week."

"I know. You missed a good show, though. This year there really weren't any clunkers in the lineup. Well, Sage Sherer shouldn't be allowed to sing a solo. And yesterday, in the final show, Graham Oyama went missing during the second half. Mr. Schulteis looked like he was going to have a stroke. You know how that vein pops out in his neck when he gets mad?"

"I do. So where was Graham?"

"Probably out back smoking weed. He bolted in to the backstage area and slid onto the stage. The audience thought it was funny."

"I bet." Cassie pushed her bowl away and put her feet up on the kitchen chair beside her. The house felt different now that finals were over; the tension had drained from the air. Olivia, Cassie, and Ellie had the house through the summer and would be joined by three new roommates in September. "So people are clearing out of here. Amelie flies back to Denmark tonight, and Olivia's mom picked her up yesterday, so we've got some empty beds. Why don't you come visit me, Boo?"

"I can't. There's prom this weekend, and after that graduation. Maybe I can come in June."

"That would work. I'm thinking about summer school."

"Really? I thought you were coming home."

"I'm leaning toward staying. They'll give me longer shifts at the café. Since we have to pay rent on the house through the summer, I figured I'd make the most of it." And avoid Ariel's craziness. "Besides, Andrew is going to be here."

"Well, no wonder you want to stay."

"I don't want to leave him."

"Aw. So you really like him."

"Things are going well for us." That was putting it mildly. Actually, the real L word had been used, though Cassie wasn't ready to share that with her sister yet. Scientifically, it seemed too soon to know she was in love, having been hooked up for only a few weeks, but what was the magic time span for knowing definitively that someone was a good match? Wasn't it enough to crave his company, to feel her spirits lift whenever he was near, to share physical pleasure without embarrassment or awkwardness? Yes, yes, yes, she loved him, but it sounded dorky to let anyone else in on the secret right now.

"I want to meet him," Remy said. "Why don't you bring him home?"

"Please. Ariel can be so emasculating."

"Ooh. Big college words."

"You know what I mean, Boo."

"I'm just trying to get you to come home. Don't you miss Timbergrove?"

"Not really. I miss you guys, but I feel like I belong here." She hadn't felt that way for all of freshman year, and last summer she could not wait to get back to Timbergrove. But now, with Andrew, things had shifted. "This is my home now."

"Aw. You're all grown up, Cass. You've flown the coop."

"Sort of. But I worry about you guys." She constantly felt the tug of home; those kids were her responsibility. They needed her, or at least that was what she felt in her heart. Andrew kept reminding her, in the sweetest way, that Trevor and Maisy were not her children, not her responsibility. "You have a life here at college," he always told her. "This is where you need to be now."

"We're fine," Remy said, pulling Cassie's attention back to the conversation. "But wait—you have to come home for graduation. You could make that a long weekend."

"Definitely." Cassie opened her laptop and clicked on the offering of summer classes at Oregon State. "So what are you planning to do this summer?"

"Now that the Europe trip is off, I got my job back at the theater camp."

"Awesome. Believe me, the cash will come in handy next year at school." Cassie had gotten used to being perennially broke. "So when's prom?"

"Friday. Which reminds me. I have to go over to Malika's. Lady Leeks is loaning me some shoes."

"Okay. We'll talk more later." Cassie ended the call, put her dish in the sink, and headed out to the living room where her roommate grunted as she lifted her suitcase off a scale. Apparently, the weight limits were strict on international flights. "How's it going?"

"My bag is overstuffed. All these clothing, I can't fit them in my suitcase. Do you want them?" Amelie pointed to stacks of folded clothes on the worn denim couch. There were knit cotton sweaters in delicate shades of pink and oyster gray, and a pile of denim skirts and jeans.

Cassie held an orange-and-black Oregon State hoodie to her chin. "Some of these will work for me. Otherwise I'll ask around or take them to Goodwill."

Just then piggy Maya breezed through wearing shorts and a push-up bra. "You giving out stuff for free, girl?"

"Yeah, and you should wrap yourself in one of these before Keisha's father comes back for another load." Cassie tossed the sweatshirt at her. "Unless you're planning to do a pole dance out by the carport."

Amelie bit back a grin.

Maya cast the sweatshirt on the sofa but picked up a black T-shirt with a white graphic skull on it. "This is more my style."

"You can have it," Amelie said.

"Thanks. I'm gonna miss you guys," she said, throwing her arms around Cassie for a hug.

The feeling was hardly mutual, but at least Maya would be gone soon. She had flunked out but planned to move into her boyfriend Jessie's house June first. She would stay there until she sucked the life out of that boy . . . or got kicked out by his roommates. Amelie would fly home to Denmark tonight, and Keisha was transferring to Portland State. Her father and brother were hauling out loads of her stuff.

"Things are going to be different around here," Cassie said.

"I'm so depressed! I don't deal well with change," Maya lamented as she tugged on the skull shirt and tromped into her room.

Cassie and Amelie watched her go.

"She doesn't deal well with much of anything," Amelie observed. They laughed, and then hugged.

"Denmark seems so far away," Cassie said.

"We'll Skype. And you come visit me."

Keisha came in with her father. "Good thing we brought the trailer. The car is packed to the gills."

As Mr. Williams carried out a bulletin board, Cassie realized that her mother had never been in this house. She'd never picked her up or dropped her off for school. Even freshman year, Ariel had been busy with some gig and had Rachel Whalen drive Cassie down to Corvallis and move her into the dorm.

So why the hell did she feel obligated to go back to Timbergrove and get caught in Mom's crazy orbit? Andrew was her center now. Her life was here at OSU.

Ariel would have to figure out how to mother the rest of her children on her own. Cassie was going to spend the summer investing in herself.

She went back into the kitchen, opened her laptop, and found the three classes she'd bookmarked. Social Problems and 3-D Art. She couldn't take any essential nursing classes, but two electives would work. She clicked on the box to sign up for the classes. Done. She would go home for the weekend of graduation in June. Other than that, she had flown the coop for good.

That night Rachel tried to tamp down her excitement as she tugged open the door of the menswear shop and waded into the displays of sweaters, ties, and patent-leather shoes. Jared moved warily behind her, reminding her of the days when he had waded into the ocean behind her, lingering in her path to avoid crustaceans and seaweed that tumbled in on the waves.

She longed to take him by the hand and tell him not to be afraid, that this was a wonderful moment he would look back on with a smile. But, he was about to turn eighteen; he was no longer a second grader playing in the surf.

"Hey, there." A young man with close-cut hair and a big bow tie stepped out from behind a display. "What can I help you with this evening?"

She turned to Jared, giving him a chance to speak for himself. "Prom," he said in that shorthand of youth. "Need to rent a tux."

"You're in the right spot." The bow-tie dude led them over to the formals section, where mannequins in tuxedoes and morning suits took up much of the real estate. Jared muttered short answers to the clerk's series of questions.

Rachel wished her son could loosen up and enjoy the moment. These were supposed to be good times.

"So when's prom?" the man asked as he swiped a finger over an iPad.

"Friday," Jared said.

"The day after his birthday," Rachel put in with a flare of pride. "He's turning eighteen."

"Oh, yeah? Happy birthday. So what color is your date's dress?" the salesman asked.

Jared shrugged. "I don't know."

She let out a huff of breath. Why was he being so coy about

this? "Well, I do. It's in shades of blue. Indigo, royal blue, teal, and turquoise." Weeks ago, Rachel had seen a photo on Remy's phone. "Honey, you need to pay attention to these things."

"Whatever." Jared turned to the dude in the bow tie. "I want a classic tux. Black with white shirt and black tie."

"Perfect. Why don't you step over here and I'll measure you."

Jared skulked over to the spot, then grimaced when the man asked him to stand up straight.

Rachel decided to spare him some of the agony of planning. "I'm going to cut over to the florist down the street to order the corsage. Should I get a matching boutonniere, or do you think she's ordering it?"

"I don't know." Jared didn't make eye contact as he slipped on a sample jacket. "Whatever people do."

Bowtie grinned. "He's not sweating the details, Mom."

"No, he's not." Rachel stole one last look at her son being fitted, and then headed out.

A few doors down at the flower shop, Wendy showed her a sample of the roses she could choose from. Full blooms or baby roses?

Seeing the tight, petite buds restored her excitement. Remy was a tiny thing; these would suit her well.

Just as Jared did.

"And it just went on like that, the sales guy asking questions and talking up the merchandise, and Jared answering uncomfortably," Rachel said, recalling the evening over coffee with Mike the next day. "I'm telling you, he couldn't wait to escape."

"I'm with Jared. I don't go in for dressing up. All those collars and ties that are supposed to be a certain way." Mike nodded as he chewed a piece of bagel. "Sounds like appropriate guy behavior."

"It's prom—his first and only—with a girl he's crazy about. I was dying to take photos. And he was just dying."

"Yeah, it's a guy thing." Mike chuckled. "Nice of you to refrain from taking a video. When is the high school prom?"

"Friday. Nothing like the last minute. And on Thursday Jared turns eighteen. Can you believe it? Talk about timing. But the celebration for that will have to wait until this hoopla dies down." She snorted. "If he had his way, I think he'd opt out of any celebration at all. That kid is so low-key, sometimes I want to check for a pulse."

He nodded, watching as the door of the shop opened behind her and new customers came in—a mom and her two kids. His gaze eased, relaxed, as the threat of danger dissolved. More than protective instinct, his cautiousness was enmeshed with his profession; it was a quality she found very attractive. When she was in Mike's arms, she felt safe from the world, safe from her own demons, too.

"So, I'm glad to see someone else has Tuesday off," he said.

"Woo-hoo. Big Tuesday."

"Got any plans?"

"I'm going to try and get horizontal." She grinned, realizing it sounded like an invitation, which wouldn't be the worst thing in the world. "I've got some long days scheduled between now and Friday. Lots of girls coming in for highlights and trims for the big night. The shop will be like one wild hen party, and I love it that way. But today's a quiet day. How about you? What's on your schedule?"

"Got some yard work to do. Mowing and trimming."

"Do you like yard work?"

He shrugged. "It's a necessary evil."

"I could help you."

When he smiled, crinkly lines formed at the outer edges of his eyes. Those eyes—summer blue—she could stare into them forever. "Do you like gardening?"

"I've got a black thumb. But I wasn't talking about the yard work." Her resolve fluttered a bit, faltering, but she plunged ahead. "I'm wearing new underwear." She saw the lump on his neck move as he swallowed. "Little wisp of nothing. Next to nothing."

He swallowed again. "Sounds like something I should check out."

"I think so. Due diligence."

"I should be power-washing my deck, but . . . what the hell. Any excuse to get out of yard work."

Sleepless nights were taking their toll. Ariel had tried every remedy she could think of: hemorrhoid cream to clear up the puffiness under her eyes, a greenish face cream to take the pink out of her skin, and a case of Visine for her burning red eyeballs.

Tracing a line with eye pencil, she faced the mirror and recited the lines she had memorized from the partial script the producer had sent her by email. "You don't understand. They were making fun of my daughter. Laughing at her. Treating her like dirt. And I won't have it," she rasped, snarling into the mirror.

Scary. The script was a little too close to life, and she wasn't so sure she wanted her next big role on television to be a suburban shrew. Still . . . this part would be her ticket out of here.

Thank God this was just a video chat. Her agent had set up the preliminary meeting for a role in a new TV pilot, but this was just the look-see before the go-see. She would need to be on her game, rested and exuding energy, when they flew her down to LA. For today, she adjusted the lighting, bringing in the lamp with the orange glow to warm things up and soften the shadows on her face. Leaning toward the camera on her laptop for a test run, she approved of the image. Her face was a bit stark from the makeup, but the hard lines softened and her eyes came alive when she gave a big smile.

And . . . action!

"Hi, there," she spoke to the curious faces, three men and one woman. "I'm Ariel Alexander," she said modestly. Of course they knew who she was, but people got a large charge out of it when you pretended humility.

"I loved you in the singing witch," said the round man with the marshmallow face.

"*Wicked Voice,*" the guy with the geeky square glasses corrected him. "And we're pleased that you could meet with us today." He was Brent, the boss, and he was merely *pleased,* not thrilled or delighted. He was going to be a tough sell.

She was charming, smart, affable.

She got them laughing, but she also drew them in, holding them captive as she gave her interpretation of the character. They loved her.

When they ended the phone call with a simple "Glad to meet you," Ariel's heart began to thud. Was that the end of it? She shut the laptop as hope spilled out of her. She had lost her edge. No one would cast her now.

She would be stuck here forever.

By Wednesday afternoon Holy Snips was full of teenage girls, who easily outnumbered regular clients. Tiffani handed out Oreos and cranked up the music, which annoyed Hilda and her older clients. Rachel stayed out of the dispute. Hell, she had her hands full, working feverishly on her regulars and squeezing in a few prom girls. But when Tiffani went on break, Rachel stole behind the counter and lowered the volume.

Wednesday was a thirteen-hour day, and Thursday was just as busy, with anticipation of the big night crackling in the air. Rachel had tried gotten up early to give Jared his card before school, but he had left it on the kitchen counter, claiming that he didn't have time to open it. She sent a few cheery birthday text messages, but he replied with a simple "thanks" and instructions not to count on him for dinner. Disappointment nipped at her, but she kept telling herself to get over it. It was time to let go of the rituals of childhood and give her son some space.

Rachel enjoyed the party atmosphere in the shop, but she was also grateful for the chance to slip out for a bite to eat with Mike. Their lovemaking had bonded them in the most elemental way, and Rachel was taking her time each day, building the relationship one block at a time. She imagined it rising like a Lego tower the boys built together in their munchkin days. They shared an order of eggplant parmigiana and split a glass of Chianti and talked about the stupid mistakes they had made during college. The business with KJ's football dreams was still far from a resolution, and Mike, who enjoyed reading non-fiction in his spare time, supported her opinion that it was dangerous to risk further concussions. Although she hadn't told the boys much about her new relationship with Mike, Rachel looked forward to the time when both Jared and KJ could get to know him.

Of course, dating in a town like Timbergrove was a very public affair, especially when the man involved was a sheriff who prided himself on knowing most of the community on a first-name basis. By Thursday night, when the waitress at Vespa commented on the frequency of their visits, Rachel began to feel a little overexposed.

"Tomorrow, let's meet for coffee at Holy Snips. No one is around before ten, and we can hang out in the break room."

Mike's eyes twinkled as he squinted. "Are we going under-cover?"

She nodded. "Just to step out of the display window. I don't know how you deal with it, but it's pretty intense, having every-one in town monitor your every move."

"The price of celebrity."

She smacked his elbow and told him to bring the bagels.

The next morning, Mike was wearing his uniform when she unlocked the door of the shop for him. The gold star on his chest was most impressive against the dark blue fabric of his shirt. The crisply creased sleeves were accented by gold hash marks on the shoulders. "Wow. Aren't you looking official, Mr. Sheriff."

"This is all off the record, ma'am. I'm on coffee break."

"I'm not complaining," she said as she ushered him toward the backroom. "There's something about a man in a uniform. Makes a girl want to rip it off him."

"I'll need to wear it more often."

The bagels he'd brought were still warm, and Rachel tore into hers without butter or cream cheese. As they chatted, the radio on his collar squawked a bit.

"Sorry." He turned down the volume. "I can turn it down, but I need to listen in."

"I don't know how you can understand a word they're saying."

"You develop an ear for it."

They talked about prom, how Rachel wanted to take pictures, but Jared was still keeping her at arm's length. It bothered her that Jared's eighteenth birthday had been overshadowed by prom, but she had given him a card with a hundred dollars yesterday and was determined to celebrate in some way next weekend. For now, she was considering going over to Ariel's house tonight, maybe getting a few shots once the kids sprang the surprise on her.

"Sounds like a plan." Mike was nodding, but his body had straightened over one of the chirps from the radio. He held up one finger and turned up the volume.

"Confirm, lockdown at Timbergrove High School."

The mention of the school caught Rachel's attention.

Mike keyed the radio. "Command to central. Is the lockdown a drill?"

"Negative. Assault in progress. Man with a knife."

"I'm on my way," Mike said, already on his feet.

"Oh my God! The high school? What's happening?" Alarm jangled her nerves as Rachel hurried to the door alongside Mike.

"It may be unfounded, but I need to get there." His voice was calm, but the tension showed in the tight set of his jaw. "Sorry."

He squeezed her arm, and then dashed out before Rachel could ask him to watch out for her son.

Chapter 21

Ariel noticed her hand shaking as she held Remy's prom dress over the steamer, smoothing out every wrinkle in the delicate fabric so that Remy could knock everyone's socks off tonight. It wasn't like Ariel to fuss over her kids' clothing. In fact, she couldn't remember the last time she had steamed or ironed a garment for someone else in the house. But this was important. All eyes were going to be on Remy, and Ariel needed her daughter to kick ass in this dress.

She was totally stressed—a hot mess. Usually, she didn't let things get to her, but she was just sick about this. It wasn't her fault. She'd been driven to it. It wasn't as if she had any choice. She had to fend for her daughter, even if that meant finding Remy a date and making sure she looked fabulous.

But her strategy was flawed; she knew that. It had made her a little sick inside when she'd strong-armed Jared into asking Remy to prom. He had not been happy about it, but he got it. He could see why Remy had to go with a date, and he agreed that it would throw people off the trail, divert the eyes of the watchers: all those neighbors and parents and teachers who drank a little too much, neglected their children whenever possible, fooled around with someone they met at happy hour, and then had the nerve to point out the problems in other people's lives.

Those sanctimonious moms and lecherous dads. If they got

wind of the way Ariel satisfied her most basic needs, she was going to be ruined in this town. Her business, her livelihood . . . and Maisy and Trevor. People around here were going to make their lives miserable.

So no one could find out. That was why the plan was so important. She kept emphasizing that, and for once he seemed to believe her. She hung up the dress in the laundry room and sighed. Remy was going to look sensational in that. Okay. Deep breath. Remy and her date were going to kick ass at the prom, and Tootsie and Cooper and Angela Harrell and any other bitches out there would burn. Burn and eat their words.

Upstairs she had just started the shower running when she saw that her cell phone had exploded with messages.

What the hell?

Three from Rachel, and a bunch from the high school . . . and the police. She scanned them for information, but after one robo-message saying the school was on lockdown, all the other voice mail messages just asked her to call. Her knees were trembling, and she huddled over the bathroom counter, holding on for support as she shot a few text messages to Remy. When there was no immediate answer, she called the school.

"This is Ariel Alexander. I'm returning Mr. Enrico's call?"

There was a pause as the secretary on the line, Janice something or other, sucked in a breath. "Ms. Alexander! There's been an incident. I think it was the vice principal who called you? But he's not here in his office right now. He's over with the police."

"What's going on there?"

"We were in lockdown?" Janice made every statement a question. "But the police called it off? Mr. Enrico said that Remy was hurt? I think he wanted you to come down here?"

Her heart began to thud in her chest. "Wh-what happened to her?"

"I don't have any information? But if you can't come down, I'll take your number and have Mr. Enrico call you back?"

"Never mind. I'll come over." Ariel hung up, hoping that moron Janice had her details jumbled. Giving up on her shower, she slipped on a pair of jeans and called Rachel, who picked up immediately. "Do you know what's happening at the school?"

"A lockdown. Mike just ran out of here to see what was going on."

"The vice principal called me. Sounds like Remy got hurt. I'm going over there."

"I'll pick you up," Rachel said quickly. "I'm at the shop. Hold tight."

Quickly, Ariel mopped perspiration from her face and blended in foundation and blush. No time for the eyes; she would have to wear sunglasses.

By the time she came down the stairs, Rachel's car was in the driveway.

"Are you worried?" Rachel asked as Ariel got into the car.

"I just want to know why they called me," Ariel said, clinging to the notion that this was all a mistake. "That moron Janice, who works in the office, was a total dead end when I called."

"I'm sure everything is going to be just fine," Rachel said as the Subaru zipped down the road. "I can feel it in my bones, and my bones don't lie."

"Thank God for your bones," Ariel said, grateful to have Rachel there. She could not imagine driving in this cold state of dread. She checked the screen of her phone; still no answer from Remy.

From a quarter of a mile away, the high school was a throbbing cluster of chaos, with flashing lights, police cars, and emergency vehicles strewn over sidewalks and lawns, and cars of eager parents jamming the entrance to the parking lot.

"Crap." Rachel eased as close as she could and then swung the car into a spot in front of a hydrant on the main road. "It'll be faster to hoof it from here."

They started out walking briskly, but the flashing lights and line of gathering parents prodded Ariel to run. Two cops tried to step into her path, telling her to stop, but she skirted around them. She had to get inside. "The school told me to come," she said breathlessly. "My daughter was hurt."

The officers backed away, letting Rachel through the human barricade, too. They blew through the doors into the office, where rattled employees huddled behind the counter with a handful of cops from different jurisdictions. Ariel recognized the principal, Glenda Balducci, a buxom woman with shoulder-length brown curls, whom she'd met through her dealings with Gleetime. Actually, it was Dr. Balducci now. From their hushed tones, Ariel sensed that they'd been shaken up, but if the lockdown had been called off so soon, it couldn't have been that bad.

"I'm Ariel Alexander. I was told my daughter was hurt."

"Right." Dr. Balducci pressed one palm to her chest in an odd gesture of earnestness as she skirted around the counter. "It's good that you came."

"Where's Remy? Is she okay?"

"She's over in the music wing. I'll take you there. Right this way." Dr. Balducci took long strides for a woman in platform sandals.

Dazed, Ariel let herself be escorted down the hall, past a bank of lockers and the stairs to the glass-walled library where the lower windows had been glazed for security after the lessons of the Columbine shootings. The thought of that violent rampage made her throat ache, and her peripheral vision went dark. "What happened to her?"

"They say she was attacked. A student with a knife." The principal paused, as if giving Ariel a chance to absorb it.

"I can't believe it," Rachel said from the dark tunnel beside Ariel. "Everyone loves Remy."

"She's a good kid," the principal agreed. "She seems to be friends with all the students."

"Not everyone." Ariel's lips hardened. "It was Cooper Dover, wasn't it? That little bastard."

"I don't have much information on the attack." Dr. Balducci seemed apologetic. "James was handling the incident. James Enrico, our vice principal. I was coordinating the lockdown."

"Cooper is the only one with a grudge against Remy. Everyone knows that. He . . . he dropped her on the stage and his mother's a raving lunatic." She was babbling—Ariel knew that—but it was her way of working through panic, a tactic she'd learned as a child when her home seemed to implode on a regular basis. Sweat pooled behind her sunglasses, and she lifted them and took a swipe at her eyes. "It was definitely Cooper."

"The police will have more information on that." The squeak in the principal's voice revealed that she was nervous, too. Probably afraid of a lawsuit. "They have the alleged attacker in custody."

Alleged. It infuriated Ariel that any attacker would get the benefit of the doubt.

"Do you know if it was Cooper Dover?" Rachel asked.

The principal shrugged. "I just know that a male student turned himself in soon after the attack. The police searched the school and determined that he acted alone. We ended the lockdown, but held the students in their first-period classes."

The methodical approach of Madame Principal was beginning to piss Ariel off. "Would you just help me find my daughter so we can get the hell out of here?"

"Of course."

When they rounded the back of the auditorium, Ariel was in familiar territory. Dr. Balducci paused to ask two cops about James Enrico, and they pointed the women toward the staircase leading down to the rehearsal rooms for choir, orchestra, and band. Ariel knew her way around these parts. "Remy's probably downstairs," she said, her stress easing. "She and her friends hang out in the choir room. They usually meet there before school."

Cops lingered at the top of the stairs, their radios squawking. Their eyes fixed on the passing women, and one officer moved to stop them until the principal flashed her ID at him. Ariel followed the principal down the stairs, then paused at the sight of the yellow tape barring the second landing.

"James. There you are." Dr. Balducci was introducing Ariel to an administrative type draped in a gray suit. Olive-skinned and jittery, he clung to the wall a few steps up from the yellow tape.

Ariel vaguely recognized a very pissy James Enrico, who was telling the principal that they shouldn't be here. Their voices slipped through Ariel's consciousness like a handful of sand as she spotted the pool of blood on the landing.

So much blood.

"Jesus! What the hell happened here?" Ariel asked. Her annoyance with this wild-goose chase had begun to sizzle into a panic. A throat-squeezing, heart-racing wave that compelled her forward into the blood-splattered stairwell.

She stepped down, one stair, and then another, her eyes fixed on the deep dark pool. That couldn't be blood. So dark and sticky and . . . so much. The red splatter on the adjacent concrete wall was another story. It resembled photographs she had seen from true-crime shows on television. Surreal. Her heart was pounding, her pulse thrumming in her ears as she gaped at the catastrophic scene. All that blood couldn't be real. It had to be some prank. Typical teens.

But the smell was unmistakable . . . the earthy, dank odor of blood. Her daughter's blood. No, no, no. No one walked away from a bloodbath like this. Someone else had been hurt. Or maybe it was the attacker's blood. Remy was a strong girl; she could hold her own. . . .

Ariel's racing heart seemed to swell in her chest, constricting her breathing, her balance, her rational thought. Dizziness swirled around her as she struggled to breathe. She swayed, reaching toward the steel handrail to steady herself.

"That's it. Don't come any closer." An overweight cop held up his hands, but he seemed to speak from a distant place, beyond the bell jar that confined her. "I can't have you folks tramping through my crime scene."

His words brought attention to the bright light fixed on the scene beyond the dome of her control, casting ghoulish shadows. The crime scene tape was doubled from wall to bannister at Ariel's waist. Little plastic markers with numbers on them were placed in seemingly random spots.

Just like on television. Except here, in the real world, the earthy smells of blood and sweat hung in the humid air. And she was caught, suspended in a real-world panic, with racing heart, damp palms, and trembling knees.

She felt a hand on her shoulder. "Come on, honey," Rachel said. "Let's get out of here."

Ariel turned away from the ghastly landing, closing her eyes against the image branded in her mind. Oh my God. Oh My GOD! "Where's my daughter?" She had to push the words through her constricting throat. "*Where is she?*"

Some male voice muttered to get her away from here as Ariel collapsed against her friend, her knees giving way. Darkness closed in from the edges, accentuating the throbbing tattoo of her heartbeat pounding in her chest. She felt herself being dragged up the stairs, nearly carried from the stairwell, delivered into the school corridor.

"Take a breath," Rachel said gently as Ariel's feet touched ground once again. "A deep breath."

Ariel braced herself and stood upright as her heels grazed the carpet of the hallway. The air was better here. As soon as she drank it in the horror sharpened again, regaining focus, and her breath came out in a painful moan. "Where's my girl?" Ariel demanded. "Tell me, damn it!"

"The paramedics transported her to the hospital." The vice principal was addressing her, at last. His eyes seemed thoughtful. Or haunted.

"Is she all right?"

"I am not a doctor," Enrico said, "but I can tell you they were taking excellent care of her."

"Then why are we traipsing around here?" Ariel shook off the cop, who was holding on to her on one side. "Jesus, you're wasting my time."

"I'm sorry. You should have been told." Enrico's voice was polite, but he glared at the principal with thinly tethered anger.

Ariel would sue them all when this was over. For now, she felt the tug of urgency to get to her kid. "I need to get to the hospital. Now."

"I'll drive you. Come on." Rachel darted down the hall, then paused and turned back. "Wait. Jared's going to freak."

Jared. Ariel didn't have time to worry about him now.

But Rachel, mother of the year, turned to Dr. Balducci. "Are you going to release the students early? My son's a student here. Jared Whalen."

"We'll let them go as soon as the buses get here." The principal's strained, tight voice revealed her tension. "We're looking at a ten o'clock dismissal."

"He'll be fine," Ariel told her friend. This was no time to mollycoddle Jared. "He'll find his way home. Let's go."

"Wait one moment." The vice principal held up his hands. "I'm sorry, did you say Jared Whalen?" Sweat beaded the man's forehead, and his mouth was a line of distress.

"Right. He's a senior here," Rachel explained. "A member of Gleetime?"

Enough with the small talk. Ariel grabbed Rachel's arm, backing away. "We gotta go."

"I apologize. I didn't know. . . ." Enrico pressed the back of his hand to his brow as he turned and stared at Rachel. "There's no easy way to say this. Your son, he's talking to police right now. Jared Whalen, he was the one who attacked Remy."

Chapter 22

Rachel's spine stiffened with indignation as she glared at the vice principal. "You've got that wrong. Really. Jared wouldn't hurt Remy." She turned to Ariel for confirmation, but her friend's face was a pale mask, her mouth drooping open. Probably in shock. "Jared and Remy grew up together. Like brother and sister. Good friends. In fact . . ."

They were dating. She stopped short of revealing the secret. What would it matter to the school staff? They were not in control of any of this.

"He turned himself in," Enrico said succinctly. "The police are questioning him now."

"This is ludicrous." Rachel's outrage hardened to fury as the knot in her throat swelled. First the lockdown, then Remy's attack and all that blood, and now Jared was getting dragged into the nightmare? Tears stung her eyes and a glaring panic threatened to overwhelm her, but she took a breath and tamped the fear down.

"Where?" She flung her arms wide. "Where's my son?"

"Downstairs." He nodded toward the arts wing. "We must use the other stairway. I will take you there."

"But . . ." She turned to Ariel. "You need to get to the hospital."

Ariel waved her off. "Go." Her glassy eyes held the same bewilderment that plagued Rachel. "I'll find a ride."

She couldn't believe it. This had to be a terrible mistake. Maybe they had gotten the name wrong or Jared had come along to save Remy from the assailant . . . something like that. But she withheld conversation and followed the vice principal down the corridor, determined to sort things out quickly so that she could get to the hospital. Ariel needed her support, and Remy, God bless her. Rachel had been praying under her breath since they'd stepped into that gruesome stairwell. She called on the blessed Mother Mary and St. Jude, patron saint of impossible causes, to intercede and watch over Remy.

Following Enrico to the opposite end of the music wing, Rachel imagined Remy back here in a few days, laughing with her friends and hurrying off to a class. Please God, that would be the best possible outcome.

The second staircase was vacant, clear of cops, its landing spotless but for two smudges of old chewing gum. Rachel tackled the stairs with fervor, ignoring the panicky pulse that roared in her head, driving her forward, down the hall past the band room. A handful of kids were scattered there, talking with cops. Chatting? They were talking quietly, almost normally.

As if anything would ever be normal again.

The officers stared curiously at Rachel and the vice principal, but did not try to stop them. Enrico tapped on the door, then opened it.

As soon as Rachel stepped beyond the frosted glass of the teachers' office, she saw her son slumped forward in a corner chair. One cop sat with his body angled toward Jared, while another stood back, leaning against a wall. One craned his neck around and asked, "What is it?"

The pulse thrumming in Rachel's ears blocked out the conversation of the men around her as she rushed into the office. She squatted with one hand on the desk, close enough to see the blood on Jared's hands. Dried and sticky, it clung to his cuticles, rimmed his fingernails. His favorite shirt, the plaid button-down that he usually wore over a T-shirt, was drenched so that the white background was now brown. "Jared. What happened?"

He lifted his head slowly, her son, her baby. Tears pooled in his eyes and ran down his cheeks, streaking through the blood that stained his chin, neck, and shirt. From up close she could see that he was covered in it, and the magnitude of what had happened in that stairwell hit her all over again.

Gaping at her silent son, she stumbled through a prayer for Remy, half silent words, half inarticulate wishes for a positive outcome. Healing. Survival. Peace.

"Jared," she breathed. "Talk to me. Did you try to save Remy? What happened?" Although he refused to meet her gaze, there was no mistaking his misery, his horror. Tears pooled in his eyes and slid down his cheeks. When tears fell to his hand, the blood on his knuckle became liquid and she suddenly wondered at its source.

"Are you bleeding?" Rachel said, suddenly sure that none of this was what it seemed. "He needs a doctor." She twisted back toward the men and realized that Mike McCabe was one of them. His arms were folded, his gaze soft, as if he were a million miles away.

"He's not hurt," the other cop said. "That's not his blood."

She turned back to Jared for confirmation, but he had lowered his head to his forearms once again.

"Jared." Rachel moved closer, her hands on his shoulders, her forehead tipping against his soft brown hair. "Honey. What happened? I know you would never hurt Remy."

He sobbed silently, his shoulders shaking beneath her hands.

"You need to tell the truth." She kneeled before him and rubbed his arms gently, trying to transmit love and support to her child. She had never seen him in such a state, so distraught and broken. But then again, she could not begin to imagine the trauma of witnessing such an attack on the girl he loved.

"I did it."

She couldn't believe that. She wouldn't. "Jared. Don't take the blame for someone else."

"It's true, okay? I stabbed her." Without lifting his head, he reached up and peeled her hands from his shoulders, pushing her away.

Rachel sat back on her heels and bowed her head, unable to breathe in this new vacuum of hope. "No."

The hush in the room only verified that all logic and life had been sucked away.

Dear God, how can this be?

There would be no heavenly intervention, no quick answers. She knew that in this brief moment of grace, she could only do her best to protect whatever life her son had left.

"Okay." She looked up at him, restraining herself from touching him. "We're going to get you through this," she promised. There was no telling what the outcome might be. She still did not understand what had happened in that stairwell. But no matter what, she was going to be Jared's advocate. "Don't talk right now. Don't say anything else." She used the desk to pull herself to her feet and steady herself.

"Mrs. Whalen, your son has already confessed," the cop said from behind her.

"I don't care." Rachel wheeled toward the cop. Ramirez, according to his nametag. He was a fortyish guy, baby-faced, with a dime-sized birthmark on his cheek. "He would never hurt another person. Especially not Remy. He's a good kid. He's never been in trouble before."

"Please, ma'am, I have to ask you to step outside and let us finish the interview."

"But I'm his mother."

"He's eighteen. Legally, he's an adult."

"Barely! And he still has rights. I'm not going to let you do this to him. Where's his lawyer? He wants a lawyer," Rachel said quickly, recalling the protocol from a crime show on television. "So now you can't talk to him anymore, right? Right?"

"Fine." Ramirez sneered. "We'll finish at the jail, with a lawyer. Okay, *Mom?*"

After that, things moved quickly. Jared was handcuffed and taken away. Hunched over and silently sobbing, he seemed frail and broken and young. A boy. Yes, he was eighteen now, but in so many ways he was still a child.

Her heart ached for him as she followed the passel of officers up the stairs and out the nearest doors of the school by the auditorium to a waiting patrol car. A female cop patted his head. A tender gesture? Rachel wondered. No. She was just making sure he bent down low enough to clear the roof of the car as he climbed into the backseat.

Rachel turned away from the cops and blinked back tears. There was no time to cry. She had to get to her car on the other side of the school, where there were, no doubt, packs of students and parents recalling their fear and terror over the lockdown. Probably satellite news trucks and reporters jumping on the sensational story. Swiping obstinate tears from her eyes, she noticed that the wall before her was filled with headshots of the Gleetime kids—the remaining decor from last week's performances.

There was Jared, eyes round as quarters and smiling with more mirth than she'd seen since he'd started junior high. He had hit his stride recently. He'd been happy. How could this happen to him now? And to Remy?

With a murmured gasp Rachel pressed a hand to her mouth. God, she hoped Remy was okay. Her cell phone was back in the car; she'd run out without it. Please, please, let there be a text from Ariel saying that everything was fine. And then this thing, whatever had happened, could all just dissolve away.

"Rachel." Mike's voice came as his hand landed on her shoulder.

He looked miserable. Washed out, with new creases in his face. Such hard lines. "Jared will be at the jail in Oregon City, and I don't know if they'll allow you to see him now, but..."

"Of course, I'll be there." That knot was back in her throat, throbbing and swelling, pushing her to tears. "Mike. He's a good kid, and I can't believe he would really do this. You need to look into Cooper Dover, Remy's ex-boyfriend. He was bitter about the breakup, and not beyond hurting her."

"We'll follow every lead, but..." He looked down, folding his arms across his chest. "Honestly, it looks like Jared is our guy."

"How can you say that, Mike? What about due process?"

"His rights will be protected, and he'll be treated fairly, I promise you that. But Jared confessed, and there were witnesses. Girls who'd been hanging out with Remy downstairs in the choir room."

"And they saw Jared . . . *my Jared*—"

"They saw enough, Rachel. I'm going to spare you the details right now, but it's not good."

She held his gaze, her face tipped up toward him in challenge. She wanted to argue her son's innocence, but knew that Mike was doing his best to deliver the truth. "Was anyone hurt besides Remy?"

"No physical injuries, but a few kids in shock. One of the girls was so traumatized she ran back downstairs and hid. We found her in the closet where they keep the choir robes."

"I don't get it. This is not my son."

"Some of the kids heard Jared and Remy arguing. He wanted her to go to prom with him, and she kept saying no."

She shook her head. "And then he stabbed her?"

"With a carving knife. Why would he have a carving knife at school?"

She closed her eyes against the realization. Those damned Flashco knives.

"Look, I've got to get over to the jail, but I wanted you to hear it from me first."

She forced herself to breathe, slow and steady. "Thanks."

He shook his head. "That's not the worst of it. From the crime scene I suspected that . . . shit. There's no easy way to say this. Remy didn't make it. I just got word from central dispatch that the paramedics pronounced her dead. Remy's gone."

No amount of time in Mike's arms could stop the crying jag that began at the news of Remy's death. Her chest was a thick jumble of pain, a hot mess of fear and loss and guilt that pressed on her lungs and throat. When Rachel could finally breathe again, she assured Mike that she was okay to be alone. He had to get to work, to meet with the prosecutor, to prepare for a press conference. "Besides, how would it look to have the sheriff consoling the killer's mother?" she said, trying to pull herself together.

"Everyone needs compassion; I don't have to make any excuses for that."

He apologized for leaving her, but she assured him that she understood. As soon as he turned away she stepped back into the school, grateful for the temporary shelter of the cool shadows as she took tiny breaths and wobbled on weak legs. She had planned to cut through the school to get to her car, but she couldn't make it there right now, not with this dense core of pain in her chest, throbbing like a festering wound. New tears ran down her cheeks as she considered the public spectacle she was about to make of herself here in the school hallway, just steps away from the chaos.

God help me.

She staggered into a nearby girls' room. The sight of her damp, bloodshot eyes and puffy face in the mirror made another sob rise in her throat. She retreated to a stall, locked the door, and collapsed on the toilet seat to cry in privacy.

Her muscles bunched, taut with tension, as images of the little girl who had come into her life fifteen years ago flickered through her mind. Barely two, Remy had been cheerful and amenable, a good napper, quick to smile. That sunny disposition had not wavered over the years of pigtails and braids, braces and pink sneakers, stars on the ceiling of her bedroom, happy dances on the coffee table and selfies. Selfies everywhere, all the time.

How could such a bright light be snuffed out?

By your son, your flesh and blood.

Dear God, it doesn't make sense for him to kill her. He loved her. They grew up together. And Jared is not a violent person.

She dropped her head into her hands as denial rose and flared inside her. Denial was a cop-out, and she knew that, but right now, it was the only avenue she could travel.

An early memory of Remy came to mind . . . the toddler dressed in a pull-up diaper, her back lathered with sunscreen as she wobbled along the lawn at the swim park, chasing the ducks with a toothy smile. "She doesn't even need the diaper," Ariel said. "This one potty trained at eighteen months. Just about did it herself."

"Adorable," Rachel said, trying not to compare two-year-old Jared, who had no interest in the typical benchmarks of development. Even now, he sat in the sandbox alone, lining up cars, while his brother, KJ, took a swimming lesson with friends. Meanwhile, Remy wandered from blanket to picnic table, offering a smile and handfuls of grass, which sunbathing moms wholeheartedly enjoyed.

"Yeah, Remy's the model baby," Ariel said. "The good daughter. And I know, because I got the bad seed, too." With a bitter laugh, Ariel had looked back to five-year-old Cassie, who cowered at the picnic table. "Would you just get over it and come down to the water with us?" Ariel called to the frightened girl. "Those ducks aren't going to hurt you."

A tearful Cassie shook her head no and curled herself into a little ball.

"You know, sometimes the ducks do nip a little," Rachel said.

"Don't tell Cassie. It'll give her one more thing to whine about. That kid is a royal pain."

Not one to judge, Rachel had changed the topic and vowed to offer those girls a little positive mothering whenever possible. As it turned out, over the years she'd had plenty of opportunity to calm their fears and nurture their dreams.

During those years of single parenting, Cassie and Remy became the daughters Rachel never had, and Ariel was always generous with sharing their affections.

Maybe I should have spent more time raising my own kids, less time obsessing over Ariel's mistakes.

Hugging herself, Rachel bent over her knees and willed herself to breathe through the pain that gripped her chest. Keep breathing. It was the best she could do for now.

The door creaked and the flurry of loud girl voices began to fill the lavatory.

The last thing she needed was a bunch of students staring at her. She pulled on the stream of toilet paper and wound it around her hands. Pressing the mound of stiff paper to her eyes, she snatched at bits of their frantic conversation and felt herself sinking lower into the abyss.

These were not students taking a bathroom break. They had seen the stabbing.

"I'm still scared," one girl gasped in a breathy voice.

Rachel crept forward, peering through the cracks by the door. The girl who was talking had long brown hair that nearly covered her black tank top from the back. "I know the police took him away, but what if he comes after us, too!"

"He won't. He just had a thing for Remy. He was out to get her, and no one else mattered to him," said the other girl, a striking African American girl with a low voice. Under the black minidress she wore, her legs seemed to be a mile high. Rachel recognized her from Gleetime. Malika.

"Did you see his eyes?" Malika asked, the pitch of her voice rising. "God! I never knew that Jared Whalen had crazy eyes. He was, like, blind to the rest of us. All he could see was . . . getting Remy."

Rachel sat back on the toilet and died a little inside as the truth pressed down on her. These girls had been in the stairwell. Malika had seen it happen.

Jared was a killer.

Malika was crying now, and Rachel felt an odd sort of communion with the girl as tears ran down her cheeks.

"I didn't see that much," the other girl admitted. "I mean, I was behind you and Shanna, so I didn't see it happen. I told the police everything I saw, but it wasn't much. Oh my God, why did Jared do that?"

"Because he's mad at her," Malika said through a sob. "He's mad at her because she won't go to prom with him."

"Did you hear him say that?"

"Well, first he took her aside and asked her to prom, and she was giving him a hard time, teasing him. It seemed normal, so we just sort of walked by. And when she said no, he . . . he grabbed her and cornered her. He pressed her up against the wall and kept ordering her to go to prom with him."

"Was she scared?" the girl whimpered.

"Not really. They've known each other forever, like brother and sister."

Like brother and sister. Rachel pressed the crushed paper to her eyes to stave off a sob.

"She was pissed," Malika went on. "She was fighting back. She told him he wasn't her boss. It seemed like every other hallway confrontation in this place. And then . . ." Her voice trembled for a moment. "She screamed. She called him a sicko-psycho, and . . . and he snapped. That was when he did it."

"Oh my God!" the other girl wailed. "I saw the blood. I was coming up the stairs behind you guys and . . . when I saw it, I ran back down."

"I know. I ran, too." The two girls wrapped their arms around each other, hugging until their sobs calmed to whimpers.

"I hope Remy's okay," said Malika. "That knife . . . what the hell was he thinking, bringing that thing to school?"

"Do you think she'll be able to come to prom?" the other girl asked hopefully.

Rachel's head swayed to the side as the girls talked of that night's prom, as if it were a vital world event. They didn't know that Remy was already gone. They had no clue that the killer's mother was lurking in the lavatory stall.

She waited, calculating Jared's defense. Eighteen as of yesterday; he would be tried as an adult. There would be no attempt to plead not guilty; she knew that now. Now, it was about lessening his sentence, sparing his life, and preserving whatever life he might have in prison.

Long after the girls left, Rachel remained in the stall. A breakdown chamber. A cell of sorts.

There was no reason to rush.

PART 2

Chapter 23

Cassie had to work hard to keep her mind in the present as she drove home from the morgue in a nearly blinding fury. The task of keeping her trembling hands on the wheel, slowing for stop signs and maintaining her lane on the road, was more important than railing at the shell of a woman riding with her in the car or rolling back the images of her afternoon. Her sister, so pale . . .

She couldn't go there now.

And it would be useless to blast her mother right now. Ariel was so out of it that arguing with her would be like pummeling a zombie.

So Cassie kept to twenty miles per hour in the school zone, and slowed on the curves in the country road that constituted the back way home from the hospital.

"Take the back way," Ariel had said as she had settled into the rear seat like an Uber cab client. Those were her mom's first words after Cassie had emerged from the room where she had viewed the body. No questions about Remy. No sympathetic pat on the back. No whispered thanks for taking care of the horrible task that Ariel refused to do. "I can't bear to do it," she'd said, as if they were referring to washing windows or scrubbing a toilet. Ariel was reverting to the same hermit existence she'd slunk into when Oliver died. Amazing how easily she could slip into her cocoon, block out the pain, and let

Cassie take over the family. Damn her. Cassie had stepped up when Oliver had died, but now . . . no. No, no, no.

Rage burned hot as she gripped the steering wheel, clenched her teeth, set her eyes. The only good thing about fury was that it kept her from crying.

"I'm calling on your mother's behalf. There's been an incident with your sister," the person on the phone had said. Was it the school principal or a cop? Those details had been blurred by panic, but the caller had asked her to come to the hospital, and that was how she knew. They never told you over the phone that someone was dead, because they were afraid that you'd wreck the car while you were driving. They just said, "There's been an incident."

And before Cassie could throw underwear and her toothbrush in a bag, she had gotten the text from her mother. **Remy is dead. Come now.**

For the first horrific hour of her trip home, she had freaked out as she tried to call Ariel for details, but there'd been no answer.

Thanks, Mom, for all the love and support.

Thanks, Mom, for making me be the one to look. The image would be with her forever, indelible and nightmarish. A scar on the inside of her eyelids. A forlorn shop mannequin with a sheet pulled up to her chin, her beautiful hair stiff and matted and way too dark. Dark with blood.

Little Remy was nowhere to be found in that pale face.

That was not the way Cassie wanted to remember Remy. That empty shell! That deflated body had barely resembled her sister. Remy had been more than lean muscle and bone. Energy had swirled around her, sparks flying from her heels, vibrations radiating from her and richocheting like a rubber ball bouncing into infinity. The squeals of delight, the hugs and tears and smiles of encouragement. She kept telling herself that Remy's life had amounted to so much more, but her perverse mind kept flashing on the dead body she'd had to identify.

That wasn't Remy.

No! That couldn't be her little sister. The girl she had taken by the hand a thousand times to guide across the street or through a parking lot. The long, thick hair that she had brushed and tied into ponytails. The kid who loved the way Cassie made grilled cheese with pickles and chicken potpie with biscuit crust. The young woman who strung gems along the walls of her room and sprayed her underwear drawer with perfume. The intuitive sister who recognized that Cassie had mad talents that were untapped here in Timbergrove.

"College is going to be your time to shine, Cassie," Remy had told her late one night at a graduation party that a bunch of kids in Cassie's class had thrown for themselves. One of the guys lived in a big house on the Willamette River, and after the sun went down, kids had flooded the yard with its kidney-shaped pool that backed into the dark, tree-lined riverbank. Cassie had been sitting with Olivia and some other graduates on a boulder overlooking the water when Remy had breezed in like she owned the place. Like a fairy dispensing pixie dust, she had danced to the song of the summer as she handed each girl a cold bottle of Mike's Hard Lemonade—the drink of choice for girls, who didn't go for the soap-sud taste of beer. . . . Then she plopped down next to Cassie for a heart-to-heart.

"I'm so excited for all the great things that are going to happen to you in the next few years," she told Cassie. "You have so many talents and gifts that people here just don't see," Remy said. "High school kids are way too into themselves. But out in the real world, people will notice. You're going to be a rock star, Cass."

Ironic, because everyone knew Remy had been the one destined for stardom.

But not anymore.

A wave of sorrow washed through her stomach. A sick feeling that would probably never go away. None of this could be reversed. It was a red band of alarm tight around her stomach, a harness that would forever reel her back to the sorrow of losing her sister.

When she turned on Cedar Lane, signs of commotion loomed ahead. A news truck parked a few doors down from their house, its satellite tower jacked up and spiraling thirty feet into the sky, announced that big news was happening here.

"Look at that." She turned to the empty passenger seat as if Remy would be there to see it all. This was right up Remy's alley! Gaggles of people cluttered the street, slowing traffic and giving the neighborhood a festive feel reminiscent of the Fourth of July when people came out front to set off firecrackers.

"All we need now is a lemonade stand," Cassie muttered as she braked to ease through the crowd. A shuffling noise in the backseat made her glance over her shoulder; Ariel had removed her seat belt and flopped onto the floor, where she huddled facedown.

"I don't think it's quite that extreme, Mom." They were crawling toward home when Dinah Lambo, a neighbor, tapped a TV reporter on the shoulder and pointed toward Cassie's car.

"Traitor," Cassie muttered.

The reporter began to jog alongside the car, pointing a microphone toward Cassie's window. "Jazz Milkin, from News Seven." He was a thin, rangy, mocha-skinned dude with a soul patch and square red glasses. Fun-loving and animated. Cassie had always liked watching him on TV. "Can we get a statement, please? Our viewers want to hear from the family."

Cassie just kept easing the car toward the house, repulsed by the media circus. The last time Cassie had been on television it had been because she had led the high school food drive at Thanksgiving. Back then, the reporter hadn't been half as enthusiastic as Jazz.

With relief she pulled into the driveway, waited as the garage door opened, and then eased into the shadowed protection of the building. She cut the engine and slumped in her seat, waiting for the door to descend behind the car. Home . . . but not really. It would never be home again, not without Remy.

With sunglasses on, her mother moved lethargically, stumbling out of the car as if she were drunk.

"Mom?" Cassie stopped her at the door. "Did they give you something at the hospital?"

"They're so tight with drugs these days." Ariel frowned. "It's a good thing I carry my own supply of Valium."

"How many did you take?" Cassie asked.

But Ariel stumbled into the house like an old grandma, palming her way along the wall as Maisy and Trevor called from the dining room table, where they were sitting with their grandfather. Their eyes were puffy and red, but Cassie felt a little better just seeing them gathered together. Misery loved company.

"Mommy, you're home." Maisy came over and threw her arms around Ariel, who wavered with the weight. "We need your hugs." Her voice broke as she pressed into Ariel's blouse.

The tiny whimper tore at Cassie, who hadn't really cried. She'd misted over a few times in the anxious moments of waiting to view Remy's body at the morgue. Mostly she was feeling anger, a hot fury that took all her strength to subdue, but she kept a tight grip. Someone had to keep things together for Trevor and Maisy.

"My darlings." Ariel kissed the top of Maisy's head. "Eli. Thank you for coming."

Cassie was relieved to see that Mom had called in Oliver's oddball father. There were so many choices for child care that would have been worse than the hippie poet and wood-carving stoner. Besides, Eli Ward was actually family, and he had a big heart.

"I'm here as long as you need me." With a gray fringe of hair, a shiny bald pate, and round glasses that gave him an owlish look, Eli projected a mixture of wisdom and rebellion that reminded Cassie of Gandhi. "We were just noshing a bit." Eli gestured at the table where an eclectic assortment of fruits, vegetables, dips, and desserts were laid out.

"Granddad took us to Trader Joe's," Trevor said. "We got Japanese ice cream balls in dough."

"Mochi. Can I interest you in a little something?" Eli asked. "You must be spent."

"Not really hungry, but thanks." Ariel ruffled Trevor's hair, and then headed upstairs.

That would be the last they would see of her for days ... maybe months. That band of alarm closed tighter as the rule of the house landed sharply on Cassie's shoulders.

Gotta keep it together. Hold on.

"Cassie, do you want some hummus?" Maisy asked. "It looks like poo, but it tastes much better."

A stilted noise came from Cassie's throat. "I might. I'll be right back." Desperate for escape, Cassie ran upstairs to scrub her face and hands, wanting to remove any essence of that sterile morgue where she imagined toxic microbes lingering in the air.

Drying her face, she choked up at the sight of Remy's box of makeup on the corner of the vanity. Hands clutched at her gut, tugging her down into misery. Remy's fingerprints were all over this house, all over Cassie's life. There would be no escape. Now she understood the mythology of ghosts.

Downstairs she found Trevor crying over a text he'd received. "I hate David Green," he said, glaring at his cell phone.

"I don't blame you," Eli said. "With friends like that, who needs enemies?"

"I hate him, too." Maisy's lower lip jutted out in a pout as she drew swirls in the hummus with a baby carrot.

"What did David do?" Cassie asked as she cracked open a can of ginger ale and took a seat beside Trevor at the table.

"He said this." Trevor flashed the screen of his cell toward her, and she read the text.

I heard he cut her head off.

The soda went sour on Cassie's tongue, and she had to force herself to swallow. "This David kid is a little shit." The urge to snatch Trevor's cell away and toss it out in the backyard was fierce.

Trevor's round eyes beseeched her. "Is it true?"

Cassie braced herself on table as the image of Remy at the morgue floated back to her mind. A blue sheet had been pulled up to Remy's chin in an unnatural way, covering up the gash in her neck.

"Her throat was cut." A nurse named Sally had helped Cassie through the trauma at the morgue. Sally's voice was firm but calm as she rubbed the center of Cassie's back. "There's a major vein in the neck, so she probably went quickly."

"The jugular," Cassie said, remembering her anatomy class.

"I'm just telling you because you asked how she died, and I want you to be armed with the truth. The technician will do his best to cover the wound, but it's not always possible."

Although Cassie held her breath as they opened the shade to reveal the body, she could not stop the little moan that came from her throat as she viewed the still form that had once been so vibrant. The sheet covering Remy was a beautiful shade of blue, a cross between robin's egg and indigo, like Remy's prom dress. Drawn up and draped around her neck, almost lovingly, it framed her heart-shaped face. Cassie had studied the wide lips, the cute little "puggy" nose, the shaped brows and lashes so dark against her pearl-gray skin. Remy had seemed comfortable, but not angelic or really peaceful like you'd think. It was more like she had fallen into an exhausted sleep.

"It's her." Two words that slammed a life shut.

"I'm so sorry." Sally put a hand on her arm to lead her away, but Cassie didn't budge. "I'll give you a minute, then."

Although she didn't want to stare, Cassie kept looking, as if in search of the essence of her sister. When did the spirit leave a body? Was Remy long gone, shot off to the distant heavens, or hovering a few feet above them, sharing in Cassie's pain?

And I didn't get a chance to say good-bye. I didn't think this would ever happen. I didn't appreciate her enough. Did I ever tell her that I loved her?

"Is that true?" Trevor asked again, jarring Cassie from her thoughts. "Did Jared really cut off her head? That's what the kids at school are saying."

"And David is the rotten messenger." Cassie looked to Eli, who held up his hands in an expression of utter loss and left the table. She wasn't ready to think about Jared's role in this yet, but she couldn't let her sister be the center of gruesome rumors.

"He didn't," Cassie assured them, figuring it was as close to the truth as she could get.

Trevor and Maisy seemed to sag in unison, as if the news had softened the horror of Remy's death.

I can do that for you, Cassie thought. *I can help you focus on the good memories.*

"So you can text David that it's a nasty rumor. And he can tell the other kids to cut it out."

Somehow, that made both kids feel better. Cassie took another slug of ginger ale and regretted it as it burned all the way down.

"Let's put that nasty rumor behind us and never speak of it again," Eli said as he rattled around in the kitchen. Tipping her chair back, Cassie saw three pans and a griddle on the stove, butter sizzling on the griddle.

"What are you making, Gumpers?" asked Maisy.

"Breakfast for dinner. Who's going to help me?"

Trevor volunteered, and minutes later Eli had him turning bacon and stirring pancake batter, "just thirty turns," so that the batter didn't get tough.

Watching them, Cassie realized what Eli was doing: carrying on, feeding the family, taking care of the basics. Ariel had always said Eli was a crazy man, but Cassie was grateful for the older man's eccentricities now. Crazy like a fox.

Holding a cluster of grapes, Maisy squeezed into the chair beside Cassie. "Is Remy going to have a funeral?"

Cassie hadn't thought that far ahead. "Yes. Or at least a memorial."

"I don't like funerals. They're too scary." Maisy's mouth puckered and she began to cry.

Putting an arm around her, Cassie held her close and stroked her hair and let her cry. She hated it when people tried to get you to stop crying, as if that would end the suffering and despair. No one wanted to be bothered dealing with your pain. Cassie held her youngest sister and told herself that it was better not to join in the tears. Stay strong. Don't let on that her entire body was now squeezed in alarm. Pretend everything would be fine when she knew that nothing would be fine, ever again.

Thirty minutes later, Eli brought out plates of bacon, pancakes, and cheesy eggs that made Cassie's mouth water. "Make way, my children," he announced, his bass voice rumbling through the kitchen. Cassie helped clear some things off the table and tuck them away in the fridge. When she sat down and forced herself to try the eggs, she was surprised at how easily they went down. Eli was a kook, but he knew how to cook, and he brought an odd comfort to the house.

After dinner the kids went upstairs, Trevor to do his homework, such a creature of habit, and Maisy to visit Ariel.

Good luck with that, Cassie thought as she saw Eli open the sliding glass door.

"Hey, does this fire pit out here work?" he called, turning back to her. "That's a nice addition."

"Stosh bought it." Cassie stepped out in her socks and showed him how to turn on the propane.

"I am going to dig that." Eli sat back with his moccasins on the edge of the pit and lit a joint.

Watching him, Cassie felt a twinge of envy. How she craved escape, especially here, where Remy seemed to linger in every corner of the house. In the corner of the yard, where she had learned acrobatics on a rope swing that Oliver installed. In the hallways, where her songs lingered in the empty spaces. No one had touched her empty chair at the table, and her mac and cheese pot from last night had been left soaking in the kitchen sink.

"Want some, sweetheart?" Eli offered.

"No, thanks. It'll only make me freak out."

"Yeah, you don't want that." He took another hit, holding it in.

"Don't let Mom see you."

"She'll get over it. But I will be discreet around the youngsters. Should we see if your mother wants a plate upstairs?"

Cassie scowled. "She's probably asleep with her boyfriend, Valium."

Eli lifted one brow. "And she thinks *I'm* a bad example. Should we check on her?"

"I'm not her keeper."

"Ah, but Cassie girl, you take good care of everyone you love."

She squinted into the flames, trying to ignore the knot in her throat. "Looks like I didn't take very good care of Remy."

"Looks are deceiving." He stubbed out the joint and put it in a silver case from his pocket. "Take yourself, for example. You look fine. A little tense. But I know you're breaking inside." He let out a breath. "You did your best for Remy, but sometimes, like the Beatles said, you've got to let it be. The thing you learn when trying to protect young people is that you can't really protect anyone. We've all got an expiration date here. But it hits hard when someone dies so young. Especially someone we love."

She did love her sister, damn it. You fell in love with a kid when you raised her almost single-handedly. In some ways, Remy was the greatest accomplishment of Cassie's life. Staring into the fire, Cassie swallowed against the lump in her throat.

"I can't believe she's gone," Eli went on. "A good kid. Kind and gentle. And sheesh, she loved to sing. What a crooner."

When she looked over at him, his cheeks shone with tears. He lifted his glasses to wipe his eyes with his hands.

The sight of Eli crying tore at her. Jaded, weathered Eli. Suddenly, the knot of resolve and prickly defiance eased and tears flooded her eyes. She brushed at them with her fingers, but more tears formed just as quickly as she could wipe them away.

Eli didn't say anything, thank God, and he didn't try to console her or make her stop crying. He let her be.

They sat together in silence. When Eli got up to check on the kids, he paused and dropped a hand on Cassie's shoulder. "I almost forgot, kiddo. I talked to a funeral director about arrangements. You'll need to pick out something for Remy to go out in." Practical Eli; he always seemed to know the next step.

She sniffed. "What kind of outfit?"

"They recommend a nice dress, but that sounds a little stiff to me. Remy wasn't a fancy person, was she? Whatever you think, kiddo." He patted her shoulder and headed inside. "At this point, it doesn't matter to Remy."

Chapter 24

After nearly six hours spent corralling a criminal lawyer and reminding the desk officer that she wanted to see her son, Rachel's nerves were shot. It didn't help that she had to refuse to be interviewed by the police. She was eager to vouch for Jared's reputation and fill the police in on the way he had suffered at the hands of bullies. But George Hunt, Jared's new lawyer, had told her to refuse all interviews. "Absolutely not. No way, no how," he'd said with a burly scowl. "They can give you a subpoena, and then we'll do it right. A deposition, with me there to prep you." Although she heeded Hunt's expensive advice, she longed to set the record straight now, today.

There had been a few times when her resolve had cracked, and tears had filled her eyes at the thought of Remy's shortened life or Jared's anguished future. But she had held on, calm and restrained, repeating her mantra of "I can do this" until it became part of every breath she took.

Damn, these molded plastic chairs! She pushed to her feet and ventured outside for some fresh air. They were heading into the long days of light—the Oregon summer—and the vista over the distant treed hills revealed streaks of pink and lavender in the western sky: nature's glorious finish to the worst day of her life.

Exhaustion and stress made her tight and wobbly. Pressing her palms to the warm stone wall behind her, she soaked up the distant sunset and wondered if good souls rose up into beautiful skies like this.

In many ways, Remy had been an old soul. Rachel remembered a visit from Remy one wet autumn day, more than a year ago. Her dark hair tumbled over her shoulders as she shook off her rain slicker and hung it on the rack by the shop door. "I come bearing gifts," she said, producing two Peppermint Patties from her pocket. "One for each of us."

As Rachel trimmed Remy's hair, the girl opened up about her stepfather, Oliver, and how the whole family had been stunned by his death. "When things were at their worst, I remembered something Oliver used to say. He said there was a foolproof solution to every problem."

"And what was that?" Rachel asked.

"Keep breathing." Remy explained how she and Cassie embraced his philosophy. "And then I figured you could stretch it out. Keep going. Keep dancing. Keep singing. Keep loving. Keep living."

It took Rachel hours, until long after Remy left her chair, to realize that the girl hadn't needed a trim at all. She had come to help Rachel grieve for Jackson. How had the girl known that Rachel had been stuck in regret and sadness, unable to move through her days or endure the nights?

Keep breathing. Keep singing. Keep loving.

Hugging herself, Rachel breathed in the sunset and said a little prayer for Remy. She prayed that she was in a better place now, and that she had died quickly, without pain. Rachel imagined her spirit entwined with the colors in the sky, soaring upward into space. She wanted to think of the poor girl rising to the heavens because the reality of what had happened here on earth was intolerable.

Throughout the afternoon she had tried to call Ariel. When she got no answer, Rachel texted her, sending questions and words of condolence.

I'm so sorry.

There are no words.

Want to talk?

She had half expected Ariel to answer because she knew her friend had no one else to turn to. But Rachel's phone had remained quiet, except for calls from KJ and a few local reporters. News scavengers.

The tragedy was the perfect fodder for scandal. Lifelong friends. A prom proposal gone bad. She said no, and then he killed her.

Rachel had seen a few headlines on the Portland newspaper's blog before she clicked off the site and promised herself to stay away from the media right now. The sordid comments would tarnish the memory of Remy and make Rachel feel even more ill about Jared. Since the encounter at the school, she had tried to ignore a pinched feeling in her stomach that was leaching fear through her body. Misery. This would be her new normal.

Sometime after seven, she received a call from KJ, who had been driving home from college. "Are you back, safe and sound?" she asked.

"I got here two hours ago, but that's not it. Mom, you'd better get home. The police are here with a search warrant. I couldn't stop them. They're upstairs, going through Jared's room."

"You're kidding." Phone pressed to her ear, she marched inside and went right up to the desk officer. "Is this what you do to people? Send a squad over to ransack their house while they're here, waiting to see a child in jail?"

The cop, a new one since the change of shift, held up his hands. "Ma'am, I don't know what you're talking about. We are a criminal lodging facility, and I've never been to your house."

With a groan of exasperation Rachel hurried to her car. "I'm on my way. Don't worry, honey. This is all probably standard." Though she wished that George Hunt had tipped her off that this might happen.

As she drove home, pulling back on her anxiety to stay close to the speed limit, she wondered what the police might find in Jared's room. Illegal drugs? A collection of guns and knives? She didn't think so. Hunting and weaponry held no appeal for Jared.

Although it was after eight, the neighborhood was still bathed with light as Rachel parked beside KJ's car in the driveway. The house welcomed her with a warm, golden glow that contrasted with the propped-open screen door and the cops carrying bagged items from the house to a white van.

Slamming the door of her car, Rachel went straight to the van. "What are you looking for?"

A man in a shirt and tie straightened, revealing a large gold star pinned to his chest. "Rachel Whalen? I'm Detective Lou Shives from the homicide division." He was lean with a shaved head and that squared-away attitude of a former soldier. "I've already spoken to your son Kyle James. We have a warrant to search the premises."

"Really?" She put her hands on her hips. The fortitude and self-control she'd been exercising all day gave way, releasing a torrent of fury. "Were the knives, the blood, and his confession not enough? I can't even imagine how much more evidence you might need against my son." Exhilaration buzzed in her chest at the chance to unleash her anger.

The detective's eyes opened wide. He'd probably never seen a suburban mom lose it before. "Mrs. Whalen, this is procedure."

"Really? And where was your procedure when my son was bullied and almost killed by a pack of brutes on the football team? Where were the cops when those all-stars bound Jared's wrists and turned him upside down and held his head underwater in a toilet bowl? Tell me, Detective Shives, where the hell were you then?"

"Mrs. Whalen . . . please. Calm down. I'm investigating a homicide now, but I'd be happy to pursue these other claims." Detective Shives had lowered his voice to a soothing pitch. A sympathetic tone. Dear God, she couldn't take his sympathy. "When did these things happen to your son?"

"Freshman year," she said through tears. "Three years ago. But it's too late now. Just finish here. Strip the house and go."

Shives cocked his head to one side like a concerned counselor. "We'll be out of your way in a moment. We're just about done here."

His tone was so even and cordial, she felt sheepish for clobbering him with her frustration. "Okay. Good."

"And let me give you my card. That's my cell number, right there. But you don't need me to file a complaint. You can share your concerns with any officer at the sheriff's office. And it's not too late to investigate an assault."

She nodded, unwilling to say another word. She had just spilled her guts out to the saint of the Timbergrove sheriff's office. George Hunt was not going to be happy.

Shives stepped back from the van as two other cops came down the walkway with white plastic evidence bags.

"That's the last of it," said a woman with the creased skin of over-tanning, clear blue eyes, and tawny hair pulled back into a braid. A middle-aged Heidi.

"Great. Thanks." Shives nodded. "We'll be on our way, Mrs. Whalen. Sorry for your troubles."

That seemed like a kind thing to say. Rachel watched the van drive away, hoping that she hadn't revealed too much.

Inside the house, KJ had the gas fireplace going in the living room as he worked in the kitchen. "Are they gone?" he asked.

"Just left. I hope they didn't find anything, but that part is beyond our control." She stepped out of her shoes. "Something smells good."

"Grilled cheese and cream of tomato soup." KJ stood tall, commanding the kitchen even as he seemed to be a stranger in the house. When he stepped forward to hug her, she clenched her lips together, biting back a surge of emotion at the great irony. She had spent so much of the past few months worrying about KJ, not knowing that the quiet son under her roof would be the one to melt down.

He let her go and reached for the spatula. "I thought you'd need some sustenance."

"You didn't have to come, but I'm glad you did," Rachel said quietly. His presence would help keep her from going to the dark places. "I've been meaning to call you." She didn't really want to discuss football, but any topic would be preferable to today's crisis. "How've you been feeling? Are all the symptoms gone?"

"I'm fine. Not really here to talk football, Mom." He poked at the pan with the spatula. "It's just about ready if you want to wash up."

Appreciating the role reversal, Rachel went upstairs to press a warm washcloth to her face and change into sweatpants. As she passed by Jared's door on the way down, she paused in the shadowed hallway and peeked inside. The places that had once been occupied by his file cabinet, computer, and storage bins now seemed like empty pockets. Missing teeth. Out of habit, she pulled open the desk drawer to find that the binders had been taken, but the football remained.

She palmed the ball, then cradled it against her chest. Had it been just hours ago that she had stood here, realizing he wasn't home? If only she had stopped him this morning, forced him to connect. That had been part of his therapy as a child when the pediatrician had noticed a problem. Eye-contact therapy. Rachel had learned to hold his chubby cheeks and talk to him as she tried to entice him to look her in the eyes. It had always been hard to connect with Jared, but she had learned how to get in. Or so she'd thought.

It was too quiet when they first sat down to eat, so she switched on the television for background noise, turning to a channel that showed a million ways to remodel your home.

"The arraignment is tomorrow. A special Saturday arraignment." She picked up a piece of sandwich, touched by the way KJ had sliced it into triangles, as she had when the boys were kids. "Do you think you'll go with me?"

He shrugged. "What did the lawyer say?"

She told him about her meeting with the attorney, George

Hunt, who had spoken to her for only a few minutes. Rachel had asked the lawyer about the death penalty. "Is it possible?"

"Possible but not probable," he'd said. "Even if he got that sentence, and I doubt he would, the state of Oregon hasn't executed a prisoner for years. But we're jumping ahead here."

George had explained that he would collect most of the information directly from Jared. Although Rachel would be paying Hunt's retainer, his relationship would be exclusively with Jared. "Since he's eighteen," Hunt had said, "I need his consent to share information on the case with you." Rachel had agreed. What choice did she have?

KJ's voice brought Rachel back to the present moment. "That lawyer sounds like an asshole. Did you ever get to see Jared?"

"Finally." She swirled a spoon through her soup, recalling the endless day of waiting. "Hunt arranged it before he left, but it was only for a few minutes, and we were separated by a screen. It was . . . awful." Jared had cried the entire time, silent tears punctuated by occasional bouts of sobbing, and she had longed to hold him in her arms and offer some comfort, some simple compassion. But no contact was allowed, and no words could penetrate his hysteria.

"How did he seem?"

"Sad. He was crying."

KJ kept his gaze down, as if the grill marks on his sandwich were homing beacons. "Did he tell you anything?"

"No." And she had needed answers. "I begged him for something, some kind of explanation. I know there's more to this, KJ. I tried to find out."

"*Did you do it?*" she had asked him, her voice waffled by the vented Plexiglas. When he'd nodded, his face contorted in a sob, she had pressed closer, beseeching. "Why? Why did you attack Remy? Please, Jared, I just need to know why."

She had to know. She deserved an answer. And somehow she believed that if he opened up, the explanation would mitigate the circumstances of the attack.

But she would have to wait for his answer. "He's admitted to stabbing Remy, more than once. The real question now is why." Forcing herself to go through the motions, she took a bite of the sandwich and chewed.

"He's gone over the edge." KJ shook his head as he wiped up soup with the bread crusts. "You got him a good lawyer, and you held a freaking vigil at the jail. All that waiting around, and he didn't even talk to you? What the hell?"

"He's in crisis."

"A crisis he brought on himself. Come on, Mom. Don't defend him."

"He's my son, and we don't know all the circumstances yet," she argued, furious with KJ, although she knew he was right. She was the deluded one, holding on to false hope that somehow her son would be vindicated. "And no matter what, I'll never give up on him. He'll always be my son and . . . it's my job to fight for him and wait around all day, if that's what it takes. I would have stayed the night in one of those plastic chairs if I thought it would make a difference. It felt horrible, leaving him there alone."

"To be honest, I'm glad he's behind bars," KJ countered. "It would be pretty scary having a killer in the house with us."

When Rachel flinched, Kyle pointed to the television. "Wake up, Mom. It's all over the news, trending on the Internet. Your little darling is a killer, and he's just torn the heart out of this family."

"KJ, please . . ." She felt like she herself was under siege now. "What can I do here? I feel like I need to defend Jared. But at the same time, I hate him for what he did to Remy. It's a heinous act. And I'm sick that my own child, my flesh and blood, has become a monster."

"It's not your fault." KJ got up and gathered dishes, leaving a barely touched bowl of soup in front of Rachel. "It's not your fault that he's become an animal. But you've got to accept that the Jared we knew is gone. He's either really sick or really evil. He may be my brother, but right now I wouldn't be able to sleep in the same house with him."

* * *

From her bedroom window Ariel saw them down in the backyard, gathered around the fire pit. Cassie and Maisy were huddled together in a blanket and Eli wore a fleece overshirt. Trevor, in his hoodie, jumped up to demonstrate a move. Ariel's forehead bumped the glass when she moved closer to sniff for weed. Was Eli turning them on? No. Eli wouldn't do that. At least not until they were all teenagers.

Pushing away from the window, Ariel swayed a bit as she staggered toward the bed. No. Not yet. There was something else.

A bath. Yes, she needed a hot soak with lavender salt.

She swung around a little too quickly and braced herself against the dresser, where her pills were spilled out beside a glass with two fingers of whiskey.

"Time to take your pill?" Or had she already taken it?

"Oliver?" she called. He would know if it was time. "Ollie?" Where the hell was he? Probably down by the fire pit.

Well. One wouldn't hurt. She gulped down a pill, wincing as the whiskey burned a path down her throat. The edges of her vision were hazy, making her dizzy. She had to feel her way along the wall to get to the bathroom, where the tub loomed, gleaming white, slick, and slippery. Ha. Maybe a bath was not such a good idea. She could drown. Then again, maybe that was what made it an excellent idea.

The rushing water reminded her of that waterfall in the Gorge, where she and Oliver had gone swimming that hot summer day. So hot. She turned the cold-water spigot; that was better. Breathing in the steam rising from the surface, she waited for the lavender to calm her rattled nerves. Lavender was so soothing. But why was she so upset?

He would be here soon, and sex was always a great distraction for her.

And Remy . . . Remy was so talented, with such a bright future ahead. She was going to be a star. Maybe Ariel would find a role for her daughter on the show. She wouldn't mind sharing a bit of the spotlight with her girl. The singing witch's daughter.

She closed her eyes and laughed.

When she opened her eyes, the water had grown cold, her fingertips wrinkled. She slithered out, wondering why he was so late. Well, fuck him. She scowled, then giggled. She already had. But there were others out there. So many others.

Still damp, she crawled into bed and passed out.

Chapter 25

After the dinner dishes were done and it was decided that KJ would stay the night, Rachel made two mugs of tea with honey and they settled into the living room. KJ stretched out on his belly in front of the fireplace just as he had on school nights a few years ago, a tactic to delay homework. The scene looked cozy and tranquil—a family evening at home—until she realized that he was crying.

"KJ...honey..." At a loss for any means of comfort, she went to him and rubbed his back. "Someday we'll look back on this and...it'll always be a shitty memory."

He lifted his head and rested his forehead on his fist. "I feel like I've lost a sister," KJ said. "But it's even weirder because my brother killed her."

"I know." She sat on the hearth beside him, choking up as he sobbed into his arm.

When he could speak again, he talked about Remy. She'd been a toddler when they met, and KJ was only five or so, but he remembered how she seemed to speak in full paragraphs when other kids were dropping one or two words. "She would babble on with this weird, almost mystical tone," he said, "and sometimes she didn't make any sense, but she thought she did. She would hold up a seashell to her ear and say it was magic, that it spoke to her and told her stories of where it had traveled. Remember that?"

"I do. And I remember how you used to carry her on your shoulders and toss her in the air."

"Yeah. I grew like a tree, and she was always so little."

Rachel cradled her mug and reminisced about the old days. In the crush of grief, she reached to recall a better time—the "wonder years" when Remy, Jared, Cassie, and KJ were little. Summers were loaded with golden afternoons picnicking at the swim park and vacations at the coast, where the kids dug in the sand and biked into town after dinner for ice cream and saltwater taffy. "And the school days," Rachel recalled, "I never would have survived those PTA meetings and Portfolio Nights without Ariel's blunt take on it all. And all the holidays we spent together. I used to love shopping for girly gifts for Cassie and Remy. We were a giant family . . . all of us together, telling stories or singing. Those were good times."

"If you say so," KJ said, raking at the rug with his fingertips.

"Come on, now. Didn't you have a storybook childhood?"

He shrugged. "Sometimes. You were a great mom, but I didn't always like hanging around with the Alexanders."

She rested her mug on her knee. "Why are you doing this?"

"Nothing personal, but I'm really uncomfortable around Ariel. I know she's your friend and all, but there's something a little off about her."

"That's not very kind—especially now—and I didn't raise you to be so critical of other people. Ariel is my friend because she doesn't fit the mold. She's a refreshing change from the other Timbergrove moms."

"Maybe for you, but it makes me uncomfortable when she's around. The way she looks at me. And once, I think she tried to hit on me."

Rachel had never heard this before, but KJ's ego was sometimes a bit overinflated. "When was that?"

"When I was in high school. Like, sophomore year."

"Maybe you misread her intentions."

"No, it was real." KJ stood his ground. "She was the reason

I wouldn't audition for Gleetime. There was no way I was going to do private sessions with her in that studio."

A pale scrap of memory flickered in her mind: Ariel dancing with Graham Oyama the night of the rehearsal, his hands on her body, possessive and familiar. Had Ariel had been crossing sexual boundaries with these boys?

No. Ariel could be wild and unconventional, but she was not depraved.

Shifting on the couch, Rachel worked to keep her voice level. "Memory can be so subjective. When I think of you in sophomore year, football comes to mind. You were all about getting on the varsity team. Football was your world. You wouldn't have taken time away from it for something like Gleetime." She put her mug on the table. "How's that all going? Have you talked with the coach?"

"Yeah, and I think it's over."

"Oh?" She braced herself for more bad news. "Your choice or theirs?"

"Mine, I guess. They said they would play me, but . . . I don't know. It's killing me, but I don't want to take the chance of having mush for a brain. At least, that's where I stand right now. I've got another month to make a final decision."

"That sounds like the responsible choice." An expensive choice for Rachel, but worth every penny. "I'd be very happy with that. Just say the word, and I'll move some investments around to cover things."

Tuition, room and board, on top of Jared's legal fees. She would need to liquidate her rainy day funds.

"I'll let you know." He raked a hand through his dark hair. "But now my issues are small shit compared to Jared's. What the hell happened to him, Mom?"

She shook her head.

He snorted. "Maybe we should've let him kill himself when he wanted to go."

"Kyle James!" Tears filled her eyes at the suggestion. But then, in a perverse way, KJ was right. If Jared had committed suicide, Remy would be here today.

She would be alive.

And Jared would be at peace.

Cassie rolled onto her side, pulled the sheets over her head, and breathed in the smell of lavender and orange. Remy's scent, on the sheets, in the bed all over this room.

She whipped down the covers and stared up at the Day-Glo stars covering the ceiling. How was she supposed to sleep with signs of her sister everywhere she turned?

She scurried to the edge of the bed to turn on the lamp. In the safety of the light her old room was now unfamiliar and eerie. When she'd gone off to college, Remy had taken it over, redecorating cheaply with a corkboard strung with lights, neck-laces and jewelry and tie-dyed tapestries on the walls. Now it was psychedelic. Every time Cassie sat on the bed under the ceiling covered with Day-Glo stars, the song "Feelin' Groovy" popped into her thoughts, and the video Remy had sent her from the Gleetime showcase played in her mind.

The big upstairs bedroom had become Remy's in life; in death, it still was very much Remy's territory. Her scent, her music and laughter, her colors and moods hovered here, rush-ing and receding like a human heartbeat. Her breathing, soft and steady, filled the spaces in the restive house.

Cassie was afraid to open the closet, as if Remy were hiding amid the hanging clothes, waiting to scare her and insist she wasn't really dead and take a selfie with Cassie so that every-one would get a good laugh at her eyes popping in fright.

Always a skeptic, Cassie wondered about ghosts. Was Remy haunting the house, trying to tell her something? But no mes-sage was coming through, just vivid impressions and whispers of her sister—but none of them were reassuring. One thing Cassie knew for sure: She had to get out of this house.

She grabbed her cell phone from the nightstand, then put it back. Too late to call Andrew. Earlier that night, on the phone with Andrew, she had gone through possible timelines for get-ting back to Corvallis. She had to wait till the coroner released Remy's body. Then the funeral. Then, once the kids were resettled, maybe she could go back. Would that be Friday or a week from Friday or in a month?

Her summer classes began in two weeks. Would she make it back in time? Andrew insisted that she should take time for herself. The school would let her drop the classes without a fee. He didn't understand that she wanted to get back to the safety of her college life. That she needed to escape this tightly woven web before she became ensnared and weakened.

Now she grabbed a comforter and started for the stairs, thinking of the couch in the den. But halfway down the skunky odor of raw weed reminded her that Eli was bunking down there.

Frustrated and exhausted, she returned to the room with the luminescent stars. Hugging the comforter to her chest, she sat on the bed and looked up to the artificial heavens above.

"What are you trying to tell me?" she asked.

There was no rush of wind, no blinking light from the hall. This was not going to be a simple task.

"Okay. Tomorrow I'm going to do some digging. Talk to your friends. Go through your stuff, and I don't know ... search for clues?"

Silence. Well, what did she expect? A talking ghost? She plodded down the hall to Maisy's room and pushed her little sister aside to claim some space in the single bed.

Chapter 26

The next morning, Rachel's hand shook as she brought up Kit's number on her cell. "I'm sorry, but I need you to cancel my afternoon appointments, too," she told the shop receptionist. "I thought I'd be able to come in after the arraignment, but..." The truth was that she could not hold her hands steady, and she could not bear the inevitable looks and whispers. There would be questions from the bold, sympathetic pats on the shoulder from the others. No, not today. "I've just got this stinkin' headache," she told Kit. With the throbbing pain between her eyes, it was only a half-lie.

"No problem." Kit was a rock; she would make the calls and chitchat when necessary, but she would not let the conversation spill into Rachel's current dilemma. A former suburban heroin addict, Kit understood the value of privacy. The resolve to keep things buttoned down was one of the reasons Rachel was prone to hire a person with an illicit past. "I'll take care of it. You just let me know if I need to reschedule your Monday clients."

As she massaged shampoo into her hair in the shower, Rachel wondered if this numbness would wear off. Most likely she was feeling residual effects of the double dose of over-the-counter sleep aid she had taken last night. She wasn't generally a pill popper, but last night it seemed to be the only way she could find even a superficial level of sleep.

As she turned off the shower and toweled off, she realized that it had been years since she'd missed a Saturday at the shop. Not since Jackson's death. Part of her believed that the shop would crumble to pieces if she wasn't on site, holding up the posts and beams. In reality, gals like Kit and Hilda could manage while she took care of family business.

While crossing the courthouse parking lot with KJ, Rachel recognized Jared's lawyer getting out of a Toyota. With a squat, strong build, bushy reddish hair, and a thick beard to match, George Hunt looked like he might work as a lumberjack in his spare time. She hurried over to talk with him. "Do you think there's a chance he'll be tried as a minor? He's barely eighteen. He just had a birthday?"

"Barely eighteen is hardly a mitigating factor." He stared ahead, as if he couldn't spare her a look. "He'll be tried as an adult."

"What about bail?" she asked. "Maybe we can get him released for a while?"

"Not likely. This is an extremely violent crime your son is charged with. But we'll be in and out today. This is very routine."

She introduced KJ and asked if there was a chance that they could talk with Jared today.

Hunt stopped walking and leaned in, stroking the side of his beard. "I'm sorry, Mrs. Whalen, but he doesn't want to see you."

Stunned, Rachel gestured to her oldest son. "What about his brother, Kyle James? Maybe he'll see him?"

KJ's shoulders went up as he arched back. "Not sure I want to go there."

"I'll ask." Hunt continued walking toward the entrance. "But no promises."

"Can I ask about the case?" Rachel hurried alongside him. "How are things looking?"

"It's all preliminary still. Let's just say I've got my work cut out for me. And no, I can't give you details. Remember what I said about client privilege?"

Rachel let the man go. "Don't forget to ask about KJ," she called after him, thinking that even a distant connection to Jared was better than none. Hunt disappeared into the shadows and was swallowed up by the courthouse. So that was that; Jared didn't want to see her. Tears began to blur her vision as she turned back to KJ. "When this is all over, remind me to ground your brother."

"Yeah, Mom." KJ put his arm around Rachel and led her into the courthouse.

They didn't get far before they came to a cluster of people blocking the corridor. TV reporters, looking bigger than life in their makeup, spoke into cameras, setting up their story. And at the center of the group was the sun—Ariel Alexander, looking chic in an enormous black hat with dark netting that swept down to cover her face. Always a woman of mystery. Cassie stood beside her, appearing distinctly uncomfortable with all the attention. Looking sophisticated in high-heeled sandals, black jeans, and a print top with a high waist and scoop neck, Cassie ran her fingertips over the hem of her shirt, tugging on it nervously. Eli, Oliver's father, hunched against the wall, hands in his jeans pockets and the collar of his corduroy jacket folded inside.

Rachel approached Ariel and paused, trying to see beyond the veil and dark glasses.

"Mom," KJ muttered. "Don't. Just keep going."

"I have to stop. I have to say something."

But with reporters shooting off questions, it was impossible to get a word in. Although in an odd disconnect, Ariel wasn't answering anyone; she simply stood in the center of the corridor like a queen holding court.

Rachel raised a hand and mouthed, "I'm sorry," but Ariel did not acknowledge her. A moment later, when Cassie waved her away with a look of warning, Rachel continued on with KJ.

Inside the courtroom it seemed that half of the town of Timbergrove had found a new spectator sport. She recognized her neighbors, Walt Finley and Mrs. Abduljuwad, as well as a bunch of the high school supermoms. Tiffani from the shop fluttered her fingers at her, though something sinister gleamed in her eyes. Were these people here to support Jared or crucify him?

One row seemed to be filled with teachers and school administrators, looking dutifully somber. Rachel recognized Dr. Balducci and Mr. Enrico. None of the teachers met her eye as she and KJ came down the aisle, but then most of them didn't even know who she was. Until yesterday, she had been an inconspicuous parent of an unremarkable student in their school.

KJ found seats for them near the front, and Rachel braced herself. She wanted to appear strong and supportive, just in case Jared got a look at her.

But the minute the bailiff brought her son out, Rachel began to cry. His dark eyes were hollow and haunted, and the way his lower lip jutted out in his attempt to stave off tears cut her to the quick. He moved slowly, obviously uncomfortable in the handcuffs, and the orange prison jumpsuit made him resemble a beanpole, but he was *her* beanpole of a boy, her son.

She could not bear to look at him in that jumpsuit, a reminder that he would be tried as an adult even though he was not truly a man yet, not really. Couldn't they make an exception for a kid like Jared who had not reached that level of maturity? He had just turned eighteen! If all of this had happened a week ago, he would be treated quite differently by the criminal justice system.

He was a kid, damn it. It seemed like yesterday that she was taking photos of him in his First Communion suit. Closing her eyes against tears, she saw his freckled face, his grin missing a few teeth as he handed her the homemade Mother's Day card that held three coupons entitling her to a kiss, a smile, and a week of making his bed all by himself. She saw him banging on the back door, just home from football practice, crying as he held aloft the cleats that he had to retrieve from the urinal of the boys' locker room.

No . . . not a man yet. Barely eighteen. Opening her eyes, she tried to focus. She knew she should focus on what the attorneys were saying, but she could not stop crying over what would not be. His adult life, his second act, his happy ending.

At the mention of Remy's name, a visceral pain traveled through her. She hadn't even scratched the surface of misery over losing Remy. She closed her eyes and saw Jared kissing Remy's boo-boo when they were both in preschool. He was always a gentle person, kind and tentative.

Sniffing, Rachel turned toward her best friend, hoping for a glance, a nod, some sort of connection. But the black-brimmed hat hid her well.

The charges were read: "Jared Whalen is charged with premeditated manslaughter."

Rachel sobbed quietly into a rumpled tissue.

That tiny whimper seemed to catch Jared's attention, as he glanced back over his shoulder.

With a deep breath, Rachel tried to calm herself. She could tell he'd been crying, and she didn't want to make him feel even worse. Straightening, she gave him a brave smile.

But when she silently mouthed, "I love you" she realized he was looking beyond her.

Chapter 27

Manslaughter.

The word seemed to hang in the damp air of the courtroom.

Cassie realized it was incorrect. It should have been "woman-slaughter." He had cut her sister's throat, killing her on the morning of prom, even before the first classes of the day had begun.

Cassie had learned some of the details from Remy's friend Malika, when they talked on the phone in the morning. That day at school, Malika had been downstairs in the choir room, hanging out with Remy and other girls who were going to prom in a group. They were making plans to meet early, at Sophia's house, do their hair together, and feast on sushi, pizza, and ice cream. Girlfriends together. No need for dates. All very nontraditional.

They were still talking prom when the first bell rang. Malika and Sophia were a few steps behind Remy, who got pulled aside in the stairwell by Jared. Apparently, he'd been doing a Flashco sales pitch for a teacher, and he still had his knife kit in his hands when he flipped out.

Jared, Jared, what the hell is wrong with you?

Staring at the back of his head, Cassie couldn't think of an adjective to describe him. Desperate Jared. Despondent Jared. Pathetic Jared. Borderline Jared. Killer Jared.

No, that didn't sound right, but then again, nothing did. He'd always been a quiet kid, the last person you'd expect to hurt someone. But that was the thing about people: From the outside, you couldn't see their secrets.

One night in senior year when they were absorbed in a school psych class, Cassie and Olivia had stayed up late trying to diagnose the people in their lives. With his preoccupation with being the star quarterback, they had deemed KJ Whalen a narcissist. Olivia swore that her dad was a sociopath, because he didn't have a moment's guilt over anything. He spent his entire weekend golfing, and she was sure he was having an affair with some woman at work. Cassie got a little nervous when Olivia brought up Ariel, but Cassie quickly pointed to her mother's Native American background as partial explanation for her drinking problem. If Olivia realized that Ariel's real addiction was for sex, she didn't bring it up.

While Olivia proposed that Jared was on the spectrum for autism, Cassie argued for borderline personality disorder. Jared was very sensitive to changes in environment, and he definitely seemed to have abandonment issues. Over the years she had observed him, mostly because he was so easy to observe. Usually, Cassie steered clear of Jared because they were so different. When they were little, she thought he was a big baby, so easy to disturb, so sensitive. "Just get over it," she would mutter. She could not understand why he didn't grow a thick skin and get over his fears.

Although Jared had seemed to get better in the past few years, Cassie realized that was a myth, like growing out of being Caucasian or shedding your Navajo heritage. Certain things just stuck with you for life. For Jared, it was his frantic need to avoid rejection, his panic-button heart, that would now define him forever. Remy had been the unlucky one to reject him at a bad time.

Diagnosis by Dr. Cassie. But just because she understood what made him tick didn't mean she couldn't hate him for killing her sister. He deserved to fry. And it hurt to feel that way about someone she'd grown up with.

Cassie felt bad that she couldn't *engage* with it all—with Remy's funeral, with the people who'd dropped by with food, with the lawyers talking right in front of her about her sister's murder. Cassie was crushed by Remy's death, but guilt could be crushing, too. She wanted to figure out a few things, put her sister to rest, and get the hell out of Timbergrove.

But it didn't look like that was going to happen. Cassie was now the center of the universe at home. She could deal with Trev and Maisy, but there was also Mom being comatose, Stosh calling and trying to be Mom's boyfriend again and trying to butt into their family, and Eli coming in from the garage stinking of weed and spouting off words of advice for the grandkids. He tried to pitch in with the dishes and stuff, but he didn't believe in dishwashers and the man didn't know how to clean.

Cassie wanted to run. Slam the door behind her and go back to school, back to her separate life, away from the memories that her home in Timbergrove held. Was that denial? Hell, yeah, but she welcomed it. Everything here was steeped in memories of Remy. Back in Corvallis, Cassie could pretend that Remy was still alive and doing her thing. Graduating and finding a summer job and picking out a comforter for her dorm room. Cassie wanted out of here, but she couldn't leave her siblings in the lurch.

When was Mom going to step up and return to the land of the living, take responsibility for the family again, so that Cassie could extract herself? It was hard to imagine Ariel bouncing back without Rachel's help, but Ariel refused to talk to her. Cassie got that, though Rachel wasn't really to blame. She didn't kill Remy. Why couldn't people see that?

Why couldn't Mom see that?

She let her gaze wander to Ariel, who sat beside her, a silent shell of a woman in the courtroom. Ariel could be so clueless when she was tanking. Cassie had to force her mother to come today. Ariel was not going to be Cassie's savior.

Cassie was looking beyond the immediate pain of losing Remy to a lifetime of disappointment. A bleak landscape. How many years had it taken Ariel to get over Oliver's death? How many years of Cassie playing mother to the others? She could not do it again. She could not, would not. But looking at her mother, who could pass as a movie star under the veiled hat and dark glasses, Cassie was not sure that she had any choice in the matter.

The threat of the courtroom was dissolved by the filters of a single veil and two Vicodin. Although Ariel had not wanted to come, she felt surprisingly secure in her nest of black material and dark glasses. It allowed her to close her eyes and tumble back to a time when she was happy but didn't even know it yet. Remy was barely two, and Paul had already flown the coop. It didn't matter because she had adorable, soulful Remy. Remy, who narrated sweet magical lives for the floaty toys in the tub and made up songs about the friendship between a carrot stick and a raisin. Everyone had adored her.

And Ariel was not biased just because Remy was hers. She realized that people had a harder time learning to like Cassie, who dutifully picked up all the tub toys and placed them in the bucket. Cassie, who ate her vegetables without fanfare and put herself to bed. Cassie was a good kid, but Remy was amazing—a wondrous girl.

Someone stood up in the courtroom—the judge was leaving the bench—and Ariel immediately sensed the shift. Something changed in the air, like a front coming in from the Pacific, and suddenly, it was over. A guard emerged from the woodwork and motioned for Jared to stand. People began to talk, their voices rising like a flock of starlings lifting from a field, blocking out the sun. Reporters swooped in, buzzing flies. They stabbed the air with their microphones, ramming them toward Ariel's face, breaking the barrier of privacy.

How ironic that she had spent so much of her life eliciting this sort of attention, and now she couldn't handle it. Panic made her heart trill in her chest, and she looked to Cassie and Eli for a cue. When Eli offered her his arm, she hooked on to him and rose to her feet. She was an actress; she knew how to take direction and make an exit.

Chapter 28

Just as George Hunt had speculated, the arraignment pro-
ceedings had moved swiftly: The charges had been read, a
court date set for discovery. The lawyer had told Rachel that
nobody wanted to be in court on a Saturday, but with a high-
profile case, sometimes it was necessary. Hunt had also been
right about the outcome: Jared was being held without bail.
Rachel had been warned that the judges did not release sus-
pects like Jared, but still, when she heard the edict issued, she
burst into tears again.

And suddenly, it was over, for now.

Rachel waited in her seat, holding tight as the guard waited
for Hunt to say something to Jared. The attorney was leaning
close, his hand clamped on Jared's shoulder in a fatherly gesture.

*It should be me. I should be by his side, supporting him, reas-
suring him.*

But Jared didn't want that. She stared at the two men, hungry for answers. What had happened? What had happened to
her son, her boy, the kid who used to catch spiders in a cup
and set them free outside? For the past twenty-four hours she
had been badgering herself with these questions. She longed to
ask Jared, give him a chance to explain, but her access had
been brief, and her son had turned his back on her.

She watched with a heavy heart as the guard took Jared's

arm and led him away. Jared stared down at the floor, his shoulders slumped, his spirit broken. A sob escaped her throat as the side door closed behind Jared and the guard. He was gone. Beyond her control. Locked up beyond anyone's reach.

"Your honor, Jared Whalen confessed to killing Remy Alexander."

She had heard the prosecutor's words, but somehow she had not processed them until this moment.

"He confessed."

The cop had told her yesterday, and KJ had reiterated it last night, but Rachel had let their words slide off her, like rain off a duck. She had claimed to be waiting for an explanation, some extenuating circumstances, but now she saw the truth, bold and blinding as the sun.

He had killed her.

No wonder Jared refused to see her. There was no explanation, no circumstance that could justify killing Remy. He could not deliver the words she wanted to hear.

"All right, then." George Hunt's ruddy face appeared before her, his long whorls of eyebrows reminding Rachel of a daddy longlegs spider. "Jared says he'll see you, brother, and we have about ten minutes until he gets transported back to the jail. Come with me. What's your name again?"

"Kyle James . . . KJ. But I'm not sure this is a good idea." KJ was on his feet, glancing back at Rachel. "We need to get the hell out of here. I'll do it another time."

"It's not so easy, kid." Hunt scratched his furred cheek, annoyance flickering in his eyes. "Another meeting might take days."

"Just go," Rachel begged, rising to place a hand against KJ's smooth cheek. "Please. Tell him I love him no matter what. Even if the worst is true. Tell him I love him to the moon and back."

"Do I have to?" KJ's mouth was taut, but the soft drawl of his voice told her that he was relenting. "Fine."

As she watched him follow Hunt out of the courtroom, Rachel suddenly became aware of the attention she was getting from having talked with Jared's lawyer. The reporters were piecing together her identity. Just as she began to turn away she saw Tiffani beside the window, blatantly pointing at Rachel as she spoke to a female reporter from a TV station. The woman— Cissy something—waved at Rachel as she turned away.

"Aren't you Rachel Whalen?" a man asked. He had come out of nowhere, and he held a microphone that said KZTV.

Rachel shook her head, backing away from him. She had thought to wait here for KJ, but suddenly people were closing in on her, pressing closer. Could they smell her panic? She could imagine the footage they would run of her with her swollen, bloodshot eyes and red nose. The killer's wreck of a mother. She had wanted to wear sunglasses, but did not want to look like she was hiding something.

"Can you tell us what brought on the attack?" one woman probed.

"Was your son experiencing behavior problems at school?"

"Is it true that your son was a childhood friend of Remy Alexander?"

"Please." Rachel held up a hand to block the glaring light and their cameras. "I have nothing to say." She kept backing away, desperately wishing she could bolt out the exit, but now a crowd had amassed between her and the door. "No comment." A hard barrier behind her stopped her retreat. She'd hit the railing blocking off the front of the courtroom. She could go no farther.

"Is it true he was angry with Remy for refusing to go to prom with him?"

"That's enough, now." A low male voice came from behind her.

Mike McCabe. He stood on the other side of the railing, his face impassive, his hands on his gun belt. "Ms. Whalen is not answering questions, and I believe the bailiff is trying to clear the courtroom."

Rachel gaped up at him in relief.

He moved to the center of the rail, opened the gate, and

ushered her inside. She nearly fell against him as he took her
arm and whispered, "We're not supposed to be in here, but I
won't tell anyone if you don't." He escorted her through the
door leading to the judge's chambers in the back. It opened to
a corridor, where the bailiff sat at a desk.

"Hey, Mike. Getting kind of crazy out there?"

"It is. We're going to cut out this way to avoid the crowd. If
that's okay with you, William."

The bailiff waved them off. "Anybody asks, I never saw you."

Dazed, Rachel let herself be led down the stairs and through
a few roundabout turns that brought them to the parking lot.
She fumbled for a pocket on her green dress, then realized that
KJ had the keys.

"I feel so helpless. KJ drove me here, and he's meeting with
Jared."

"I'll take you home," he said, pointing to the row against
the wall. "I'm parked over there. Why don't you shoot him a
text. Tell him you got a ride so he doesn't worry."

"I didn't even bring my phone. My hands have been so shaky,
I didn't want anyone to see me fumbling. Besides, who would
call me now? My whole life was in that courtroom."

He handed her his cell. "Use mine."

Once inside the car she sent KJ a text, then let her head drop
against the seat. The smooth leather was a far cry from the patrol car. "Thank you for saving me. The second time, I guess."

"It was only a matter of time before the media surrounded
you. It's a big story for them."

"I know that. No one can understand why a talented, kind
teen would snap like that. All over a prom date. At least, that's
what they seem to think."

"There's more to it. There always is."

"But what? What happened? I'm his mother, dammit. I need
to know. Why did he do it? I won't be able to rest until I know
the answer to that."

"That's like asking why the sky is blue. It just is." He braked
at a stop sign, waited for a truck to pass, and then turned onto

the entry ramp for the highway. "Sometimes people do terrible things. And I'll let you in on a secret. Even when you know the reason why they do it, you don't feel any better."

"You have experience with this."

"I have a brother. Justin. Considering all the abuse he's done to himself, he should be dead. But he's still kicking around. Still out there, stealing and dealing to feed his habit."

"Meth?"

"Mostly booze. A legal high. Except in his case he's resorted to illegal activities to support his drinking. Anything to carry on the mission. I used to look up to him when I was a kid. I thought he was just the coolest dude. He had a line for everyone, and he could make people laugh. But he used that charm to get over on people. Stole from our parents. He was running a fencing operation out of our family garage." He let out a heavy breath. "Look, I'm not trying to dump on you. Though maybe I am. My point is, I know what drives him. I know he means well when he says he's sorry and he's going to pay me back the money he's borrowed or taken from me. It's the addiction—that's the beast in his soul. But even knowing that, I can't do a damned thing about it."

She rubbed her finger along the edge of the seat belt, letting it cut under her nail. A man was mowing a field with a tractor, leaving a cloud of green dust in his wake. The scent of new-cut grass and gasoline reminded her of hot summer days when the kids would dash through the sprinkler, stomping around until the lawn turned into a swamp. Back then, when Jared and KJ were kids, she knew what made them tick: their favorite foods and birthday wish lists, their strengths and weaknesses. But adolescence drove a wedge between parent and child.

"Is it wrong that I want to console him? Even if he's guilty, I'm still going to love him." Her voice broke. "I don't think Jared believes that, but it's true."

"I know. I love my brother, but we can't have a relationship while he's drinking."

She was crying now, and he reached over and rubbed her thigh, a familiar but comforting gesture.

"He's my son," she sniffed. "He'll always be my son."

There was comfort in the silence as the car sped on the freeway, winding back toward Timbergrove. By the time he pulled up in front of her house, she felt exhausted but grateful. This was not something she could discuss with the other stylists in the shop. Ariel was not returning her messages—she probably never would—and KJ was too young to understand the complexity of the situation.

"Thanks. For listening," she said.

"I think I did most of the talking."

"So, does this mean we can't see each other since you're on Jared's case? Aren't *we* a conflict of interest?"

"Just to set the record straight, I'm not working Jared's case. There's a special homicide investigator, a guy named Lou Shives, and a detective working with the prosecutor. This is not like television where a cop works on his girlfriend's case."

"But you were there yesterday, at the school."

"I'm the Timbergrove sheriff, and a crime was committed in my jurisdiction. But I wasn't the arresting officer. I'll testify if they call me, but I don't have much in the way of evidence. From here on, the case is out of my hands."

"You don't want to be involved with me," she croaked out. "After this, I'm going to be poison around here."

"Pretty poison." He tucked a lock of hair behind her ear and kissed her cheek. "I'm willing to take that chance."

Chapter 29

When Cassie answered the door Saturday afternoon, a handful of teenage girls stood on the front porch in the rain. "Hi, Cassie." Remy's friend Malika Little stood at the center of the group. With mocha skin, a willowy build, and a stud in her nose, she had an exotic look that always seemed composed. "I hope you don't mind. Some of Remy's friends wanted to come along."

"That's fine." Cassie recognized some of the faces popping from hooded jackets; some she'd seen here, hanging with Remy.

"I remember you. I'm Sophia." The ginger-haired girl with the large doll head was the obvious leader. "And this is Rosie and Tia. And Kristina brought you something."

"Well, my mom said to give your mom this." A pair of hands reached between the two girls in front and handed over a covered foil pie plate. An Asian girl with dark hair swept back from her face peeked through behind it. "It's spinach quiche."

"Thanks." Still warm, the quiche smelled good, though Cassie knew the kids wouldn't touch it if they saw the telltale green of vegetables. It would join the leagues of casseroles that had landed on the dining room table.

"We're really sorry about your sister," said one of the girls in the front, a pretty girl with blond bangs that hung in her eyes. Cassie recognized Tia from Gleetime. "Is there anything you need?"

"Like we could run errands or wash dishes," Kristina added.

"We have a dishwasher," Cassie said, staring down at the foil-covered pie pan. "But if you seriously don't mind, there's something you guys could help me with." It wasn't like she could ask them to help her figure out if her sister was haunting her or to help her look for reasons why Jared Whalen went crazy. But she could use their help de-ghosting Remy's room, which was proving to be a little overwhelming, with over a hundred glowing stars to remove from the ceiling.

The girls filed into the house, seeming nervous but eager to help. Leading the way, Cassie worried that this was a bad idea. Up close she could see their puffy eyes and shaking hands. Everybody was off-balance, on the verge of tears. If this turned into a crying fest, Cassie would have to leave the room. She was not up for a group hug. She had to keep moving, had to stay distracted by stupid trivial tasks. Upstairs, they entered Remy's bedroom with gaping mouths and wide, shiny eyes. Did they feel Remy's presence lingering here, too? Like a cool mist, it hung in the air, thick and stalled.

"What happened to her tapestries?" Malika's lower lip jutted out in a pout as she touched a blue-and-green tie-dyed print that dangled from two pushpins.

"I started taking them down. They . . ." Cassie caught herself before she said that the room gave her the creeps. Remy's friends might not understand the strong compulsion that had tugged her out of bed that morning—the urge to purge. "They remind me so much of her, and I . . . I can't handle that right now."

"This whole room reminds me of Remy, but that's a good thing, right?" Sophia picked up the bright zodiac tapestry that Cassie had folded and shook it out. "She made it pop with color and life . . . so *her*."

"Aw. I know what you mean." Tia sat on the bed and puckered her mouth, fighting tears. "I can *feel* Remy here in this room."

That's exactly my problem, Cassie thought. No way could she stay here in this shrine. Her sister's death was bad enough; right now Cassie couldn't live here surrounded by artifacts of Remy's life, by her lingering spirit.

"It's weird to be here without Remy. I'm not sure I'm feeling this, Cassie." Sophia moved toward the desk and opened Remy's laptop. "What exactly do you want us to do?" she asked as she clicked the mouse and typed on the keyboard.

"I need help with the stars." Everyone glanced up at the ceiling as Cassie explained that the fluorescent stars were keeping her up at night. "I started taking them down but there are a hundred, at least. I just can't."

"We can do that." Rosie balled up her jacket so that the wet part wouldn't drip. "It shouldn't take too long."

"Okay, but I'm hanging this up first." Sophia grabbed some pushpins from the desktop and pressed a corner of the zodiac tapestry to a bare spot of wall. "Come on, girls. Let's get this done."

Cassie bit back her objection as Sophia tacked up one corner. Cassie could undo it again later. As she took the quiche from Kristina and ran it downstairs, Cassie wondered why everyone else was so intent on preserving everything about Remy. Didn't they understand the pain that flared at the sight of constant reminders? Didn't they realize that some people needed to put the pain behind them?

When Cassie returned to the room, music rose from Remy's computer, where Sophia was bringing up playlists, trying to keep the mood chill. Rosie manned the ladder, handing flowers down to Kristina and Tia. Malika stood alone, hugging herself as she stared out the window. Did she feel the bad aura here? Cassie thought the girl was kind of brave to come here after the trauma of yesterday.

Cassie moved past the ladder and joined Malika at the window nook. "How's it going, Leeks?" she asked, feeling a surprising tenderness for her sister's friend.

"I can't stop thinking about her, Cassie." Malika's amber eyes were shadowed, haunted by the memory. "I keep going through the details in my head, spinning the scene like a bad video, playing it over and over again to see things I wish I could forget. I . . . maybe I should go. My mother told me to stay home, but I wanted to be with my friends."

"Does it help to talk about it?" Cassie asked. When Malika nodded, she said, "Then tell me again."

"We were on our way up the stairs. The first bell had already rung." Malika twirled the rings on her fingers as she spoke. Banded silver rings, some with amber and jade and moonstone. Although her narration was a bit jumpy, she was totally tuned in to the bits of conversation she had heard between Jared and Remy.

"Remy was happy to see him at first. Like, 'Hey, buddy, how's it going?' She did that teasing thing with him. Then she was all, 'You're asking me to the prom? What's your girlfriend going to think?' She said it in that sweet Remy way, but you could tell it was a little dig."

"Does Jared Whalen have a girlfriend?" Cassie asked.

"Not that any of us know." Malika shrugged. "Maybe someone from another school. I dunno. Some of the juniors in Gleetime were crushing on him this year, but he never made a move."

Aunt Rachel would know the answer to that. Cassie had wanted to talk to Rachel at the courthouse today, but that would have made Mom sizzle like an angry feline, and Cassie was not up for a catfight.

"I couldn't hear everything they said, but I got the gist of it. Remy told him she was going to prom with her girlfriends, and she was chill with that. And then he started getting upset, like, 'You gotta go with me. Seriously. For real.' "

The details held Cassie spellbound as she imagined herself watching this from the school corridor. The truth was in the details. If she could understand that moment, how things had transpired, she believed it would be easier to lay it all to rest.

"Remy stood her ground, and she told Jared that he was

really sick. Like a sicko-psycho. That made him crazy mad. He kept telling her that she had to go to prom with him. When Remy screamed, I ran upstairs to get help." Malika's lips puckered, and she pressed a hand to her mouth, trying to keep from sobbing. "I ran away. I was scared, but I should have stayed and helped her. But I ran."

"It's not your fault," Cassie said, though Malika didn't seem to hear. "You tried to help."

Lost in her own grief, Malika sobbed quietly. Cassie opened her arms for an embrace that was, surprisingly, not awkward at all. It no longer seemed to matter that these were popular girls embracing someone who had straddled the lines of geek and zero in high school. The lines of division were blurred and broken now.

Most of the stars were down in the first half hour. Noticing the playlist playing from Remy's computer, Cassie asked Sophia how she got in. "Isn't it password protected?"

"Her password is HAPPYDANCE. She uses that for everything."

"That's good to know."

Sophia swept her hair back as she tipped her moon-shaped face up to inspect the room. "Tell me you're leaving the corkboard up. Remy and I put it up together." She ran her fingers over the fake jade stones of a necklace, and then lifted a pendant depicting metal hands holding a blue stone. "You have to keep this stuff exactly as it is."

"Maybe her jewelry," Cassie said. She longed to scoop all the shiny necklaces and earrings into a bag and be done with them, but these girls would think that was irreverent.

"There are some things you just have to keep forever," Sophia said reverently.

For what? Cassie wondered. To turn the room into a memorial for Remy? A holy shrine? That seemed wrong to Cassie. To dote over the scraps of Remy's life would be a waste of time. Her instincts told her to clean house, try to move on, to donate Remy's clothes and things to someone who could use them. That was what Remy would want. She would take care of that when the girls were gone.

In the meantime, Sophia shared a few tips on how to navigate Remy's computer. She showed Cassie the folders where Remy had stored photos and videos of herself and her friends. Although the police still had Remy's cell phone, there was a ton of stuff here. While Sophia was talking with the others, Cassie found a folder marked *jared n me.* She clicked on a doc that opened up to an old junior high video of Remy and Jared in clown suits, singing and dancing to "Popular." It was riveting to see them having fun together so many years ago, but there was also something horrifying about it, and she clicked it closed before anyone noticed. From the names on the folders she realized that there were many recordings of Remy and Jared performing together. Cassie would take a closer look later.

When Sophia played the "Feelin' Groovy" video, the girls melted. There were tears and hugs as they recalled stories about little things Remy did to make them laugh or help them through a bad day. Observing from her spot on the bed, Cassie felt that familiar knot of emotion in her throat. She was starting to find that tears were contagious. Malika was sobbing while Rosie hugged her tight, and Kristina's voice broke as she finished a story. Everyone was crying, including Cassie. Farewell, Queen of Numb.

"I know what we need. Something to remember Remy by." Sophia turned to the computer once again, scrolling through the thousands of selfies Remy had downloaded. Looking back through them was like going through a timeline of Remy's high school years. Cassie allowed the girls to e-mail copies of the photos to themselves, figuring Remy would want that.

When the girls headed out, Cassie breathed a sigh of relief to be alone again, minus the drama and teen angst and high emotion. She worked voraciously then, filling a dozen grocery bags with Remy's clothes and stacking them by the door. Her schoolbooks were in a stack to go back to the school. Most of her school papers and notebooks went into the paper recycling bin, though Cassie did pull out her creative writing notebook to hang on to. Tomorrow she would tackle the junk in her closet baskets.

"Someone's been busy," Eli commented when Cassie dumped a load of papers into the recycling bin. He was sitting in a lounge chair, holding his hand behind his back.

"I've been cleaning up. And you don't have to hide the joint."

"You want?"

She shook her head. "But I could use a hand, carting this stuff down to my car."

"You're moving fast. You know, once you give her things away, there's no getting them back."

"It's now, or in a few weeks. And I don't want the task looming ahead. I'm not like my mother. I'm a doer, Eli."

"I see that."

A shriek from upstairs sent them both running inside.

Maisy and Trevor stared, horrified, at the piles of bags collected for donation.

"What are you doing with Remy's stuff?" Trevor demanded.

When Cassie explained that she was passing the clothing on to people who needed it, both children burst into tears.

"You're throwing Remy away!" Trevor accused in a sullen voice.

"But I want Remy's clothes," Maisy insisted as she plucked a tank top and a flouncy skirt from the bag and held it up to her. "I'm going to wear this stuff. I'll wear it all someday."

"No, you won't," Cassie insisted. "It will be out of style by the time you grow into it."

"I don't care."

Cassie bit back her impatience. Of course, she didn't want to throw Remy away, but it was ridiculous to hold on to her possessions. "Listen, guys, I know this is hard, but we need to clear these things out."

"No!" Maisy demanded, tears shining in her eyes.

"Why are you being so mean?" Trevor asked.

"I'm not mean, I'm practical!" Cassie insisted, but the sight of their sad eyes peering up at her broke her resolve. A sudden surge of emotion overtook her, causing her throat to thicken, her eyes to tear up. "Fine!" she roared. "Do what you want. Keep this stuff until it rots away." Throwing up her hands, Cassie stormed downstairs, took Eli's seat on the lounge chair, and began to sob. She missed her sister, she hated being the bad guy in all this, and she was furious that no one understood how she was feeling. And where was Eli now that she could really use that joint?

When the glass door slid open a few minutes later, the worst of the storm had passed. Eli shuffled out and perched on the chair beside her knees. "I told Maisy to pick out what she wants."

"None of that stuff is going to fit her for years." She sniffed. "And by then, it will look ridiculous."

He shrugged. "So you'll store it in the attic and throw it out in a few years. Let Trevor pick out some mementoes, too. No harm done."

"I was just trying to move forward," she said, her voice cracking with pathetic emotion. "I'm not going to soak in the tub and cry like Mom. I'm taking action."

"We all grieve differently. For you? You need a clean sweep. So you'll move the bags out of the house as fast as you can. You're doing the right thing, but that doesn't make it any less painful."

That night, Rachel didn't want KJ to realize she was pushing him out the door after serving him up two turkey burgers and a green salad.

"Are you sure you don't want me to stay?" he asked as she hugged him in the kitchen. She would have walked him to his car, but the news trucks parked on the street prohibited free movement in front of the house. They were waiting, watching.

"You've got your own responsibilities back at school. If you're leaving the team, you'll definitely want to keep that job through the summer. I'll be fine." *I can do this, I can do this.* "Drive safe, honey. You should be there before dark."

"Love you," he said, pulling the side door open.

"To the moon and back." Rachel closed the door behind him, bolted it, and leaned back with her eyes closed as the impact of the latest development set in.

When KJ had his ten minutes with Jared, there had been only one odd request. Jared wanted to see Ariel.

"Ariel?" Rachel had winced. "He might as well have asked to see the Pope. Or the President. Or Lady Gaga. It's not going to happen."

"I told him he was crazy, but that sort of backfired. He kept crying and begging me to talk to Ariel."

"Ariel? That's crazy. She'll never talk to him again, and I can't say that I blame her."

"Well, that's what he wants, and he held firm when I tried to talk him out of it."

"Why does he want to see her? Do you think he wants to ask for her forgiveness?"

"Who knows?"

The conversation replayed in Rachel's mind as she set to scrubbing her house. Wiping the stovetop, she tried to imagine Jared's face as he asked for Ariel. As she Swiffered the kitchen floor, she tried to imagine what Jared was thinking, where he expected his case to go.

Pausing only to send a text to Ariel, she moved upstairs to Jared's room and dusted the nearly vacant surfaces. Buffing the dresser to a high gleam and leaving a scent of lemon in her wake, she flashed back to better days when this room was inhabited by Remy and Cassie while Jared bunked in with his brother. When commercial gigs came up for Ariel, she had needed to be in the Los Angeles area for a week or so, and had relied on Rachel to watch the kids. Having a houseful, Rachel had been reminded of the big family she'd grown up in. Always someone around and underfoot. Comforting and a little crazy.

She stripped the bed, put on clean sheets, and puffed the pillows as if Jared would be returning any day. Her instincts told her no, but she could always hope.

* * *

After her prolonged cleaning spree she fell into bed and slept, with the help of some Advil PM. In the morning, the tidy, lemon-scented house made her feel more in control of her life.

I can do this.

Over coffee and whole-grain toast, she noticed that the news satellite trucks were still there, the cameramen shooting her house from the foot of the driveway. When were they going to back off? For now, she would risk attending the eight o'clock Mass. Although she wasn't up for a public appearance, she needed to be in a place of hope today.

After a quick shower she slipped on her simplest black dress, wrapped an emerald-green scarf around her neck, and checked herself in the mirror. She added her sunglasses. If she had to go in public, she would allow herself the safety of shades.

Stepping out the side door, she heard the rising voices of the reporters and neighbors assembled in the street.

"There she is!"

"It's so awful!"

Ignoring them, she turned toward the garage and stopped in her tracks. Someone had tagged the garage in red paint that read: *KILLER*.

Chapter 30

"I like this picture of Remy sitting on the kitchen counter," Maisy said. "She was so little then. Why was she sitting by the sink?"

Cassie leaned close to her sister to peer at the laptop screen. "That was in Rachel's kitchen, probably when we were staying with her. Remy was, like, five or six then. She used to hop onto the counter so she could watch the birds in the feeder outside the window."

"Aw. I want a copy of this one, too," Maisy said fondly.

"Let's put it on your list, peanut," Cassie said.

Trevor craned his neck to take a look. "I'll write it down for her." He shoved a forkful of waffle into his mouth and reached for the pen.

"Don't get syrup on the computer," Maisy said, sounding too grown-up for her years.

Cassie was relieved to have made amends with her younger siblings by offering to help them make up memory books with photos of Remy from the collection on her computer. They had spent most of Sunday morning looking through photos. Eli had made waffles with fresh blueberries, and although Trevor had gone overboard with the whipped cream, the morning had gone much better than yesterday's fiasco. After discovering the gathered clothing, Maisy had run into Mom's room to complain about Cassie, and Ariel had yelled at all three of them to leave her alone. That had subdued Maisy quickly, and Cassie had found herself hugging and consoling Trevor and Maisy. Ariel's outburst had reminded Cassie that she needed to be here for her siblings right now.

The photo project was a good diversion, though Cassie was careful to keep the kids away from some of the files on Remy's computer. In a folder marked *secrets,* Cassie had discovered a collection of odd images that she still hadn't had a chance to sort through. With Remy's habit of documenting her life through selfies, her archives were extensive.

"Do we get to miss school this week?" Trevor asked. "Chance Hamilton got to miss two weeks when his mother died."

"That's nuts. Besides, don't you want to go to school and be with your friends? It'll get kind of boring, hanging around here." Cassie thought it would be good for them to stick to the routine and be around friends. Besides, she needed some time to sort things out on her own.

"But I don't want to go to school," Trevor complained. "Kids will be staring at me and asking me questions."

"You don't have to tell anyone anything," Cassie said. "Remember what we talked about with the photos? You have to take your memories and hold them in your heart."

He shook his head. "I'm never going back."

Never say never, she thought as the phone rang.

Five minutes later, Cassie headed upstairs to roust Ariel from her cocoon. The bed was an island of twisted sheets and deflated, tousled pillows.

"Mom, you need to get up. The detective working on Remy's case called and he's coming over to talk with you."

"What?" The mound in the sheets moved slightly. "Who's coming over?"

"Detective Shives. He's coming over to return Remy's stuff." Her *personal effects,* the detective had said on the phone, sounding like a caricature from a crime show.

"Can't you take her things? Tell Eli to talk to him," Ariel muttered into the mattress.

"He needs to talk to you. You're her mother." Her next of kin.

"I can't get out of this bed."

"You have to. It's not just this, Mom. The kids need you. And there's a vigil for Remy tonight down by the school."

"I'm not going."

"Well, I am. And I'm taking Trevor and Maisy. Eli thinks it will be good for them." Cassie moved toward the bedside, flinching as she stepped on pills scattered on the carpet. "God, Mom." She wanted to tell Ariel to pull herself together before she killed herself and traumatized Maisy and Trevor for life. But they had been down that road before, and right now any lecturing from Cassie would not penetrate Ariel's coma.

"Come on." She had to yank on the sheet to tug it loose, but finally she had unsheathed her mother's head and shoulders. Thank God Ariel was wearing a nightgown. "Do you want a bath or shower?"

"Go away."

Cassie pulled the sheet off completely, then slid Ariel's feet off the mattress so that they hovered over the floor. "Bath or shower?"

"I hate this," Ariel hissed.

"I hate it more."

Ariel sat up with a groan, then rose unsteadily. Cassie put a hand around her waist and guided her into the master bathroom. The shower seemed like a safer bet, so Cassie got the water started and left the room when Ariel felt her way into the tiled stall.

One bottle was empty, turned on its side, but Cassie snatched up the long-neck bottle of whiskey, then put it down again so that she could gather the scattered pills. She had to pick them out of the shag carpet, and she dropped them back into the container, fuzz and all. Whiskey and pills in hand, she tromped down the stairs to the kitchen, where Eli was scrubbing the griddle from breakfast.

"These were on her nightstand. She may have more hidden up there."

"Thanks, doll." Extracting one sudsy hand from the sink, Eli picked up the pill bottle and frowned. "These things are toxic. She'll do better once the system clears out."

Cassie had her doubts; she'd been through this with Ariel before. But this time, she realized she could lean on Eli. Kooky, psychedelic Eli. Underneath his eccentric veneer, he was solid as a rock.

After her outburst with the police Friday night, Rachel felt a little sheepish calling them to her rescue Sunday morning. But beneath the simple malice of the vandalism she perceived an underlying threat, and she was concerned that the culprit was angry enough to encroach on her property and paint a vile message nearly under her bedroom window.

Fortunately, Mike was one of the occupants of the two police cars that arrived, splitting the crowd of reporters and neighbors nearly simultaneously in a dramatic display that could have been featured on reality TV.

The other officer, an African-American woman with a soft voice but a stern demeanor, let Mike take the lead.

"Are you okay?" Mike asked first. When she nodded he asked if there'd been any other damage, any sign of a break-in. "Any idea who might have done it?"

Rachel glanced toward the street, where one reporter was talking in front of the camera and the other was calling her over while neighbors and steely-eyed strangers pointed and gawked. "It could be anyone in Timbergrove."

As they spoke the side door of the house next door opened and her neighbor Valeria crossed the driveway.

"This is terrible," she said as she joined the group. With thick, dark hair down to her waist and a petite body, Valeria Calo always seemed more like a child than a suburban mother of two. "I'm so sorry," she said, shaking her head at the sign. "Anything I can do to help you out, let me know."

Rachel was overcome for a moment by the kind gesture, the first from her community. Swallowing over the knot in her throat, she thanked Valeria, who was watching her own side door like a hawk. When it popped open and a little head peered out, she ordered, "Stay inside. I'll be right there." Turning back to Rachel, she added, "I'm serious. Just give a holler."

While Officer Willis took information for the police report, Mike circled the house, checking the windows. "No signs of forced entry," he said when he returned. "Looks like the goal was to tag your garage."

"The way they painted it in red, with dripping paint." Rachel turned away from the graffiti. "It looks like blood."

"That was probably the effect they were going for," Mike agreed.

"I have everything I need," the officer said. She told Rachel to call if she had any other concerns. Rachel took her card, thinking that she had a thousand concerns, but none that could be solved by the police.

As Willis headed back to her patrol car, Mike nodded at the garage. "I've got a buddy who paints houses. Maybe you want to call him, see if he can come out."

They went inside to get "offstage" as Mike put it, and Mike put her through to his friend Marcos, who promised to be there in a flash. "I'll have the door at least covered with primer by this afternoon," he promised.

After she ended the call, Mike took her hand in his big mitts, his eyes searching hers. "How are you holding up?"

"I've been keeping a low profile, but I was trying to get to Mass. I can't let those people out there keep me from church. I don't know what it is, but the sameness of the prayers, the tranquility there, it's reassuring."

"Then you'd better go. Or is it too late?"

Drawing in a breath, she checked the kitchen clock. "I can make the twelve fifteen."

He opened his arms and she fell against his chest, grateful for the security of his embrace, never wanting to leave his arms. "I'm going to talk to some of the reporters out there about backing off. Jazz Milkin is a good guy; he'll understand. You shouldn't be victimized."

With a promise to check on her later, he left, and Rachel followed him out the door. He corralled the crowd at the foot of the driveway, clearing a space for her to ease her car out and head off to church.

She parked on the street, avoiding the congestion of the parking lot for a quick escape. In the church vestibule she paused, dipped her fingertips in the holy water, and made the sign of the cross.

"That's her." A raspy voice echoed through the entryway. "Her son . . ." came the whisper. "He was the prom killer."

The prom killer. What a dynamite headline. Now Jared would be notorious for killing a girl and ruining the entire school's prom night. *He hath murdered prom,* she thought, hearing the rasping voice of an Elizabethan player. Even if the tides turned and it was discovered that Jared was innocent, he would loom large as a scourge upon this town.

Trying to put distance between herself and the gossip, she moved quickly down the aisle, genuflected, and took a seat at the end of the pew. But it wasn't long before other voices cut through the low organ music.

"What kind of kid carries a carving knife around?"

A kid who sells them to make money for college.

"He's just damaged. A bloodthirsty animal."

He's a teenage boy who wants to apologize to Remy's mother.

She wanted to turn around and snap at them that her son did have a conscience. He did not plan to ruin the entire school's prom. And he did not mean to hurt anyone.

Dear God, she prayed, *let that be true.*

Showered and bolstered with makeup, Ariel found that she could strike the right balance with the cops: cordial and polite, but not afraid to reveal her wounds, her fragile state of grief. It was simply another role to play.

"Did you bring Remy's cell phone?" Cassie asked, breaking Ariel's concentration.

Ariel did not like having Cassie in the scene. Too unreliable, always forgetting her lines.

"My sister had a lot of photos on her phone," Cassie said. "Pictures we'd like to have."

The uniformed officer, a youngish African-American man, held up a paper bag. "We've got it here. We'll leave these things here with you."

"But first, we just have a few questions," Detective Shives said, his authoritative tone preventing Cassie from rifling through the bag.

Ariel liked a strong-willed man. He wouldn't be her first bald man, either. What was that saying? *God made only a few perfect heads. The others He covered with hair.*

"Was your daughter Remy dating Jared Whalen?" asked the detective.

"No, she was not." Ariel firmed her lips in a stoic look.

"So they were friends?" Shives persisted. "The reason I ask is, Jared was seen leaving this house at night."

"Oh. That." Ariel swatted away the concern. "Jared was here for voice lessons. I'm the voice coach for all the high school singers in Gleetime."

"Is that so?" Shives's brows rose.

Ariel knew he was impressed.

"And what about Cooper Dover? Did Remy date him?"

"They dated off and on," Ariel said, feeling foggy again.

"It's more complicated than that," Cassie said. "They were supposed to go to prom together, but Remy changed her mind. She wanted to go with her girlfriends. So she broke up with Cooper, and he couldn't get over it. He was pretty mad at her." Then Cassie went babbling on about some prank Cooper had done to get Remy back. Yadda, yadda, yah.

"Mrs. Alexander—"

"You can call me Ariel."

"Ariel. We have a few photos here that we captured from your daughter's cell phone." He handed her some large photos, magnified, like inflated beach toys.

Something pinched deep in her belly at the sight of the glimmering shards of glass, remnants of the crystal vase that had once sat on her piano. Rose petals were scattered amid the debris, along with the stems of the torn flowers. "Oh, that." She tried to downplay it. "That was a vase in my studio that broke one afternoon. I left the glass on the floor because I was in a rush to get back to the Gleetime rehearsal."

"But Remy was really scared by it," Cassie piped up. "I know. She texted me."

Little Miss Know-it-all.

"Who broke the vase?" asked Shives.

"A student." Ariel's heart was drumming in her chest, but she tried to cover up. Acting.

"Remy seemed to think the vase was broken by Nick Anastasio."

"How could . . ." Ariel struggled to keep her cool as a bead of sweat trickled between her breasts. "How do you know that?"

"It's in her text messages to Cassie, here." Shives drummed his fingers on the kitchen island, and suddenly Ariel saw him for who he was: a fidgety tight-ass. He would never be her boyfriend.

"There's a police report of a domestic dispute at this address a few weeks ago. You were the complainant, Ms.—sorry. Ariel. Based on that incident, we know Anastasio has displayed violent behavior. And Remy's text message states that Anastasio was back in town. It seems that Remy felt threatened by him."

"I'm telling you, the vase was an accident," Ariel insisted.

"Did Anastasio break that vase and threaten your daughter?"

"No!" Ariel clapped her hands over her ears. "I can't believe I'm hearing this. I lost my daughter. Jared Whalen killed my little girl, and you come in here and accuse me of, what? Dating a man with a temper, weeks ago?"

"We're not trying to upset you, Ariel, but we need to know your most recent association with Anastasio."

"He's long gone," she insisted. A lie, but they wouldn't know that he'd called her a few times since it happened "The vase was an accident; I'm sorry Remy misconstrued it. What has that got to do with my daughter's murder?"

"We want to be sure Jared Whalen acted alone."

Ariel began crying, real tears. It wasn't difficult with pain so close to the surface.

That did it. The police thanked her and left. And scene.

Chapter 31

When Rachel returned home from Mass, the sick feeling lifted slightly as she turned on her street and found that the news trucks were gone, the crowd dissipated. Mike had truly taken care of it, or else the reporters had realized there would be nothing else to see, no one to talk to. She imagined that they would run footage of her garage with the gory graffiti. That should tide viewers over for a while. It was exactly the reason she had avoided news broadcasts and social media in the past two days.

Marcos's van was parked in front of the house, and the painter was just finishing up a primer coat, rendering the graffiti invisible under a large white square of paint. Rachel thanked him, and he told her he would send his crew back the following day to finish the job.

With a clean house and the afternoon looming ahead, Rachel couldn't help but think about Jared. Somehow, if he would let her in, confide in her, she would be able to help him. She knew she could do it. But he had to let her in.

And he was asking for Ariel.

Such an impossible task. But Rachel had to make it happen. If she could bring Ariel to Jared, it would be the first step toward getting him to let Rachel help him.

Sitting in front of the television while actors went through the paces in an old romantic comedy, she noodled around composing a letter to Ariel. It would have to appeal more to Ariel's sense of friendship than her weak maternal instincts. At first Rachel struck out everything she came up with. Too trite. Too bold. Too whiny. But what was the correct tone for apologizing to your best friend for something like this?

When she finally came up with two paragraphs, she printed the page but left it on the coffee table to mull over. Knowing Ariel, she would probably just rip the letter into little pieces and blow it into the air like confetti.

As darkness came over the house, she changed into her tights and a T-shirt. She would go for a run. Under the cover of darkness she would be able to move through town with relative anonymity. She laced up her sneakers and headed out the side door. This time, she would stay off the isolated path and keep to the streets.

The cooler evening air eased the tight bands of repression—all the hours of holding in her feelings. Pumping her legs, she flew down the street and mounted the hill, moving into the street to cut around an elderly couple—not the kind of people who were usually out after dark.

As she jogged up the hill she passed other people carrying flashlights or lanterns. It wasn't until she crested the hill that overlooked the school that she saw the conflagration of lights—dots of white floating around the school like fireflies in a jar. Her footsteps slowly dissolved until she stood there, staring down into the bowl of the little valley drawing shape from the light of the half moon. The lights and electric candles were held by people of all ages. Little children raced through the gathering crowd, making some of the lights zigzag in the darkness below.

It was some kind of vigil, no doubt a service for Remy, and there seemed to be hundreds of people gathering. For a moment she stared, mesmerized, longing to join her community in grieving for the loss of a generous, talented young woman. She should be down there, telling stories about Remy and crying, arm in arm with her neighbors.

That was not going to happen.

Deciding to cut away from school and run toward town, she turned back and started down the hill. She passed people headed to the memorial, disks of light bobbing over the ground as they swung their arms. She stepped off the sidewalk to avoid running into two women pushing a stroller. That sent her stomping over the lawn of the park just as a couple hurried around the fountain, stepping into her path.

Letting out a yelp, she scrambled to a stop, the sleeve of her jacket grazing the woman, who was older than she'd seemed at first. Was it . . . ? She glanced back.

Yup. Tootsie Dover, with her son, Cooper. Headed toward the vigil, of course. She turned away, hoping to go unrecognized. No such luck.

"You!" Tootsie looked ghoulish in the glow of the lantern held under her chin as she marched over to Rachel. "You desperate bitch. You told the police terrible things about my Cooper."

Rachel reared back as if she'd been physically assaulted. "I—I only told the truth."

"According to you! And we know that you'll do anything to get your son out of jail. But to stoop so low as to make up lies about my Cooper! That's unforgivable."

"That's me," Rachel said under her breath. "The unforgivable."

"What? What are you muttering?" Tootsie demanded.

"I told the truth. Cooper, here, was organizing kids against Remy. He was targeting her, weren't you, Cooper?" She looked to him for confirmation, but he remained pale and silent.

"That's total nonsense. My boy loved Remy. He adored her."

"Your *boy* was pressuring her into getting back with him."

"You're talking about adolescent angst." Tootsie let out a huff of breath. "It's no reason to send the cops to our place. Unlike you, I don't enjoy having the police in my living room, and I don't like them grilling my son."

Welcome to my world, Rachel thought.

"I won't have it. You put them onto us; you call them off."

"The cat's out of the bag," Rachel said. "But don't worry. Cooper has nothing to fear if he did nothing wrong."

That made Cooper squirm.

"That's it!" Tootsie hissed between her teeth. "I am through with you. Finito! You've just lost one of your best clients."

"Pity to lose such a sour lush. How will I fill my days?" Rachel mused quietly.

"What did you say?" Tootsie lunged toward her.

"Mom." A subdued Cooper pulled his mother back. "Come on. Let's go."

As the Dovers walked away, Rachel felt a burden lift. She should have dropped Tootsie long ago. "And by the way," she shouted after them, "you're a rotten tipper."

Tootsie turned back in a fit, but Cooper kept tugging her forward. Hands on her hips, Rachel watched them go, grateful to be done with Tootsie Dover. Who needed that negative karma?

Rachel crossed the little park on the ridge in search of a vantage point and decided on the purple-and-red slide. She climbed to the top and wedged herself in between the guardrails. Below, hundreds of voices joined in singing "Amazing Grace." The song made her heart ache, though it seemed fitting for Remy, a girl with that rare balance in a world of extremes.

Hunkered down at the top of the slide, Rachel watched through a blur of tears. As the lights swirled and twinkled, assembling into a beautiful glow down by the school, she said a prayer for Remy's sparkling spirit. Long live that joy.

"Why do you think the police asked about Stosh?" Cassie was talking on the landline with Andrew late that night as, cell phone in hand, she scrolled back through messages she had gotten from Remy.

"Well..." Andrew drew the word out. She imagined those crinkly lines forming between his brows as he gave it some thought. God, she missed him. "They found reference to him in Remy's cell phone, right? They picked up on Remy's perception of Stosh as a threat. They're just following through on that possibility."

"You're so logical. That's what we need around here. Everyone else is blinded by emotion."

"I suspect this is a very emotional time."

"Yeah, I keep losing it. Every time I cry, the raw edges feel so close to the surface. It feels real now." She hated losing control, especially in front of the kids, but there was no denying that each little breakdown brought some relief. "There was a lot of crying going on at the vigil. It's kind of contagious."

"Aw. Babe, I wish I could be there for you. Are you sure you don't want me to come up?"

"Not now. You can't miss your summer classes. Maybe Thursday night, for the weekend."

"I'll plan on that."

"Then you can be here for the funeral. Or life celebration. However you want to look at it."

"Are you sure you don't want me to drive up? I'm looking at my car keys now. I have gas in my tank."

"No." She did want him to come, but it would be wrong to wreck his summer term. Andrew's classes were intense and demanding, and she wasn't going to suck up his time and energy by making him drive four hours round trip. "Anyway. Back to Stosh. Remy was sure he was the one that broke the vase. What if Mom is covering for him?"

"Covering for him, as in, he killed Remy?"

"Yes! No. I don't know. There's just something stinking false about that broken vase. It did not happen by accident during a lesson, I can promise you that. I can tell when Mom is lying, and she was telling the cops a whopper."

"Is there a way that Stosh could have killed Remy and made it look like Jared was guilty?" asked Andrew.

For a moment Cassie let herself pursue the fantasy. It would be wonderful to see Jared vindicated, released from jail, saved from the hell of life in prison. It would be a huge relief to know that brother hadn't turned against sister. But the reality painted a different picture. "The evidence against Jared is so strong," she said.

"He was there in the stairwell, but what if someone else killed her and he stumbled upon the scene?" Andrew suggested.

"He was covered with blood."

"As he would be if he tried to stop the bleeding."

"And his knife was used to cut her."

"Someone could have stolen it from him."

"You are so brilliant," she breathed. "I'll bet the police are thinking the same thing. That's why they wanted to talk to Mom."

"Did you find anything pertinent on Remy's cell phone?"

"Not really, but I downloaded all of her recent photos to her laptop. I spent part of the afternoon going through a file called *secrets*. Some of the shots are goofy mistakes. A few of them show the ceiling, cut-off hands, photo bombs. Ariel is in a lot of them. Sometimes she's posing with Gleetime kids, and a few of them show boys grabbing her ass."

"Really? That's kind of sick."

"I told you. No boundaries. An even bigger *eeew* factor because Mom seems to like it. A lot of the photos are just silly. They show Remy having a bad-hair day, and there are a few where she and her friends have blacked-out teeth."

"Weird. I wonder why Remy bothered to keep all those pictures," he said.

"I know. You'd think she would delete them right away. Instead, she kept them all. Hundreds. It's going to take me awhile to go through all of them."

"Well," he said in that low, logical voice. "There's a reason for everything. We just need to discover it."

Chapter 32

Rock music poured out of Holy Snips when Rachel opened the door Monday morning and stepped into cool air. It was Sondra's morning to open, and her usual ritual was to put on a pot of coffee and crank up the music.

"Good morning," Rachel called, and heard a blurred response from the break room.

At the reception desk, Rachel hit the message button on the answering machine while she opened her appointment book. She had a fairly full schedule today. Good. That made it worth dragging herself in. But as the messages played, she saw a pattern.

Her customers were canceling.

"This is China Kenyon. Just calling to say that something's come up, so I won't be able to make my two o'clock with Rachel."

"I'm calling to cancel my appointment with Rachel. I'll call back to reschedule. . . ."

By the end of the messages, more than half of today's appointments had canceled.

"Dammit." No big surprise, but somehow she had expected more from her clients. She found Sondra in the break room, rummaging through the fridge. Today Sondra's hair was the color of a copper penny, tied off into low pigtails like a junior high cheerleader. "How's that coffee coming along? I desperately need it."

"It's brewing, but there's no milk or creamer." Sondra looked up from the fridge. "Oh, Rachel. I didn't think it was you. How's it going?" She shook her head and slammed the refrigerator door. "Bad question. But what should I say? How ya holding up?"

"I'm trying to keep my head up. I just keep telling myself that I can do it. Whatever 'it' might be." Rachel shook her head, feeling the sting of tears. "My kid . . . he's got a long road ahead of him."

"I know, honey." Sondra opened her arms and enveloped Rachel in a hug. "Come hell or high water, he's still your son."

A sob escaped Rachel's throat at the truth in Sondra's words. Why didn't the rest of the world get that? Grateful, she patted Sondra's shoulder. "I'll probably be working the rest of my life to pay for his defense. Guess that's just how it goes."

"You do what you gotta do."

"True. The problem is, I don't know what that is." Besides coaxing Ariel to see Jared. She had tried to put that heinous task out of her head, probably because she saw no way to make it happen.

"Well, you're a trouper," Sondra said. "I sure didn't expect to see you here today."

"I didn't want to let my customers down again," Rachel said, swiping tears from her eyes. "Although half of them wouldn't have cared. I've got a ton of cancellations."

"Yeah, people are hinky. They think it might be awkward with you."

"Or they blame me for what my son might have done."

"Yeah, that, too." Sondra let out a sigh. "Not to kick you when you're down, but I'm afraid I've got more bad news. Tiffani cleared out her stuff on Saturday."

"What?" Rachel ducked out of the break room to examine Tiffani's corner. Sure enough, the counter was empty, the cupboards bare. "Wow." She sat down in the client chair and patted the armrests. "This may be the first time Tiffani has ever cleaned up after herself."

Sondra snickered. "Funny and true."

Rachel squinted. "Is she planning to rent that place across the square?"

"That's her story. Said she's going have all new stuff. She's sick of working around old things."

"And was she referring to the furniture or the people?" Rachel asked wryly.

"You haven't lost your sense of humor. I'd be so pissed off. Some people don't have a loyal bone in their body."

"Honestly, I'm relieved to have Tiff out of here. Let her stir up trouble across the square or in someone else's shop. And I'm grateful to have the support of people like you."

Sondra looked up at the clock. "I've got a client in five minutes. Do you mind watching the shop while I grab some creamer?"

"I'll go. I wanted to get a latte, anyway."

Grabbing her purse, Rachel stepped back into the sunshine, heading to the coffee shop as if the day were like any other. It was going to be a hot one. Except that she was sick to her stomach, sleep deprived, and trembling. Beads of sweat formed on her upper lip, more from her own nervousness than the heat. As she walked she considered going to Ariel's house. Cassie had to be there. Cassie would let her in, wouldn't she?

Inside the coffee shop, the familiar rich coffee smells and the buzz of conversation restored her sense of hope. But as she stepped into line, the barista stiffened. Conversation became strained before it dropped off as people in line glanced back and recognized Rachel.

The killer's mother has arrived, Rachel wanted to say.

Perspiration misted up Rachel's glasses, temporarily clouding her vision. When they cleared, she recognized familiar faces. Two of the women in line were Gleetime moms—Nan Lee and Patti Cronin—but they whispered to each other, refusing to acknowledge her.

A handful of teenage girls at a nearby table stared and whispered. Of course. The high school was closed today. Rachel recognized one of the girls from doing her hair for prom. Aubrey something.

In another life, that girl might have dated Jared. In this world, she would be reading about his sentence on social media.

Rachel's hand shook as she tried to swipe her credit card. Desperate to get out of there, she held the half-and-half and to-go cup to her chest and strode out the door. Back at the shop she bypassed Sondra and her client, shoved the creamer in the fridge, and escaped. Her hands were still trembling as she drove home, as she drove through a stop sign, as she parked in the driveway and put her head down on the steering wheel.

She couldn't bear to go into the empty house. She had to see Ariel. Now. Right now; everything was riding on that.

Ariel, Ariel. I never could rely on you, but you've got to come through for me now.

Fumbling with her keys, she left the coffee and got out of the car. She would walk to Ariel's house, braving the stares of neighbors and people passing by.

Her walk of shame.

Rachel forced herself to move forward through the oven air of an eighty-degree day, taking the familiar route to Ariel's house. One step at a time. The day felt ripe and rotten, far too hot for May. Sunlight warmed her shoulders, but not enough to melt the disgrace locked in her muscles. The air was thick with pollen kicked up by the breeze, a mixture of sweet honeysuckle and sour criticism from the eyes of the watchers.

Although the street seemed quiet, Rachel knew they were there.

Ginny Newkirk, strapping the kids into their car seats. Probably dumping them at day care so she could have a spa day in Portland.

Mrs. Abduljuwad, staring from her garden of spring tulips. She had a green thumb, and a husband who'd been hauled off for sexual abuse of their granddaughters.

Mother-of-the-year Angela Harrell peered between slats of the plantation shutters. Probably looking for someone new to castrate when her youngest headed off to college in the fall.

And there was Walt Finley, owner of the hardware store, sitting on his porch rocker, his bum leg stretched out as he hid behind the headlines of today's paper. Everyone knew that was not coffee in his travel mug.

They watched. They sniffed for news. They knew Rachel's shame, her horror, her secrets unmasked. She knew these neighbors had secrets of their own, but none could come close to the horror that had emerged from the once-pretty closet of her life three days ago.

The walk was laborious, a lead-footed exercise, an unwanted public spectacle, but she didn't trust herself to drive. Too much stress, too little sleep, her mind pinned down under the weight of an elephant. All these evils combined to form a surreal frame of mind, a stiff zombie walk. She plodded past a median strip chockful of color: pink impatiens punctuated by heavy-headed red tulips. A basket brimming over with purple pansies and yellow petunias hung from the old-fashioned lamppost. From her vantage point on the corner, she could see similar bursts of colored baskets hanging from every light post in sight, neat and orderly and utterly charming. The town of Timbergrove knew how to get it right. A suburban haven.

Too bad it was populated by snakes.

"We find that many family members want an open casket. Oftentimes it helps advance the grieving process." The funeral director spoke in a hushed voice that spooked Cassie, making her want to dance through this sleepy office and shout, "Some of us are still alive!"

"We are definitely having a closed casket," Eli said with surprising authority. "Honestly, Chuck, if it were my choice I would have her cremated and simply hold a celebration of her life. But her mother won't allow that."

Cassie had overheard that discussion between Eli and Ariel.

Eli had advocated cremation, but Mom had freaked out at the thought of it. Something about the fires of hell. In her weakened state, Ariel got freaked out by a lot of stuff.

"So we're going with a closed casket," Chuck confirmed. Eli had befriended the guy, chatting him up about the sixties and draft dodging. Apparently, Chuck was a lot cooler back then. "We'll go with the simple gray box you picked out. We'll do the ceremony at the Unitarian Church. It seats eight hundred people. That ought to give all the high school kids and whatnot a chance to say good-bye."

Since they had entered the funeral parlor, a floral-scented house that looked like it was stuck in an old television show, Eli had totally stepped up to handle the details. But even before today he had been on the phone many times with the medical examiner, trying to get them to release Remy's body. Eli kept saying that a funeral was a part of the healing. Cassie didn't really see that, but she would be glad to have it behind her.

"All right, then." The funeral director looked up with his stoic expression. "There's just the matter of clothing for the deceased. Did you bring a dress?"

Cassie handed over a paper bag, watching as the man lifted out a pair of fleece pjs.

"Pajamas." There was a tired patience in his voice. "Most people want their loved ones buried in nice clothes. A pretty blouse. Maybe a formal gown or prom dress. Something nice."

"I want my sister to go out in comfort." Remy had loved those pjs. It had been the first item of clothing to come to mind when Eli had asked her to find something.

"I understand, but maybe she'd be better off in a—"

"Use the pajamas already," Eli barked, and the man nodded solemnly.

As the two men discussed the contract, Cassie felt a new glow of protection over her shoulders. For the first time since Remy was killed, Cassie felt like someone had her back.

On the way home, Cassie kept her eyes on the road as Eli sighed into the seat. "We're doing our best for her, Cassie. That's all we can do."

She stole a look at him: the owlish glasses, the long gray hair, the love beads. This man who wasn't even her grandfather, no relation to Remy, either, had proven to be their hero.

"Do you remember after Oliver died?" she asked. "We wanted you to stay but you left soon after the funeral."

He nodded. "Those were sad days, too, but a different shade of sorrow. You kids were sweet, but your mom wanted me out of her hair. I think I was cramping her style."

"This time, don't listen to her," she said. "This time, I hope you stay."

Rachel sat on the stoop in front of Ariel's house, mulling over a plan as she willed her friend to open the door and let her in. Didn't fifteen years of friendship account for anything?

Apparently not in Ariel's book.

However, there had been times over the years when she'd had to help Ariel adjust her moral compass. When she'd had to insist that her friend repay a loan. When Rachel had argued that it was wrong to take money for sex, even if the millionaire on the other end was perfectly fine with forking over for the "widows and orphans" fund. And there had been that time, after Oliver had died, when Ariel had returned from working in Los Angeles and wanted Rachel to keep her kids indefinitely. That was not going to happen.

So maybe this was one of those times; it was up to Rachel to show Ariel how to do the right thing. She brushed the dust from her dress and headed over to the studio door. Rachel knew where the spare key was.

She was going in.

The air in the studio was stuffy and it smelled of dust and sorrow. Rachel put the key back in the vestibule and pushed through into the house.

"Ariel? Where the hell are you?" There was no sign of Cassie and the kids, which was perhaps all for the best. Getting Ariel to the county jail was her focus right now.

Swallowing back any reservation, Rachel climbed the stairs and began to detect the smoky smell of burning weed. She followed the scent to the master bathroom, where Ariel sat on the edge of the large Jacuzzi tub, blowing smoke out the open window.

For all that Ariel had endured, she still looked pretty darned good. Her hair fell around her face, straight and unkempt, but giving her that disheveled chic seen in fashion magazines. Even in gray sweatpants and a T-shirt her bombshell of a body was apparent. She simply looked rattled, a little teary, like someone who had witnessed an accident.

"I am so sorry." Rachel realized that was an admission of guilt, but she didn't know where else to begin.

"You didn't do anything to be sorry for." Ariel turned the joint in her hand but didn't offer it to Rachel. That was all for the best, as the last thing Rachel needed right now was to further splinter her disjointed sense of reality.

"Well, I'm sorry about Remy. Devastated." She stepped closer, but Ariel still did not look her in the eye. "She was such a good kid. So loving and . . . and loved by everyone."

Ariel took another drag, breathing in deeply as the house stirred to life downstairs.

Someone else was here.

"Who's that?" Rachel asked.

"My boyfriend."

Moving tentatively down the stairs, Rachel saw Cassie and Ariel's father-in-law, Eli, in the kitchen.

"Hey, there. You startled me." She embraced Cassie in a tentative hug and nodded to Eli. Cassie, who hugged her back, did not seem surprised to see her.

"I'm sorry about Remy," Rachel said, fighting the knot of emotion in her throat. "So sorry."

Eyes averted, Cassie nodded. "Is the queen holding court?" she asked. "Or is she still talking gibberish?"

"I'm trying to talk with her," Rachel said.

"Yeah. Good luck with that."

"I have something really important to ask her." Rachel took Cassie's hand. "Come with?"

Cassie rolled her eyes but followed Rachel up the stairs.

Back in the master bathroom, Ariel sat in the same spot, hunched over like a wounded bird.

"Smoking weed now, Mom? Really?" Cassie picked up the burning stub of the joint from the edge of the tub and ran water over it to dowse the smoke. "Well, I guess it's better than whiskey and Oxy."

A toxic combination. It was a wonder Ariel was conscious at all. "At least weed won't kill you," Rachel said, trying to sound sympathetic. Her pulse thrummed with anxiety at being here, and she kept reminding herself that she had come for Jared. Circling Ariel as if the woman might flee like a wild animal, Rachel moved to the opposite end of the empty tub and perched there. "This has been a nightmare for all of us. I never expected this... any of this, especially since Remy and Jared were a couple."

Ariel didn't look up but her head jerked up and froze.

"That's not what I heard," Cassie said slowly.

"They kept it hidden," Rachel went on, "probably to avoid trouble with Cooper, but when I saw him leaving here late one night, and I realized they were together, I was thrilled. I wanted to tell you, but Jared made me promise to keep their secret. That's why I still find it hard to believe that Jared snapped. It's so hard to believe, so hard to accept. I need to know why."

As if she were alone in the room, Ariel yawned and lay down on the lip between window and tub. Resting there with her eyes closed, she looked gray and waxen.

"Ariel, I need your help." Rachel's nails dug into her palms as she pressed on. "Jared refuses to see me, and he's not cooperating with his lawyer. He won't talk to anyone but you."

Her eyes flew open, and Rachel felt as if she'd just awakened the dead.

"I'll drive you there," Rachel offered. "Right now, if you want. If you'll talk with him, tell him to let us help him... It's the only way that he'll get through this with his life. The thing is, I think he wants to ask your forgiveness. That's the first step toward dealing with all of this."

"You should go." Cassie spoke up at last, God bless her.

"He probably wants to apologize. That might help you, Mom. You should go talk to Jared."

"No."

The word came so suddenly, Rachel was sure she had misunderstood. "It doesn't have to be now. Maybe later today, if that's better for you. Give yourself some time to come down."

"No." Ariel lifted one arm over her eyes and sobbed. "I'll never do that, so stop begging me. Just stop it right now. He's the last person I want to see." She sat up and faced Rachel for the first time. And just like that, her mood flipped. A hollow smile replaced her somber expression. "But you, you're still my friend. Forever and always."

The dead stare in her eyes chilled Rachel to the bone.

Chapter 33

Cassie wished that Rachel had stayed.

While she had no patience for Ariel's depression, Cassie worried about what would happen to Rachel with her trembling hands, red eyes, and sloping shoulders. With KJ at school, Rachel had no one. Cassie longed to hold Rachel in her arms and rub her back and tell her that everything would be okay, which was a total lie, of course. It was strange that Cassie cared about Rachel after what Jared had done. It didn't make any sense, but you couldn't help how you felt.

After Rachel lammed out, Cassie was left to mull over what Rachel had said about Jared and Remy being a couple. That was news to Cassie, and it didn't match the bits of conversation that took place before he killed her. Besides, Remy would have told her if she had a thing for Jared; that would have been big news.

Cassie opened Remy's computer and continued to sift through the *"secrets"* folder. Today she focused on photos of Remy with Jared, which were sparse but for some Gleetime photos and a few old shots from when they were kids on family outings. The Jared thing didn't make sense. If Remy was seeing him, she would have had a bazillion pictures of Jared and her on her phone. Which she didn't.

Remy's most recent photos showed her with a football-player type, a dark-skinned guy with broad shoulders and a winning smile. From the school yearbook Cassie had learned that he was Isaiah Denton, a football player and performer in Gleetime. Apparently, they hadn't come out as a couple, but it made sense for them to keep things quiet with Cooper Dover still smarting. Cassie suspected that Isaiah was the guy who had come over to help her feel safe the night Remy found the smashed vase. Probably. Knowing that Remy was fiercely loyal— she never dated more than one guy at a time—Cassie surmised that Isaiah was the new boyfriend.

Not Jared. Rachel meant well, but she was wrong about Remy and Jared. Cassie would hit Rachel with that news. But first, it was about time that Ariel did something to pull herself out of this funk.

Cassie closed the computer and pushed her way into Ariel's room without knocking. Ariel was curled up on the unmade bed, twisting a strand of hair around and around her fingers.

"It's time to get dressed." Cassie went to the open closet and pulled a black-and-white print dress from its hanger. "I'll drive you over to the jail."

Her mother squinted up at her. "For what?"

"To see Jared. Didn't you hear anything Rachel said?"

Suddenly, it clicked, and Ariel's eyes went wide, sizzling with alarm. "Oh no. I can't go there. No, no, no."

"Come on, Mom. It'll be good for you. Forgiveness heals the soul."

"Can't you understand that I can't do it?" Ariel snapped, rocking herself rhythmically.

This was not Ariel's typical stubbornness, but full-blown panic. "Dammit, Mom. You're such a mess." Cassie tossed the dress on the bed and stormed out, knowing this was not a battle to be won today.

Realizing she wasn't getting anywhere with Ariel, Rachel returned home to find two young Hispanic men—Marcos's crew—painting her garage. She offered them water, reminding them to stay hydrated on this hot day, but they politely declined. Since yesterday she had become resigned to her image as a marked woman in this town. In a way, she understood the condemnation of the person who had painted that graffiti. If that was the worst censure she received, she could take it. In fact, she had embraced it. She was, and always would be, Jared Whalen's mother, and she would own that title for the rest of her life.

Inside the kitchen she forced down water and yogurt as she tried to think of a way to assist Jared without Ariel's help. What had the lawyer told her about building a case? Character references. He was going to hire an investigator to compile positive statements about Jared. Maybe she could get that started.

The high school would be a gold mine, but Rachel couldn't bear to go near it. She'd accidentally taken the route past it on her way back from Ariel's and had noticed the sign in front saying: CLASSES CANCELED AND CANINE GRIEF THERAPY TODAY. The teachers would be there, as well as teams of dogs that the students could hug and talk to. The prospect brought her to tears, and she let herself cry as she rinsed out the yogurt container.

When the wave of emotion had passed, she opened the kitchen drawer and found the school directory. Her first call was to the counseling office where she reached Tim Hoddevick, Jared's counselor, a man who played by the rules but showed genuine compassion for students.

"Tim, I'll cut to the chase. I'm trying to come up with a list of positive character references for Jared, and you came to mind."

"Oh. Hmm." His hesitation made her aware of her beating pulse. "Jared was a good student. I could say that. And he worked well with other kids."

"Thank you, Tim. That will be helpful."

"But just to be clear, I would also have to disclose the issues Jared had on the football team."

A ball of fury rose in her throat. "You mean the bullying?"

"That was never documented."

"Whoa . . . wait. You're not siding with the victim?"

"It was his word against the other players'," he said.

"But you know it happened. They vandalized his locker and accused him of being gay, Tim. They threw his cleats into the urinal and nearly drowned him in the toilet."

Tim sighed. "That was what Jared said, but he didn't help us pursue the investigation. Understandably. Still, I can't be sure that any of those things really happened. Sometimes kids exaggerate."

"Like he would make that sort of thing up. Make himself a target. Create an environment so hostile that he had to quit the team."

"Rachel, please don't make this about bullying. You know we interviewed everyone involved. We did our due diligence."

"It will be up to our lawyer to argue the case."

Another pause. Tim wasn't happy about this, but who was?

"There's something else in my notes," he said. "From my conversations with Jared, it was clear that he idolized KJ and felt that he'd let his family down by quitting the team. He seemed depressed. I gave Jared a list of therapists who worked with teens. And then I gave you a call."

"Right. We spoke a few times." Rachel remembered. She had offered to make an appointment with a psychologist on the list, but Jared had shut her down, saying that he could never share his problems with a stranger.

"I hope you got him some help," Tim said.

Jared's refusal rang in her memory. He didn't want to see a shrink; he wasn't crazy. Guilt prodded Rachel, and she wondered if she should have pushed her son back then.

Those damned football players. Sneaky bullies. They had no clue about the pain they inflicted on other kids.

She ended the call with Hoddevick and called the school athletic director, who was also currently the junior varsity football coach.

"Jimmy Wilcox."

Rachel took a breath, preparing to ream him for managing a herd of reprehensible bullies.

And then she hung up.

Shouting at the football coach would only make Jared's case worse, and Coach Wilcox would have no information for her, no enlightenment. He had been working at another high school when the hazing had been going on, and since he had joined the Timbergrove staff a zero tolerance policy had been implemented. Many of the previous football coaches had been let go.

The truth about what happened to Jared would never be completely clear, and badgering the school administration would only hurt his case. She had reached another dead end.

Eli and the kids were watching some talent competition on TV while Cassie tinkered on Remy's computer, scrolling through her archive of photos.

A new discovery was the videos listed by song title in the "*secrets*" folder. She had found nearly two dozen recordings of "Singin' in the Rain" and snorted when she saw one titled *Singin XRated*. Somehow, she doubted that.

It turned out to be a recording of Jared and Remy rehearsing in the studio, with Ariel on the piano. Bracing herself to see something sordid between her sister and Jared, Cassie watched and found that it was not X-rated at all.

The number ended, and Ariel gave then some instruction on the tempo. Then Remy left the studio, but the recording continued. Apparently, she had left her computer behind with the camera going, though it was focused on the empty part of the studio.

Cassie was about to turn it off when Jared said something about being bad, and Ariel laughed. Cassie pulled the laptop closer to her ears and walked it into the kitchen.

"What is it about you bad boys that makes sex so good?" Ariel asked.

"It's because I'm forbidden fruit," Jared said, his voice low and sexy. "You can't get enough of me."

The empty space that followed was punctuated only by breathing and sighs—or at least that's what Cassie thought she heard.

Then Ariel said, "Oh, shit." A blur flashed over the screen and then it went black.

"Oh, shit," Cassie repeated.

Cleaning had become Rachel's new therapy.

She moved the mop around the base of a chair and then pushed into a corner under the vanity in that station, stopping to rub repeatedly over a sticky spot. There was satisfaction in making things white and shiny again, and the physical exertion helped her fall into bed at night.

After her canceled client appointments, she had not been too surprised when Kit told her that the husband-and-wife crew that usually came in to clean Holy Snips Monday nights had also bagged out.

"For now, or indefinitely?" Rachel had asked.

"We'll need to find someone else," Kit said. "They mentioned something about not wanting to offend their other accounts."

Edie and Chance cleaned many of the big McMansions in Timbergrove's Green Hills section. Rachel understood their worries about holding on to those accounts.

She went into the break room to rinse the mop. Almost done. She just needed to clean off the countertops and sink in there, and then she could head home. That empty, sad house. Rachel had so much trouble getting past Jared's room that she had taken to sleeping downstairs.

She was just spraying down the countertops when a thunderous noise came from the front of the shop. Rushing out, she jolted to a stop at the sight of the floor covered in sparkling shards of glass. A jagged edge of glass was all that remained of the shop's window.

On the floor lay the brick that had smashed through the front of the store.

Chapter 34

Adrenaline kept Rachel going for the next few hours. Through the police report, the cleanup, the application of a plywood board by the owner of the hardware store, an alien survivor instinct pushed her forward. It helped to have Mike, one of the first responders, there by her side. After his shift ended he stayed, helping her vacuum the fine bits of glass while Rachel's neighbor, Walt Finley, drilled screws into the plywood window covering.

"Thank God you weren't hurt," Walt said as he fished in a can for the right size screws. Rachel hadn't wanted to wake him so late at night, but he seemed glad to come to her rescue. "But you could have been. You could have been standing right here by the window. I'm telling you, the world has gone to hell in a handbasket. I've lived in Timbergrove all my life and never seen anything like this. Not even close. This is a town that works and plays together. Live and let live, I say. I mean, you got some bad people in the world, but things like this don't happen here. Maybe in Portland or Seattle. Big cities have crime and all. But not Timbergrove."

Rachel had never known her neighbor to be a chatterbox, but conversation seemed to soothe him. From the way his steady hands placed the screws, she suspected that he had sobered up.

"This window was an antique, right? I can see from those

stained glass panels at the top. Why in the world would any-one do this?"

Rachel figured he deserved an answer. "It appears that some-one, or a few people, are very angry with me over Remy Alex-ander's murder."

"And that's just craziness." Walt drilled one screw in, then paused. "Did you see anything? You know who it was?"

"I ran out the door in time to see a white SUV pull away. That's all I know."

"Well, Mike here will find your guy. Right, Mike?"

"We'll sure try," Mike said. Then he turned on the vacuum, blotting out conversation for the time being.

That night, Mike insisted that Rachel stay at his house. "Even if it means me sleeping on the sofa so you can have your space," he told her. "I'm keeping you close."

"No one is sleeping on the sofa," she said. "If you're going to protect me, you'd better stay right by my side." As she rode home with him, she saw that she had a text message from Cassie. **I really need to talk to you.** That could mean anything. She texted back: **I'll call you in the morning.**

Mike told her to pick any side of the bed she wanted and then went off to brush his teeth. Her body ached as she pulled the summer quilt of Mike's bed up to her chin and considered the next day. She would call the glass smith first thing. And then get back to Cassie. And then, what? Could the shop stay open during repairs? Not that she had any morning appointments, but the other stylists had their clients. And what about the re-pairs? The stained glass window was irreplaceable, but maybe it was time to move on. Maybe a more modern look, as Tiffani always said. Maybe safety glass.

But that would cost extra. And no glass was safe enough if someone was out to get her. Someone determined. Someone possessed by fury. Having seen Ariel's dull state, she knew it wasn't her former friend. And that left her suspecting half the population of Timbergrove. Everyone had loved Remy, and a few were vindictive enough to believe that you could have an eye for an eye.

"I won't be able to stay here." A tear trickled down one cheek as it hit her. "I could have been hurt tonight. One of my customers could have been injured. I'm a walking target around here."

Mike shook his head, still brushing.

"It's true. Someone's trying to punish me, and they could hurt someone else in the process. I can't let that happen."

He ducked into the bathroom. When he returned, he sat beside her on the bed. "Give it some time, Rachel. Asher lifted some prints from that brick. That might lead us to the perpetrator. And the furor will die down. People move on and forget."

She shook her head and pressed her face to the pillow. When Mike got into bed and pulled her close, she wondered if he would go with her, leave Timbergrove and move far, far away. She hoped he would start a new life elsewhere with her. Hope flared like a sparking match, then died in the darkness.

Why did men always leave?

Fathers and lovers, Oliver and Stosh and Jared. They all left her in the end.

Ariel rolled over in bed and felt along the nightstand for her bottle of pills. Her fingers floundered and knocked into something substantial—a glass. The nightstand was suddenly soaked, the tumbler hitting the carpeting with a thunk.

"Cassieeeee!"

That little brat thought she knew what was best for Ariel. Miss Know-it-all. She was just like Darla, always telling her to do this and do that. Never a nice thing to say, never a smile.

Darla was Ariel's foster mother, the one who took her in after Ariel had been left abandoned in a playpen. They had only found her because the postman kept hearing crying from the front window, day after day, as the mailbox got jammed up with bills and catalogs. Nobody home but baby Ariel, all dehydrated and stinking in a diaper about to explode.

Of course, Ariel didn't remember any of that, but one of her therapists said that it was the beginning of her abandonment issues. Ariel used to joke that she wished she had been abandoned totally by Darla and her real mother, Jeannie, because being on her own would have been preferable to growing up under the claws of those two psychos.

And now Rachel had turned out to be a psycho, too, expecting Ariel to do the impossible. Jared had killed her girl. No way was she granting him forgiveness. He could rot in his own teen angst.

But first, she would seduce him one last time. Nice and slow. And then she would take one of those knives he carried around, a long, brutally sharp knife like the one that she had thrown out the window. She would tease him with it and then . . . one deep thrust. The last.

Before sunrise the next morning, Rachel was pacing in front of the store, willing the glass repair man to find the right-sized window in his inventory, when her cell phone rang. It was Cassie.

"You've got to come over, Aunt Rachel."

The old nickname tugged at Rachel's heart.

"I—I can't talk about it on the phone," Cassie went on. "Can you come over?"

"What is it, honey?" A new wave of panic washed over Rachel. "Do you need an ambulance?"

"No, no, I need you to help me talk to Ariel. I can't do this alone anymore."

The strain in her voice stirred Rachel. She glanced over at the repairman, who seemed a little annoyed by her anxiety. He would probably be relieved to have her out of his hair. "Give me two minutes and I'll be right over."

Ariel's studio seemed stale and empty in the stark light, but Rachel followed Cassie into the hollow room. "Is your mom around?" she asked as the heels of her sandals clicked on the wooden floor. "How about the kids?"

"Everyone is in bed. Eli will have the kids up for school soon. Mom will spend most of the day in her new hermitage."

She plopped onto the yellow velvet sofa and propped her laptop on her thighs. "Thanks for coming over. I hope I didn't
wake you."

"Oh no." The shattered window loomed in Rachel's mind,
but she didn't want to burden Cassie with that. In this town,
she would hear soon enough. "I'm not sleeping a lot these
days." She settled on the sofa next to Cassie. "So what's going on?"

"Some of the stuff you said yesterday really threw me. Like
when you said Remy and Jared were seeing each other?"

Rachel nodded. "Right. And?"

"And, no disrespect, Aunt Rachel, but if Jared told you
Remy was his girlfriend, he was lying to you."

Rachel wasn't offended, but she wasn't ready to buy
Cassie's theory.

"Remy was seeing someone else," Cassie insisted. "A kid
from Gleetime. You might know him—Isaiah Denton? I think
he was on the football team."

"I do know him." Rachel remembered how Isaiah kept a
level head when Cooper was having a tantrum. "But why do
you think he was involved with Remy?"

"I did some more poking around in Remy's files, looking on
her computer and through the selfies on her cell phone. I
found these photos of her with Isaiah."

Though skeptical, Rachel took a look at the pictures. From
the way Remy leaned into Isaiah's broad chest, smiles lighting
both of their faces, there was no denying the affection between
them. "I see what you mean." Her resolve dissolved to shock
as Rachel stared at another photo of Remy planting a smooch
on Isaiah's broad jaw. "But I don't understand. Jared had a
girlfriend. I know he did." She flashed back to those days.
There were tangible signs like condoms disappearing from his
room, as well as his improved attitude. She had begun to hear
him singing in the shower. "And that night when he didn't
come home?" Rachel turned to Cassie. "I saw him coming
from your house."

"Yeah. About that." Cassie took her phone from her pocket and scrolled through a few pages. "That was the night of the broken vase. Here's the photo Remy sent me."

Rachel frowned as they both peered at a photo of the piano that sat a few feet away from them, only in the picture it was covered with shattered crystal.

"We thought that Stosh smashed the vase, but that was our mistake. Now, in retrospect, I think Jared did it."

"What?" Rachel squinted in disbelief. "Why would Jared break Ariel's prized possession?"

"Because he was mad at my mom for going home with Craig Schulteis. Jared was jealous and mad, thinking he might lose her to the drama teacher."

Rachel's heart sank. "You're telling me that my son was involved with your mother?"

"I'm sure about it now," Cassie went on. Rachel was shaking her head, wanting Cassie to stop, but the girl was on a roll. "Yeah, I know it's really sick, but it's the stinking truth. Jared and Ariel were hooking up. Ariel was Jared's secret girlfriend, not Remy."

Rachel pressed a hand to her mouth as she tried to swallow back the onslaught of disgust and hatred. "Ariel and Jared? Oh, God no." How could her friend betray her that way? Violating her boy, sneaking around with him, taking his innocence when he should have been exploring with young women his own age, women in his peer group.

Not a woman who had been a second mother to him.

"Poor Jared." Rachel let out a breath, floored by Ariel's actions. She had crossed a line, ventured too far. This time, there would be no repairing the damage.

Lolling like a wounded animal, Rachel took a deep breath. She had to pull herself together; she was supposed to be here to support Cassie. Bracing herself for more, Rachel lifted her gaze. "You've done your research, Cass. So do you have evidence to prove they were an item?"

"A couple of compromising photos. Actually, Remy saved a lot of photos of Ariel getting frisky with the Gleetime boys.

Makes me wonder what she was really doing behind closed doors in here for the past few years."

Rachel groaned. "Those poor kids. I'm sure a few of them felt pressured."

"There's one video that Remy took. She was recording a rehearsal of 'Singin' in the Rain,' but afterward she left the camera running." Cassie clicked a few times on the computer, then turned the screen to Rachel. "Just saying, it's pretty bad."

Again, Rachel braced herself as the drama unfurled: the ending of the brilliant song, the mundane, teasing conversation that gave way to something earthy and wanton.

"*What is it about you bad boys that makes sex so good?*" Ariel's kittenish voice oozed with seduction.

"*It's because you can't get enough of me,*" Jared said, taking the bait.

"Good Lord!" A sickening feeling tugged at Rachel's gut, and her shock gave way to revulsion as the guttural noises of lovemaking filled an excruciating minute. It dragged on until Ariel cursed, and the camera was turned off.

Cassie closed the frozen image from the video. "I'm sorry. That's got to be hard for you to see."

"At least it's giving me a sense of what Jared was dealing with . . . where his mind was." Revulsion left a bitter taste in her mouth as she considered that this could have been going on for quite some time. "She's a sexual predator, going after kids." She pressed her fingertips to her temple to ward off the acute tension there. "How long has this been going on? Obviously, she seduced Jared when he was underage. . . . When he was seventeen. But how long? Did it happen when he was even younger?"

"That I don't know." Cassie cocked her head to one side and closed the laptop. "But the bitch is right upstairs. I think it's time we find out."

It was just after eight a.m. when Cassie led Rachel up the stairs. Armed with the truth and ready to strike, Cassie flung open the door of the master bedroom.

"Time to wake up, Mom. Rachel's here."

"I'm awake." Ariel's body in repose looked peaceful, except for her wide-open eyes, glowing and bulbous in the dim room.

Cassie went to the window and cast the curtains aside, letting in a stream of sunlight. "It's a beautiful day for an intervention."

"Over what? You took my pills. And there's nothing left to drink in this house. But I'll bet Eli has more weed."

"Never mind that. Rachel and I have some questions. Some stuff that we're wondering about." Cassie turned to Rachel, who was uncharacteristically quiet. The bomb Cassie had dropped had knocked the wind out of her. It was up to Cassie to forge ahead.

"The thing is, that night when the vase on the piano was shattered, Aunt Rachel saw Jared leaving the house. I know, I know, everyone jumped to conclusions about him hooking up with Remy. But that was wrong. I know from the photos on Remy's cell phone that she was into one of the football players. That black kid with the big smile."

"Isaiah Denton," Rachel offered.

Ariel pushed herself up to lean against the headboard. "Isaiah?" Her nightgown drooped drunkenly over one shoulder. "I didn't know she liked him."

"Well, she did." One of Remy's friends, Sophia, had confirmed it.

"That means that the night Rachel saw Jared sneaking out of here, he wasn't with Remy." Cassie watched her mother for a reaction, but Ariel didn't flinch.

"So, what? He was probably just . . . hanging out with her or something."

"Yeah." Trying to keep it casual, Cassie pushed back some clothes on the upholstered chair and sat down. "But I don't think so. Actually, probably not, because Isaiah was here with Remy."

"No, he was not," Ariel insisted.

"How would you know?" Rachel said. "You got home late

from Craig Schulteis's house. I remember that night like it was yesterday."

"You went home with Mr. Schulteis," Cassie said slowly, "and then what? You came home and the vase was broken because Jared . . . Jared was upset with you. He was jealous, because he thought you hooked up with Mr. Schulteis."

"Which I didn't," Ariel insisted.

"*Because you were having sex with my son.*" Rachel's sibilant voice was loaded with fury, each word a quiet barb. It snapped Ariel to attention and seemed to suck the air out of the room.

"What kind of trash are you talking now?" Ariel said in a singsong voice designed to lighten the tension.

"I am talking about my son, my baby. And you seduced him. You had an affair with my kid, Ariel."

"You are so wrong," Ariel said, sincerity swimming in her green eyes. "I would *never* do that."

"You did," Cassie said. "Apparently, more than once. I've got it on videotape on Remy's computer. That time in the studio when the camera was recording during 'Singin' in the Rain,' and it kept recording?"

Ariel folded her arms and sank down against the headboard. "All right. Fine. We had a thing. But it wasn't my doing, and he's eighteen. So you can think what you want and condemn me and give me that pissy look of disapproval, but your son was an adult man making his own choices. You can't stop a boy from growing up, *Mom.*"

"He just turned eighteen!" Rachel growled, her jaw set in fury. "You took advantage of my boy."

Cassie had never seen them fight. She half expected Rachel to lunge forward and slap Ariel in the face, but instead she turned away and pressed her hands to the dresser, as if the scattered jewelry and coins there were mesmerizing.

"Tell me." Rachel's voice was husky. Was she crying? "How did it start?"

"It was all very innocent in the beginning. He started it, of course, and I, well, at first I went along with it to build up his confidence during a difficult time for him. All that stress over football. Those assholes on the team. And you weren't available. Not your fault, but you were dealing with Jackson's diagnosis. A difficult time. But I made it better for Jared."

Cassie squinted at her mother. Really? This had been going on for three or four years? Since the time that Jared was bullied by those football players?

"Rachel, I swear, I tried to end it out of respect for you. And he stayed away when I started seeing Stosh. He knows I'm a one-man woman. But after Stosh and I broke up, Jared kept pressuring me, staying after lessons or coming over late at night, and I had trouble denying him. He's a very deep person. Dark and edgy. But I had no idea how disturbed he was. He became infatuated . . . obsessed with me, and honestly? I liked the attention. But I knew we were on dangerous ground." Ariel pressed her hand to her chest. "I was the one with a reputation at stake."

Cassie wasn't buying it, but she let her mother ramble on. "Jared wanted to continue our relationship, reasoning that it would be somewhat socially acceptable once he graduated high school. He's a very determined person. Stubborn under that mild façade. And he kept pointing out that it was all going to be legal once his birthday came around. He's eighteen now and, honestly, he couldn't wait to be out from under your control."

"You're full of shit," Cassie interrupted. "You seduced him when he was a freshman. That's not so legal. Not to mention the other boys from Gleetime that you hooked up with."

"What are you talking about?"

"I saw it in Remy's photos. Jared wasn't the first Gleetime boy, and some of them were definitely under eighteen."

"Cassandra," Ariel hissed. "Whose side are you on?"

"Just speaking the truth."

"Which is all relative. The world according to Cassie," Ariel said with a sneer. "You think you're in love because some guy finally hit you in the bloomers. Really. Don't count on anything. He'll drop you like an old used tissue."

"Oh, fuck off." With a scowl, Cassie tugged a blanket from behind her and leaned back in the chair. Ariel could be such a bitch.

"That's enough." Rachel turned around and leaned on the footrest of the bed. "I'm not going to stand here while you vilify your daughter."

Ariel swept one hand toward the door. "Then you're free to go."

"I'm here for our children. For Remy and Cassie. For my son, who was young and impressionable enough to be wrapped around your finger. Caught in your fucking witch spell. I need to know about Jared. I need to know why he stabbed Remy."

"As if I know." Ariel pulled the covers toward her and focused on turning back the sheet. "He's your son. You should know what presses his buttons."

"He was your lover," Rachel responded. "And I'm not leaving here until you tell me what made him freak out."

Rachel stood her ground as Ariel vacillated and postured, portraying herself as the lonely widow, explaining that the boys she had bedded from Gleetime had lifted her spirits after Oliver died. She claimed that no one understood what it was like to suffer suburbia when you had an urban mentality. She lamented over the terrible waste of her talents, stuck here giving voice lessons to gawky teens.

Like a marooned mariner waiting for the tide to come in, Rachel waited. None of this was new material. She had suffered Ariel's stories of discontent for nearly fifteen years. This, today, would be the last time.

"You've got a million excuses for yourself," Rachel said. "But I still need to know what set Jared off."

Ariel pulled the covers up to her chin, her eyes shiny green stones. "It was you, actually. He freaked out when you saw him leaving here in the early morning."

Sure. Try to blame it on me, Rachel thought, her eyes steady on Ariel.

"Jared was sure we were caught. But then you assumed he was seeing Remy, and Jared figured it would be a good idea to play along. I wasn't really into it at first. And then I ran into Tootsie Dover."

Another person to blame, Rachel thought, letting out a whisper of breath. But she kept her mouth shut. She couldn't afford to alienate Ariel now.

"Tootsie got in my face. She said that Remy couldn't find a date for prom. She claimed that was why she was going alone. Can you imagine anyone thinking that? Remy was a beautiful girl."

Physical beauty had always been important to Ariel. Rachel cast a sidelong glance at Cassie, whose worth had always been diminished in Ariel's eyes. But the comment didn't seem to faze her.

"Tootsie made it sound like my daughter was hopeless without her fat-assed son to save her. That did it. Tootsie pushed me to the edge. I had to do something."

"So I told Jared to ask Remy to prom. I figured it would kill two birds with one stone. It was going to be a good cover for our relationship, and it would show that bitch that my daughter was desirable. Jared's star was on the rise after the showcase. Guys finally accepted him. Girls fell for him. I saw those little girls watch him onstage with stars in their eyes. They wanted him. I wanted him. So I promised him to find a way to see more of each other if we could get through to graduation. He had already enrolled in community college, and—"

Ariel pulled her knees up to her chest, her face lit with a daydream. "I couldn't wait to tell Tootsie about Remy and Jared. She was going to eat her words. And it should have worked." She scowled. "Remy was going with her friends, and I figured she would jump at the chance to have Jared pay for everything. I told Jared to sell it as a free night. I never thought Remy would say no to a prom date. And I never thought he would snap like that."

"You selfish bitch." And this woman had pretended to be Rachel's friend.

"I'm not responsible for your son's lunatic behavior," Ariel protested. "How was I to know he'd turn violent?"

"He killed Remy for you." Cassie sat upright in the chair. "He was so afraid of losing you because he couldn't deliver Remy as his prom date. And then, when Remy let on that she knew about the two of you, he must have thought she had to be stopped, or else he would lose you. I think he had the knife in his hand, and he struck her down—a knee-jerk reflex. All because he was afraid of losing you."

Ariel grunted, rubbing the back of her neck. "Here's the lesson in that. Men do crazy things when it comes to defending their territory." She looked up, straightening her shoulders so that her breasts were two perfect round points beneath her nightgown. "I'm just one of those women cursed to drive men to do crazy things."

"Oh my God!" Cassie clapped her hands over her ears. "You keep making this about you, Mom!"

"It was all about you, Ariel. You selfish bitch." Rachel's voice trembled with rage. "You took advantage of kids . . . boys. In most states you can be arrested for having sex with a fourteen-year-old."

"That's not going to happen here." Ariel scoffed. "Because you are going to keep your pretty little mouth shut." Ariel shot a look at Cassie. "Both of you. If anyone finds out about this, I'll lose all my clients."

"Ha! And let my son rot in jail to cover your ass? We've got to go to Jared's lawyer with this. It will show his motive. It will help George build a defense."

"I'm not telling the lawyers anything," Ariel snapped. "And if you breathe a word of this to anyone, I'll deny it. Deny, deny."

Rachel swooped down on Ariel. Her fingers sank into her shoulders, her thumbnails digging into the skin above the clavicle, so temptingly close to her pretty neck. "How dare you?" Her voice was raw with fury. "You would really let my son rot in jail for twenty years to life just so you can maintain your reputation? You made him your pawn. You used your own daughter as a sacrificial lamb. Your own daughter!"

"Stop it!" Ariel wriggled back and forth, trying to wrest free. "You're hurting me."

Blinding rage closed Rachel's fingers around Ariel's neck as she thought of Jared as a boy, building a Lego creature or diving into her bed on a Saturday morning, and Remy as a little girl singing a song and pedaling her tricycle as her long curls trailed behind her. They had been good kids. They had been on a path to becoming complex, kind adults until Ariel intervened.

"Stop!" Ariel gasped, her eyes bulging.

"Aunt Rachel . . ."

Suddenly, Rachel felt herself being pulled back. Cassie was out of her chair and leaning in, breaking Rachel's grip, easing her away.

"That's enough, okay?" Cassie broke the spell. "You." She pointed to her mother. "You're going to get dressed. And the three of us are going to the police or the lawyers or whoever we need to see to help Jared."

"I'm not going." Ariel's lower lip jutted out in a pout. Good God, the woman was reverting to five-year-old behavior.

"If you don't, I'll bring them the Ariel sex tapes." Raking tousled curls out of her face, Cassie frowned down at the bed. "I think you might want to own up to a few things instead of having them aired on YouTube."

Chapter 35

September

Rachel pressed her palms to the conference table in search of coolness. The air conditioner chugged away over the window in the law offices of Rathburn and Hunt, though it did little to break the heat that promised to push the thermometer into the nineties this week. She checked her phone for messages, then went to a crossword puzzle app to pass the time. Over the past three months, she had learned to wait. She'd had no choice.

At last, the door opened and George Hunt trudged in and plopped into a chair.

"That went better than I'd anticipated." His ruddy face puckered, puffing out his beard. "The prosecutor reduced the charges to manslaughter one, and Jared agreed to a plea bargain."

"Oh, dear Lord." Rachel pressed a hand to her mouth, alarm and relief fluttering in her chest at the mixed news. "So there won't be a trial."

"Nope. I told you that. And though Jared gets a mandatory ten-year sentence, that's a heck of a lot better than twenty-five to life, which he'd be getting with a homicide charge."

She let out a heavy breath. So the legal battle was over.

"Your son is fortunate to have you advocating for him, Rachel. The deposition from Ariel Alexander was a gold mine.

It painted a picture of Jared as a preyed-upon youth. Dynamite info. Really filled out his profile. A jury would have at least understood where he was coming from. And since we showed that he was under the influence of extreme emotional disturbance, well, hell, that's straight out of the Oregon law books. It's a reason to knock a murder rap down to manslaughter one."

She nodded. They had gone over these details before, when everything was speculative, pending, tenuous. "How is Jared taking it?"

"Same as ever." George bounced a fist on the arm of his chair. "He's holding out hope that he'll get out in ten and get with Ariel again." He shook his head. "By then, he probably won't even want her anymore."

Not true, Rachel thought. Ariel would still be beautiful in ten years. A stunning, morally vapid bombshell. And Jared? Rachel feared that in ten years her son would be a stunted individual, locked in teen angst, navigating by single-minded desire.

"And it's good that you got those two young men to step forward," George went on. "Luchter and Oyama. Graham Oyama was especially convincing. Poor kid. He said that after Ariel seduced him the first time, he booked lessons five days a week, hoping to get with her again."

"I'm grateful that they came forward." Rachel had avoided the news accounts of Ariel's exploits, though she'd picked up enough conversation around the shop to learn of Ariel's sexual abuse of local children.

"Their depositions helped us. Eighteen-year-olds. When I was that age, hell, I wasn't quite as savvy as these guys. But even so, it must have been tough for them to testify." He bumped his fist on the armrest again. "Tough choices all around."

The past few months had been filled with difficult choices for Rachel. She had decided to sell her house, where guilt and memories of family life seemed to dwell in the creak of the floors and the empty spaces. But she had held on to the shop, where there was a groundswell of community support for her. Her loyal customers did not waver, and a week after the incident she went to work to find them all there, waiting for an appointment, her schedule jam-packed.

"Why, Mae, you were just here a few weeks ago. And, Glinda you're not due for highlights for another month or two."

"Then maybe I'll try something new," Glinda had told her. "That blue hair. Or maybe purple. My grandkids will think it's a hoot."

Customers like Mae and Glinda as well as coworkers like Hilda and Sondra had rallied local ladies to show some understanding toward the woman with the troubled son. Holy Snips would survive the scandal, and the prospect of hot competition in town had waned. Tiffani had moved to Idaho when she couldn't pull her new shop together.

The disapproval Rachel had sensed did not seem to run deep in the veins of Timbergrove, and the culprit behind the graffiti and broken window had been unveiled. One evening while Rachel was jogging, a white SUV had slowed alongside the trail and pelted her with an egg. This time she got the license plate information, which Mike traced to Tootsie Dover.

"Why are you attacking me?" Rachel asked outright when she got Tootsie on the phone.

"Because you're going to drag my son into all of this . . . this hornet's nest of sex. You put the police on him and . . ." In the garbled explanation that followed, Rachel understood. Tootsie feared that Cooper would be revealed as one of Ariel's "victims."

Another victim. Rachel agreed not to press charges as long as Tootsie stayed the hell away from her. Mike told her that she didn't have the authority to drop criminal charges, but he understood. That was the thing about Mike: He got her.

Rachel found herself burrowing into her new home with him, hanging a picture, organizing a cupboard. Each day she tottered ahead, one more baby step. She was starting to move on, beginning to forgive herself for the things she did wrong when she was raising Jared and KJ. Although Jared was still angry with her for going after Ariel, maybe he would soften over time.

She was not going to give up on him.

A lot could happen in ten years.

Stretched out on a lounge chair near the pool, Ariel shielded her eyes from the sun to peer through the glass doors at the movers working inside the house. Just finish, already. It seemed like they were taking an inordinate amount of time moving her things into Stosh's Sherman Oaks bungalow; she had a feeling that they were dawdling to get an eyeful. Gawkers. She could have sworn she heard the click of a cell phone camera as she sat by the pool, trying to even out her tan for an upcoming audition.

The pool was the best part of Stosh's house, an old one-story structure with tacky features like a pink toilet and mirrored closet doors. "Hey, real estate is killer expensive in So-Cal," he'd told her when she pointed out the deficiencies of the house.

It would be better to sell this place and start over with a bigger place. One with a grand entrance: marble floors and a double staircase that rose from both sides like a celestial cloud. They would get a house like that when she landed a part.

But for now, this definitely topped the life she'd been leading in Oregon. She'd been a fool to want to hang on there when the scandal broke. Although there had been no court testimony, her depositions were public record, and reporters had splashed her statements on every form of media with headlines like "Singing Witch Seduces Boy Warlocks" and "Singing Witch Now Singing Cougar."

"They're making me out to be a monster," she had cried to Stosh when he called her one night. He had begun calling every night, just like old times. "I'm not a bad person. I have my standards."

"Babe, it's all good." Stosh had chuckled, that gurgling sound deep in his chest. "That's what I'm telling you. The whole suburban-seductress, vocal-coach-vixen thing might get you drummed out of East Bumfart, Oregon, but it totally plays down here. Your star is on the rise. Everyone knows your name again."

"Then I should be living down there." It was an offhand remark, but he jumped on it.

"Maybe you should."

Ariel had rationalized that the move to Southern California was her only means of survival now that her vocal training business had crashed and burned. After the scandal broke, none of her clients had remained loyal to her. Maisy had been excited by the prospects of "moving to Hollywood," but Cassie had been sad to see her little sister go. That Cassie was always complaining about something.

Trevor had been the only one to balk, desperate to hold on to his friends and reluctant to leave the little town. "This is our home, Mom!" he kept telling her. After many nights of tears, Eli had stepped in with an offer. He would move to Timbergrove—to a small cottage that fit his budget—and Trevor could stay with him. Ariel had declined the offer, unwilling to lose her son. Then, when she saw Trevor jump for joy at the prospect of staying, she backed down. Trevor didn't want to go with her; she had already lost him. Abandoned, once again.

The slider opened and Maisy popped out, followed by her friend Tessa and Tessa's father Bruno.

"Mom, can Tessa stay and go in the pool with me?"

"That's fine."

The girls cheered in delight and started stripping down to their swimsuits. Apparently, they had planned ahead.

Ariel looked up at Bruno, who definitely was not looking at her eyes. "How did your pitch go?" she asked, lazily stroking back her hair, pleased with its new warm highlight called "Ginger Bite." "Last time I saw you, Fox was talking to you about your Rehab Rebel idea."

"They were interested, but not greenlighting anything right now." Bruno sat down on the chair beside her, facing the girls in the pool. "You know, I could sell a reality show featuring you in twenty-four hours."

"I'm sure you could." Ariel adjusted the lounge chair and rolled over onto her tummy. "But I'm not interested."

"It sucks to have classes when the weather is this nice." Olivia nudged Cassie, who was sitting beside her on one of the campus lawns. "Hey. It's so annoying to talk to people who aren't listening."

"Sorry. I'm just reading an article online." An article about Jared Whalen pleading guilty in exchange for a reduced charge carrying a ten-year sentence.

"Is that Jared?" Olivia was leaning in. "What did he do now?"

"Apparently, he copped a plea." She read a bit of the article to her longtime friend from Timbergrove, one of the few people here at Oregon State who knew of Cassie's connection to the "prom day murder," as the media had begun to call it.

"Ten years doesn't seem like a lot of time for killing someone," Olivia said.

"The charge was reduced because of mitigating circumstances. That would be my mother."

"Yeah." Olivia raked back her ash-blond hair and let it drop onto her back. "Ariel turned out to be flakier than anyone realized."

"Yup." Cassie put her phone away, not sure how to feel about the sentence. Jared was definitely messed up, but prison was not going to cure that.

"Are you and Andrew going to the poetry slam tonight?"

"We are. Andrew has a poem he's going to read." A love poem. Yeah, it sounded nerdy, but Andrew's approach was multilayered and highly symbolic and she doubted anyone would recognize her in the piece. Cassie enjoyed her anonymity here on campus. Here she was just another nursing major who liked poetry slams and loved her adorable, geeky boyfriend. It was a very comfortable place to be, and when she wanted a touch of home she visited Trevor and Eli in Timbergrove, sleeping on the futon in the little cottage that backed up to the woods along the river.

She missed Maisy, but it was probably a good thing to get Maisy away from the house, where thick memories of Remy lingered in every corner. Cassie had been home the day the movers came for the furniture, and when she sensed the lingering ghost, it seemed to be a helpful spirit, a poltergeist who helped you find your missing car keys, one who saved children from tripping over a crack in the sidewalk, one who made flowers bloom brighter. More like a guardian angel than a howler.

Sometimes, walking between classes or goofing around with Andrew, Cassie became aware of all the things Remy had missed out on. Remy would never go to college or travel to Europe. There would be no career or family for her. When sadness seeped in, the ache was eased by knowing that Remy would not have wanted people to cry for her. She would have told them to dance.

One night while stargazing in the backyard, Eli mentioned that all people were made of stardust. Since then, Cassie imagined Remy as a star flickering in the distance, watchful, steadfast, shining bright into eternity. A star. Remy would like that.

Chapter 36

February

Outside the sky was a pallid shade of gray, but inside the shop, laughter flowed as Hilda told a story of how she and her sister had sneaked out of boarding school in Germany, changed their minds about meeting older boys in town, and then had so much trouble sneaking back into the school that they ended up ringing the doorbell.

"My sister stood at the door and opened her arms to the headmistress and said, 'Do with me what you will.'" There was a splotch of rosy color on Hilda's cheeks as she doubled over in laughter.

Rachel chuckled as she set a customer under the hair dryer with a stack of *People* magazines.

"I always have such a good time when I come here," said her customer, an accountant named Diane. "Whenever I tell my husband about it, he gets jealous."

"Well, he could come here for a haircut," Sondra said. "I have a few male clients."

"Ha! Over my dead body," Diane exclaimed, and they all laughed again.

When Rachel went back to her station to clean up, she saw that her cell phone was rumbling and lit. Assuming it was KJ, who had started an internship at a clinic during his final semester of college, she snatched it up.

"Mrs. Rachel Whalen? This is Lieutenant William Danelski

from the Oregon Department of Corrections. Ma'am, there's no easy way to say this. Your son Jared Whalen was found dead in his cell."

Her mouth seemed to drop open of its own accord as the broom slipped from her hand and clattered to the floor. She walked down the aisle, past the surprised and curious glances of her friends and coworkers, and strode straight out the door into the sloppy rain of a dull winter day.

No. It couldn't be true. Jared had hope. He was counting the days until his release. He saw the light at the end of the tunnel.

She walked briskly down the street, phone pressed to her ear, escaping to nowhere in particular. On her left was World Cycle, the bike shop Jared had adored as a kid when all the boys were going through X-treme mountain bikes with specially shaped helmets and expensive accoutrements for the bike. "Mom, do you think there are bikes in heaven?" he'd asked her. "Why not?" she'd responded. "When I grow up, I'm going to have a job at World Cycle," he'd said. "And then I can stay there all day long and they'll pay me."

Her baby boy. How could he be gone?

"Ma'am?" The officer's voice mixed with static on the line. "Are you still there?"

"Still here." Although her pulse was thrumming and her eyes were blurred by tears, she was still here. She would always be here for Jared. Although her logical mind would try to process the fact that he was dead, part of her would always half expect to open the side door to his quiet smile, his gentle hug.

"What . . ." Her voice was breathy, unreliable. "How did it happen?"

"It seems that he tried to hang himself. We will have more information once the autopsy has been done. For now, we suspect that it was a suicide."

Suicide. The word returned to that familiar groove in her mind like a forgotten adversary, the cool, slick friend who hurts you and laughs at your pain. He laughs, and all you can do is brace yourself and keep moving. She lifted her face to the rain and continued down the street. Keep moving.

* * *

"Cause of death: asphyxiation." Mike put the report on the kitchen table and removed his reading glasses. "The corrections officers seem to think that he hung himself, but the medical examiner also found that he had endured a blow to the head."

Rachel sniffed back tears. "So someone could have killed him or . . . or rendered him unconscious. And then they set it up to look like a suicide."

He nodded slowly, drumming his fingers on his thigh. "That's possible."

Rachel drew in a shaky breath. "He was murdered. I'm sure of it." In the eight months of his incarceration, Rachel had sent him at least one letter every week. Sometimes it was just a short, cheerful note. Other times she waxed introspective, writing to him about life choices and redemption and hope. In all that time, she had received three notes back from him, all of them asking her to have Ariel get in touch with him. "Jared wanted to live," she said. "He told the whole world about it when he did that prime-time interview with Sawyer Swift. He wanted to live happily ever after with Ariel."

"Maybe he lost hope. Prison can break a man's spirit."

She shook her head. "He could be stubborn as the day is long, and he was determined to win Ariel back. You saw the interview. That was the only thing I heard from him, all about Ariel. He was counting the days and months and years till his sentence was ended. He was planning to walk out through those prison gates and reunite with Ariel."

"Rach." Mike covered her hand with his. "It's going to be really hard to prove that it was a homicide."

"I know." She closed her hand around his. "That's not a battle I want to fight. It won't help Jared now. I just pray that he didn't suffer. And I wish that I'd been able to get on better terms with him."

"You tried."

She did. But Jared had dodged her, and now it was too late.

* * *

April

Sometimes Ariel thought it was all a trick of the mind; she wondered if she believed Jared had been one of the best because she couldn't have him anymore. But when she parsed out their moments together and really tried to analyze it, she realized that it was the tenderness and anger, all mixed in an intense force, that had made their lovemaking so exciting, so edgy and breathtaking.

They had been a volatile match, a fire that had burned bright but flamed out too fast. It was easy to wax lyrical about their love. So much easier to romanticize a person who had succumbed to death.

But Jared had also brought her trouble, dragging her into that scandal back in Oregon. He was stubborn and persistent, hounding her from prison with countless letters that begged her to visit him or write. He had carried a torch for her, which was sweet in a way. It was nice to be wanted.

He had made his wants and desires very clear when she had visited him in prison. Oh, yes, Rachel had blackmailed her into that fiasco. She'd been forced to enter that disgusting, smelly place because Jared refused to cooperate in his defense unless he had a visit with his beloved.

Fortunately, Ariel's disguise of dark sunglasses, hat, scarf, and trench coat had kept her visit out of the media. But the prison had been deplorable and the meeting with Jared just broke her heart.

"I'm sorry about Remy," he had told her, his beautiful eyes round as quarters. "Really sorry. But I did it for you, Ariel. She knew about us, and she was mad. She turned on me, called me a psycho. I think she was going to tell people, and there was no way she'd go to prom with me and . . . and I'd promised you." He had pressed his palm to the glass, his eyes lulling her into those long-ago hours of seduction and pleasure. "I couldn't break my promise. I couldn't do that to you. So I tried to coax her. I thought it would really scare her. And . . . the rest of it happened so fast. She wouldn't stay against the wall. Trying to get away, she pressed herself into the knife. It happened so fast. One second I was holding her there, the next, the blade had gone in really deep. Just like that, it was over."

Just like that.

She had loved him more than ever that day when he told the story. There was something pure and beautiful about a love that knew no boundaries: his love for her.

But reality, cold and dank as the concrete prison walls, set in before she made it out through the final gate. No matter how you cut it, he had killed her daughter. Accident or not. She had a career and a future to pursue, and he was stuck behind those walls. Nothing was going to come of that beautiful passion.

But Jared did not give up so easily. A few months later he did the prime-time interview with Sawyer Swift, and the whole scandal seemed to crack open again like a rotten, sticky egg. Parents at Maisy's school began to eyeball Ariel as if she were a dark seductress, ready to snatch up their little ones and drag them off to hell.

Stosh insisted that the controversy had upped her ante in Hollywood, but so far she had not seen her new notorious status pay off with a single job. She kept getting callbacks, but she suspected that the producers were looky-loos. The final straw came after a frustrating audition when she locked herself in a bathroom stall and sat with her head on her knees. While she was composing herself in the busy restroom, two women came in and gossiped about her. They picked at her, calling her a pervert and an abuser and a sex addict. "I thought that Andre liked her," one woman said. "He likes to look at her, the old perv," the second woman replied. "But he'll never give her a part. No one in this town is going to hire a woman with a convicted killer breathing down her neck."

Jared's image throbbed in Ariel's head as she drove home that day. Those big brown eyes. That teddy bear smile, so huggable. He had won people over in that interview, attracting attention. Now those hypocrites were turning a critical eye on her.

This was so unfair.

She had wanted him to be gone; she had needed him to be gone so that people would begin to put all that nastiness behind her, where it belonged.

But when she learned of his death, it was devastating. The news was underinflated and short-lived, bumped from the headlines by a senator who had been caught stealing water for his pecan ranch in California.

"The infamous prom day killer has died," said the television reporter. That night Ariel cried in the tub, but she never said anything to Stosh, and she hoped the report was right when they mentioned that Jared had committed suicide. She liked thinking that he was that noble.

When Bruno came knocking on her door again with his reality show pitch, she was in a vulnerable state. He told her that her experience, gruesome though it was, would land her a starring role on his TV crime show.

"A starring role?" Ariel liked the sound of that.

"You would be the host, and we would love to have you in some of the reenactments." Bruno accentuated each word with his flying hands. "It's called *Damsels in Distress,* a show about preyed-upon women."

That seemed a little weird, considering that people thought of her as a predator now. But then her daughter had been a victim of a violent crime. She could lead that charge.

Ariel signed on for sixteen episodes. Hell, she had kids to support for a few more years. And there was an adorable production assistant working in Bruno's office. He was dark and exotic looking, and more than once, she had caught him watching her, his gaze lingering. He wanted her; she could tell. Well, maybe he would get lucky.

Epilogue

Although a year had passed since it all happened, Rachel still had trouble going near the high school. Whenever she had to drive down that street, something about the truth of that fatal moment took her breath away. Each time, she held the wheel steady as she honored Remy with a silent prayer for everlasting peace or maybe a new life through reincarnation. $E = mc$ squared, and all that. Einstein claimed that molecules do not disappear. Matter was not destroyed but transformed . . . a solid to a gas, a gas to a liquid. In Rachel's dreams, Remy's spirit had lifted away before there was any pain and had dropped into the body of a newborn at Good Samaritan Hospital. Or maybe she was floating in the atmosphere, waiting for the right fit.

Rachel had stopped torturing herself over the frantic thoughts of the pain and horror Remy must have known, as well as the desperation and brutal fury of her Jared. For Rachel, the high school would always be Remy's place of passing, her portal to the afterlife. A very public cemetery.

In the weeks after the killing, some parents had lobbied for some kind of reconstruction at the school to demolish the stairwell where the crime had occurred. After meetings and debates, the school board decided that it was not an act of domestic terrorism but "a domestic quarrel." They painted the stairwell and erected a plaque in the theater to commemorate

Remy Alexander's contribution to the drama program. Rachel was glad the plaque hung in the theater. Remy had always liked the bustle of activity there, the emotional highs and lows, the laughter and applause. And plenty of music.

Of course, no one had asked Rachel's opinion. She had followed those developments in the *Timbergrove Times,* but had not discussed them with anyone but KJ. It didn't make for upbeat dinner conversation with her new husband, and the ladies at the shop avoided the topic altogether. KJ listened with interest when she talked about the ripples in the community, but his head was elsewhere these days, deep in his studies. With the time commitment of football out of his life, he had switched his major to biology and was applying for postgraduate programs to become a physician's assistant. Oregon Health & Science University had one of the top ten programs in the country, and with top grades in tough courses like Chemistry and Physiology, KJ's counselors thought he had a good shot.

Rachel didn't talk about Jared much, either. Not that Mike couldn't deal with it, but the time and place of Jared's death left Rachel with a disconnected sense that he was still on this earth. Still waiting, still planning to pass through those prison gates one day and find his true love. So Rachel did not discuss her dead son, but she thought of him often. Her teddy-bear boy, awkward and curious and quiet.

And Jared's restless spirit? Her son was still avoiding her. Sometimes she imagined that he'd flown south like a western tanager, coursing through the sky over Southern California in search of Ariel.

Ariel's house had a different vibe from the high school, and Rachel drove by the place nearly every day on her way to the shop. Another family lived there now, an optometrist, she heard through the grapevine, with his elegant, dark-haired wife, whom Rachel had seen in passing. They had two boys, maybe five and eight, who played in the driveway, aiming a ball at a hoop or kicking goals toward a net or rolling around on the lawn.

One summer day they had a lemonade stand set up—two chairs, a TV tray, and an ice chest—with a sign that boasted ONLY FIFTY CENTS A CUP! Rachel stopped. She couldn't resist.

"It's weally good," the younger one told her, while his older brother dipped a paper cup in a bag of ice in the cooler. The pitcher trembled as he lifted it, and a bit of liquid sloshed over the side. Seeing the crease in his brow, the familiar worry and self-doubt, Rachel quickly looked away and handed the younger boy a dollar bill.

"Uh-oh. Clive, she needs change."

"Okay, okay, give me a minute," Clive said in a parental voice.

"Keep the change." Rachel smiled as she accepted the cup. "I'm just happy for a cool glass of lemonade on such a hot day."

"Yay." The little boy waved the dollar bill through the air, a scraggly butterfly. His smile, his whimsy, his moon-shaped face reminded Rachel of the early days with her boys, before the torment of adolescence and a cruel world had torn away at their innocence.

She pressed the cup to her lips and drank the lemonade, sweet and sour to match the memories.

"You forgot to say thank you," Clive scolded his younger brother, and the boys chimed a thank-you together.

"You're welcome. Do you like living here?"

The little one shrugged, and Clive drew closer to his younger brother.

"Where did you live before?"

"California." Again, the little one answered freely while the older brother, forehead creased, took the dollar bill from his brother and opened a shoe box, their till.

"I have a good friend in California," Rachel said, wishing she could retract the lie the moment it slipped out.

Just then the front door of the house—a new door of clear glass with a cedar frame—popped open, and their mom emerged. A slender woman with chestnut hair down to her waist, she was smiling despite the unmistakable vibe of maternal instinct that made Rachel feel like an intruder. And rightly so. "Hey, there. I see you stopped to support our neighborhood entrepreneurs."

Rachel nodded, lifting the cup in a toast. "I always shop local, and I was thirsty."

"She gave us a dollar," Clive told his mother.

"That's very nice of her."

"I had to stop," Rachel said, wanting to come clean. "I used to know the people who lived here and, well, it's been so nice to drive by and see your family enjoying the house. I love the teal paint on the trim, and the new door is gorgeous." The open glass panel allowed a clear view into the living room, where inviting chairs and a fireplace waited. As if visitors were welcome. As if this family did not possess terrible, twisted secrets that had to be concealed from the neighbors. "You've given the house great curb appeal."

"Thanks. We're settling in." Her smile was cautious. Was she afraid Rachel would talk about the tragedy in front of her kids? No chance of that.

"Timbergrove is the perfect place to raise a family. I hope you like it."

"So far, so good."

"I know, I probably sound like someone from the chamber of commerce, singing the town's praises. But it's true. My name's Rachel. Rachel McCabe." The new name had seemed to be an awkward fit at first, a jagged departure from the name she had maintained for years to match her sons'. But her therapist had suggested the image of a hermit crab that grew out of its shell and moved on to one that was bigger and better suited to its needs.

"Nice to meet you, Rachel." The mom introduced herself as Ellie Henrico and explained that her sister was a longtime resident of Portland.

As they chatted, Rachel's gaze strayed to the boys. How quickly a lifetime cycled through: babies, toddlers, soccer games, graduation. Rachel wanted to tell Ellie Henrico to enjoy it now, to seize the moment, but that was the sort of greeting card advice that washed down the drain. Still, Rachel stared at the children, struggling to tamp down the warning.

Hold your boys in your arms, every night, she wanted to tell her. *Hold them close and let them know how much you love them.*

KJ and her therapist kept reminding her that Jared's meltdown was not a product of bad parenting, but guilt kept knocking on her door, reminding her that the question remained. Was it mental illness? Social isolation? A twisted misconception of Ariel's orders? A symptom of his infatuation with her?

Realizing she would never know the answer, she was trying to let her wayward son go. Making an earnest attempt. If trying were any measure of success, she would be as rich as Donald Trump.

Even when you know a life is over, the love remains in your heart. To the moon and back.

Please turn the page for a Q&A with
New York Times–bestselling author
Rosalind Noonan.

What prompted you to write this novel?

The seed of the story came from a terrible event: the fatal stabbing of a Connecticut teen in the school corridor after she rejected a prom date. In so many ways that story is too appalling and horrifying to believe, and it started the thought process of how that might have happened. How could a teen be driven to such an action, and what impact would it have on the community? While I continued to research the Connecticut killing, there came a point when I needed to let the true details go and begin to create a new story with original characters and organic motivations.

Would you say that the book is inspired by a true story?

Not really. Although I followed the details of the true crime, I placed the story in a completely fictitious world. By the time I finished writing I had made the story very much my own. The issue of mental illness simmering in suburban homes and erupting into violence is the take-away from the original news story. Some reviewers have written that my books are "ripped from the headlines," but generally I take a timely topic and plant it in a fictitious setting. I have written about postpartum depression, the reunification of a family after the return of a hostage, the question of nature versus nurture, and posttraumatic stress.

Do you begin writing each book with a theme in mind?

Usually, the theme drives the story. In this novel I was working with the theme that we all have secrets; no family is free of strife. As I'm writing I latch on to motifs, sometimes obvious, sometimes subtle. In this book, one of the more obvious motifs is motherhood, as I saw Rachel, Ariel, and Cassie handling the care of children in very different ways. Although Cassie was not literally a mother, in some ways she possessed the strongest parenting instincts.

What was the most compelling thing to you about this story?

The ripples caused by a violent incident touch an entire community in a variety of ways. Ariel reacts with denial and numbness. Cassie strives to protect the survivors and easily forgives a killer who was like a brother to her. Rachel seeks answers and tries to protect her son's rights. The complexity of human reaction to such a tragedy fueled the novel for me.

How did you come up with the book's title?

I am fortunate to have an intuitive editor who had a fine sense for marketing books; John came up with *Domestic Secrets* as the title. My working title was The *Short Life of Remy Alexander,* which I knew wouldn't last. As I was writing I lobbied for titles like *Out of the Blue, Shattered,* and *Fallen Stars,* but Kensington thought *Domestic Secrets* was the most compelling choice. Once I saw it with the cover art, I thought it was serendipity.

DOMESTIC SECRETS

Rosalind Noonan

ABOUT THIS GUIDE

The suggested questions are included to enhance
your group's reading of Rosalind Noonan's
Domestic Secrets.